Pippa Roscoe lives in Norf[
and makes daily promises t[
day she'll leave her compute, ω ιακε a ιοng walk
in the countryside. She can't remember a time when
she wasn't dreaming about handsome heroes and
innocent heroines. Totally her mother's fault, of
course—she gave Pippa her first romance to read
at the age of seven! She is inconceivably happy
that she gets to share those daydreams with you.
Follow her on X, @PippaRoscoe.

Clare Connelly was raised in small-town Australia
among a family of avid readers. She spent much
of her childhood up a tree, Mills & Boon book in
hand. Clare is married to her own real-life hero,
and they live in a bungalow near the sea with their
two children. She is frequently found staring into
space—a surefire sign that she's in the world of
her characters. She has a penchant for French food
and ice-cold champagne, and Mills & Boon novels
continue to be her favourite ever books. Writing for
Modern is a long-held dream. Clare can be contacted
via clareconnelly.com or at her Facebook page.

Also by Pippa Roscoe

Twin Consequences of That Night
Forbidden Until Midnight

The Greek Groom Swap collection

Greek's Temporary 'I Do'

Filthy Rich Italians miniseries

Inconveniently Wed

Also by Clare Connelly

Unwanted Royal Wife
Billion-Dollar Secret Between Them

Royally Tempted collection

Twins for His Majesty

A Greek Inheritance Game miniseries

Billion-Dollar Dating Deception

Discover more at millsandboon.co.uk.

WANTED: A FIANCÉ

PIPPA ROSCOE

CLARE CONNELLY

MILLS & BOON

All rights reserved including the right of reproduction in whole or in part in any form. This edition is published by arrangement with Harlequin Enterprises ULC.

This is a work of fiction. Names, characters, places, locations and incidents are purely fictional and bear no relationship to any real life individuals, living or dead, or to any actual places, business establishments, locations, events or incidents. Any resemblance is entirely coincidental.

Without limiting the author's and publisher's exclusive rights, any unauthorised use of this publication to train generative artificial intelligence (AI) technologies is expressly prohibited. HarperCollins also exercise their rights under Article 4(3) of the Digital Single Market Directive 2019/790 and expressly reserve this publication from the text and data mining exception.

® and TM are trademarks owned and used by the trademark owner and/or its licensee. Trademarks marked with ® are registered with the United Kingdom Patent Office and/or the Office for Harmonisation in the Internal Market and in other countries.

First published in Great Britain 2025
by Mills & Boon, an imprint of HarperCollins*Publishers* Ltd,
1 London Bridge Street, London, SE1 9GF

www.harpercollins.co.uk

HarperCollins*Publishers*, Macken House, 39/40 Mayor Street Upper, Dublin 1, D01 C9W8, Ireland

Wanted: A Fiancé © 2025 Harlequin Enterprises ULC

The Rossetti Ring Requirement © 2025 Pippa Roscoe

Tycoon's Terms of Engagement © 2025 Clare Connelly

ISBN: 978-0-263-34485-1

10/25

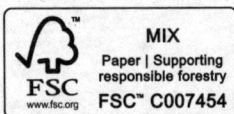

MIX
Paper | Supporting
responsible forestry
FSC™ C007454
www.fsc.org

This book contains FSC™ certified paper and other controlled sources to ensure responsible forest management.

For more information visit www.harpercollins.co.uk/green.

Printed and Bound in the UK using 100% Renewable Electricity at CPI Group (UK) Ltd, Croydon, CR0 4YY

THE ROSSETTI RING REQUIREMENT

PIPPA ROSCOE

MILLS & BOON

PROLOGUE

PLEASE LET THIS WORK.

Please let this *work*.

Erin Carter nibbled anxiously on her top lip as she tried to ignore the heavy glare from the receptionist peering over her spectacles at her as if surprised that Erin had the temerity to *still be here.*

As if others would have taken the hint and left by now.

Erin looked at the gold script imbedded in the double mahogany doors fronting the office she desperately needed to enter.

GIO GALLO.

The octogenarian Italian billionaire owner of Gallo Group had resisted every single one of her numerous attempts to meet with him in the last three years. Until now. Which was why Erin had accepted, rather than questioned why he had finally agreed to meet her. It was enough that she was here. Even if he was keeping her waiting.

This is a bad idea.

Oh, she wished her mother's imagined voice wasn't so clear in her head.

They'd argued about this off and on for the last three years, ever since she'd shared her hopes with her mother.

It's gone, Erin, and good riddance. All it ever did was bring us pain.

But her mother was wrong. If Erin could just get her fam-

ily's company back, if she could just convince Gio Gallo to let her buy just the *name* of the company, then she'd be able to honour the promise she made to her mother and fix what her father broke when he sold it ten years ago.

And it wasn't just a wild hope either. Erin had worked hard at school to get grades not only good enough to get into university, but also to secure a full scholarship for her business management degree. A scholarship that was very much needed after her father's grand schemes and hideous debts had quickly burned through the funds from the sale of the small publishing house that had been owned by her family for generations.

Erin had worked hard, learned voraciously through placements and even started her own business, all the while attending university full time. She'd used Gio Gallo himself as the business model for her dissertation and could quite likely write an unauthorised biography of the man. Gio Gallo, she knew, was a man ruthless enough to disinherit whatever family member had upset him that month, something he had done twice at least.

Which was why she also knew that *this*—keeping her waiting—was a tactic with the sole purpose of making her uncomfortable.

'Ms Carter?' the perfectly presented assistant said, without deigning to look in her direction. Red talons pointed her towards the large double doors to the left of her desk.

The door opened to reveal Gio Gallo standing in the doorway, his hand outstretched for her to shake.

When she reached him, she found his grip firm, even if the skin on his palm was smooth in a way that spoke of age rather than youth. He was smaller than she'd imagined, but the piercing gaze he shot her reminded her not to be fooled by his appearance.

'Ms Carter.'

'Mr Gallo.'

'Have a seat,' he said, gesturing to the buttery soft chesterfield that faced another glass coffee table. 'Coffee?'

'*No, grazie.*'

'*Parli Italiano*?' Mr Gallo asked.

'*Mi scusi*,' she apologised. 'Not really, no.'

Gio nodded once and waited for her to sit before he did. She felt as if it were a habit for him, a hangover from a different time. Which it probably was, she realised. His manners and his morals made him a law entirely unto himself—and it had garnered him great success.

'Mr Gallo, thank you for seeing me,' she started, hoping that he couldn't hear the tremor in her voice. 'I'm here to talk to you about Charterhouse.' He nodded, yet still remained silent. She took it as her cue to continue. 'As you know, you bought it from my father ten years ago, yet what was once a household name, recognised and familiar for its publication of crime novels, is now all but forgotten,' she said, swallowing the hurt. 'And I want it back.'

Not even a twitch appeared on Gallo's wrinkled face.

'I don't,' she rushed on to say, 'want any of the authors or contracts or staff, or even assets. I just…' She swallowed, knowing that she was revealing herself far too much to the man who was called a shark on a good day. 'I just want to buy back the *name*.'

'And you plan to fund this purchase with the proceeds of the sale of your own business?' Gio asked, his accent leaning into his words.

Erin frowned. She opened her mouth to ask how he knew that, but he pressed on.

'You sold a lucrative business that you started up in your first year of university in order to buy back the name of

your father's company?' The Italian's voice was sharp like a whip, the tone, clear as a bell, incredulous.

'My *family's* company,' Erin stressed, before biting her lip at the overshare.

Of course, Signor Gallo would have done his research, so he knew about HomeJames, the sober-driver app she had started at uni. What had started as a favour to her flatmate had quickly spun into a way of earning money to counter the exorbitant costs of student living that no scholarship could fully cover. Being a 'sober driver' for drunk peers quickly spiralled into a hugely successful country-wide business. Students, it seemed, were far more likely to trust other students to get them home safely. It was a win/win for everyone. A friend of a friend had wanted to test their app development skills, and they had worked together on the design as coursework for both their degrees. They'd sold the company six months ago and split the profits. Profits Erin wanted to use to buy back her family's company—in name if nothing more.

'Yes, sir. I did.'

Gio shook his head as if disappointed.

'It is the one thing that seems to run contrary to the fact that you are, by all accounts, a sensible, intelligent, promising young businesswoman. You are letting sentimentality get in your way.'

It was horribly close to the argument she'd had with her mother the last time Erin had seen her. And she said to Gio what she had said to her mother. 'I'm comfortable with that.' Because sentimentality was what kept her on the right side of the line, what kept her from being too much like her father.

After a period of time that would have made most grown men weep, Gio Gallo grunted and sat back in his chair, reappraising her through narrowed eyes.

'I have a counter-offer,' he announced.

She hadn't expected anything less, but it still hurt. She'd wanted this to be easy. Just a simple transaction so that she could go home with the company name and start to work in earnest.

'I will do as you've asked. More so in fact. I will sell you Charterhouse—the publishing house *and* all its assets, for one million pounds.'

Shock blanketed her brain. *He'd do what?*

It was beyond her wildest dreams. And after a few quick calculations, she realised she would even have a little money left over from the sale of her startup to cover the costs of operations to allow for the smooth transition in ownership and revenue. She could—

'On one condition.'

Her heart sank. She should have known it was too good to be true.

'What do you know of Enzo Rossetti?' Gio asked, his hawk-like gaze penetrating hers.

Surprised by the hard left turn of the conversation, Erin wracked her brain.

The Playboy of Amalfi? The moniker slipped into her thoughts.

'Enzo Rossetti—famous for being infamous. Early thirties, American-Italian,' she recalled. 'Itinerant playboy. Always breaking hearts and climbing out of the wrong bed,' she said, calling to mind the many headlines that had delighted in his bad behaviour. And she had scowled every single time she had seen it. The man was everything she hated about celebrity and money. Wasteful, careless, arrogant, promiscuous.

'And...' Gio prodded.

'He is the son of American actor Luca Rossetti and an

Italian heiress… Amelia *Gallo*,' Erin said as she put the pieces of the puzzle together. 'The daughter you disinherited just over thirty years ago.'

'Mmm,' was Gio's response to her scathing description of his grandson. 'I want you to marry him.'

'Pardon?' she asked, knowing that she couldn't have heard him correctly.

'I want you to marry him,' Gio repeated in exactly the same tone.

Erin's gasp turned into a shocked choke, and Gallo waited for her to recover.

'I am not here to find a husband, Mr Gallo,' she said trying to regain her composure. 'I am here to buy back my family's company.'

'And I am offering you terms,' he insisted civilly, as if he'd not just asked her to prostitute herself. 'I will sell you back your family's company, whole and as it is, for one million pounds if you become Enzo Rossetti's wife.'

Erin fell back against the soft leather of the sofa.

'I… I'm not that kind of person, Mr Gallo.'

'I don't know where you got your principles from, Ms Carter. It certainly wasn't your father.'

She felt his words like a slap. There were few people that still remembered the man who had frittered away the small fortune he'd exchanged for a company that had been in his family for generations, and she had let it slip her mind that Gio was one of them. A company Gallo was offering to sell her back…in its *entirety*.

'Why?'

'That is my business and not yours.'

'You are making it my business by trying to marry me to your grandson,' she pointed out, not unkindly—still un-

sure as to whether this was all part of some age-related cognitive decline.

'He's not my grandson. He is the child of someone who was once a member of my family.'

The cold, ruthless, way in which he spoke of his daughter cut Erin to the bone. But she couldn't afford to get lost in Gio Gallo's convoluted family drama. She was here for one reason and one reason only.

As if sensing that she was beginning to bend, he pressed on. 'If you agree, then Enzo Rossetti is not to know of my involvement or the entire deal is off. Do I make myself clear, Ms Carter? Tell him whatever you need to in order to get him down the aisle. Make up whatever story you like. I don't care,' Gio Gallo said with an Italian shrug of his shoulders. 'I just want him married.'

Erin blinked. And then she laughed, because the situation was utterly hopeless. But even though it felt that way, she couldn't stop thinking her way through how she might actually pull this off.

'And then I can divorce him? Or get an annulment?' she asked, needing to be sure of what he was saying.

'You think you can resist the charms of the Playboy of Amalfi?' Gio asked, something a little like amusement lighting his eyes.

'That won't be a problem, I assure you,' Erin replied confidently, thinking of all the sordid headlines and brokenhearted women he'd left in his wake. 'But, just so I'm clear, you're not asking me to…sleep with him?' Erin asked.

'I'm manipulative, Ms Carter, not crass,' he replied disdainfully. 'I don't care whether you sleep with him or not, only that the marriage certificate is signed. Once that happens, I will appoint you CEO of Charterhouse and you can

take over operations. Six months following that I will approve its sale to you.'

'But what does that *achieve*?' she asked, thoroughly confused by Gio's intentions.

'I have my reasons. I do not need to explain them to you.'

It was the least patronising way she'd ever heard 'don't worry your pretty little head about it', but it still grated on her. Even though she recognised that he was right. What did it matter to her if she could do what he needed her to do? She'd still get Charterhouse.

'Even if I did go through with this, wouldn't he have to *agree*?' she asked, the thought of Enzo Rossetti—never seen without a model, a royal, or an heiress on his arm—finding any interest in her whatsoever almost ludicrous.

'You do yourself a disservice, Ms Carter. I believe that you are resourceful. Intelligent. Beautiful, in that English way that some people find...appealing,' he said in a way that made it abundantly clear that he was *not* one of those people.

But Gio's offer had already begun to sink its claws into her. She could get the family company back. With the staff, with the author list. With all the things she wanted to do with it, her wildest dreams were beginning to play out in her mind.

But she had to get married to do so? Could she do that to someone? Could she abuse their feelings like that?

Like Enzo was known to abuse the feelings of the women he used?

As if he sensed her prevarication, Gio glared at her, his gaze ice-cold, sending a shiver across her shoulders.

'Ms Carter. It would be remiss of me not to inform you that should you refuse my offer, I will take Charterhouse and break it down piece by piece, asset by asset, until there is, and never will be, anything left of it. Do you understand?'

A cold shiver tripped down her spine. Oh, yes. She understood perfectly. She had been manipulated into a corner by the man before her. Oh, she had been a fool! A fool to think that she could go head-to-head with someone like Gio Gallo.

And the other thing she understood perfectly was that if she had any hope of reclaiming her family's business then she might have to do what Gio Gallo wanted: marry the world's most notorious playboy.

CHAPTER ONE

IT TOOK A while for Enzo Rossetti to realise that the thumping in his head was not the bass line to music still playing from the night before, but instead the pounding of a well-earned hangover.

Thump. Thump. Thump.

He groaned, turning onto his back and in doing so, retrieving his arm from beneath the blond-haired woman lying beside him to fling it across his eyes. The sun had dared to slip through the cracks in the blinds that hadn't been fully pulled down over the windows and was now creeping, unwanted, into his suite.

Wincing and restless, which only made the thumping worse, he turned onto his other side, only to come face-to-face with a brunette.

Svetlana. Agata.

Had there been a third? He really couldn't remember. He'd met them at a bar in the marina last night and they'd cajoled him into taking them back with him. Although, he conceded, it wasn't as if he'd taken that much convincing.

Raising his head, he risked a squint at his surroundings.

A bottle of champagne balanced precariously on a sideboard beneath a Renoir, a glass half full of whiskey perched beside it. A bra hung on the corner of a Matisse, his briefs directly below *another* bra lying over it. A feminine sigh

fell from kiss-bruised lips and he felt the blonde behind him snuggling deeper into his side as the brunette before him slipped a slender foot around his calf.

Normally, he wouldn't have minded the continuation of the mutually pleasurable pursuits of the night before, but unusually he had things to do—all of which were most especially unpleasurable.

Thump. Thump. Thump.

This time he couldn't be sure whether the thumping came from the hangover, or thoughts of his father. The man had been trying to reach him more insistently than usual, which meant one of two things. Either he was looking for money, or he wanted to tell Enzo that he was getting married. Again.

With that disturbing thought, Enzo raised himself up on to his elbows, unsettling both of his companions into varying states of complaint. He smoothed his palm over a thigh possessively hooked over his hip, flattered but not tempted.

Cries of 'not yet,' and 'come back to bed' fell on deaf ears as he threw back the covers and removed himself from the handmade larger-than-king-sized bed and stalked, naked as the day he was born, out of the room.

The need to clear his head drove him down corridors lined with small round portholes, letting an almost unforgivable level of light in. Sunglasses. He should have brought his sunglasses. His feet padded on the warm varnished teak as he passed several members of staff, all of whom were familiar enough with Enzo Rossetti to be nonplussed at their boss's lack of attire and simply continued to maintain their gaze at eye level.

He was a man of no small ego, yet in the matter of his appearance, Enzo Rossetti had every right to be confident. At six foot two, broad-shouldered, thin hipped, with smooth skin that tanned easily and deeply, and dark hair that some-

one had once poetically described as the colour of a raven, the man was hard to ignore. And while he might have been known for his excess and largesse, when it came to his body Enzo may as well have been sculpted with surgical-like precision in the vein of the Italian grand masters whose work graced the Galleria dell'Accademia in Firenze. Women had, in fact, been known to moan in orgasmic delight just from the sight of the musculature of his backside.

Continuing up the stairs into the main quarters and passing a living area already spotless despite the extensive partying from the night before, Enzo stepped out onto the back deck of the superyacht that was his home for the summer and inhaled deeply.

He cast a lascivious gaze over the beautiful Sorrento coastline that was more familiar to him than perhaps any other place in the entire world. The colours so rich, so vibrant it was as if a painter had been overly zealous with their palette. Despite the jagged and rough hillside, villages clung defiantly to the coastline that was one of Italy's most famous tourist destinations.

In all his extensive travels, *this* was the place that called to him the most. The unique smell of the Tyrrhenian Sea whispering of a heart home that he'd never actually had. The scents of the salt from the ocean and citrus from the *Sfusato Amalfitano*—the elongated bright yellow lemon particular to the region—promising something undefinable that he yearned for in his deepest veins.

He opened his eyes and tried to peer down the coast to his next destination, Positano. Usually he would have moved on by now, but an old friend from Oxford was throwing a party on the island of Capri and had convinced him to attend.

'You can't *not* come, Rossetti. You're the main attrac-

tion! Girls come from all over just to get a glimpse of the Ravenous Rossetti!' Marcus had whined.

Enzo had flinched at the moniker that was his father's, not his.

He walked to the edge of the deck free from the safety rail, the area often used to access the number of jet skis, eFoil boards, or the speedboat. However, in this moment Enzo had nothing so complicated in mind and, taking a deep breath, dived straight into the frigid depths of the sea.

Shock drenched his body in shivers of icy heat and burning cold. His heart pumped frantically as it struggled with the oxygen locked in his lungs. It had become a competition with himself, to see if he could last longer than previously, the pressure building and building until he finally propelled himself upwards, breaking the surface with a gasp for air. Enzo flicked his hair back from his face and wiped away the droplets clinging to his eyelashes and mouth.

He felt the heavy gaze of Agata—no, the brunette was *Svetlana*—and gave his most charming smile before closing the distance to the side of the boat with an easy three strokes.

He hauled himself from the water onto the deck and reached for the fresh towel already being handed to him by a member of staff. Another held a tray on which sat a Bloody Mary with enough of a kick to worry the World Health Organisation, though it was spice rather than alcohol that provided the powerful punch this morning.

'*Bella mia*, must you go already?'

Svetlana nodded. 'Sorry, *amore mio*, Agata has a meeting at nine and I have to be at the consulate by eleven.'

'You're happy for Jensen to return you to the mainland?' he asked.

'*Naturalmente*,' Agata said, blowing him a kiss that he caught with much affectation in one hand.

The sound of their laughter tickled his ears as he headed back to his suite, checking his watch to ensure he had time to shower before his phone call with Dubai.

While most of the world believed—and in fact, Enzo worked hard to make it so that they did—that he lived off whatever money his parents deemed fit to give him, Enzo Rossetti had his own, startlingly impressive income.

However, it benefited him to keep his investment company hidden behind several layers of obscure shell companies and false figureheads, primarily in order to keep his fortune away from the parents whose pursuit of money was almost as vicious as the pursuit of one-upping the other. If there was one thing Enzo hated above all else, it was the pursuit of material things above common decency.

Both Luca Rossetti and Amelia Gallo had done so, making not only a lifestyle but a career out of messy divorces and relationships, all under the heated gaze of a very public spotlight. A spotlight he had grown up under and been burned by more than a few times. But like any adversary, Enzo had eventually bent the spotlight to his will and now it was a tool that he used, cloaking himself in it and using it to his advantage.

And with that thought, Enzo stalked back into the belly of the boat, still naked but feeling immensely better.

Despite the fact that Enzo Rossetti had disappeared into the depths of his obscenely expensive yacht a full minute ago, Erin was *still* holding the binoculars to her eyes, frozen, irrevocably marked by the sight of his naked form. And Enzo Rossetti had a lot of…flesh. Toned, and tanned and—

'Erin, is he still there?' her friend Samara asked through the Bluetooth headphone in Erin's ear.

'No,' Erin replied, shaking off the afterburn of the images seared into her mind's eye. She cleared her throat before dropping into the seat on the small balcony of the hotel room in Capri that she'd booked just two days before, and puffed her cheeks out with the breath of air that had become stuck in her lungs.

Oh god. She was never going to be able to pull this off.

'You can do it,' Samara insisted, as if she'd heard Erin's innermost thoughts.

'Sam, he's six years older than me, a whole volleyball team more experienced than me, and he's literally everything I dislike in a man.'

'You don't have to like him to marry him.' Samara's reply sounded defiant, almost too defiant, and Erin cursed herself for forgetting Samara's own impending nuptials, to a man she'd never even seen, let alone knew enough to like.

'Has Gallo been in touch?' Samara asked, staving off Erin's apology.

'No,' Erin replied, pushing aside the newspaper she'd picked up that morning, with pictures of Enzo and two women splashed across the front page. 'And I don't think he will be until either I marry Enzo Rossetti or give up on Charterhouse.'

'Which you'll never do…'

'Which I'll never do,' Erin confirmed, looking out at the superyacht moored just outside of the marina. It was obscene, ostentatious and near offensive as far as she was concerned. It was rumoured that Enzo didn't possess a single piece of property. That he spent all of his time flitting from one hotel room to another, and that even though he'd spent every summer since his eighteenth birthday on some

form of luxury boat, he couldn't even be bothered to buy one for himself.

Wasteful.

Enzo was wasteful and Erin did *not* approve. Which had been firmly put down on the 'For' column of her For and Against list, when she had been debating with Sam over whether to agree to Gio Gallo's hare-brained scheme. In her mind's eye she saw the list again:

FOR
He is amoral.
He is careless.
He is wasteful.
Ownership of Charterhouse.

AGAINST
It's wrong.
I can't do it.

Sam had, quite rightly, pointed out that whether Erin could do it or not was not a reason for or against, but merely something to be worked around.

'So we're sticking to the plan then?' Sam asked.

'Yes, we're sticking to the plan,' Erin replied.

'Good. I like a plan, and yours is sound,' Sam insisted, the support and confidence she offered to Erin more welcome than Sam could ever imagine.

Erin had discovered the invitation for Samara's network, Conxion, in her email inbox in the second year of university, just as her sober-driver app had begun to take off. Working flat out on the app and studying for her bachelor's in business management hadn't left room for making friends. And just when Erin had been at her loneliest,

over two hundred miles away from home and her mother, Conxion and the women in the network had made her feel seen and supported.

Linking business-minded women across the globe of all different nationalities, ages, and experience levels for support, problem solving, and the opportunity to see other women doing what they were doing, had been a literal lifeline.

A lifeline that she was using even now to help with the plan she had come up with, just like one of her beloved detective fiction heroes.

'Step One…'

'Catch his eye,' Sam added knowingly, having been heavily involved in the plan herself.

'Which will happen at the party tonight,' Erin concluded.

A party that, despite the money she had from the sale of her startup, she'd never have been allowed into if Marcus Rothsburry, the British billionaire whose party it was, hadn't hired Angelique Xavier to plan it. Angelique was one of the first members of Conxion that Erin had come to know and the guest list she'd secretly added Erin's name to only proved the truth behind the running joke about Conxion: that between them, they had the power to topple heads of state and small countries should they wish to.

Erin looked back to the yacht, where a speedboat was waiting for two female passengers to board from the deck. Erin picked up her binoculars but no matter how hard she looked, she couldn't find a trace of Enzo anywhere.

He couldn't even be bothered to see his guests off after a night of what—if the rumours were to be believed—would have been orgasmic delight. Multiple times.

'Are you sure that this is something you want?' Sam probed gently.

Erin narrowed her gaze through the binoculars, considering the question.

Was she sure that she could marry a man she didn't like in order to get her family's business back from an owner who was willing to shred an entire business just because he could? Outrage and anger whipped through her like a sudden sea squall.

She hadn't been sure. Not really. Not until she'd done her research on the man who seemed to *revel* in his reprobate antics. Who ignored the reams of verbiage printed about the women who had loved and lost the Playboy of Amalfi. Convinced of his heartlessness, Erin was only too happy to do the women of the world a favour and teach Enzo Rossetti a lesson.

'Yes,' she answered truthfully. She could. And she would.

Which was how she found herself, several hours later, arriving at an ultra-exclusive, deeply private party on a beach far down below the rocky heights of the island of Capri.

Erin exited the lift that had brought her and all the other guests down the several hundred feet of cliff face with more than a little relief, having had her eyes clamped shut throughout the entire ride. She'd never liked heights and this had tested her. But still, when she stepped out onto the beach she had to stifle a gasp.

It wasn't a large beach by anyone's standards, but it was truly beautiful. Not far from the shore, great husks of rock reached into the sky. Some of the more adventurous revellers had stripped down to swimwear and were perched at various places, or hurtling down into the water. Beyond the three jagged bluffs, the sea stretched out to the horizon where the sun kissed the sea in a blaze of molten pinks and oranges.

Behind her, men and women glittered like jewels in silver and gold, their tans deep, their clothes expensive and

their alcohol levels high, dancing on a concrete platform around a sunken pool beside the bar that was hewn out of the rock wall itself.

This was how the glitterati partied: in luxurious hedonism.

Music rippled over the crowded beach, hands held high beneath a sky already pincushioned with stars, and excitement and joy heavy enough to taste in the air.

Almost immediately she saw him in the heart of the crowd.

Enzo Rossetti. Hair, darker than the night, slicked back thickly on top and faded at the sides, the closely cropped beard sharp around his mouth and chin. His dark blue shirt was open at his neck, the shimmer of a silver chain glinting in the night, and a whisper of the dark chest hair that she'd seen earlier slick against his torso from the water. The midnight-coloured suit clung lovingly to lean hips and broad shoulders, and the crowd all but shivered as he danced with them.

She watched him as he threw his head back and laughed, fascinated by the way he moved. Until he turned, his eyes opening straight onto hers, and even though she was prepared, even though she didn't like anything about him, the breath was *still* punched from her lungs.

Who was that?

The question circled in Enzo's mind as he searched the crowds for any sign of the woman he'd just seen. From the corner of his eye, he'd caught the dramatic sweep of red hair—not light strawberry, but a deep fiery red—followed by a powerful punch of confident turquoise. But neither had eclipsed the magnificent clarity of her sparkling gaze.

She was tall. Unusually so, her features fine, nose just

a little snub, between high cheekbones and a narrow chin. Eyes were the kind of blue that made him think of curaçao, his mouth near watering just at the thought of the sweet orange liqueur.

The blush that painted those cheeks when their eyes had connected was young, innocent. It was one hell of a combination with the dress and the hair. One he didn't see very often. His fingers itched to wind a curl around his finger, and when she bit her lip, he fisted his hand, regretting the way she cut the connection a moment later, to slip invisibly into the crowd.

Marcus stumbled into his side.

'Who is the redhead?' he shouted into his friend's ear, his gaze still scanning the crowd.

Marcus craned his head and peered in the woman's direction, frowning, and offered him a shrug. 'No idea. Why?'

'No reason,' Enzo dismissed as Marcus grinned and said, 'there's *always* a reason with you.'

Marcus turned back to him, his gaze sobering.

'You should probably know that Jeremy is here.'

Enzo frowned, unsure why that was of any significance.

'Kayla's husband?' Marcus pressed.

The faint stirrings of his memory began to shake free.

Kayla. London.

'Wait, Kayla Masters?' Enzo asked.

'*Yeah*,' Marcus said, wide-eyed as if he should understand the warning inherent in his gaze.

'The one I gave a lift to? After her husband got in a snit and stormed off leaving her alone at the opera house in Covent Garden?'

'That's the one.'

'But nothing happened,' Enzo said.

Not that her marriage vows had stopped Kayla from try-

ing it on with him. Disgust shivered across his skin from the memory. Despite what everyone seemed to think of him and his proclivities he would never cross that line. Unlike his parents who made a mockery of the institution, *repeatedly*, he respected the sanctity of marriage and abhorred anyone who didn't do the same.

'I don't think he believes that.' Marcus winced.

Enzo dismissed it as very much not his problem with a shrug, and turned back to find the stunning redhead weaving her way towards him. Oh, she wasn't making a beeline for him. Her movements were more like a dance. Subtle. They created...*expectation*.

She was going to make him work for it, he instinctively knew. And he *liked* that.

They locked eyes again, and again he felt it. That fizz, bubbling in his veins, as if someone had dropped baking soda into water. The crystalline blue was so unusually bright, it made her gaze almost startling.

They skirted each other, the distance between them getting shorter and shorter. He wondered where she was from. She looked almost Celtic in her colouring. He swept two glasses of champagne from the tray of a nearby waiter, and inclined his head towards her in an offering.

Her gaze brightened, the smile broadening, before frowning slightly, with a slight look of alarm on her features, when her eyes focused on something over his shoulder.

It prompted him to turn, just in time to see a large, red-faced man bearing down on him. Now, Enzo was tall, but this man looked like a door, and while Enzo could probably have held his own in a fight, he also didn't *have* to and instead simply chose to sidestep the oncoming force.

This, however, was a near fatal mistake.

Because while Enzo had successfully managed to avoid

the bull-sized charge, it had left the other man with nothing stopping him from careening straight into the large sunken pool that the guests had been dancing around, taking both the redhead and another poor innocent bystander with him.

Genuinely shocked, Enzo looked around to find somewhere to put his glasses down so that he could at least help the red-haired woman, whose name he still did not know, out of the pool. She had emerged from the water with a gasp, and was all but indecent as the turquoise silk, now a dark forest green, clung desperately to a lithe, toned body of subtle, but no less delicious, curves.

Laughter and cheers broke out from the fringes of the gathering from people who had clearly not seen the entire situation, but above them all, Kayla Masters arrived and turned her not inconsiderable ire on *him*.

'This is all your fault!' she screamed, as Enzo realised that the large man must have been her husband.

Utterly taken aback, Enzo peered at her. 'Are you drunk?'

'No, I am not! None of this would have happened if it wasn't for you,' she shouted accusingly, causing Enzo to question his sanity.

Because while he enjoyed his fun, skirting the edges of what most would call common decency in his *private* life, this was quickly becoming very *public*.

He felt the wide-eyed furious gaze of the wet woman in the pool, and *Dio mio*, he *hated* this. The drama, the hysteria. It was all too close to home for a man who had witnessed his parents' dramatic and often very public exchanges, one too many times. The memory was strong enough to blot out all thoughts of red hair and turquoise silk, of pleasure-filled evenings and simple fun.

'Did you tell your husband that we slept together?' he forced out through gritted teeth.

Kayla's eyes glittered for one moment, as if she'd suddenly realised that she might have made a mistake.

'I…no, I…'

The lie was as clear to him as day.

'That was a monumentally stupid thing to do,' he said succinctly, before knocking back both glasses of champagne in his hands.

'Are you just going to leave me here?' she demanded.

'It's your bed. You lie in it.' And with that he stalked off without a backward glance.

Erin pushed the long thick wet ropes of her hair back from her face.

This is all your fault.

Did you tell your husband that we slept together?

Oh, the man was a beast!

He'd gone and left that poor woman alone to face *his* music, while her husband splashed about furiously making things worse.

Someone handed her a towel which she gratefully accepted. She walked, rather slowly because of the way that the water pressed against the silk skirts of the gorgeous—and now ruined—dress, towards the steps and awkwardly hauled herself from the pool.

Everyone was in paroxysms of gossip, pointing and staring, and just like that Erin's cheeks flamed. Oh, she knew they weren't talking about her, but the staring and the pointing, the pity, and the sniggers… It was all a little too much like what she had experienced as a taller-than-average sixteen-year-old new student with a posh British accent in a Cornish state school.

A painful, ugly blush rose to her cheeks from her throat, and reached out across her chest. And no matter how much

she tried calm thoughts and slow breathing, nothing worked to dim the red stain of humiliation.

She looked into the crowds just in time to see Enzo running away from a chaotic scene of his own making, after his extra-marital affair had been discovered.

And she was supposed to marry this man?

If there had been even the slightest hesitation, any twist of conscience, left over from the concerns about manipulating or using Enzo Rossetti for her own means, there were none remaining.

Enzo Rossetti deserved everything he had coming to him.

CHAPTER TWO

IT WAS NOT every day that Enzo Rossetti found himself on the back foot. But from the moment he'd left Marcus's party last night, he'd not been able to get the haunting image of cool blue eyes and thick dark wet ropes of rubies from his mind.

The woman had been unacceptable collateral damage in a war he'd had no idea had been raging. But he should have handled it better, at least ensuring that no one got caught in the cross-fire.

He puffed out a breath of air as he looked up at the pale yellow building wedged, like its neighbours, as tightly up to the cobbled streets as possible. Real estate was a limited commodity in Capri, and every inch was used to its full potential. He craned his neck back to peer up at what appeared to be a very neat B&B rather than the more expensive hotels in Anacapri.

Oh, it was still in a very beautiful part of the island, but it just hadn't been what he'd expected from the fiery siren he'd encountered, albeit ever so briefly, the night before.

Still, he'd paid a high price to discover Erin Carter's name and location, facilitated by various incredibly efficient members of staff. He'd considered asking Marcus what he knew of her, but dismissed the idea. The man would be in-

comprehensible for at least another twenty-four hours. He'd never handled his alcohol well.

Enzo entered through the glossy white doorway, and found the Signora at the small wooden reception. He explained his predicament, and she gave him an assessing look. He imagined that a grandmother would have looked at him like that, had he ever had one. He'd long ago given up the childish habit of searching for information on his extended family. His father's parents were no longer alive, and his mother's? Well, the Gallo clan were just as famous as his parents and not a single one had ever come looking for him, no matter the stories about him and his parents in the press. And Enzo certainly wasn't going to go begging for their attention.

'*Allora*,' she said with a nod of her head, before explaining that she would let Signorina Carter know that he was here and she could decide for herself whether she wanted to see him.

He found himself hustled into a courtyard with much flapping of hands and, biting back a smile, turned to wait for the woman that would come down to meet him. He was sure of it.

The courtyard was pretty, ancient bougainvillea twisting up to the roof and out across the building. Large terracotta pots barely containing small-leafed plants in need of a good trim. In the corner an olive tree's silvery leaves rippled in the soft breeze. It was, he could admit, in its own way quite beautiful. And then he laughed at himself for the fanciful thought.

He crossed over to the pots that contained the lavender, curious about their scent, and inhaled for a moment, letting the calm it brought him hit home.

In the background he was conscious of the sounds of

the hostel, the windows open and the balconies above that looked down on the area.

'It was unspeakable.'

The words drifted down from a balcony somewhere above. The disdain so evident it caught his attention as much as the English words.

'No, it hasn't changed my mind at all. I'm more determined than ever.'

He found himself smiling—because he realised that it was highly likely to be the voice of Ms Carter. Her English was crisp, her accent untraceably regional so it was probable that she grew up in London. But it was that fire, the one that heated her words, that had drawn him. The blaze in her gaze that he'd—

'Once he marries me, I'll get what I want and the rest is history.'

Enzo blinked. Once. Twice.

'I just have to engineer another way to meet him, before he gets back on his yacht and disappears off down the coast.'

If Enzo had been in any doubt, if he had been willing to give her the benefit of the doubt, her next words sealed her fate.

'I don't care that Enzo Rossetti is obnoxious, arrogant, and clearly immoral if not *depraved*,' Ms Carter continued blithely, his faults highly exaggerated in his honest opinion. 'I'll just have to grin and bear it. At least until the ink of his signature is dry on the paperwork.'

He reared back as if he'd just been slapped.

Marriage? He nearly barked out a laugh. *Nothing* would convince him to marry. And she thought that she could, what, entrap him?

For what reason? Money? Fame?

'No, that's okay, Sam. You've done enough already.'

Sam? Who was this Sam? Her lover? Her *real* lover, in on this scam?

Gritting his teeth so hard he was in serious risk of breaking a tooth, he turned on his heel to leave, but—

But what if he didn't?

Anyone looking at Enzo Rossetti at that exact moment might have had the urge to shiver at the sight of his narrowed gaze, the furious intelligence radiating from those dark eyes, the stillness of a predator very carefully assessing his options.

What if he *didn't* turn and leave…?

What if, he wondered to himself, he instead chose to teach Ms Erin Carter a lesson? Perhaps she should get her just deserts. As the Masters had found out this morning, when they'd woken to discover several of their business associates had cut ties with them following last night's scene, Ms Carter would come to see that he was known to the world as an itinerant playboy, but that he was not a man to be messed with.

Grin and bear it, indeed.

Oh, this, Enzo Rossetti assured himself, was going to be *fun*.

Erin ended the call with Sam at the knock on her door. She'd woken up that morning and thrown herself into the shower determined to head down to the marina to see if she could get hold of Enzo and had only stopped to take the call from Sam.

But when Mrs Agostino explained that there was a gentleman here to see her, a Signor Rossetti, Erin knew her luck had turned. She told the hotel manager that she'd be down shortly, closed the door and promptly sank against it.

Don't panic. Don't panic.

Enzo Rossetti was downstairs and asking for her. Oh, she didn't bother wondering how he'd found her. A man with that much money and free time could do pretty much anything, she was sure. But *why*? Maybe all that practice making eyes at herself in the mirror had worked! Could it be that the Italian billionaire had fallen for her charm? She all but laughed at herself for having even considered it.

But no matter. She had to be more...*calm*. More like Rin, the fictional femme fatale she had created to ensnare the Playboy of Amalfi. *Rin* wouldn't rush down to meet him. She'd make him wait. So even though it went against every fibre of Erin's being, she took her time choosing—with very specific intention—what to wear.

She riffled through 'Rin's' half of the wardrobe with something very close to nerves. Her research had shown her where Enzo Rossetti's sartorial tastes ran, and it appeared to be either very low or very high, depending on the body part in question. Erin pulled out a pair of high-waisted blue shorts, and a very low-cut white shirt that seemed to cover more than it actually did.

She gave one last longing look in the mirror at the elegant, sophisticated trousers and cool cotton jumper she had been wearing before getting changed. She might not be sure why Enzo was here, but she was going to take full advantage of it. He'd slipped through her fingers last night, but she wouldn't let it happen again.

A short while later she entered the courtyard to find Enzo Rossetti on the small wooden bench, ankle crossed over knee, head tilted back in a ray of sunlight, reminding her for some strange reason of a fox. But not red in colour. Black. A wolf then, Erin decided, and took it as a warning to be on her guard. Despite that, her mind was still able to cata-

logue all the ways in which he was one of the most aggressively handsome men she'd ever encountered.

'Ms Carter,' he said without opening his eyes. 'Are you spying on me?' he teased.

She suppressed the instinctive shiver that rolled across her body, his English heavy with an alluring Italian lilt. They hadn't spoken the night before, and the tone he used now was markedly different to what he'd used last night with the husband and wife he had so badly wronged.

'Mr Rossetti,' she said, inclining her head, 'I was going to ask you the same question.' His eyes opened on hers and, to her immense satisfaction, widened in surprise.

He licked his lips as he took her in from head to toe, lingering on the rather shocking amount of leg on display thanks to the shortness of the shorts and the height of the wedged heel. It was almost indecent, but at least Enzo Rossetti wasn't tacky, she'd been relieved to discover. Even if she was still uncomfortable about the lack of her attire.

He slapped his hands on his thighs in a way that nearly made her jump.

'I could hardly allow you to be left with such a terrible impression of me after the events of last night, now could I? Your beautiful dress, ruined, my reputation, tarnished beyond repair,' he said, shrugging as if it were that easy to dismiss.

'So, the solution was to track me down and mysteriously appear at my hotel?' Erin asked, trying to keep her frustration at his carelessness as to the very real damage of the night before out of her voice.

'Oh but of course. Isn't that what all beautiful young ladies like? A little bit of...*excitement*? And I simply must make amends. So, come have breakfast with me,' he commanded, coming to stand at his full height.

The small courtyard that had seemed perfectly service-
able, suddenly felt constrictive and entirely impossible for
two people. She had a seesawing sense of déjà vu as she
looked up into his eyes, the world tilting just a little, just
enough to nearly have her swaying on her feet. Without a
word, his arm appeared, not reaching for her, but at her side
for her to take if she needed it. Oddly, the gallant gesture
reminded her of Gio Gallo.

Instead, she rolled her shoulders, and smiled. Or at least,
Rin smiled.

'Excitement *and* breakfast. Why, Mr Rossetti, you really
are spoiling me.'

She held out her arm for him to take.

He looked down at her arm and for a moment she wondered whether she saw hesitation in his gaze. A slight quirk
of his brow, before it was masked completely by a look that
could hold no other description than mischievous.

'Oh, Ms Carter, you have *no* idea,' he relied with a toothy
grin.

He'd brought Erin Carter to a small café, out of the way of
the tourists that filled the main drag on Capri from the time
the first boat moored in the port, to the last. The waiter that
showed them to their table had nearly had a heart attack
when he'd caught a glimpse of Erin Carter's very long legs.

He knew the feeling. Still, Enzo had glared at the man,
the warning to control himself understood, if the hasty head-
ducked-apology was anything to go by.

Erin was telling him about the places she'd visited since
arriving on the island, and he listened only with one ear.

Money. She must be after his money. She wasn't the first,
but she would be the last if he had anything to do with it.
The hastily formed plan beginning to take shape in his

mind would make sure that no one would dare mess with him again. He needed time to do this properly, but he also couldn't let her escape.

'Oh yes, I totally agree,' he inserted into a suitable break in the conversation, as she relayed a stereotypical tourist experience of Capri. 'Have you been up to Monte Solaro?' he asked.

'I don't really like heights,' she confessed with a genuine enough grimace and continued to describe where else she had been. He tuned out the highlights of her holiday so far and instead took her in.

Unquestionably beautiful, she had long rich red hair— almost dark enough to be auburn—that shone like rubies in the morning light. She was tall and lean, rather than the curves he was used to finding pleasure in.

She shifted, pulling at the near indecently low-cut shirt, her discomfort subtle but evident, making him wonder if she had worn it for him. That perhaps this was something she believed that he might like. He only just managed to stifle the bark of laughter at a woman so determined to get her hands on money that she would put herself out so much.

But if that was the case then she had very much misread him. While the press usually portrayed many of his companions as vapid and brainless, they were wrong. Agata and Svetlana were currently on attachment with the UN, and many of his previous lovers were either businesswomen or powerful global players in their own right. However, this did not fit the image that the world's press preferred to paint of him.

An image that Erin Carter seemed to be trying to fit into at this present moment in time.

As she tried to pull discreetly at the hem of her shorts, there was—he admitted—the smallest possibility that he'd

misunderstood the conversation he'd overheard in the courtyard. That he'd somehow got his wires crossed. It was possible, he forced himself to concede. Even though it rarely happened, if ever, and he was one hundred percent sure of what he'd heard.

Perhaps he needed to put Erin to the test, he thought as she expounded the many glamorous things she'd done since arriving on Capri, fluttering her eyes, and giggling in a slightly grating high-pitched way. It was generous to give her the benefit of the doubt, he thought, giving himself a pat on the back for being so gracious.

'So, tell me about Erin Carter,' he said, putting his espresso cup down and leaning back in his chair, all the better to see her every action and reaction.

Her mouth hung open just a fraction and he realised that he'd been so focused on his thoughts that he'd interrupted her. Irritation quickly masked, she shrugged her shoulder, the move causing the shirt to slide a little down her arm.

Intentional? Likely.

'Oh, there's not much to tell,' she said coquettishly.

It would, of course, be nothing for him to find out more about Erin Carter. He had the money and connections to root out every single fact about her.

But this would be more fun.

And, he realised, this *was* fun. Pitting his intellect against a worthy opponent. It wasn't as if it would interfere with his summer plans. The next three weeks at least were free and clear.

'I don't believe that, Erin. Marcus wouldn't invite a *nobody* to the party,' Enzo insisted, though he was beginning to suspect that Marcus hadn't invited her.

His gaze narrowed on the slight straightening of her pos-

ture. Mmm. No, it was unlikely that Marcus had invited her at all. Internally, he grinned.

'Rin, please call me Rin,' she said, with a seductive grin that momentarily short-circuited his brain.

He nodded. 'Rin,' he confirmed, honestly not caring what she chose to call herself. 'What do you do, Rin?'

'Oh, as little as possible,' she said flirtatiously. 'I like shopping, travelling, *partying*,' she said.

All the things that anyone who'd read half a dozen newspapers about him would think that he'd like.

'And what about you, Enzo? What do you like?'

'Games,' he said with a little more vehemence than necessary. 'I like to win.' He'd lost too much in his childhood to allow anything less.

'How deliciously...*aggressive*,' Rin replied as if it most certainly was *not*.

Enzo let loose the laugh that built in his chest. Her eyes were her tell. They were what gave her away.

'Oh, but it can be so much fun, Erin. Especially with a willing partner.'

'Well, happy day that they're not *un*willing,' she replied, her tone just a little tart.

He slapped the table. 'Oh, you're just delightful!'

She'd jumped a little at his exuberance.

But he saw how her gaze landed on his wristwatch, widening in recognition at the expensive item.

'Where in England are you from? I want to know *everything* about you,' he insisted, pulling her attention back to him.

'I grew up in London.'

Would she feed him some sob story? A family that had wealth—because that was evident in the way she moved, in the way she talked, despite the words coming out of her

mouth. She'd had money at some point. And presumably was after it again.

'And is that where you live now?'

'I…am staying with friends. They're currently out of the country and it's so *convenient* to be on the river,' she said offhandedly.

The Thames; the lifeblood of London. But he'd noticed her hesitation.

A lie, he decided.

'And you?' she asked in return.

'Where do I live? Wherever the winds take me,' he said, and shrugged. He'd never owned a property, had never really seen the point of it. After all, he'd quickly learned that it was something that could be taken away in a heartbeat. He'd stopped counting the houses he'd lived in with his parents when they sent him to boarding school. Between the new starts and the divorces, they hadn't stayed anywhere longer than eight months.

'So, you just flit from place to place?' she asked, apparently genuine curiosity in her gaze.

'*Flit*?'

'Ah, move around a lot,' she clarified.

He knew what it meant, after all he'd spent three years at university in England, but he was quite happy to play the fool if that would help him achieve his aim. And that aim? To make sure that Erin Carter paid for thinking she could take advantage of him like that. To make her punishment so big and so loud that *no one* would do such a thing again.

A sunbeam bounced, once again, off the obnoxiously expensive watch on Enzo's wrist and right into Erin's face, causing her to blink, and she shifted in her chair.

Only when she did that, the damned shirt gaped and she had to pull it back to protect what little was left of her mod-

esty. She bit back a curse. She didn't think she'd be able to dress like this again. She'd already burned the backs of her practically bare thighs on the metal chair when she sat down.

'I guess you could say that I like to *flit,'* Enzo said with what he surely believed to be a winning smile. 'And are you about to flit?' he asked.

She opened her mouth to say no, when she realised that she needed to move to Step Two of the plan. Rin was doing well, had caught Enzo's attention, but now Rin needed to play a little hard to get.

'Well, there's a party in Spain that—'

'No! *Non è possible,*' he said. 'I *cannot* allow it.'

'Why not?' she asked, a little alarmed by the vehemence of his response.

'Because I *need* you,' he implored. 'I want to see Italy, to see this beautiful place of my ancestors through your eyes… it would,' he said, laying it on a little thick, 'give me *life*.'

Good god, what a line, Erin thought. *Does that really work on women?*

'Maybe…' Rin dangled. She couldn't make it too easy for him.

And then she looked into his imploring gaze and despite herself, she saw it. The handsome Italian billionaire, the charm, the attraction…

'Tell me you can stay,' he cajoled.

'I couldn't possibly,' Rin demurred coyly.

'Oh, but you *could*,' he insisted, just as she'd hoped he would. 'I've been positively bored for the last few weeks. You could join me on my tour of the coast. We'll go to Positano, Amalfi and then on to Sorrento, it will be marvellous! I just can't wait to show it all to you. We can start tomorrow. *Sì?*'

Rin bit her lip and nodded.

'Wonderful. I will pick you up at nine am.'

'Really?' Erin asked, as if it had all been that simple.

'Yes. And wear something...*else*,' he said, casting an eye over her clothes.

Oh, she'd definitely be doing that. Erin couldn't pull her plan off dressed like this. It was too uncomfortable and distracting. But despite that, this morning had been more than she could possibly hope for. The chance to get Enzo on his own, away from other distractions. Step Three already achieved and she'd only been in Italy three days! She couldn't wait to tell Sam.

Enzo reached a hand into the air and clicked his fingers and Erin tried to hide the flinch of disdain that shivered down her spine.

Her father had done that when she was younger. Ordered people around as if he was better than them, than anyone. But he hadn't been. It had all been lies. And when those lies had come tumbling down, his promises as empty as their bank accounts, she and her mother had been forced to go it alone, in a new home in a new area.

Erin would *never* allow herself to be that dependent on a man. Ever. And Charterhouse was how she'd do it. For her mother. For herself. Once she got Charterhouse back, everything would be okay.

The waiter came with the bill, and a profusion of Italian passed between Enzo and the man before he bobbed his head and scurried away. Enzo reached for his wallet and retrieved an unnecessarily thick wad of notes before throwing them carelessly onto the table.

'Well, then it's settled,' he said launching himself up from his chair, startling her a little. *Again.* The man was entirely too unpredictable.

He escorted her back to her hotel, for which she was almost thankful. The high wedge heels were a balancing act on the narrow cobbled tourist-filled streets. Arriving at the door to the small boutique hotel, he picked up her hand and brought it to his lips gently and slowly enough for her to stop him if she wanted to.

For just a moment, his eyes locked on hers, his lips hovering above the back of her hand, her heart thumped painfully in her chest.

Oh.

This was the charm. This was the Playboy of Amalfi.

This was the man she needed to be wary of. Because while Rin could handle a man like Enzo Rossetti, she wasn't sure that Erin Carter could.

CHAPTER THREE

WHEN ENZO MESSAGED to say that he'd arrived the following morning, Erin had chosen to compromise between what she would wear and what she imagined Rin would wear. She knew that Enzo was unlikely to appreciate her *usual* choice of clothing—which alternated between business suits and lounge wear with a conservative, but comfortable, leaning.

So, she had chosen a pair of wide legged trousers, comfortable but pretty sandals and paired them with an off-the-shoulder cropped linen loose-knit top from Rin's side of the wardrobe. Dressing the part, hopefully, would aid in her deception. And if she ever felt a moment's guilt, then she called to mind the snap of his fingers, the careless toss of money on the table, and the headlines about the heartbreak he left in his wake.

Mrs Agostino smiled knowingly at her as Erin left the hotel and came to an abrupt halt on the narrow pavement.

Opposite her, Enzo Rossetti leaned lazily against the side of a metallic baby blue convertible that looked like something out of the 1960s. His legs crossed at the ankles, breeze playing with the linen shirt, sleeves rolled back to the forearms and the tendrils of thick dark hair just above the pair of dark sunglasses bent towards his phone screen.

He tapped away aggressively, belying the adopted appearance of casual carelessness, and thrust it into his pocket

when he was done. But the moment he looked up to find her waiting for him, all traces of anger were erased.

'Rin! *Bellezza*! What a sight for sore eyes, as you English say.'

Oh god. Enzo was like the Duracell bunny. He just didn't stop.

Pasting a smile to her face, she crossed the road and allowed him to air kiss each cheek.

'Allow me,' he said, walking her round the car bonnet to the passenger side door, as if she couldn't have found it herself. No, that was ungracious. His manners...they reminded her once again of Gio Gallo, and she wondered whether they'd ever met, even though Gio had severed all ties to Enzo's mother.

'Thank you,' she said, as he closed the door for her and returned to the driver's seat. 'Where are we going?'

'It's a surprise, *cara*.'

'Wonderful. I *love* surprises,' Erin lied as she settled into the plush leather seat as Enzo guided them out onto the narrow streets.

As Enzo expertly manoeuvred the gorgeous car that, at any other time she would be delighted to be in, around the tourists and the small narrow cobbled lanes, Erin realised why the use of cars was so strictly monitored. But just a little way out of the main town, the road opened up and the dramatic island views began to take over.

Stunning. There was no other word for it. Clear blue seas surrounded them on all sides. In the distance, she could just make out the Amalfi coastline, as wild and dominating as the man beside her.

With the top down, the wind thundered around them, making small talk impossible, so she allowed herself to take in the moment. The easy way with which he drove, guiding

the car around curves in the road, the way the muscles on his forearm flexed as he changed gear. The subtle catches of his aftershave—tempting hints of amber and musk—tasteful and not overbearing as she'd expected. The powerful line of his jaw dusted artfully in dark stubble and the sense that while he was utterly focused on the road ahead, he was also completely aware of *her*.

And that awareness…she felt it on her skin, heating her cheeks, and in the fluttering of her pulse.

Oh, she could see how women could fall for his charms.

But she needed him to fall for *Rin*.

'Might we be going to a café?' she tried to ask over the roar of the wind as she felt her stomach twist a little. She hadn't had time for breakfast and she was beginning to get a little hungry.

'What was that, *cara*?' he asked, raising his voice but pointing to his ears.

She shook her head in an 'it's okay' gesture. She was sure she'd find out where they were going soon enough. No doubt there would be some posh restaurant overlooking the rest of the island and she could eat when they got there.

Only when they got to the surprise destination she realised to her horror that it wasn't a restaurant, but a helipad. With a helicopter waiting for them.

And the twist of hunger in her stomach morphed into nausea and fear. Because while Rin might have enjoyed a helicopter ride, Erin Carter was very much afraid of heights. And she was pretty sure she remembered telling Enzo that, too.

'Enzo?'

'Yes, *cara*?' he said, turning off the ignition and leaning back in his seat, his sunglasses and easy smile utterly at odds with the creeping fear that was beginning to take hold.

'Why are we here?' she asked, trying to keep the shiver

of revulsion at the sight of the death-trap behind him from her voice.

He looked at her, then to the helicopter and then back at her.

'Why do you think? I want to show you *all* that Capri has to offer.'

'But...' She hesitated. She was *sure* that she'd told him that she didn't like heights. *Sure* of it. He had either not been listening or hadn't cared. And while Erin would have found an excuse to back out of it, Rin knew that it was too good an opportunity to pass up. A man like Enzo would *love* to display his prowess, and this was a perfect opportunity for Rin to convince him that she was utterly charmed by him. All Erin had to do was keep her fear in check. *Surely* it wouldn't be that bad?

'Is something wrong, *cara*?'

'No... Not at all. I can't wait,' Erin said with a forced smile.

Enzo did the handover with the pilot as the flight assistant helped a very nervous looking Rin into the passenger seat of the chopper. He'd expected her to back out. To make an excuse, or even remind him that only just the day before, she'd told him that she disliked heights.

He'd been utterly prepared to be gracious about it and even had other plans ready to execute. But no. The silly woman had decided that it would be better to put herself at what could only be described as clear discomfort just to get what she wanted.

It had been a test of sorts. To see how far she would go to draw him in. Which, presumably, included her losing all her brain cells and agreeing to something that would clearly make her miserable.

He didn't know whether to be infuriated or impressed.

He slipped into the pilot's seat and donned the head-phones that would allow him to talk to Rin through the microphone, as well as connect him to the control tower in charge of the airspace above and around Capri.

She glared at him in alarm. 'You're flying this thing?' she demanded.

'What self-respecting billionaire doesn't know how to fly a helicopter?' he shot back with what many around the world considered to be a winning smile.

He explained to Rin what he was doing as he went through the pre-flight checks, wondering just how far her dislike of heights went. He had no intention of scaring her to death, he wasn't a monster. Surely if it was a genuine phobia she would have told him—she'd only said she wasn't a fan.

He frowned, casting a glance at the white-knuckled grip she had on her handbag.

'Rin, are you sure you're okay?' he asked.

'Absolutely,' she insisted, even as she paled.

He'd given her all the opportunities he could to let her back out and she had taken none of them.

'*Va bene*,' he proclaimed, and lifted them into the air, nearly jumping when she thrust a hand out to the window beside her.

'Rin—'

He was fully willing to put the bird back down on the ground, when she said, 'No, it's okay. Keep going.'

If he didn't have his hands full of controls, he would have scratched his head in confusion, now most definitely frus-trated *and* impressed with her.

By the time he got them into the air properly, she had prised her eyes open about a centimetre and then shut them again and he almost felt sorry for her. Almost, because

clearly she was prepared to do *anything* to get her hands on his money.

'You can open your eyes, *cara*,' he said into the headset, his voice in her ear apparently shocking her from the way she jumped in her seat.

'I will,' she said and he couldn't help but smile. 'How long have you been flying?'

'Oh, my licence just came through the other day.'

This time her eyes *did* open, along with her mouth, and he let loose his laugh. 'I'm joking, *amore mio*. I've been flying for nearly eight years now.'

'That wasn't funny,' Erin chided.

'It was a *little* funny,' he prodded. 'You should have said something,' he said.

'I did. Yesterday.'

'No, I mean today.'

'But you've clearly gone to so much trouble.'

Oh. He hadn't considered the fact that she might have agreed because she hadn't wanted to disappoint him. Had he misread things?

No. He was sure of himself and what he'd heard yesterday. Erin Carter wanted to marry him, to get her hands on something. His money, probably.

It had been confirmed when last night he'd called Marcus to ask about whether he put her on the list. Marcus hadn't even heard of her before and had no idea how she'd managed to get in to the party.

'Shall I take her back down?' he offered, and she shook her head.

'No, it's okay, really. It's not as bad as I thought it would be now that we're...' she took a breath '...up here.'

'Okay. Well then, if you're sure, let me give you the tour.'

Enzo angled the helicopter gently to bank out to the left

and took them around the island. As he pointed out the spots on the island she had visited already and some that she hadn't, he thought back over the plan he had decided on the night before.

He couldn't let people like Kayla, like Rin, like his parents continue to think that they could get away with taking liberties. He had expected it from his parents, was doing anything and everything he could do to ignore their antics.

And while the charming, easy-going playboy persona he had adopted had been one kind of armour, the unfortunate side effect was that people thought they could get away with taking advantage of him and his good nature. The fact that he even had a good nature was miracle enough after the mind games of his parents throughout his childhood.

No. He needed to put a line through it all now, once and for all. And Erin was how he would do it. Because that kind of hubris, that kind of cold calculation to seduce and take advantage of certain strong emotions, was untenable.

So yes, Enzo would play along with the pretence of a quickly escalating romantic relationship, even an engagement, even to the extent of planning and holding a wedding. He would follow through, all the way to the very moment where he could leave her standing at the top of the aisle and reveal her perfidy to the world.

And no one would ever dare take advantage of him again. No one.

After a not inconsiderable time in the air, when Rin had seemed to, if not relax, then at least relinquish the death grip she'd had on her handbag, he took them back down to the helipad and powered down. The heliport staff appeared and took over, allowing Enzo and Rin to get back to the gorgeous convertible he'd borrowed while he was in Capri.

He escorted her to the passenger seat and checked his

phone before taking his place behind the wheel. He deleted the four messages from his father, who had apparently ignored Enzo's angry message from earlier telling him not to contact him again, and opened the one from Marcus.

How did it go?

Smirking, he typed back his answer.

Perfectly. She has no idea that I know.

He slipped his phone into his pocket, looked over at Rin and smiled at her, even as he plotted her downfall.

'Oh god, Sam, it was *awful*. My heart is still pounding,' Erin hissed into the phone, pressing her hand to her chest and trying to keep her voice down as Enzo ordered them drinks at the bar of the swanky hotel he'd brought them to.

'Why didn't you just tell him?' Samara asked.

'I didn't think his ego would handle the rejection.'

A bark of laughter shot down the speaker and into Erin's ear.

'From what I hear his ego isn't the only big thing about him.'

'Sam!'

'Sorry, just teasing!'

'The thing is that I'm *sure* I told him that I was scared of heights.'

'You don't think he knows, do you?'

'No,' Erin insisted. 'I don't see how. And besides, surely if he did know, he'd have left me in the dust, right?'

'Yes? Maybe?' Only Sam didn't sound that convinced.

'I have to go, he's coming back.'

'Be safe!'

Sam's warning rang in her ears as Enzo returned to their table on the edge of a balcony that reached out from the cliff face and over the sea far below.

At least one good thing had come out of her flight with Enzo in the helicopter...*this* was nothing compared to the heights she'd just been to.

She took her glass from him, gently clinking it against his in a toast '*to them*,' and took a long mouthful, allowing the alcohol to soothe the frayed edges of her nerves.

He watched and her and smiled and she couldn't help herself.

'Are you always such a daredevil?' she asked, genuinely curious. There had been nothing about his penchant for helicopters in any of the articles on him that she'd read.

'There's nothing wrong with a healthy dose of adrenaline,' he said with a shrug. 'I didn't realise you liked to play it so safe,' he chided teasingly.

'I...' She was about to refute his claim, but she *did*. She did play things safe. She didn't go out, she didn't attend wild parties. She did watch her pennies, and pay her bills on time.

Probably because she'd had to. After she had moved down to Falmouth with her mother and her father had stayed behind in London, desperate to pursue yet another crazy scheme to recover all the money he'd lost, it quickly became clear how much her mother had adapted her life to her husband's. How much she'd relied on him for everything. *Everything.*

Arla Carter had been in such a state of shock, starting over again, that she'd been frozen and overwhelmed. And at fifteen Erin had learned pretty quickly how to set up online accounts for bills, or food orders, for the TV licence and the council tax.

And that had been when it started. Their little game. Something they would say when things got a little too hard. It had started as a story that Erin would tell her mother.

When we get Charterhouse back, everything will be fine.

When we get Charterhouse back, we can return to London.

When we get Charterhouse back, we can eat out in fancy restaurants.

When we get Charterhouse back, Erin could return to St Paul's Girls and Arla Carter could return to the friends that had disowned her.

When we get Charterhouse back, everything will be fine.

And then she remembered that she had to answer as Rin, not Erin, and cursed herself for forgetting.

'I don't always play it safe,' she teased instead.

He smiled, and just then his phone vibrated with an incoming call. She just about managed to see his father's name on the screen before he rejected the call and put his phone back into his pocket.

'It's okay, you can—'

'No. That's okay, *cara*. You have my undivided attention.'

It rang again, background music to a now awkward silence.

'I'm afraid my father isn't the kind of man to take no for an answer,' Enzo admitted. 'And I will probably have to take this after all.'

Enzo raised his hand and clicked his fingers in the air again, missing the narrowing of Erin's eyes at the gesture. She watched him say something to the waiter and hand over another very thick wad of notes.

'You have my sincerest apologies, but I've arranged for a car to come and pick you up and return you to your hotel.'

'You're leaving?' Erin asked in surprise. Was it because of his father, or because of her?

'Yes, but don't look so devastated, Rin. I'll be seeing you tomorrow,' he said with that charming smile, picking up her hand again, and hovering an air kiss just above her skin. After the briefest of pauses, he closed the distance. His lips gently pressed against the back of her hand, the touch little more than that of the wings of a butterfly, but the impact was instantaneous. Goose bumps shoot across her skin, her pulse fluttered and her cheeks pinked.

She pushed the startling sensation aside and tried to focus on what he was saying about seeing her tomorrow.

'I will?'

'Yes. We have plans, *cara*.'

Plans indeed. Over the next four days, they toured the Amalfi Coast's greatest hits. Enzo had taken her to Spiaggia di Tordigliano, a stunning little beach where they'd swam and eaten the gorgeous picnic prepared by the chef on his yacht. He'd driven them to Sorrento where they'd eaten a spectacular spaghetti carbonara, they'd visited San Lazzaro, overnighting at a hotel that clung defiantly to the edge of the coast, and gone swimming at the *Grotta dello Smeraldo*, which Enzo had presumably paid an exorbitant and hugely wasteful amount of money so that they could have it to themselves. In aquamarine waters, enclosed with ancient rocks but beautifully lit, she'd never admit to a living soul how much she'd had to resist the intimacy and charm of the moment.

For the little girl to whom a shocking change from London to the dark, damp cold shorelines of Falmouth that had dominated her winters, this contrast of this beautiful sun-drenched, near perfect moment, was almost seductive.

Filled with exquisite food, and more maddeningly polite charm from Enzo, they had visited the Valle delle Ferriere

near Ravello. The walk cut through rich green forestry and magical waterfalls, the earthy scents refreshing after the salt of the sea, as dappled light ticked her skin through the leafy canopy along the path.

During that time, she had learned that Enzo liked chocolate so dark it was bitter, that he probably had more coffee than blood in his veins, and that he drove like every Italian stereotype she'd ever seen—heavy on the horn and loose on the wheel. He was like Peter Pan, utterly careless about anything remotely serious and she was half fearful of what would happen to him when his money ran out, the charm fell flat and the good looks faded.

Was that why Gio wanted her to marry him? To ground him somehow? Play Wendy to his Peter?

If that was the case then Gio Gallo had clearly never read to the end of the book. And if she didn't get herself under control, the book of her and Enzo's romance would end up as a murder mystery—without the mystery. He was driving her out of her mind with his affectations. Affectations that she had to pretend to be utterly enthralled with.

But that wasn't enough, was it?

She was, she recognised, being dated. But she needed *more*. She needed him ravenous. Desperate. Madly in love.

You need to give him a ticking bomb.

She read Sam's message and typed out a reply.

I think the police take that kind of thing quite seriously these days.

Sam had sent back a string of laughing emojis and her last bit of advice.

You need to threaten to take away his toy.

And, to clarify, YOU are the toy.

Enzo was beginning to get frustrated. He hadn't minded wining and dining Erin all over the Amalfi Coast, but he was wondering when she was going to try and take things further. Not that he wanted to sleep with her. That would be taking things too far considering the plans he had to leave her in such a humiliating way.

No, no matter how beautiful Erin Carter was, he would not knowingly or willingly allow a woman to prostitute herself in such a way. There would be a way round it, he was sure. Because he doubted that Erin would want that for herself either.

He tapped his finger on the white cotton tablecloth of the restaurant he'd told her to meet him at. She was a little late, he thought, checking his phone, which was unusual given her punctuality so far.

At least his father had finally stopped calling. A harshly delivered warning during their last phone call cautioning him not to ask for money, had put paid to that. The sooner his father realised that he'd get nothing more out of him, the better.

Some would perhaps consider it ironic that the moment Enzo had finally severed financial ties with both his parents, along came a gold-digger trying to sink her teeth into him. But no. Enzo had decided it was just the universe making sure that he'd learned his lesson. That people who professed love too easily and quickly were not under some strong emotional sway, but a financial one. Only and always.

And when there was a commotion near the door, he—like the other diners—looked to see. And Enzo was *sure* that it was someone else's gasp that filled his ear when he caught

sight of Erin being escorted towards his table. He coughed to clear the thickening of his throat, and stood when she reached the table he was sat at.

She looked...*incredible*.

There was nothing of the overt, revealing clothes she had worn to breakfast that first time. No. This was...sophisticated elegance. This looked like the real Erin Carter. The white jumpsuit clung lovingly, but not overly, to every long line of Erin's body. The draped sleeves, slashed between the shoulder and wrist, hinted at strong, toned arms, and although the V-neck was low, it was very careful about what it concealed. She had drawn not only his attention, but that of many of the other dining guests that evening.

Erin, it appeared, had decided to take things to the next level. And it was about damn time.

'You look *bellissima*, Rin. Truly,' he said as he held out her seat, ignoring the amusingly resentful gaze of the waiter who had clearly wished to do the same.

'Thank you,' Rin said, blushing prettily, but her eyes were awash with regret.

'What's wrong, *bellezza*?'

'I... I've had some sad news. I must return to England,' she confessed haltingly. And there it was, that look: chin down, gaze up, designed to engender the maximum sympathy.

Such sad news, he reflected, that she had to dress herself up to the nines to deliver it. Well played, Ms Carter, well played. Because he *felt* it. The natural twist in his gut, the one that he had been prepared for, but was still a slave to. The one that had him wanting to beg her to stay. Emotional manipulation of the highest kind.

'No, *cara*. Why?' he demanded as if he hadn't expected some kind of ruse like this.

'It is a work thing. A project that really needs my attention.'

'A work thing, *cara*?' he questioned. 'And there I was, thinking that all you did was shop, travel, and party!' he proclaimed, repeating her words back to her.

She blinked, unexpectedly caught out. 'It's for a friend, really...' She gamely tried to recover.

'*Eh*, who is this friend? Tell them no. And tell *me* you can stay,' he cajoled.

'But, even if I could, I have nowhere to stay,' Rin explained. 'The hotel is booked out for the rest of the summer.'

'No room at the inn?' Enzo teased, and her smile wobbled a little in response to the saccharine sweetness of his tone. But he could hardly help himself. He was having so much fun.

'Sadly not,' she replied helplessly.

'But that is no problem at all!' Enzo insisted. 'Stay with me. On my yacht.'

'Mr Rossetti,' Rin cried indignantly. 'I don't know what kind of women you usually associate yourself with—'

Intelligent, beautiful, sensually confident, he mentally answered. *Not vipers like you.*

'But I am not that sort of woman,' she proclaimed with vehemence.

That's for sure, Enzo thought, but instead, he put his hand on his heart, pretended to be hurt by the implication and declared, 'Of course not! I would *never* think such a thing.'

She glared at him in a way that very much reminded him of an old-fashioned schoolmarm and he just about stopped himself from laughing.

'I was raised in a very traditional household and I have very traditional views on those sort of things.'

Those sort of things being... *Ahhh. This* was how she was

going to get around not sleeping with him. There would be no sex before this carefully orchestrated marriage. Clever. Very clever, Ms Carter. He was half thankful that she had brought it up herself, and while it might have been amusing to see her bend over backwards to avoid the kind of physical intimacy that was almost expected these days with a serious relationship, he was pleased that they didn't have to do that particular dance. It would have been a step too far for him, given the brutal punishment he planned to dole out. Oh, she was beautiful, very much so, but the thought of tangling himself in all that cold calculating avarice left him with frostbite.

'Have no fear, Rin. There are more than twelve rooms on my yacht, and a full contingent of staff at all times, any of whom would be willing to act as chaperone. Why, it is nothing short of a floating hotel! We would simply be suite-mates,' he said with a wild gesture of his arms that nearly took out one of the restaurant's waiters.

'I couldn't possibly,' Rin demurred coyly.

'Oh, but you *could*,' he insisted, deciding to go all in. 'I've never met a woman like you before,' he said, reaching for her hand and placing it on his heart. A heart that was beating quicker with mirth rather than sincerity. 'And I am not ready to let you slip through my fingers just yet. Are you?' he asked, throwing it back to her. 'Because I thought… I thought perhaps that we were building something special…'

Special was one way to describe it, that was for sure.

He let the implication dangle, sure that she wouldn't be able to refuse the bait.

'Oh, I had thought it was just *me* that felt that way,' she said, doing the doe-eyed thing again.

'Not at all, *cara*,' Enzo said, with a grin that was beginning to hurt his cheeks. 'I am as deeply touched by our…

friendship…as you are. And it would mean more than you could possibly imagine if you would do me the honour of joining me on-board my yacht.'

'Well, I suppose I could defer my project.'

'Would you? Could you?' he asked eagerly, pulling back at the slight flare of alarm in her gaze at his flamboyant response. It wouldn't do to scare her off now. Not after how much he was invested in this. How much—to his surprise—that he'd enjoyed this. It was the most daring competition he'd had to date.

'Oh yes, that would be utterly darling, wouldn't it?' she said, finally giving in.

And it felt like the most natural thing in the world to kiss her. He'd meant it as little more than a way to seal the deal, the punctuation mark to their decision. Nothing more than a light, almost friendly kiss. But the moment that his mouth met hers, every thought, every intention went up in flames, and all he was left with were *feelings*.

The jolt in his heart, the slight gasp from her lips that he swallowed, the way that after just a moment, they opened to each other instinctively, the hint of a growl in his throat and a sigh of surrender in hers, the delve of tongue and the way his hands moved, one gripping her hip, the other cupping her jaw, the sigh that she made as he turned something easy into something heady. He felt her hand press against his thundering heart, heat spreading like wildfire through his body, until he was breathless and she was wide-eyed with wonder. He pulled back, her cheeks flushed, blinking as if Erin was as shocked as him at how quickly things had escalated.

It had been a mistake, he realised, to be so smug. He had been unprepared. But he wouldn't let it happen again.

CHAPTER FOUR

ERIN'S HEAD WAS SPINNING, her mind oscillating between being so close to what she wanted, and losing herself to the memory of the sudden and utterly inexplicable kiss.

She pressed her fingers to her mouth, still bemused at the way that she had so easily succumbed to the shocking pleasure. She'd been unprepared—it was that simple. Surely if she'd expected it, it wouldn't have had such an impact?

She'd returned to the hotel and packed her suitcases, the entire time still feeling the tremors that had spread from his touch, from his *possession*. As she'd messaged Sam to let her know of her success, still she caught the scent of his aftershave as if it had become imprinted on her clothes.

Even now, as she got out of the car that had brought her and her cases down to the marina to meet the speedboat that would collect her and bring her to Enzo's yacht, she was still back in the middle of the restaurant, her hand on his chest, her mind unspooling at their feet. The port was still humming with tourists streaming on and off boats, even at this late hour, but she saw none of it. Instead, a pair of dark brown eyes with golden flecks consumed her. But she could *not* let him distract her and she could not lose herself like that again. And she wouldn't. She would know better now, she would be prepared.

Her phone beeped as the driver placed her luggage down beside her.

If I don't hear from you in two days, I'm calling Interpol.

Erin smiled at Sam's response to the message she'd sent earlier, letting her know that she'd accomplished Step Four. Getting on his yacht. It was nice to have someone worried about her. It was…she swallowed, unfamiliar. Her mother, following her father's fall from grace and subsequent abandonment, had retreated into herself. Losing everything they'd had and known seemed to have taken a large piece of Arla Carter and what had remained had been focused on getting through the day. Erin had sworn to herself by the age of seventeen that she would never let a man do that to her. She would never let a man determine the choices she made about her life.

Where her father was now was anyone's guess. She hadn't heard from him since he'd called just before her twenty-first birthday to ask her for money to invest in the *best* new business idea.

The toot of a moped's horn cut through her thoughts and she tuned back into the signs of life around her, inhaling the scent of the sea. She turned back and took in the Capri nightlife, loud and vibrant and bright, even at this hour. Couples lounged at café tables that had sprawled onto the streets, friends laughed and chatted, and even a few lovers danced beneath the stars to music wafting out of restaurants and bars.

Enzo hadn't even waited for them to start dinner, let alone finish it, that's how eager he'd been to get her onto the boat, she thought, amazed that she'd got this far in her plan. Of course, she'd have to make sure he understood, *truly* understood, that she wouldn't sleep with him, just because she had agreed to stay on his yacht.

Especially after that kiss.

She noticed her hand rise towards her lips and ordered herself to get a grip.

As for how he would feel about the line she would be drawing about no sex before marriage—or even after, if she had her way—that remained to be seen. It wasn't that she was a prude. Erin had had boyfriends in the past, both of whom had been very nice and considerate of her feelings. But they hadn't been able to compete with the attention she'd needed to give to HomeJames, or everything that she was doing to get Charterhouse back. And she'd not been able to bend for them like her mother had bent for her father... until there was very little of herself left.

So no, it wasn't that sex was abhorrent to her. But what *was* abhorrent was the idea of using sex to get what she wanted. She just couldn't bear to lie to him while sharing such an intimacy. That felt like a betrayal that she might not come back from. So, she had decided, before she'd even agreed to Gio's outrageous offer, that she could only go through with this if she *didn't* sleep with him.

As for how to go about that? She would use his reputation against him, insisting on waiting until after they were married to prove that he only wanted her for one thing— that she could not be just another flash-in-the-pan relationship like all his others. She imagined that his ego would be up for the challenge.

And after the marriage? Well, she'd explain to him that she had to return to London to assume her role as CEO of Charterhouse, and she doubted that the Playboy of Amalfi would be happy to sit idly by in London while she worked all hours god sent to turn around the failing publishing company. She'd be 'so very sorry' that it had come between them, but 'it wouldn't be for long'...just, oh, say, the six months that Gio Gallo has insisted upon?

And when she got the publishing company back from Gio
Gallo, she could begin to claw back a little of what they'd
lost. The family business. The security. Their identity. And
all she needed was—

'*Bellissima*,' called a very recognisable voice and she
opened her eyes to find Enzo standing at the large cream
wheel of a classic speedboat that *gleamed* in the lights from
the harbour.

He'd taken off his jacket, rolled back his sleeves, and
the white shirt, open at his neck, offered just a peek at the
spattering of swirls of dark chest hair. Combined with the
rakish grin across devastatingly handsome features, it had
a near heart-stopping lethality.

He seemed to revel in the attention that he and his boat
were getting, yet despite that, his focus remained solely on
her. He threw a rope up to a marina employee who tied it
off for him while Enzo climbed the stairs, stopping almost
directly in front of her. He held the two top rungs and leaned
back, as if to take her in fully.

'You are beautiful,' he said, as if he hadn't seen her but
twenty minutes before. The effect was quite unnerving for Erin
who had spent a significant portion of her teenage years trying
to avoid attention. However, *Rin* accepted it with a wry smile.

She leaned forward a little, to where he was looking up
at her.

'So are you,' she said truthfully and Enzo threw his head
back and laughed.

This one sounded different to many of the others she'd
heard from him in the last twenty-four hours. It sounded
free. And something in Erin preened to have made such an
impact, even as she reminded herself to be on her guard
against his charms.

'My lady,' he said affecting an upper-class British accent.

'Allow me,' he said, holding out his hand for her to take. Her luggage was already being passed down by harbour staff, so she let him lead her towards the metal ladder clinging to the side of the stone harbour wall. But when she'd expected him to move away, he didn't. And she found herself being turned in his arms and stepping backwards and down almost directly into his hold.

Her heart pumped as she was encased in the heat of his body. And though he wasn't touching her, she felt him envelop her. His aftershave, warm on the currents that flowed back and forth between them, bringing amber, salt, and citrus deep into her lungs when she breathed.

And then it was gone.

He jumped the small distance from the ladder to the boat below, his arm still outstretched to guide her.

'*Va bene*,' he said, when she and her luggage were stowed safely on the deck of the speedboat.

She was about to ask whether he was going to pilot the boat, before she realised that of course he would. After the helicopter, she shouldn't be surprised. But there was something nerve-wracking about the boat navigating its way out of the harbour into the darkness of the open sea.

Yet despite her discomfort, he seemed utterly in his element. Strong powerful hands guiding the wheel, the wind ruffling the dark hair that was longer on the top and shorter on the sides.

A pirate captain.

The fanciful description suited him.

As if he sensed her attention he turned slightly—eyes still on his destination—to ask, 'Do you want to have a go?'

'Driving?' Erin squeaked, and then remembered that she was supposed to be cool and sophisticated.

'Well, we say "steering," but yes,' he said with a smile.

* * *

He'd sensed her hesitation, but whatever had caused it was clearly thrust aside as she rose from the seat at the back of the speedboat, and came to meet him on unsteady feet, which was understandable given the way the boat wedged into the choppy waters.

He stood back to give her enough room to stand in front of him, and placed her hands where his had been. He noticed the shiver that passed across her body at the same time as sparks jabbed at his fingertips.

It was no matter that the woman was a conniving gold-digger out for whatever she could get from him. His body clearly hadn't got the message.

'But how do I know where I'm going? It's so dark,' she said, almost in awe of the expanse of night around them.

'Can you see that light in the distance?'

She nodded.

He bent his head to her ear and wondered if he imagined the shiver he felt from her body. 'Aim for that,' he whispered.

Determinedly, she put her hands on the wheel, flexing her fingers, and eventually took the cream leather in a firm grip.

'Like this?' she asked, and he couldn't tell whether the nervous excitement was for his benefit or real.

'Exactly like that. Just hold her steady.'

She nodded, the wind whipping at her hair, casting it free from the long line of her neck. And while there were many more places on a woman's body that he found erotic, the swanlike sweep of Rin's neck into her shoulder fascinated him for far longer than it should have done.

'You really are an adrenaline junkie,' she said to him, without taking her eye off the yacht's light in the distance.

He hadn't considered himself one before, but he was be-

ginning to agree with her. Being with Rin, playing this cat-and-mouse game, it was *thrilling*.

She squeaked in alarm when the speedboat hit a particularly determined wave, the *thunk* sending the nose upwards and in shock she pulled her hands off the wheel. He caught it almost immediately, laughing as she turned into him, hiding her face into his chest as she groaned in embarrassment.

Now *that*, he decided, was most definitely an act, but it only served his own cause. He anchored her with a hand around the back of her head, holding her to him for comfort.

'I think I'll let you do the driving,' she admitted with a smile, looking up at him with those incredible bright blue eyes.

'Your wish is my command.'

She turned back to face the horizon, but stayed in the circle of his arms, leaning back against his chest and he wondered whether it was natural to be so impressed with someone so treacherous.

They reached the yacht shortly after, a bright glowing beacon in the night seascape, where they were helped aboard by two uniformed deck-hands.

He'd already warned his staff of Rin's perfidy—namely so that they too could keep an extra eye on her. He had instructed them to treat her with no less respect or courtesy than any other guest, and he wasn't surprised to see the captain and crew welcoming her with wide, eager smiles.

'Shall I show you around?' Enzo asked, after the introductions were done.

'Please,' she said with a wide-eyed glance at her surroundings.

With one of the deck-hands already having swept away her luggage, he held his arm out for her to take. Rin was unable to keep the look of awe from her eyes—no one was

that good an actress. Though to be fair, the *Sea View* was a spectacular ship.

'She's one hundred and seventy-one feet, with five suites that can sleep eleven,' he said as he followed her out of the glass elevator and onto the sun deck that offered a dining area that could seat thirty people, a BBQ, and a protected Jacuzzi. She gravitated towards the rail at the back of the deck, to where in the distance the lights of Capri danced as the yacht began to muster its engines, ready to move them further on down the coast.

'The bridge is directly below us, along with many of the staff quarters and facilities. Below that is the lounge, more entertainment areas, and an office.'

'Do you use that office much?' she asked turning her back to the view, her arms stretched out across the railings and a wry smile across her lips.

'Never,' he lied, intensely private about the income he earned given just how many people wanted pieces of it. *Including Rin.*

'And where's your cabin?' she asked, the hint of flirtation in her raised eyebrow.

'Oh, Rin. I have nothing so small as a *cabin*,' he teased, an almost nauseatingly lewd innuendo. For a second he thought he saw her mask slip, as if she too had thought the same thing, but it was blinked away almost immediately. 'The *Sea View* boasts five *suites*,' he clarified. 'Would you like to see yours?'

She nodded, and he thought he saw relief in her gaze this time. As if she had thought he might try and install her in his. And distaste rolled in his gut. He might be willing to play this game, but he had never, would never, force someone against their will like that.

He took her down three floors to the deck that housed

the sleeping quarters. The interior design was all Art Deco, and he appreciated it anew through her eyes as she unconsciously ran her fingers across the smooth cherrywood polished to a glittering shine. The owner had been trying to sell it to him for years, but that spoke of a permanency that Enzo disliked intensely and would, he presumed, continue to reject for many years to come.

He led her down the corridor to the open door to the Queen suite and was satisfied to hear her gasp of surprise.

'It's *huge*,' she couldn't help herself from saying and he bit back a retort that would have had them both in hot water.

'As we missed dinner, I've arranged for something to eat back up on the sun deck, in say…thirty minutes?'

'Uh-huh,' she said, not quite paying attention as she walked around the spacious room with the double bed and the large sofa, chairs, and coffee table, opposite a desk and the wardrobe where her bags had been unpacked for her already.

'Then I'll see you soon,' he said with a smile, backing away from her room. He enjoyed making her speechless with his wealth. Because it revealed her true colours. Oh yes, he was very much looking forward to playing this game with Erin Carter.

Erin wasn't entirely *unfamiliar* with money. Before her father had sold the family business, they'd been one of the wealthiest families in London. With an address in Mayfair, she'd been to school at St Paul's Girls, and it had taken her father just the first fifteen years of her life to burn through the money and assets he had inherited.

Charles Edward Carter had made the grave mistake of falling foul of believing his own hype; that bluff and bluster could hide his own mediocrity and bad business sense.

He'd chased one dream after another until finally, one too many bad investments brought debt-collector to their door.

Oh, nothing so uncouth as large scary men in black clothing with rough accents. No, this creditor was as eloquent as her father. He'd worn a suit, just like her father. And he'd smiled while he'd stripped them of every single one of their assets, except the house that had been put in her mother's name down in Cornwall.

So, Erin Carter *did* remember a time when money was rife. But this? She swallowed as she walked, wide-eyed, around the spacious suite that would fit nearly the entire top floor of her mother's house in Falmouth inside it.

And yes, in some respects, Erin had her own money— from the sale of the HomeJames. She had just over one million pounds sitting in her bank account. But that money was earmarked for Charterhouse. She'd never even really considered it *hers* given that it would take every penny of that money to bring the small publishing company back to life and regain all that her father had cost her and her mother.

She pushed through to the en suite bathroom, with a claw tub. A claw tub! The Art Deco mirror above a basin so large she could wash her hair in it was nothing short of beautiful. Shaking her head, she returned to the main suite and collapsed onto the impossibly soft bed.

And he didn't even *own* this. He just rented it for the summer.

She shook her head in awe. Enzo really got all this wealth just from his parents? she wondered, surprised. Yes, she knew that his father had been an actor with a series of wildly successful films in his heyday. But these days he was known more for the increasingly younger women he dated. And his mother, Gio's daughter—strikingly beautiful, dark hair and unusually pale skin—had been cut off

from the family coffers when Gio disowned her following her marriage to Luca Rossetti.

Was it possible that there was more to Enzo than he portrayed? So far she'd seen the daredevil, the itinerant playboy, the autocratic charmer...but there was nothing mean in his carelessness, not intentionally so. She sensed nothing *cruel* about him.

She sank back into the bed. The last few days had been a whirlwind. And really, the hard work was only just beginning. Tomorrow, she'd have to set out to snare more than just the Playboy of Amalfi's attentions. She needed his ring.

She rubbed a hand over her sternum, willing away any sense of guilt she may have had. She needed to do this. For her mother, for herself. She *needed* to. So that she would never experience again the kind of hurt and betrayal that her father had shown her.

She sighed and checked her watch. If she was *really* quick, perhaps she could have a bath in that amazing tub before heading back up for dinner.

Thirty minutes later, punctual because Erin couldn't concede that personality trait to Rin, she arrived on the deck in a dress from Rin's side of the closet, determined to kick things into gear now that she was that much closer to getting what she needed.

The burnt orange silk of her dress pressed seductively against her skin from the warm breeze that flowed around the upper deck, as she exited the glass elevator and she stopped in her tracks when she saw what awaited her.

Enzo stood with a bottle of champagne beside a table set for two with a thick white tablecloth, twinkling glasses and rose petals scattered everywhere.

Her hand flew to her mouth to stifle the gasp of genuine shock. Because while in some ways it was beautiful, it

was also as if Cupid had gotten a little carried away with himself. Garlands of red flowers hung in strands, amongst fairy lights that changed from white to red. There were even paper love hearts strewn about the deck, pressed up against pink lanterns.

'Champagne?' Enzo asked exuberantly.

'Yes please,' she squeaked, coughing to clear the shock from her throat.

Enzo popped the bottle and poured the champagne into two flutes, thoroughly pleased with himself.

'Do you think it's perhaps a little too much?' Frederick, the deck-hand, had asked when he'd stood back to admire their efforts.

'Absolutely,' Enzo had replied. 'It's *perfect*!'

He wanted to drown her in romance, pretend to be the besotted fool all just to convince her that she had him dangling on her hook. He wanted nothing to jeopardise his own plan of vengeance.

'What do you think?' Enzo asked Rin now.

'It's...' She swallowed. 'Very romantic,' she said as if it was anything but.

'Just what I was aiming for,' Enzo replied truthfully.

He passed her a flute and raised his in a toast.

'To all the fun and adventures we are about to embark on, *together*. To us!'

'To us,' she repeated and when she went to take a sip, he stopped her with an 'op!'

She paused, the glass an inch from delectably pink lips.

He adopted an expression that could only be read as '*silly girl*', and held out his arm in a hook.

It seemed to take her a moment to realise that she was

supposed to weave her arm around his and that they were to sip together.

But the nauseated look that crossed her features for just a second was an utter delight to him and worth every moment of the ridiculous act. An act that brought her close enough for him to see the swallow of her throat as she took a sip, the breeze bringing just a trace of the complex heady scent she wore.

Cirtus and pepper. Sharp and hot.

He liked it. It suited her.

'So,' he said, pulling out a chair for her at the small table, already laid with crostini covered in mouthwatering toppings, 'tell me about this project that would have stolen you away from me,' he commanded with mock officiousness as he took the seat opposite.

'What do you want to know?'

What you're after, he thought.

'Everything,' he replied instead. He could find out of course—at the drop of a hat. There were any number of highly skilled and extremely discreet investigators he could turn to. But Enzo felt somehow as if that would be cheating. And besides, he wanted to know what she would tell him. But he was sure that her excuse hadn't been some whim, some easy lie. He couldn't exactly explain why, but there had been something about it, about her, that had rung *true*.

'I…'

Was she going to continue the charade or give him something real? He was almost on the edge of his seat.

'I have an opportunity to purchase a company I've been looking at for quite some time.'

Oh really. Was she just laying foundations for the long con to relieve him of his well-earned money? Or was there something genuine here?

'It probably wouldn't mean much to you,' she said, as if he could not understand such sentimentality. 'It's just a small, floundering publishing company whose name few remember. But it was excellent once,' she said, the smile gracing her lips both sad and beautiful at the same time. He'd not seen her wield this one before. 'It published crime novels full of murder and mystery from authors all over the world.'

'You like these books,' Enzo saw.

'Yes,' she replied, nodding her head definitively.

'Why?' he couldn't help but ask.

She hesitated, as if choosing her words. 'I like… I like that the murder is symptomatic of something that is inherently wrong with society,' she said, surprising him a little with her philosophy. 'I like that it reflects a societal failing that has resulted in the death of the victim. That while the detective can identify the criminal, the murderer, whose reasons are almost always selfish, he can also point to a moral failing inherent in society.'

He wondered if she realised that her syntax had changed. Her use of language. This, Enzo was beginning to suspect, was the real Erin Carter. And he was just a little frustrated, because *this* Erin, he might have actually have enjoyed even more.

'That is important to you? Moral judgement?' Enzo asked, trying to keep the scepticism out of his voice. This seemed to run so contrary to everything about Rin's scheme to marry him and use him for his money.

'Yes,' she said. 'Is it not to you?'

'I think we may have different morals,' he replied, using a smile to cover his reaction to her audacity.

'Does your publisher do any other genres?'

She struggled to hold onto her smile. 'It's not my publisher yet.'

'But it will be. Of that I am sure. I can see the determination in your eyes,' he said, gesturing to her with his glass. 'How did you come to know of it?' Enzo asked, wanting to hear a little more of *this* Erin Carter.

Erin shifted in her seat. She probably shouldn't have told him about Charterhouse. It was too personal. Too real. But she had started, and now she couldn't quite unring that bell.

'I knew the family who once owned it. I've been…notified the current owner is willing to sell.'

'It means a lot to you,' he observed.

She nodded, knowing her voice would break if she spoke.

Charterhouse had been in her family for generations before her father sold it, when she was fifteen. It hadn't just been a business to her. It hadn't just been financial. Her grandfather and great-grandfather, and even great-great-grandfather had loved the business. Using local printers, employing local artists, but publishing all around the world. And yes, while she understood that there were better business models, quicker, cheaper, they were also heartless and soulless and that was exactly what she didn't want.

But her father had sold it to cover the debts he had incurred with the many side hustles he had ventured for, all just to avoid putting in the work that Charterhouse needed. He had always chased the big break, the quick buck, bouncing from one failed idea to the next, uncaring of the impact on anyone else around him.

She didn't need Charterhouse to make huge amounts of money, she just needed it to make enough so that she could put the things her father had wronged to rights.

When we get Charterhouse back, everything will be okay.

'Well, then how could I possibly compete with such a heart project?' Enzo said, tilting his head to one side, mak-

ing her feel as if he were studying her, watching for her reaction.

You aren't, she thought. *You are my way of securing it.*

'You must do whatever it takes to secure it,' Enzo insisted.

'You think?' she asked, knowing that he was utterly unaware of the implications of what he was saying.

'Oh absolutely. Whatever it takes.'

She nodded. *Okay then. Whatever it takes.* She would be *everything* Enzo Rossetti expected in a lover—spoilt, rich, silly—to get him to take their relationship to a more serious, permanent, level for Step Five; getting what *she* wanted.

CHAPTER FIVE

SAUNTERING DOWN THE hill towards the centre of Positano with Rin on his arm, Enzo mentally mused over the messages he'd exchanged with Marcus last night, after Rin had gone to bed. He'd been unnerved by the conversation, doubting himself and the plan. There had been something unusually honest and natural about her responses to his questions last night. As if he'd been hearing from the real Erin Carter.

If you're worried, you just need to find proof.

What kind of proof?

Surely, if she's a real gold-digger, then she'll jump at the chance to spend your money? Just give her the opportunity and see what happens.

Marcus was right. If she proved herself ready to spend his money, then she deserved everything she had coming to her. Which was why he had come up with the plan to take her shopping. And Rin had seemed utterly delighted with the idea.

The speedboat had dropped them off at the little concrete marina serving the centre of Positano, where it brushed

right up against a small sandy strip of beach fronted by a near inconceivable amount of restaurants in the small bay.

From there, they had wound their way around the steep cobbled streets, packed with tourists of every kind. Bright boutiques, jewellery stores, trinket shops, galleries, designer clothes—there was everything that a morally corrupt heart could desire. And he'd been almost disappointed when all it had taken for Rin to revel in her newfound riches was the slightest of pushes.

'Here, *amore mio*. Whatever you like,' he said, offering her the black credit card that had no limit. 'It's my pleasure to provide.'

There had been a single moment when she had looked between him and the card in his hand, when he'd thought perhaps, just perhaps she might decline the offer. When he'd thought that she'd really wanted to. But then she'd plucked it from his hand and practically skipped into the first shop of so very many.

As he watched her trawl through silk scarves, expensive sunglasses, glass beaded necklaces, swimming costumes, and silk dresses, he could almost have been impressed. There didn't seem to be any cohesive pattern to her purchases, their styles were varied and almost erratic, in bemusing contrast to the style and elegance Erin sometimes displayed.

She stopped at every single clothing store, each more expensive than the last, jewellery stores glittering with diamonds and gold, and even tourist stores as if she were a child hunting down her favourite treats. It was almost amusing to see her behave in a way so charmingly juvenile and silly.

But he was also relieved. At least now he knew. At least now, Enzo thought, he could finally put her in the box she'd been somewhat difficult to squeeze into, now that he was sure she was a gold-digger.

He hung back as Rin trapsed off to another shop along the steep, narrow, cobbled steps as he fired off a message to Marcus.

Took the bait. Hook, line and sinker.

Three dots appeared on his screen, as Marcus composed a reply.

You have your answer then.
And my congratulations on your forthcoming nuptials!

Ahh, finally. She had shaken Enzo's limpet-like attachment to her side and found a shop that she actually *liked.* Unlike the others that had been filled with improbable silks and impractical satins, here were more wearable clothes in linen and cotton for her time on the yacht.

She breathed a little sigh of relief at her moment of freedom. It was exhausting being the perfect girlfriend for Enzo. But every time she spent his money, he seemed more and more pleased. Of course, Erin had no real intention of wearing even half of what she'd bought and had every intention of returning the items the first chance she could get in order to refund the money into his account.

One of the main reasons this entire plan was bearable was because it wasn't costing Enzo a penny. As for emotionally? Well, he'd left a swathe of broken hearts across the world. Surely his could do with a little denting in return?

Her fingers brushed along the palazzo trousers that she was drawn to, the cotton shirts that looked loose and comfortable, because she really *did* need some more clothes. She hadn't exactly packed with a long yacht trip in mind. She picked a few things off the rails. A cropped sleeveless

linen top with matching wide-legged trousers. A simple linen dress, a long-sleeved shirt and a cotton jumper. Things that she would pay for herself, she decided.

'Would you like to try something on, *Signorina*?'

Erin tore her gaze away and smiled at the saleswoman. 'Yes, please,' she said, and gave the items she wanted to try on to the woman who placed them in the changing area for her. Really, it was just a curtained-off corner, but it would suffice.

Her phone beeped with a message from Sam just as she was looking at a cotton vest.

Is it working?

Was it? She *thought* so. She just wished she didn't feel so guilty. The way that he'd listened to her last night, as if he was actually paying attention to what she was saying, the way that she had wanted to believe that he actually did support her goal for Charterhouse...it felt wrong somehow because she was using him to get it.

But she forced those doubts aside, because he was right, she did need to do whatever was necessary to get her hands on it. Because *when we get Charterhouse back*... So, she typed back a reply to Sam and sent a pic of all the shopping bags she'd amassed at his expense so far.

I think so.

Samara sent back a head exploding emoji and Erin smiled a little. Her phone beeped again just as she was about to put it back in her bag.

I hear wedding bells!

Erin then jumped when the bell across the door to the shop sounded and Enzo appeared.

'So, this is where I find you?' he asked, looking around at the clothes in the shop as if he were a little confused. They were probably too cheap for him and a part of her was irritated by his disdain.

Shoving it aside, she smiled at him and said, 'Well, as beautiful as silks and satins are, if we are going to spend the next ten days on a yacht, I might need something a little more practical.'

'I don't see why,' he dismissed. 'But as you wish. Let's see,' he said, fluttering his hand at her and sinking into a chair at the opposite end of the shop. He had a new shopping bag with him and she wondered whether he'd finally given in and bought himself something.

'You want a fashion show?' she asked, her voice high-pitched in surprise.

'Yes,' he said, crossing his ankle over his leg, as if settling in for the long haul.

She looked for a way out, but couldn't see one, and eventually retreated to the changing room, passing the shop manager who had caught sight of Enzo Rossetti and had dollar signs in her eyes.

Erin closed the curtains around her and bit her lip. There was nothing indecent about what she was doing. He couldn't *see* anything. But it felt…strange to be undressing in such close proximity to him. Not that he'd care, she realised. He could have seen hundreds of naked forms. What was one more? And with that slightly deflating thought, she changed into the first outfit.

Enzo cast an eye around the clothes, all of them attractive, and good quality, but nothing he'd have thought particu-

larly extravagant enough to catch Rin's eye. He scanned the room, coming to a halt when his gaze caught on the sliver of the changing room that the curtain had failed to cover.

It was nothing indecent. He'd seen more flesh on the beach at Capri the night they'd met. All he could see was the curve of her shoulder and the flare of her hip. He should look away, but it was impossible. Because he knew the feel of the flare of her hip beneath his palm, he'd traced the long line of her neck with his fingers. Even now his body warmed from the memory of it.

Erin's honeyed cream skin glowed beneath the spotlight above the changing area. His fingers curled reflexively, his jaw tightened. He caught sight of her face in profile as she fiddled with something—a button, a zip?—the frown of concentration and the slight flush on her cheeks. Could she tell? Could she feel his gaze? Had she done this on purpose? he wondered.

He felt like a voyeur which only served to enflame the wildfire of arousal burning across his body. By the time she emerged from the changing area to see herself in the only full-length mirror in the shop, he was wound as tightly as an unexploded bomb.

Seemingly unaware, Rin walked to the mirror and turned her back to him, and he watched her observe herself, at first critically and then with something like surprise.

The wide-legged trousers flattered the narrow lines of her curves, and the sleeveless linen top showcased the sleek lines of her toned arms.

It shouldn't have looked anything other than okay. But the rich forest-green linen made her look like a wild sprite, ready to demand his servitude.

She caught his gaze in the reflection in the mirror and stilled.

It was a strange moment, her clear blue eyes wide and on him, and with a jolt he realised that her mask had slipped. The vulnerability he saw there was not fake or imagined. It was real because he felt it like a punch to his chest.

The saleswoman oohed and aahed, and shooed her back into the changing area, closing the curtain, cutting off his line of sight completely this time.

Bereft. It left him bereft.

He waited impatiently for her to return from the changing area and when she did so, he was a little disappointed to see the sleeveless, halter-top dress that flowed down to the ground from her throat. The saleswoman disappeared to answer a ringing phone at precisely the moment that Rin turned to look at herself in the mirror and Enzo lost his breath.

It whooshed out of him inelegantly. The dress was backless. Smooth delicate skin covered the gentle slopes of the shoulder blades and spine left bare to his ferocious perusal. The dress caressed only the side of her body, hinting at— and only just stopping short of revealing—the curve of her breast. The material came back together just below the flare of her hip, hovering tantalisingly at the base of her spine.

Hypnotised, he got to his feet and came to stand just behind her. Barely inches from her, he could feel the heat of her skin draw him in against his will. She turned her head to the side, not enough to see him, not enough for him to see her, the gesture could have been one of submission, if it wasn't for the way that her hands were fisted at her side.

He bit his lip, staring down at her, every part of his body as tense as the line that drew taut across her shoulders. His pulse raged in his ears. His fingers ached to take her hips, and haul her back against him. Against the hard ridge of his arousal. Something he would not allow himself to do.

But he *did* bend down and place his lips against the curve
of her neck.

It was just a test, he assured himself. Just to see, to make
sure that he was protected against her this time, and not
taken unawares like he had been with the first kiss. But
sensation swept over him like the pull of the ocean, drawing him beneath a tide of lust that he was helpless to fight.
A drowning death he was only happy to surrender to.

Unable to help himself, he opened his mouth to taste her
with his tongue. She shivered beneath the erotic caress,
her nipples taut, her breath a sharp jerk in her chest, and he
thanked god he wasn't the only one so affected by whatever
it was between them.

He took that much because it punished them both for the
games they were playing.

He took that much because that was the price he was willing to pay for being undone by her completely.

And with that thought ricocheting around his brain like
a bullet he stepped back. The saleswoman returned to the
room and he reached into his pocket and held out his card.

'Put anything she wants on that,' he ordered, before turning on his heel, picking up the bag containing the item he'd
already purchased and stalking from the shop.

He needed some air, because he couldn't see clearly when
it came to her, and he wasn't so arrogant that he didn't consider that he might be genuinely at risk of the one thing
he'd promised himself as a child he'd never do; falling for
someone who only wanted to use him for their own ends.

He couldn't prevaricate any longer. He needed to push
this game forward if only just to get to the end.

Rin, would you come to the upper deck?
I have something to ask you.

Erin stared at the text she'd received for longer than was necessary. Was this it? Was he going to ask her to marry her?

After Positano, Enzo had been quiet all the way back to the yacht and she wasn't sure if she'd done something wrong, or…or…honestly, she didn't really know any more.

Because when he'd found her in the shop, when he'd come to stand behind her, when he'd *kissed* her… She'd felt it. The pull, the attraction to him. Even now she shuddered, felt a fresh explosion of tingles across her skin. From a *memory*. Her heart-beat raced, her skin flushed… She'd wanted him so much it had filled her chest and stifled her breath. She'd swallowed that want to prevent it from escaping, but it had only bled into every cell in her body, hot, pulsing, *needing*.

But she wasn't *that* woman, mindlessly reacting to the charms of a playboy. She couldn't be. She had one purpose here and she needed to hold onto that, she thought as her fingers curled and her knuckles whitened in determination.

Slowly, she made her way up to the deck, hugging the scarf she'd bought with her own money around her shoulders as the slight chill of the night wrapped around her.

And once again, arriving on the upper deck, she paused in her tracks.

If she'd thought that the deck had been extravagant before, this was…a whole new level.

A single chair had been placed in the centre of the deck within a circle of rose petals. Enzo stood in a white tuxedo jacket and shirt, the tie and the trousers, midnight black superfine wool, a bouquet of roses in one hand and a flute of champagne in the other.

'Signorina Carter, *per favore*,' he said, gesturing for her to take the seat amongst the pretty petals.

She opened her mouth to object, but this was what she'd

wanted, wasn't it? This would give her the chance to give back to her mother what her father had taken from them. This was everything she needed. So why was she hesitating now?

She took the seat and realised that it faced outwards towards the dark seascape that stretched for miles. In the background, a romantic song began to play, coming from invisible speakers with lyrics that spoke of everlasting love and soul mates finding each other.

Then, out of the darkness, a thousand lights began to glow, twisting and morphing like starlings, ebbing and flowing with the music, until they formed an image of hearts and the word *love*.

Drones. She realised they were drones and for a moment, lost herself in the delight of how beautiful they were. Hypnotised by the sight and sounds she was surrounded by, she almost didn't realise that Enzo had come to stand beside her and when the drones finally formed into the question she should have expected, Enzo had dropped to his knee and upheld a small velvet box with the most stunning pink diamond engagement ring in it.

'So, will you, *cara*?' he asked. Nodding his head to the sky that had 'Will you marry me?' written across it.

'I… I'm not sure,' she said with a false hesitation that had nothing to do with any last-minute doubts and everything to do with needing him to agree to her stipulation.

'You're not…*sure*?' he repeated, as if half in shock.

Even the drones seemed to wobble in the air in surprise.

'I just…this is all happening so quickly,' she lied.

This, at least, was true. It was actually a lot quicker than she'd expected. And no, she didn't really think for a single second that Enzo Rossetti, the Playboy of Amalfi, had actually fallen head over heels in love with Rin. Not in the

space of *days*. No, this was just another example of the affectations of a bored playboy with too much money and time on his hands. She was quite happy to use that to her advantage! However…

'I just don't want to think that this is happening because of what I said the other day about having traditional values.'

'You are worried that I am only proposing so that I can sleep with you, perhaps?'

Well, yes. She needed to make it clear that she wouldn't. She was 'managing expectations' as much as she was making herself even *more* tempting to a man who clearly loved to chase.

'I want this to be special. For this to *mean* something. For it not to be just another short-term fling for you,' she said coyly.

'Oh, I assure you, *cara,* that what you and I have is utterly unique. I have never had anything like this before,' he said with a glint in his eye.

'I don't want you to think that if we become engaged, that…'

'That you'll have sex with me.'

Oh, she wished he'd stop saying it like that. It made it sound so *transactional.* And then she felt guilty. Because this *was* a transaction. But despite her silly reaction to a few kisses *and* the fact that Enzo Rossetti *was* the most handsome man she'd ever encountered, she *was* using him to get what she wanted. Which was exactly why she couldn't sleep with him, even after they were married.

'So, if that's what you're after—'

He threw his head back and laughed.

'It's really not,' he said in a tone that she wasn't quite sure how to interpret as he finally got to his feet.

Why he was taking this so easily?

'*Amore mio*, I'll be clear. I will not try to seduce you before our wedding. In fact, I promise to protect your wishes, even if you beg me to change my mind!'

His arrogant confidence grated on her nerves.

'More so, I promise that I will not expect or even *allow* you to give me any kind of pleasure until we are married.'

Oh the arrogance!

Enzo was more than a little frustrated, and no less bemused. He might have expected her to do something like this, but still. He had proposed. And she was supposed to want this after all. Surely it should have been an easy 'yes'.

'As for the prenup...' he dangled, curious to see how she would convince him that it wasn't needed.

'Oh, of course. As soon as your lawyers have drawn it up I'll happily sign it,' Rin insisted.

What? She would 'happily' sign a prenup? *What game was she playing?*

Surely her plan hinged on being able to marry him and divorce him for some unforgivable trespass so that she could skip off into the sunset with half of his—admittedly incredibly impressive—wealth.

'You have no qualms about...joining our assets?' he poked, hoping to find the loophole she would presumably seek to exploit.

She shook her head. 'Only that, in the event of a split, we keep what we came into the marriage with.'

He frowned. This was not going as he thought it would. Of course, he'd not intended to bother with a prenup because there wouldn't, in fact, be a marriage. His plan was to leave her at the altar, to expose her as a gold-digger, and use her as a deterrent to anyone in future attempting to fleece him in such a way. He considered those who would

abuse the finer, softer feelings for financial purposes the highest of criminals. And as such, they deserved swift and harsh judgement.

But this seemed to suggest that she *wasn't* after his money?

As for the no sex rule, that he *had* expected. She had said as much before. Personally, he'd thought the naïve virgin shtick a bit much, but she was playing her game and he was playing his. Returning to the more pressing matter, he shook his head decisively.

'I don't see a need for a prenup,' he announced.

She blinked. '*I* would like one,' she said, a hint of steel unexpected, but welcome in her tone.

Really?

'Can I ask why?' he probed.

She opened her mouth, and closed it again. She really did have a very pretty mouth.

'Well, so that you know I don't want you for your money,' she said with a little frown.

He let loose the laugh that had built in his chest.

'Woman have wanted me for a lot of things, *cara*. Money is only one of them.'

Once again she blushed and his respect for her art, her *craft*, only increased.

'But okay, I will have my lawyer draw up a prenup,' he agreed. It would be a waste of his money and the other man's time, but if it would make her happy, then he would do it.

'Thank you,' she said.

'So, now that we have that out of the way, may I continue?' he asked.

Her eyes widened with something like an apology as she nodded, and widened her eyes even more when he got back on to his knee. Really, this was a formality on the way for

him to get her where he wanted her—at the top of the aisle, but he waited until her curaçao-coloured gaze landed on his before delivering the speech he had prepared.

'Erin Carter. Meeting you has been truly unexpected and utterly remarkable to a man like me who was just beginning to feel that he had seen all there was to see.' *Of the lengths that some people would go to*, he mentally added with a growl. 'You have shown me that there is so much more beauty to see in the world,' he continued, *and caused me to wonder if there is anything real behind the mask you wear so carefully.* 'I am utterly, and completely enchanted,' *by the skills of your deception.* 'I would have you by my side until the very end,' he said, *of the aisle, at which point you will find yourself unceremoniously dumped and you will be removed from my life with nothing but the clothes you came in with.* 'I will give you your heart's desire,' he swore, *when hell freezes over.*

His internal accompaniment seemed all the more perfect with the look of ecstatic happiness painted across her delicate features. He rose from the floor and drew her to him, his index finger lifting her chin slightly so that he could look deep into her eyes.

'You would make me the happiest man in the world,' he said, prising the box open and holding it up to her, 'if you would just say *yes*.'

She blinked, her gaze on his, holding it, and for a single, strange, suspended heartbeat, he thought that perhaps she might say no. Was startled, in fact, to discover the leap of his own heart, the thud of his own pulse as he wanted it, wanted her to say 'yes' more than he could remember wanting something in a very long time.

'Oh, Enzo. Yes! Yes, absolutely, yes,' she cried, reaching for him.

He swallowed. Of course they had to kiss. And no, the Playboy of Amalfi was most categorically *not* scared of a silly little thing like a kiss. Besides, he was forewarned now, and very much over whatever hormone-driven haze had ridden him so hard in Positano. So when he pulled her into his arms and took her mouth with his he was ready for her, he told himself.

But when her lips softened beneath his, hesitantly opening for him, offering him hints of honey and oranges that lulled him into a false sense of security, he struggled to hold onto his restraint.

The feel of her beneath him, welcoming him, breathed life into the wildfire that had been momentarily banked and he was caught in a backdraft of lust like he'd never experienced before.

Her fingers, pressing against his chest, tensed and for a moment he thought she might push him away, as if she too were struggling with the same burning inferno. Until they unfurled and sank against his heart, a sensual surrender of sorts, far less X-rated than what he was used to, but no less heady.

Good god, she'd been holding back on him. The power she had. If she only knew, he would have succumbed far more quickly than this.

But it didn't strike him until much later, how strange it was that Rin—a gold-digger hell-bent on taking him for every penny he owned—didn't even look at the five-carat pink diamond solitaire engagement ring.

Not once.

CHAPTER SIX

ERIN EMERGED INTO sunshine the next day back onto a deck completely cleared of rose petals and romance. So much so that she could almost think she'd imagined it. The proposal, the romance, the *kiss*.

It had been…overwhelming. Not that she'd said as much in her message to Sam. No, she'd simply stripped the content back to the most pertinent information. The response had been pure Sam.

Congratulations. Now get his signature and get your company back!

Erin smiled. The woman hadn't created a global women's network without being focused and determined. The staff member she'd passed below deck had asked her what she'd wanted for breakfast and by the time she was at the table on the upper deck, coffee and orange juice and hot pastries were already waiting for her.

She looked at the plates of cornetti and pistachio-filled sfogliatelle that she was becoming addicted to. She sat down just in time to see Enzo emerge onto the deck, dark glasses hiding his gaze, but making the most of the powerful line of his angular jaw. Trim hips encased in dark blue linen and a pale blue shirt, the man combined luxury and beauty to lethal levels.

Instantly she was reminded of the dreams that had kept her tossing and turning all night long. Where his lips had kissed her palm, her neck, her mouth, and where his touch had dropped from her head, to press against the outline of her body. Even now her pulse skipped, at the way in her dream he'd licked—

'*Buongiorno, amore mio*, I trust you slept well?'

'Wonderfully,' she lied. 'And you?'

He shrugged and puffed out a breath. 'Oh, restless. Too much excitement.'

'From last night?' she asked thinking of the dramatic and romantic proposal.

'Oh, no *cara*. Last night was magical, but it will be the next twelve days that will be *exciting*.'

'Really?'

'Absolutely! Later today we will stop at Isola del Giglio. A friend is throwing a party there. And then tomorrow we set sail for Cannes.'

'We're going to France?' Erin blinked.

'Absolutely. I have grown bored of the Amalfi Coast,' he said, sinking into the seat with what Erin considered to be a rather artificial 'sulk'. 'And Cannes has this *gorgeous* little chapel that I thought would be just *perfect* for our wedding.'

'In twelve days' time,' she parroted.

'Yes! Isn't it wonderful? We'll make a lazy crossing to get us there in plenty of time. The staff,' he said, pointing down to a boat that had arrived beside the yacht, 'are already preparing for our needs.'

Erin bit her lip. Twelve days. Was that all it would take? Twelve days and she could have Charterhouse, *if* she married Enzo Rossetti.

'Wonderful,' she lied.

'Isn't it just? And tonight we can celebrate our engagement. And I have the *perfect* thing for you to wear.'

She nodded absently, not really wanting to be under a public microscope with Enzo. For some reason she'd thought that after all the negative press attention he'd had over the years, he might want to keep their engagement private.

But she frowned when her thoughts caught up with his words. 'Do I not have something appropriate?'

'Not at all, *amore mio*. I just picked you up a little something in Positano and have been looking for the perfect excuse to give it to you. I think you'll look *spettacolare*.'

Three hours later as Enzo dressed in his room, Erin glared at herself in the mirror. Oh, she looked spectacular alright. Spectacularly *awful!*

Surely, he couldn't be serious. The dress was hideous. It was an organza creation of pleated material that made her think of origami, with ruffles at the neck and wrists. In some ways it *should* have been beautiful. Only the colours were absolutely dreadful on her. They seemed to make her appear green to the point of sickness.

Her suspicions were confirmed by the way that the yacht staff she passed on her way to the deck all averted their eyes within milliseconds of catching sight of her. Presumably so they didn't end up in hysterics.

Oh god.

'Rin! *Bella, molto bella.*'

His rapturous response was a little unsettling and when she suggested that she might feel a little more *comfortable* in one of her own dresses, he asked, 'Why? Rin, it is perfect, no?'

And although she very much wanted to say no, she couldn't risk offending him. Not when everything was so close to her reach.

So although the speedboat taking them from the yacht to Enzo's friend's private estate on the Isola del Giglio had to go slower than usual, *because of the dress,* they disembarked onto a jetty strewn with thousands of fairy lights just as dusk hit.

Enzo held his hand out to help her from the boat and she had to try three times to find it beneath the explosion of organza fanning from her sleeve.

'Is something wrong, *cara*?'

'Not at all, *my love,*' she added sweetly, instead of the much more derogatory term she wanted to use. She finally found his hand and stepped onto the jetty, looking up at the sprawling walled estate that stretched almost as far as she could see. Hundreds of people waited at the grand entrance to the estate that lay within the walls.

'I thought you said this was a small get-together,' she whispered to him.

Enzo looked about him. 'This is small? It is only four, five hundred people.' He dismissed her question and Erin's stomach dropped. Already she could feel the weight of people's gazes on *her*, on the *dress*. This was going to be awful. Truly awful.

This was fabulous! It couldn't have been any better. Erin Carter looked…appalling. Really there was no other way to describe it. He could almost feel bad about it. Almost. If he didn't know that she was manipulating him for her own agenda. He'd wanted to see how far she would go. And this? Well, this told him just how desperate she truly was.

He led her proudly on his arm as if he didn't have any trouble navigating the folds and fans of the dress that threatened to trip them both up if he wasn't careful. He smiled greetings to a few people he recognised, not caring in the

least that they all stared wide-eyed at the woman beside him. That was, after all, the entire point.

Over by the large Corten steel gates to the Marberry estate—a far too English sounding and appearing place for his Italian tastes, even if they had been watered down by the American quarter he'd inherited from his father—stood Marcus talking to some joint acquaintances.

Cynthia was a hanger-on who was often found sniffing around Marcus. He seemed to enjoy the attention, but Enzo was not exactly a fan. She could be catty on occasion and he was beginning to regret that she was there, realising in a heartbeat that she would take full advantage of Erin's hideous appearance. On paper—or at least, in his mind—his idea had been perfect. But now that he was confronted with the reality of what would happen, had he perhaps gone too far?

'Enzo!' Marcus called, catching sight of him, his hand raised in the air halting mid-wave as he caught sight of the dress on his arm. Or, more accurately, Rin. 'Hi!' he greeted Enzo, evidently trying to fire a million telepathic questions at him through his wide-eyed gaze.

'Marcus, Cynthia,' Enzo greeted, 'may I introduce Rin Carter. Rin, this is Marcus and Cynthia, two old friends.'

'Less of the old there, chum,' Marcus chided with a shoulder into Enzo's side.

'Charmed,' Cynthia said, with a smile that didn't even begin to reach the narrowing of her eyes.

'It's nice to meet you both,' Rin said letting the hand she'd held out drop back into the organza when it wasn't taken.

'That's a bold choice of dress, I must say,' Cynthia proclaimed when she finally found her voice.

'Thank you,' Rin said, interestingly choosing not to lay the blame at his feet, no matter how much he deserved it.

But, he reasoned, she could have said 'no' to wearing it. Surely the dress was just *more* proof that Rin would do whatever she had to, to get her hands on…on what? She wanted to sign a prenup. Well, maybe once her lawyers got their hands on it, they wouldn't be so accommodating.

'Rin has done the unthinkable, and foolishly agreed to marry me,' he announced, forcing the subject and enjoying the way that Cynthia and Marcus eyed the spectacular engagement ring on her finger.

Cynthia looked utterly confused, and Enzo shook off the irritation he felt at the obvious slight. After all, it was what he'd wanted, wasn't it? He wanted people to know. He wanted people to be confused and intrigued enough so that when it came time for Erin's punishment, it would be full and public. The press would get wind of it soon enough, and he'd prepare and deliver a press statement in about a week, to ensure maximum exposure.

'Shall we?' Cynthia said to no one in particular, apparently choosing to ignore the rather shocking news of his engagement, as she turned and led the way through the gates into the party proper.

Enzo held back and watched Rin go, not feeling delighted in the looks of shock and half-laughs that she was drawing as she did so.

'So, *this* is the gold-digger trying to fleece you for your millions,' Marcus whispered, casting an eye over her. 'What is she wearing?' he asked, half-horrified.

'A mistake,' Enzo murmured, for the first time unsure whether it was on her part or his.

The party was loud and brash, and Enzo was surprised to find it rather unwelcome after the last few days of relative peace on the boat. His gaze constantly returned to Rin who had been smiling in a way that made him think of ab-

ject misery before she excused herself. It had made him feel guilty and he didn't like the unusual and unfamiliar feeling.

He tuned out whatever Marcus was talking about and focused on what was going on further out around them. He felt people's gazes on him, saw the whispering behind hands, over champagne flutes as if that would hide the scathing attention they turned his way. He should be happy, surely. So why wasn't he?

The twinkling lights hung around the garden flashed like paparazzo cameras and he was no longer at the party here on Isola del Giglio. Instead, he was nine years old, walking alone down the steps of the law court where his parents' obscenely public divorce had taken on the weight of a show trial. The public was ravenous for the airing of their dirty laundry—the affairs, the substance abuse, the alcoholism, the neglect. In stark contrast to the near violent silence of his extended family, of the famous Gio Gallo.

No one seemed to care about the time when, aged seven, he'd been left at his boarding school over the Christmas break because each of his parents thought the other had picked him up. The time at the age of twelve when he'd been propositioned by one of his father's lovers. Or when at fourteen he'd had to call an ambulance for his mother, after she had combined too much alcohol with pills. All of that, he could have managed... Had they left him out of it. Had they not used him as some kind of points system to make the other parent look worse. Had their love for him been anything more than glitz and glamor, used to serve their own ends. So no, people like them, people like Erin Carter...they deserved what they got.

Erin washed her hands in the basin of a bathroom dominated in so much gold baroque moulding, she worried that the ceiling might come down. She almost laughed at the

ridiculousness of it, until she heard the very real laughter from the stalls behind her.

'Oh my god, did you *see* her!'

A high tittering laugh pre-empted the response. 'Jeanie, she looks horrendous. What was she thinking?'

Instinctively, Erin felt bad for whoever it was. She'd never liked the mean-girl mentality. Not after switching schools at such a difficult age.

'Is she trying to make a statement do you think?'

'What? That she could wear that and *still* marry Rossetti?'

Erin's heart dropped.

'No! No, he can't be marrying *her*. She looks like a big bruise.'

Tears pricked the back of her eyes and she bit her lip, unable to stop herself from running her gaze over her face and skin. The dress *was* horrible. And she *did* look bad.

'Or an advert for seasickness tablets,' came the callous reply.

She heard the flush of toilets and launched herself from the room as quickly as she possibly could, her heart pounding and an ugly flush creeping across her skin that would only make things worse. Heat and panic exponentially increased the flush and she rushed to get outside, pushing past people who were openly staring at her, or whispering behind their hands.

She shook her head and tried to calm herself, even though this was like a nightmare come to life. Her throat thickened and she begged herself, pleaded with herself not to cry, but her desperation just made it all worse.

She forced herself to slow down and not rush for the nearest shadowy corner to hide in. It wasn't Erin Carter who was experiencing this, it was Rin. And Rin was strong enough to handle this. She was. She had to be.

Tears blurred the edges of her vision, but she could still see people pointing and staring. Nausea crept upwards from her stomach and by the time she reached Enzo talking to Cynthia who simply gazed over her head as if looking for someone *not* beneath her notice, even Rin had been reduced to a cowering wreck.

She should *never* have worn the dress. She should never have been so desperate to get what she wanted, that she'd not only go against something she knew would backfire, but also...was this punishment? Was this deserved? Was it karma? She was, after all, pretending that she loved a man in order to marry him, just so she could get her hands on her family's business.

'Rin,' Marcus said, trying to bring her into the circle of conversation. 'We were just saying...'

But Erin didn't hear what they were just saying, because over Enzo's shoulder, someone was taking a picture of her with their phone and laughing. This wasn't going to just stay at the party. It was going to go viral. She felt the blood drain from her face, the way pins and needles were pricking her skin, her breath locking in her chest.

Enzo moved to stand in her line of sight, but she didn't quite see him. She just saw people. Laughing. And camera phones.

'Rin?' His voice sounded muffled and she knew that she was on the verge of a panic attack, but everything was spiralling out of her control even as she hastily tried to call it all back.

Then she felt his hand on her cheek, his thumb on her pulse at her neck. She was able to focus long enough to see concern in his steady gaze, beneath the barely leashed fury.

Fury? Why was he angry?

'We're leaving. Now.'

All she could do was nod, as he led her away from the people talking and whispering and laughing. Oh, she was sure that not everyone was talking about her, but it was too much. Too similar to the bullying that she'd experienced at school in Falmouth. The laughter, the jokes, the pranks. The *humiliation*.

And the way she'd been told just to ignore it. To just get over it. *Keep your head down and it'll all be over soon. They'll get bored eventually and move on.*

But they'd been so damn wrong. Because they hadn't got bored. And because it hadn't ended. Oh, she might not have seen the bullies that made her life so terrible. But that didn't mean that the impact they'd had on her life was over.

Her body was vibrating, a million tremors a second, shivering across oversensitive skin. Enzo shucked off the black tuxedo jacket as they emerged back out into the long garden.

The speedboat was waiting at the jetty, the pilot immediately jumping to attention, surprised at seeing them so soon. Enzo ushered Erin onto the boat, where thankfully the power of the engines masked the power of her body's shock.

This is stupid. Stop it. Stop it or he'll get suspicious.

She laughed bitterly at herself, as if he hadn't already seen enough.

Rin wouldn't have been so affected by this. Rin would never have been bullied. She was sophisticated and worldly and everyone would have liked Rin. No one would ever have bullied *her*. She bit her lip *hard*, hoping to shut off the spiralling thoughts. She had to pull herself out now or her panic would crash over her like a tsunami and pull her under.

By the time they got to the yacht Erin had stopped shivering and Enzo was a seething mass of helpless anger and fury. He didn't know what had happened, but it was obvi-

ous that it was because of the dress and the way that people had reacted.

He'd thought that she would be embarrassed, that a few people would laugh and point, maybe a comment or two. It had been worse than that, and he should have known that. But Rin's response had been the exact opposite of what he'd expected. He'd thought that she'd laugh it off and ride it out, brazenly owning it rather than...*this*.

Her entire demeanour had changed. It was as if she had folded in on herself and was physically beaten down. And there was nothing remotely artificial about it.

She turned to head towards the suites.

'Rin?'

She didn't stop. He wasn't sure whether he'd heard her or not, so he called her name at the same time as touching her shoulder. She didn't flinch exactly, but he couldn't let her go off alone, not now, not like this.

'I'm sorry. I'm tired,' she said by way of explanation. 'I think I'm going to—'

'I won't keep you for long,' he promised.

He guided her towards the back of the yacht, the staff giving them whatever space they needed. He leaned against the safety rail, the evening warm enough despite not wearing the jacket he'd given to Rin. The yacht was anchored so the only breeze was the one that came off the Tyrrhenian Sea.

Guilt twisted in his gut. A perverse part of him had wanted to punish her, to give her a little taste of vengeance, but not like this. *Nothing* like this. If this was how she reacted to the dress...then what would happen at the altar?

'I'm sorry,' he said, turning to face her, the moonlight making her glow. 'I should never have suggested you wear that dress.'

She shook her head, not blaming him, but also not realising that she should have.

'It's not about the dress.'

'Well, it *is*—' he insisted before she cut him off.

'It's *not*,' she said definitively, with a little more of the strength he associated with Rin Carter. 'Someone else could have worn that dress and laughed it off,' she admitted with a helpless shrug.

'But not you?' he asked, wanting to know why. Wanting to know *more*.

Her fingers stroked the black silk lapels of his jacket where she'd drawn it around herself.

'When I was younger…' she started, hesitantly, 'at school, a few children spent a significant amount of time making me the butt of their jokes,' she said, her head angled out to sea, the line of her profile as stark as her words. 'And it hurt. And it *still* hurts,' she admitted with a shrug.

'You were bullied?' he asked in surprise. 'Why?'

'I don't know,' she said helplessly. 'Because I was different? Because I was tall? Because I sounded different? Because I have red hair? Because they thought we had money when they didn't? We didn't either. But that didn't matter. I'd *had* money, and that was enough.'

'What did they do?' he asked, despite himself. This, he knew, instinctively, was the *real* Erin Carter, and it wasn't just some sob story either.

'Hid my clothes after gym practice or swimming, took pictures of me changing. Started rumours. That my father was a drug dealer in London. That I was having sex with one of the teachers. That I had STDs. I can keep going, but I think you get the picture.'

Enzo swallowed. Horrified at how cruel those children could have been. It must have been terrible for her. He knew

a little of what that was like. The lies printed in papers for the world to see. How they ate away at you. How you were advised to ignore it and it would all go away. But it didn't. If you ignored them, they just got worse.

So Enzo had forced himself to stop caring. He'd told himself it didn't matter. He'd brazened it out and made it a joke, the way he thought that Rin would have done about the dress.

But she hadn't.

Rin. His fiancée. His now very public fiancée. He cursed. Did she even know what she'd gotten herself into? Tangling with him like this? What on earth would make her do such a thing? He shook his head and looked out to sea.

'You know that marrying me will draw attention? A lot of it.'

He saw the line of her jaw tense.

'From the press. There will be articles written, photographs taken. Things that will make you look good and bad. Things will be dug up about you. They will actively put you in situations that are meant to provoke. To taunt. To do anything to incite a newsworthy response.'

When he'd been a child, the press had done everything in their power to goad him into answers about his parents, into providing his thoughts, or his feelings about their infamous arguments and public divorces. They'd tried to bribe teachers and friends and gone through rubbish bins and hacked email accounts.

'I know,' she said, determinedly.

'You're prepared for that?'

'Yes,' she said with a conviction and determination he couldn't read. A generous man would think it love. A cynical man would think it desperation.

'Are you sure?' Enzo no longer knew whether he was asking her or him.

'Of course,' she said with a shrug. 'I cannot wait to marry you, Mr Rossetti,' she said, her smile more game than anything.

He shook his head, disappointed. And shoving aside the thought that wondered what it could have been like if she wasn't trying to con him and he wasn't trying to win. And for just a moment, he gave up the fight. Wanting to give her something. Wanting to offer her some salve for her hurts.

He looked at her, gazing back at him defiantly, the moonlight lovingly picking out the curve of her cheek, the top of her ear from where the tumble of long red waves cascaded down her back, such a dark ruby red it blended with the black of his tux jacket.

'The only reason to mock,' he said, 'is because they can't bear to be mocked themselves. They lash out before they can be lashed. It doesn't make it right, but perhaps it helps a little to understand it.'

Her eyes flared at his words.

'No one deserves what happened to you,' he said with vehemence. 'And I'm sorry it happened. But what I see when I look at you is not some cowed, beaten young woman.'

'What do you see?' she asked, her words a whisper.

'A powerful, determined, fierce and beautiful woman,' he said with nothing but the absolute truth. 'The only, the *only*, reason for taunting you over your hair,' he said, picking up the end of a loose wave and rubbing the silk of her hair between his thumb and forefinger, 'is jealousy.'

He released the tendril of hair, telling himself to back away. That whatever it was between them—and there *was* something between them—was far too vulnerable that night. But just when he would have moved away, she reached up to cup his jaw. Her touch sent sparks across his skin, tighten-

ing and stretching things that really, he should have much better control over.

Her gaze flickered from his lips to his eyes, as if worried he might do something she wasn't prepared for. He waited, curious despite himself, to see what she would do.

She leaned forward and pressed her mouth to his. Another chaste kiss that drove a silent cry of need through his body.

Her lips shaped his, the slightest opening taunting him, begging him to prise open her mouth with his tongue and take everything he found within. Eyes open, he saw the minor furrow of her brow as if she were just a little frustrated, the whisper of a moan for something more on the wind between them.

He pulled back just an inch from her lips, feeling more tempted than Eve had been by the apple.

He shook his head again. 'I told you,' he said regretfully. 'I would not allow you to give me pleasure before our wedding.'

She blinked. 'That was for me,' she confessed, her words knocking the breath from his lungs, lifting the leash from his neck.

Barely before the words had even left her mouth, had he reclaimed her lips with his. His hands were sinking into her hair and drawing her against him, angling her to the perfect position, to where he could all but consume her whole. A firestorm engulfed them, his heart racing as if he'd run a marathon, her breath heaving her chest against his, her hands fisting in his shirt, pulling him deeper against her, she shifted in his hold, seeking for the very same thing he was searching for.

His hands pushed away the ridiculous volume of that damn dress to try and reach her, but couldn't seem to grasp her, breaking the moment with a frustrated laugh from Rin.

And Enzo found himself both damned and saved by a mess of his own making.

'I should go to bed,' she said, perhaps unaware of the yearning in her tone to do the opposite.

'Yes, you should,' Enzo confirmed with a nod, not looking at her, half fearful that if he did, he'd do something monumentally stupid like beg her to stay.

There was a pause, where an infinite number of possibilities passed between them and in the end only one was chosen.

'Thank you,' Rin said.

And the thin-lipped smile was all he could muster, as he stayed back by the railing, more at sea with his thoughts than he had ever been in his entire life. He just didn't know anymore. Was *this* the real Erin, or was the truth to be found in the one conversation he'd overheard? Was she acting? Was she that good? Or was he just so caught up in her wiles that he'd forgotten everything he'd learned from the games his parents had played?

CHAPTER SEVEN

ERIN LOOKED OUT from the upper deck of Enzo's yacht at the Italian coastline, dawn barely a thought at this early hour, frustrated to find her fingers pressed against her lips, *again*.

Dangerous. It had been dangerous to mess with Enzo Rossetti. Ever since she'd woken—far too early—she'd walked around in a daze, thinking only that she hadn't known a kiss could *be* like that. A kiss that *she* had initiated.

Of all the kisses they had so far shared, this—unique in its innocence—had been all the more powerful.

And what had driven her to that kiss? Him. His kindness. And her curiosity. Her desire. Her want.

You think you can resist the charms of the Playboy of Amalfi?

Gio's taunt came back to haunt her.

She had been so naïve. Last night, she had dreamed about it, fantasised about it, thoughts of it had consumed her whole, leaving her hot and breathless, flushed and deeply, *deeply* unsatisfied.

Surely it wasn't good for her to be walking around in this state of…dissatisfaction. But in a way, wasn't it a rather apt punishment? Because Erin was beginning to suspect that she was making a big mistake. Yes, she wanted Charter-house. That hadn't changed. Not one bit. And every time she thought about it, thought about having it, running it,

making something of it, it left an ache in her heart so sore and so yearning that it was hard to speak of it.

But Enzo's kindness last night, staying with her until she'd calmed, the words he'd offered her, had shifted something ever so slightly in a very old wound. It had touched her, deeply. She'd seen the shadows haunting his gaze, knew of the press that had dogged his steps since childhood, collateral damage in the chaos of his parents' divorce. That there was a link, a connection, between them…

But was that connection enough to stop her from reaching for her goal?

No. Not that alone. But could she really cling to the belief that he was just a bored, lazy, careless playboy? That he was like her father, uncaring who got hurt by his whims? Because despite Enzo's sometimes dramatic flamboyance, his constant charm and his impressive arrogance, there was something else to him that she had glimpsed last night.

A depth. A layer beneath this playboy persona he seemed to revel in.

Erin might be ready to do just about anything to get her hands on Charterhouse, but that didn't mean she could willingly hurt another person to get what she wanted. The only reason she'd come this far was because she'd been near convinced that Enzo Rossetti didn't have a heart. And last night, she thought she'd seen a little of that heart. That was why she'd kissed him. She'd…*liked* what she'd seen.

Enzo appeared on the deck, her heartbeat jumping a little at the sight of him, tall, good-looking, his white shirt glowing in the pre-dawn. His surprise at her being there was quickly masked and she regretted it, desperate to know what he was thinking and feeling after last night.

'You are out here early, *cara*,' he observed as he came to stand beside her.

'I couldn't sleep,' she admitted.

His response was a nod, the dark smudges beneath his eyes enough confirmation that he had suffered the same. For a while they stood there together in silence as the gentlest touches of dawn began to lighten the sky overhead.

'Do we...' She hesitated. 'Do we have to go off to France today?'

She wasn't ready, she realised. France was where they would get married and suddenly Erin found herself wanting to delay. To wait. She wanted time to make sure that she was doing the right thing. To make sure that she wouldn't cause damage with a scheme that was getting uncomfortably close to something that her father might have done.

'Is there somewhere else you'd like to go?' he asked.

'Not if it would cause a problem,' she prevaricated.

'There's no rush. The yacht can make the crossing in a day if needed,' he assured her. 'So, tell me. Where is it you'd like to be?'

Florence.

It had fallen from her lips before she could stop it and a part of her hoped that maybe he would say that unfortunately it wasn't possible. But he hadn't.

And just over two hours later, she was standing at the end of the Via dei Calzaiuoli looking between the Baptistry and the Cathedral, as long soft fingers of light crept slowly into a denim blue sky.

'I get the destination, *amore mio*, but did it really have to be *so* early?' Enzo complained grumpily, as if he'd been hoping to go back to bed. The man, she had discovered, was *not* a morning person.

'Yes,' she laughingly replied, ignoring Enzo's near unholy beauty and turning back to one of the most magnifi-

cent sights she'd ever seen. 'It's so early that we have beaten the tourists and we have the place nearly all to ourselves.'

Oh, her mother would have loved this. If her father hadn't frittered everything away, they would have come here. As a family. They might have even stood right here, staring up at the ornate detail of the white-and-green marble, the terracotta tiles of the dome atop the cathedral, that was much more beautiful than she had ever imagined.

'Did you know,' she asked him, 'that work started on this in the early twelve hundreds and didn't finish until the fourteen hundreds?'

'Really?' Enzo asked as if it were the least interesting thing he'd ever heard, and she smiled, because she'd seen, despite the grim mask of 'grumpy morning man', how his eyes had feasted on the stunning sight. 'Does that have any bearing on the need to be here at *seven thirty* in the morning?'

She folded her lips together to stop herself from laughing at him again. Laughter that disappeared when she turned to find him standing in a single beam of sunlight, filtered by the Italian rooftops and Cathedral tower. It lovingly caressed the planes of his face, dancing in a healthy glow across bronzed skin, sharp angles, and deliciously dark hair. And for a moment they seemed content to study each other as if they were more important than the centuries-old architecture that they were surrounded by.

He took her breath away. She'd never met anyone who'd been able to do that.

He shook his head slightly, as if trying to dislodge them from the moment. 'Is there something wrong, *cara*?'

'Why do you keep calling me *cara*?' she asked instead of answering his question.

He frowned. 'Well, if I'm honest, Rin doesn't seem to suit

you, and I presume you use it because you don't like Erin, so...' He shrugged and closed the distance between them.

Unaware of the seismic shock that threatened Erin's foundations, Enzo led them to a small café within sight of the Duomo. A waiter bustled over to greet them, ushering them into a table. His frantic enthusiasm was amusing, but went utterly unnoticed by Erin who was distracted by the Cathedral over his shoulder.

When he'd asked her if she could go anywhere, he'd expected...something else. Maybe shopping in Paris, or a night at an ice hotel in Jukkasjärvi, or well, he didn't know. But something expensive. Something not so...easy to accomplish. And by the time they had their coffees and pastries, and Enzo—with a little caffeine in his system—was feeling more human and less bear, he finally asked the question.

'Why Florence?'

Something crept into her gaze and he wondered whether he had strayed too far into the personal. And whether that was, in fact, what he'd intended all along. A little crease appeared between her brows that he wanted to smooth away with the pad of his thumb.

'We were supposed to come here. As a family, when I was younger,' she haltingly explained. 'Before...before everything changed.'

He waited, sensing that she would fill the silence.

'Mum really wanted to go. She has a thing about Giotto— the painter and architect.'

'As you do,' Enzo interjected, familiar with the English penchant for Italian art.

'As you do,' Erin repeated with a small smile.

'And when we lost everything, when the business went, the house, her friends, my school, she kept saying, but what

about Florence? What about Giotto? Erin must see it. She simply *must*.'

Enzo could see it. The blind shock of someone so confused, that they clung to a minor detail.

'I don't know whether it was important to her for me to see it because it meant so much to her, or because she wanted one thing, just one, that my father had promised to come true.'

She was telling the truth, he realised. A few days ago he would have dismissed this as a sob story—something engineered to manipulate him. But the reverberation of truth in her tone, the steadfast clarity in her gaze...the lack of her *tell*. This was the real Erin Carter. Whose life had changed dramatically as a teenager, when comfort had been replaced by loss, all ending in a move that had seen her bullied and isolated.

'Why come here? This seems like a painful memory?' He couldn't wrap his head around why she would do that to herself.

'I want to tell her that I've seen Giotto's campanile, his bell-tower. I want her to know that I've seen it.'

The sparkle in her eye wasn't delight. It wasn't happiness. It was earnest, it was sincere. It was heartfelt and he didn't want to see it.

'Do you not have somewhere like that?' she asked. 'Somewhere bittersweet?'

He clenched his teeth, intensely uncomfortable with the intimacy of the turn in the conversation. His liaisons didn't usually last long enough for them to descend into such territory. And he'd been fine with that. If the intrusive press hadn't taught him enough when he'd been younger, one girlfriend selling her story to the tabloids, another wanting an introduction to his older and richer father, and another

using him to finance an increasingly out-of-control shopping addiction, had ensured that he'd learned his lesson.

Short-term exchanges with women who understood the finite nature of their relationship was all he wanted. And despite what the papers had to say, he'd vetted those relationships with considerable assiduity.

Until Erin Carter.

'Nothing that reminds you of your past?' she asked, dealing him another blow.

Despite himself, he huffed out a bitter laugh. 'Why on earth would I want that?'

His childhood had been a car crash. A very public, very slow, car crash.

Sympathy pooled in her gaze and he wanted to look away as much as he wanted to draw it in deep. He took a sip of espresso instead, trying to wash away the bitter statement from their conversation.

'I'm sorry,' she said.

'It is nothing to me,' he dismissed, even though now he was the one who was lying, he was the one with the *tell* in this game that they were playing.

'There were no family holidays then?' she asked.

He shook his head. 'When my parents were in love, they went away alone, wanting "adult time". And when they weren't, they would fight over which one of them got to take me away, but would get so caught up in their arguments, they'd end up forgetting the holiday altogether.'

Those arguments had been furious, violent. Hurled vases and broken china. Staff had been forced to pull him out of the terrifying path of their fury. 'Outside of that, I was at boarding school.'

And it had been the only stability he had known as a child.

'How old were you?' she asked.

'Seven.'

She frowned, putting her cup back on the saucer and before she could ask any more of the questions that were shining in her eyes, he signalled for the bill and paid.

He spent the entire day showing her everything that Florence had to offer—giving her the holiday that her father had once promised and distracting them both from the earlier emotional trespass.

They scoured jewellery shops on the Ponte Vecchio and sauntered down the *Corridoio Vasariano,* famous for being used hundreds of years before by the Medici family. They peered around tourists at statues and paintings in the Uffizi Gallery, they lunched on spaghetti carbonara and dined on Bistecca alla Fiorentina with a red wine so delicious he made a note of the vineyard.

The way that Erin had groaned in delight at the first mouthful of her steak had taken him to the edge of his control, which was laughably thin when it came to this woman. But they walked the still busy streets, Enzo enjoying the bustle of it all.

He couldn't remember the last time he'd done this. Usually he'd either be at a party, or in his office, making a deal through a shell company to hide his identity. And this, he found, was a different kind of anonymity. Strangers and tourists, so lost in their own adventures that he could have been anyone.

And with the night sky a black velvet, punctured by scattered diamonds, he led her to the entrance of the hotel that had been arranged for the night—happy to give the staff the night off. They were greeted by the hotel manager who informed them that their personal concierge was waiting

for them and would show them around their suite and as the two of them entered the lift, he felt it.

It wasn't something visible, *definable*, but he felt it. The way that tension, the delicious kind, pulled something taut in her. And it was attached to him. To his gut. Suite, not suites. She didn't know that the suite had separate bedrooms and it was perhaps cruel of him not to tell her immediately. But he *relished* it, the sensual chemistry fizzing and spitting between them. He was testing himself against the strength of it and for the first time, he feared it was a game he might not win.

Erin looked anywhere but where she wanted to look. At *him*. Being in the confined space of the lift with him, his scent sweeping around her, invading her lungs, her breath, her thoughts. Thoughts that were utterly consumed by him.

Of the precious gift he had given her that day. And of what he'd shared with her too. She was beginning to understand that perhaps the playboy image Enzo had created was a little like the persona of Rin that she had constructed. A configuration born out of necessity. And in Enzo's case, the necessity had been self-protection; from the intrusion of the press, from his parents' difficult relationship. From the loneliness of being sent away to boarding school at such a horrifically young age.

Oh, she knew he didn't want her sympathy. But something had been born in that moment. The desire to reach out to him. To connect with him. He had tried to distract her from it. And it had worked…for a while. Until now. Now that they would be alone. Utterly alone. No staff, no interruptions. No one to witness whatever happened behind closed doors.

He wasn't looking at her, but she *felt* his attention. Her

body came alive beneath it. Pulse points flaring in time with her heartbeat, breath catching in her lungs, her throat thickening with a want like she'd never known.

The lift arrived at their floor, the doors opening directly onto the beautiful hotel suite, and she followed Enzo out, hoping that neither he nor the uniformed concierge that greeted them, could see the telling blush on her cheeks.

The suite was beautiful, decorated in warm creams and golds and champagnes, but really she barely saw any of it, her hungry gaze stalking Enzo with a keening desperation that she hated herself for. Frustrated desire coursed through her body, making her skin itch and her heart ache in a strange and unfamiliar way.

When had she become so *base*? She thought miserably as Enzo closed the door behind the departing concierge.

She crossed over to the window, looking out at the Florentine nightscape.

'What is it, *cara*? What is wrong?' Enzo asked from behind her, from the other side of the room, as if knowing that he should keep his distance.

How did she even begin to explain? To tell him. To put into words what it was she wanted when she wasn't sure herself?

She shrugged, helplessly, rubbing her arms, trying to feel something other than the want clawing at her stomach and filling her lungs.

He closed the distance between them and she let her head hang forward. Submission, surrender? She wanted him to take over, to make the decision, to make the move that she wasn't sure she should, but wanted more than her next breath.

He stood behind her, like he had done that day in the boutique in Positano when he had kissed her neck. A shiver ran

down her spine, not in fear, but from the memory of it. The touch of his lips against her skin…

'Are you cold?' he asked, and she shook her head.

'Do you want to go to bed?' he asked. She bit her lip and shook her head, her pulse beginning to race from the rough-textured question.

Enzo like this, stubble across his jaw, espresso-rich gaze hot and swirling, meeting hers in the reflection of the window.

I promise to protect your wishes, even if you beg me to change my mind.

Would he break that promise if she asked him to? Did she want him to?

He began to turn away and something horribly like loss sliced into her breath, and before she knew what she was doing, she'd turned and reached for him, her hand around his wrist, pulling him back to her. As if moving in a dance, his hand slid into her hair just behind her ear as her palm flattened over his heart, a heart that was racing just as fast as hers.

He shook his head, as if he were fighting something too. As if they were both still trying to deny how strong this need was that spiralled between them. He opened his mouth and closed it again and when he finally pushed past whatever had been holding him back, she wondered whether it was a mistake. Whether she should have stayed quiet.

'I can give you what you want, without breaking my promise to you. *If* that's what you want.'

She wanted to ask herself how he knew what she wanted when she didn't even know herself, but that would be a lie. And she already had too many lies in her, she couldn't bear the weight of one more.

She looked down as the flush built on her cheeks, and nodded.

With one finger on her chin, he lifted her face to his, to the scrutiny of his gaze, and in his eyes she saw passion enflamed, she saw what she felt deep down, twisting and burning her from the inside.

'You want this?' he asked again, and even as she wondered how he could do both, she said, 'Yes'.

Yes, yes, yes.

Christo, he was shaking. Shaking with need for her. But he held himself back with the fiercest restraint he had ever needed. Because he wouldn't break his promise to her. Because whether or not she was innocent, he couldn't do that to her. He couldn't sleep with her and still leave her at the altar. Her intentions didn't matter one bit, his did. And he was a playboy, not a monster.

And while it would be a lie to say that he received no pleasure from what he intended to give her, she would not for one minute be left thinking that this had been about him or his needs, because it wasn't. It was about her and her needs. And he was only too happy to meet them.

He pulled her gently with him over towards the chaise longue. If he took her to either of the bedrooms in the suite, it would be over for both of them. And even though the future he'd planned for them had become hazy, he knew at least that he wasn't ready for whatever this was to be over.

Eyes wide and far too full of wants and needs she couldn't have been aware she was signalling, he sat first and pulled her gently down onto his lap.

'You have total control, here,' he said. 'You can leave, you can move, whatever, whenever,' he explained. 'Nothing,' he stressed, 'nothing you do or say here in this moment will change a single thing,' he vowed, wanting this to be something that was utterly contained, with no impact

on a future that was so unsettled. This had to be something outside of that.

She nodded.

'I will not have sex with you tonight.'

Her mouth dropped open as if to object, and he closed his eyes so as not to see it.

'I will keep my promise. But I can also ease what frustrates you,' he said, lifting his lids and feeling punched by the lust in the shockingly brilliant blue of her gaze.

She bit her lip and nodded, questions in her eyes less about whether it should happen and more, he realised about how. *Dio mio*, this woman had been sent to undo him.

He leaned back against the leather sofa back as she shifted her knees to either side of his legs, her long dark ruby-red hair hanging down like a waterfall of fire. He reached up to cup her jaw, his thumb falling to press gently against her throat, and her pupils engorged with desire.

She rocked forward to meet his mouth, her lips covering his as she pressed against the hard ridge of his arousal, and he swallowed her moan of aching need. Her tongue clashed with his, the kiss untried but no less for it.

One hand went to her breast, the other around her backside, kneading, pulling, drawing her against him. The kiss was one thing, but the heat of her against his erection drove him nearly out of her mind.

She cried into the kiss again and he knew that it wouldn't take much to bring her to orgasm. He wanted to draw it out, to make it last for her, to make it perfect. He broke the kiss gently, and looking up at her, slipped his hand beneath the silk of her top to palm her lace-covered breast. He lost his breath when she let her head fall back, when she gave herself up to her own arousal, but it was nothing compared to

the sensations that scoured his very soul, when she began to shift against his erection.

Fingers teasing her taut nipple, he leaned back to watch her, the flush, the closed-eyed wonder, her lips, parted slightly on an exhale, the ruched skirt either side of his thighs, and he left her breast with a moue of complaint, until his hand smoothed down over her hip and towards the juncture at her thighs.

She stilled for a moment, as if this was the line, one to cross or withdraw from. He held his breath, not moving at all, until the sighed surrender sank through her and she rolled her body against his in such a way that he nearly came himself.

'You are beautiful, *cara*. Exquisite,' he praised. 'Take what you need from me,' he said, half pleading. 'Take your pleasure,' he insisted.

And when she raised herself ever so slightly, making space for his hand, his fingers slipped beneath the dampened silk of her underwear into the hot silken heat between her legs.

This time it was his head that fell back against the sofa, his eyes closing as he allowed the feel of her to satiate his own desperate needs. Her breath coming in little pants, faster and faster as she shifted back and forth against him, against his fingers, as he gently, carefully, pinched her clitoris, bringing a sob from her lips, and a punch to his gut.

He was genuinely at risk of coming himself, as he cupped her heat, pressing the heel of his palm against her as he slipped one finger into the tight wet heat of her femininity. Unconsciously she shifted to accommodate him, and he forced himself to swallow the growl of his own need thickening his throat.

His erection, painful, taut, and impossible to deny as she

rubbed herself against the length of him, left him astounded at this being the most incredible sexual experience of his entire life. Sweat prickled his skin, and he bit his lip, to stop himself from crying out as she moved sensually over and around his hand.

Enzo added another finger to her, slowly stretching and teasing her. Her fever-pitch sighs of need were the most erotic thing he'd ever heard, and he knew, *knew,* that they would echo in his mind for the rest of his life, and precisely at that point, her muscles tightened, trembled, hovering on a precipice until he thrust upwards, his hips pressing his hand into her and finding that perfect point that tumbled her into an orgasm that left her utterly satiated and him irrevocably changed.

Breathless, stunned, he waited for their breathing to return to something that resembled normality, before picking her up, sleepy and collapsed against his body, and carrying her to her room. He gently removed her from all but her underwear, tucked her into bed and left. Before he could do anything as stupid as beg to stay. Not to have sex with her, but just to sleep. Just to let him hold her.

And that was when he realised just how dangerous Erin Carter really was to him.

CHAPTER EIGHT

ERIN WIPED THE condensation from her shower off the mirror in the bedroom's en suite and stared at herself. Even this morning, her eyes were bright, her cheeks flush and she knew it wasn't from the heat of the powerful jets of water. Her thoughts were a scattered mess, and her body still hummed to the tune of his touch.

He hadn't stayed with her. She'd been aware of it, vaguely as he'd put her to bed. But, he'd left and she'd not wanted him to. She wanted to message Sam, but she didn't know what she'd even say.

She'd already deleted: *I think I'm making a mistake.* And: *I think I got him wrong.*

But she'd not quite been able to type: *Maybe I don't need Charterhouse after all.*

She dressed, feeling a strange combination of elated, pleasured, exposed, and a little heartsore, and went looking for Enzo. She found him on the balcony of the hotel suite where breakfast had already been laid out for them.

He poured her coffee, explained the different fillings of the cornetti. He'd offered her eggs, and she'd politely declined, all so very civilised when last night had been anything but. So much so that she half wanted to scream.

'About last night...' she began, but then couldn't quite find the words.

'Yes, *cara*?'

'I…you… I feel like I used you,' she confessed on a raw whisper.

His gaze was heavy on her, she felt it, even though her eyeline was filled solely with the plate in front of her.

His reaction was a stilted sigh. As if he'd part expected it.

'I did nothing I did not want to do, Erin,' he said, his tone gentle and sincere.

But you don't know. I'm using you and you don't know it.

'Do you regret it?' he asked, the concern in his voice raising her gaze to his.

She frowned and shook her head. She couldn't possibly. It had been the most exquisite night of her life. But did that make her a bad person?

'How about this. Why don't we take the day off?' Enzo offered.

Erin laughed a little. 'You make it sound like we're working.'

Though in a horrible way, she almost was, wasn't she?

'*There*. It's *that* look I want to take the day off from,' Enzo teased gently.

She swallowed her guilt. Maybe taking a day off would make things clearer for her. She hadn't done anything that couldn't be undone yet. Not really. And she thought she'd quite like to take a 'day off' with Enzo.

'So, let's, as the English say, 'bunk off'?' he asked and she laughed. 'We'll reschedule the wedding planner—'

Oh god, she'd forgotten about that.

'And Marcus can wait—'

'Marcus?'

'Yes, I promised to meet up with him in Cannes, but he can wait, *cara*.'

Marcus from the party where she'd worn that horrible

dress. He'd been nice, but Cynthia not so much. Yes, Erin thought she could do with delaying bumping into them again so soon. Even if just for a day.

'What do you say?'

Feeling a hint of excitement at the delay, she smiled and nodded in agreement.

They still met the speedboat at the allotted time, but instead of returning them to the yacht, Enzo swapped with the pilot, and took them out of Livorno's port across to the Isola di Gorgona.

Unable to help herself she had laughed as the boat bucked and rocked as they'd crested the waves from the larger tourist ferry where people had pointed and waved and taken pictures of Enzo's sleek boat. Enzo steered towards a bay far too small to interest the other tourists, and dropped the anchor in the depths of the little inlet.

The rough tumble of craggy sun-bleached rocks clearly made it difficult to access the beach by any other means than boat. Nature had claimed large patches above and around that rock with thick bright green leafy foliage but nothing was as beautiful as the dark turquoise of pristine waters lapping gently at the boat.

Beside her, Enzo slipped off his shirt and kicked off his shoes and stepped up on to the side of the boat. His head fell back, face turned to the sun, soaking in its warmth for a breathtaking moment. He looked utterly uncaring. No one to please, to serve, his shoulders relaxed, before he took a deep breath and executed a perfect swan dive into the azure waters, leaving barely a ripple in his wake.

She'd always assumed that being on the yacht for him was about money and prestige, about rootlessness. But seeing him in the water, she was beginning to wonder whether

it went deeper than that. Whether it was something to do with a connection to that worldly element.

He surfaced, flipping his hand—and his hair—one side to another, using his hands to push the water from his face and away.

'Well? Are you going to join me, *cara*?' he teased. It was an easy flirtation, without the heady intensity of last night and she welcomed it.

She peeled off her sundress and swung her legs over the side of the boat, dangling her feet into the cool—not but frigid—water. She closed her eyes. Maybe they could have this moment. Just this one. Where she wasn't trying to marry him to get Charterhouse, and he wasn't the careless playboy that pushed all her buttons. She didn't deserve it, she knew that much, but she wanted it anyway.

Enzo watched Erin slip into the water from the side of the boat and waited for her to surface.

'You looked like you're making a wish, *amore mio*,' Enzo said, treading water.

'Maybe I was,' she replied with a cryptic smile.

'What did you wish for?' he asked, curious in spite of himself, wanting to know her every thought.

'I can't tell you that,' Erin chided.

'Why not?'

'Because then it wouldn't come true,' she reasoned, before sliding from the boat into the aquamarine waters of the inlet.

'I'd tell you mine,' he stropped teasingly, when she rose from the waters.

'Go on then.'

'*I* didn't make one,' he said in the same childish tone that seemed to bring ease to her gaze. It felt playful and fun—

different and so much more chaste than what he was used to, but more importantly it chased whatever shadows had filled her gaze that morning. Was she beginning to have second thoughts, like he was?

She swept an arc of water towards him, the small wave hitting his chest and making him laugh, reminding him that they had promised to take the day off.

'Don't start something you can't finish,' he warned, shaking his finger at her, delighted when his words ignited the small spark of naughtiness glinting in her eye into a meteor shower.

She pushed towards him with two hands, letting out a gasp of frustration as he dipped beneath the water. Plunging to a depth that would make it hard for her to spot him, he closed the distance between them in long, powerful strokes, until he saw the glow of her skin in the deep blue depths.

Her legs twisted back and forth, as if she were searching for him. Hidden from her, he let the smile loose, as he grabbed her legs and instead of tugging her down, launched them both upwards, until he broke the surface of the water, to hear a high-pitched cry peppered with laughter.

She clung to his shoulders and despite his plans to carefully throw her back into the water, he kept her in his arms, her hair, thick, ruby-red ropes, coming around them like a curtain, closing out the rest of the world.

It'd be nice, he realised. To stay like that. And the part of him that knew that this was all just part of the game grew quieter and quieter.

He changed his hold, letting her slip down his chest until his arms banded around her torso and he found the ticklish spots at her ribs that sent more screams and more laughter into the air around them.

Making her laugh was becoming something addictive.

Something that he wanted to indulge in. Just today. Just this. Perhaps for just this moment, he could pretend that it was all real. That she wasn't only here because she wanted something from him. That she wasn't just like his parents.

They stayed in the water for another half an hour, splashing around, swimming, Erin doing handstands and circles under water, and him just enjoying her playfulness.

After that, they slowly unpacked the lunch the chef had prepared for them. Erin's shocked gasps of delight were fulfilling enough as she unpacked delicacy after delicacy. Champagne, caviar, smoked salmon, charcoal crackers.

'Brie?' she asked, peeling back the parchment it had been wrapped in. 'Vacherin Mont d'Or? Is that not a little heavy?' she wondered out loud.

Enzo huffed out a breath. 'The chef is taunting me. We have an ongoing disagreement as to the better cheese, Italian or French.'

'I—'

'I don't want to hear it, *cara*!' he exclaimed, raising his hand to ward her off. 'I won't let you break my heart,' he warned, his unintended use of words landing awkwardly between them. Erin seemed to take the same moment, a blink shielding the intense blue of her gaze, before she laughed and picked up the fennel salami.

'This is some picnic,' she said, stealing a thin sliver of the delicate meat, as she looked out at the slashes of blue that defined the horizon. 'Do you always do this?' she asked, her curious gaze returning to his.

'Do what?'

'Come out here with your...'

A smile pulled at his mouth, as she seemed too uncomfortable to finish the rest of her sentence.

'Lovers?' he suggested.

She cleared her throat, and nodded.

He leaned back on his elbow and considered her question, tossing an olive into his mouth and savouring the salty, vinegary morsel.

'No,' he said truthfully. Usually, he didn't have the time to spare, as he went from place to place. And he realised how peaceful it was just to come here, take the moment, to *play*.

From the corner of his eye, he saw the way her mouth lifted into a half-smile, as if his answer had pleased her, which made him feel…too damn good, he realised. But he chose to ignore the warning that echoed quietly in his mind, and instead, lay back against the cushion and peppered her with questions about her life.

Her favourite book, *The Three Dahlias* by Katy Watson. His, *The Gone Away World* by Nick Harkaway.

Her favourite play, *Arcadia* by Tom Stoppard. His, *Le Vent Des Peupliers* by Gérald Sibleyras.

Her favourite flower, a cornflower. His, an iris. His mother had always worn them in her hair, he remembered with surprise.

Her favourite place, *home*.

The word catching in his mind even as he evaded answering the question himself. Home. He'd intentionally avoided having one. Certainly not because he couldn't afford to, but because he'd not wanted something that could be taken away from him. And then he thought of how he'd feel when Erin was taken away from him…

And just like that reality hit hard, weighing him down like an anchor tied to his foot, dragging him beneath the surface of things that could drown him if he let them.

In the short time that they'd been in Florence and Livorno, Enzo's lawyers had magicked the prenup and the documents

had been waiting for Erin by the time she returned to her suite on the yacht.

She scanned through it vaguely, skipping over the legal jargon, ensuring that Enzo's assets would be protected in full in case of divorce or annulment. If she was being honest with herself, she was wavering. Each little bit of time she spent with him, her determination and drive towards Charterhouse slowed and weakened.

She called the captain, who arrived at her suite in time to bear witness to her signature.

'Congratulations, Ms Carter,' the captain said, and Erin returned a smile that she didn't feel. 'Would you like me to make sure that Signor Rossetti gets this?'

'Please,' Erin replied, before retrieving her phone from her bag. She'd had it on silent all day.

Are you okay?
I'm getting worried.
Is it time to call Interpol?

She sent a message to Sam letting her know that she was okay, or rather that she was alive. Took a selfie as proof of life and hoped that her friend couldn't read the confusion she read in her own eyes.

Enzo had wanted to take her for drinks that evening at a bar he knew not far from the Cannes marina and she was pleased that at least it wasn't another party. That it would just be the two of them. The day hadn't ended, and she found herself greedy for more of him. Just him. And just her. Before everything else got in the way.

The speed with which the yacht had covered the distance between where it had been moored just outside of Livorno and the marina in Cannes had been ferocious, and when Erin

peered out through the porthole window of her suite barely three hours later she was surprised to find herself looking out at the French harbour shortly after dusk.

She caught sight of herself in the mirror and paused. She probably shouldn't have chosen to wear the outfit she'd bought in the boutique. Not because she didn't look pretty, but because she wanted him to think that she did.

Because that had become important to her.

He knocked on her door and she went to answer it, heart thudding as he stood there in his dark linen suit with a dark shirt. Unknowingly they'd both dressed in the same midnight blue colour.

'You look incredible, *cara*.'

'Erin,' she said, clearing the slight catch in her throat. 'You can call me Erin,' she clarified. She didn't want to be Rin anymore. She didn't want him to want Rin. She wanted him to want *her*.

'Erin,' he said slowly as if trying it on for size. He nodded, and then grinned easily, offering her his arm.

She picked up her clutch and let him lead her from the suite, off the yacht, out of the marina where it was moored and onto the bustling streets of Cannes.

Wide-eyed, she took in the opulence and the architecture, similar but different to Italy. The switch from Italian to the more familiar French was strange as she now recognised snippets of passing conversations and street signs. Enzo seemed to know where they were going and she was content to be led.

Their destination proved to be a small, but absolutely packed bar, where everyone seemed to know him and greeted him with cheers and a lot of enthusiasm. People air kissed, grabbed and hugged, and met her with the same exuberant welcome, which she couldn't help but be charmed by.

They were thrust towards a small standing table parallel
to the bar and a bottle of wine and two glasses were placed
in front of them by Jean-Pierre whose name was actually
Michael, but no one called him that.

It was bright, and loud, and vivacious and Erin was utterly enchanted.

'How long have you been coming here?' she asked, having to almost shout to be heard.

'More years than I'd admit to, on pain of death,' Enzo replied with a generous smile, as he poured the rich, punchy
red into two tumblers. It struck her that this was far removed
from the sophistication of the party where she'd met him.
It felt a little as if this was the real Enzo. In France. How
controversial, she thought to herself, amused.

'Something you find funny?'

'Only the *Playboy of Amalfi* being more at home in a
French bistro—'

'Lies!' he cried out, loudly, making her laugh, really
laugh. 'Sacrilege! Slander,' he insisted dramatically with a
wink that made her think that she'd read him right.

A few people stopped by to have brief conversations with
Enzo, some chatting with her, some rushing off to see other
friends, but for the most part they were left alone. Talking
about wine, about travel, about small things that felt as real
and as important as the big thing that they couldn't share.
Her hand found his forearm often, his shoulder a few times,
swept a hair from his forehead once. He brushed her hair
from her shoulder, cupped her jaw. The easy touching building towards something else, she thought, something she
wanted. Their looks lasted longer, penetrated deeper, built
up towards a moment where she thought he might kiss her.

Until everything changed, when a tall, older dark-haired

man came to the table, seemingly worse for wear, and slapped Enzo on the shoulder.

'So, after dodging my calls for. A. Month. *This* is where I find you?'

Ice shot out from where his father had clamped a hand on his shoulder, leaving his chest locked and his mind frozen.

All Enzo could think of was how bad this was going to be.

And how damn furious he was that his father would choose here, choose now to confront him.

He looked at Erin who had leaned back a little, as if wary. God, he wished he could stop her from seeing this. He wasn't ready. He would never be ready.

'Luca—'

'Luca? What, you don't call me father anymore?'

'What are you doing here?' he ground out.

Madonna mia, he hadn't been a father to Enzo for years. But Luca had known that. This was for Erin's benefit, Enzo recognised.

Luca turned his head and whispered heavily into his ear. 'You left me no choice, son,' he said, slapping him on the back a little harder than necessary. 'You contacted my *accountant.*'

So, this was punishment, Enzo realised.

'But this is where you always come!' Luca exclaimed louder, for Erin's ears. 'The moment the press announced you were on your way to France, it was just a happy coincidence that we were too.' Luca peered at Erin. 'Are you not going to introduce me?' he said, not bothering to direct his question at Enzo.

'He doesn't have to, Mr Rossetti. Your reputation precedes you,' Erin said, not offering her hand or any other sign of welcome.

She hadn't fawned over the famous actor, she hadn't fallen for his supposed charm that was by now getting a little old. But still, many of Enzo's other friends failed to resist—and the fact that she had...

'I wanted to talk to you about invitations to the wedding.'

Enzo huffed out a laugh. Unbelievable. His father had already heard of his and Erin's engagement and this was the excuse he was using to make his approach, to ask for more money? There was no way—

'You're invited of course,' Luca pressed on. 'Isn't she beautiful? And of course, you can bring your friend,' Luca said, pointing to Erin.

It took a moment for Enzo to realise that his father was talking about his *own* engagement. He was getting married again?

'She deserves the *world*,' Luca said of the woman standing at the bar looking bored and tapping on her phone. The long hair, high heels, Enzo would never judge, but she was at least twenty years Luca's junior. This must have been what all the phone calls had been about. His father, looking for money to have another huge, over-the-top, horrible wedding.

Luca grinned at Enzo, and he'd had enough.

'No.' The word had seismic impact on the man who should have known better.

'What do you mean, no? You're not coming?'

'Not coming and not paying for it either.'

Luca bit out an angry laugh. 'I don't know what you're—'

Enzo stood from his chair, caught Jean-Pierre's eye and thrust a few notes under his glass, and held his hand out for Erin. He had to get them out of here, before his father made more of a scene.

'What kind of son—'

Enzo grabbed the lapel of his father's jacket in his fist

and dragged him close. 'What kind of *father*,' he growled into Luca's ear. 'What kind of...'

Fury cut into his words, and his control, until Erin pushed between him and his father, her cool hands seeking him out and giving him a moment's respite.

She looked up at him, her hands coming to frame his face, to lock her eyes with his.

'Let's go,' was all she said, and he clung to her as they left the café.

The reporters descended the moment that they hit the street, presumably alerted by Luca himself. They crowded around them even as Enzo typed out a message to the boat to send security.

'Rossetti!' someone yelled.

'Do not speak to them,' Enzo commanded, low and dark. 'Do not rise to whatever antagonism they taunt you with. If you can smile, smile, if not, don't, but do not engage with them, because it will only make things worse, okay?' he said, staring at her as if he could force the knowledge of what he was saying into her psychically.

'Okay,' she said, and he felt the shiver run through her body into his.

'Enzo, how do you feel about the engagement?'

'What do you think of the age difference?'

'What did your mother say?'

The shouts came thick and fast as he tried to force himself and Erin out of the circle that had formed around them. She put a hand on his forearm, as if to let him know that it was okay. But it wasn't. None of this was okay. The simple flex of her fingers let him know that she was with him, whatever he needed. And it felt...strange. Usually he was on his own, facing down the press. But to have someone there for him, not for the cameras, not for the press... But that was

all a lie, wasn't it, because she was getting something from him. He just didn't know what it was.

A dark car came speeding towards them and came to a sudden halt, and Enzo could just make out Frederick coming out of the driver's side to open the back doors for them.

He pulled Erin behind him towards the car, but she dropped her clutch in the commotion and when she reached down to pick it up, he almost heard the audible gasp of shock from the crowd.

Her ring.

'Are you engaged yourself, Enzo?'

'Enzo Rossetti? Engaged?!' came the cry as the press closed in on them, the weight and jostle accidentally, but no less for it, threatening.

Enzo bit back a curse. This was what he'd wanted, wasn't it? The press interest at fever pitch, all the better to publicly punish those who came after him for their own interests? But they hadn't found out as quickly as he'd liked, and now it just felt as if it were all going horribly wrong.

'Who are you with, Enzo?'

'Tell us her name!'

'Are you engaged?!'

A thousand flash-bulbs blinded them both as he finally pushed through to the car and got Erin into the back. He slipped in beside her, closing the door, and told Frederick to floor it. But not before he heard the final shout of one last reporter.

'Will there be a double Rossetti wedding?!'

The words echoed around the back of the car taking them the short distance between the bar and the marina, making Erin's head spin.

'Is it always like that?' Erin asked, shocked, as the car pulled up to the marina.

'That? That was nothing. You wait until after the wedding, when news of his affairs and her heartbreak come out. That's when the fun really begins,' he said bitterly with a laugh, as he got out of the car and held out his hand for her to take.

As she stepped onto the smooth concrete track that led down to the floating wooden pathway that wound between the world's most expensive yachts, she saw nothing but him. And the pain that he tried to hide.

'Are you okay?' she asked.

'Of course. Honestly? I'm just bored of it all now,' he said, turning away to walk back to the yacht.

She stared after him with solemn eyes, not making a move to follow him, heartsore and sad. She had not been fooled by his father's false charm—so different from his son's. She had not been fooled that Luca and his fiancée had just 'stumbled' across them at a bar that Enzo was known to enjoy. She had not been fooled by the easy extension of an invitation to the wedding. Enzo's father had needled him for money, and it hadn't been the first time.

She thought back over what he'd said of his childhood, what she'd uncovered in her research. The publicity around his parents' divorce. How he'd been used like a pawn...

And then it hit her. Truly hit her. She could not continue with Gio's scheme. She couldn't go through with it, she couldn't continue to pretend like it didn't matter, like Enzo didn't matter. Because he did matter. And no, she might not be getting something from him, but she was most definitely using him.

'What?' he asked when he realised she wasn't following him.

'I…' She shoved down that thought. She would deal with that later. Because right now, he was more important. He was the *most* important thing to her.

'You don't have to do that. Not with me,' she said, quietly.

'Do what?' he asked with a shrug.

The carelessness. She'd thought all along that it was how he lived, that he genuinely didn't care. But it wasn't just other people he was careless with. It was himself. And she hurt for him. She hurt, because she realised that's how people were with him. They were careless with *him*.

'You don't…' She trailed off, holding back her words. 'Have to *lie*.'

CHAPTER NINE

ENZO DIDN'T KNOW whether to laugh or cry.

He didn't have to lie? *He* didn't?

He didn't know whether it was audacity that had her saying that or something a little like the opposite.

But he couldn't help it. Couldn't help but be seduced by the romantic fantasy that they had both woven, of some kind of deeper, more meaningful relationship. And perhaps he could pretend just a little longer that she *was* there for him. That she did care.

He held out his hand to her, and together they made their way back to the yacht, the stillness of the night punctuated by the clacking of boats' metal lines slapping in the wind and the occasional bird call. They gravitated to the upper deck as if by silent agreement and as he poured them both a drink, he thought about where to start.

With her question? Was he really okay?

He crossed to join her where she stood, looking out over the Quay Saint Pierre, and the bustling restaurants and bars that bordered the marina. It was the first time he didn't want to be there, losing himself to the bright lights and happy conversations, the easy smiles and sensual distractions. No. His father was getting married. And he knew what that meant.

That meant his mother calling on the phone, determined to find her own new fiancé. More requests for interviews,

more requests for money. It meant the reminder that once again, he was nothing to them but a source of cash, or a pawn to be used on some years-old chess game between his parents.

Erin looked at him with a solemn aquamarine gaze, tendrils of the hair she'd taken down flowing in the gentle breeze. Overhead was one of the most spectacular starscapes in the world, and still she outshone it. She was, he realised, the most beautiful woman he'd ever seen.

His fingers flexed around the glass that he offered out to her.

'It's always been like that,' he confessed, and he wondered whether she would ever understand the shame of it. The raw, guttural shame of knowing that he'd never been wanted by his parents. Never been loved.

'In part, because my father is almost completely incapable of loving anything but himself. Both my parents, actually. Everything they do is about either feeding their own ego or their own bank account,' he said with a shrug of his shoulders as if he could dismiss it that easily.

'What about you?'

He looked down at the floor, wondering how much of himself to expose to her, shocked by how much he wanted to show her everything.

'They love me as a means to an end,' he said defiantly, lifting the glass to his lips, his eyes on her, watching and waiting for the slightest response to tell him of her thoughts. But her face was nearly ruthlessly blank, waiting for him to continue.

'I was an accident. That's what they screamed at each other before their first divorce. How they wouldn't be tied to each other if not for me.'

'How old were you?'

He frowned, trying to recall. 'Five? Six? It dragged on a while, so the divorce came through when I was eight. Not that it changed much. They remarried when I was ten, after their second divorce, and then again at seventeen after their third.'

And then the veil lifted and he saw everything in those expressive eyes. Pity, sadness, hurt for him. She hurt for him.

'Don't do that, Erin. Don't pity me,' he reproached.

Erin watched the man who was slowly unpicking his deepest hurts in the anonymity of the darkness of the night, wondering if he realised how much she could read on his features. Her heart ached for him, for the little boy she'd once thought of as Peter Pan so cruelly, because of that... that *lack* of emotional insecurity...

'Why not?' she asked, heartsore and *angry* for him. Why had no one stepped in? Why had Gio Gallo chosen now and not then to interfere in Enzo's life, when it felt like far too much and far too late? 'I *am* sorry for you,' she pressed on. 'I *am* sorry for what you experienced at the hands of the two people who should have protected you most. Who should have considered your needs and wants above their own. Do you not deserve that?' she asked him.

He threw his head back and laughed. 'Oh, Erin, I have spent a long time fulfilling my own wants and needs,' he assured her.

She frowned. 'I don't think you have.'

'Oh, I assure you, I have been *very* satisfied over the last few years.'

'Don't *do* that,' she insisted angrily. 'Sexual needs and day-to-day pleasures *are not* the same thing as love, and security, and safety,' she bit out so firmly it seemed to shock them both.

Enzo blinked at her once—everything torn away, the mask, the childhood hurts, the near magician-level distraction. Her fingers shook slightly and she fisted her hand, no longer really that shocked by the strength of her own feelings. For him. Her...*love*.

She had fallen for him, for *the Playboy of Amalfi*. She was...in love with him, she realised with a hand pressed to her lips, the pink diamond glittering as her hand shook.

Oh god. What had she gotten herself into?

Even having decided to refuse Gio's offer, even if she'd decided to give up on Charterhouse, she could see how impossible a future with Enzo was. She had betrayed him in the greatest of ways. Surely there was no coming back from that.

Enzo reached up to cup her jaw, his palm warm against a cheek cooled by the night air and such devastating realisations.

She wanted to apologise for her outburst, for her mistakes, for her betrayal. Her eyes welled.

'Enzo—'

'It's okay, *cara*,' he insisted.

But it wasn't.

She reached out to circle his wrist with her hand when he would have pulled away, her fingers slipping around the space between his watch and his hand with the lightest of touches, with the greatest of impacts.

'I—'

'Shhh,' he said, reversing the hold she had on him, twisting his wrist and instead, capturing hers. He brought it to his lips, pressing a kiss against the soft, vulnerable skin covering her fluttering pulse, sending warning flares across her body that pebbled her skin in goose bumps.

It stopped time, her heart, and any coherent thought she'd

had just moments before. He took her with his gaze. It devoured her, penetrated deep into the heart of her. It scoured her, seeking and searching for something she didn't know.

'I could show you. How good it can be to satisfy sexual needs. *Your* needs,' he clarified, as if refusing to allow her to think that he would use her for his own ends.

Oh, the irony, she thought miserably.

'It is a crime, *cara*, to see you hiding from your pleasure the way that you do.'

He was distracting her. She knew it. He knew it. And she shouldn't allow it, but his seduction was working.

'While I respect and totally understand your need to wait—and we will wait, *cara*,' he said, speaking of a future she couldn't see any more, 'I would like to show you,' he said, before sucking gently at her wrist.

He made it sound so reasonable; to indulge, to explore, to discover her own wants and needs with him.

'Let me give this to you?' he asked, pulling her into his arms, his dark gaze searching hers for permission, for agreement...for surrender.

'Because I *really* want to give this to you,' he said, as if it were the truth, as if he wanted nothing more in that moment. His gaze hid nothing, and she saw it all. Hurt, frustration, desire, confusions, want, and something she couldn't name.

'Say yes,' he begged, his whisper puffs of air against her lips. 'Just say—'

'Yes.'

The word was barely from her lips, when Enzo lowered his mouth to claim hers. The storm of desire he'd been holding back, released like a tsunami, a single wave overwhelming them both, leaving only the ability to cling together and hope to survive.

He walked her backwards until her thighs hit the table, lifting her in his arms, and placing her on top of it, inserting himself between her thighs, all without breaking the kiss. Her hands shaped his chest and clutched at his hips, sinking into the material of his shirt and holding her to him.

They had gone up in flames. It had taken so little. With just one word he was hers and she didn't even know it.

He bunched the voluminous skirts of her dress in his fists, as he drew it up from her ankles to her thighs, feeling the smooth supple skin against his knuckles. Her fingers sank into his hair, her nails scraping lightly over his scalp, sending a shiver down his back to grip his gut.

Frantic. He was frantic for her. And unwilling to wait any longer, he drew back from the lure of her mouth and dropped to his knees. She looked down at him, the flush of need slashed across her cheekbones.

'*Cara?*'

'Yes.' She nodded, quickly, her lip pinned by her teeth.

'Are you sure?'

'*Yes.*'

That word again. He wanted to hear it, over and over and over again.

Pinning the skirts of her dress with one hand, he drew her underwear from her body with the other, slipping them into his pocket, before placing open-mouthed kisses on the inside of her thighs.

'Lean back, *amore mio*,' he commanded, his hand reaching up to gently press her back against the table, wanting her completely relaxed and focused on her own pleasure, on the sensations he was going to give her. It opened her to him and he could hold back no longer, as his tongue dipped into the cross-hatch of curls at the juncture of her thighs and found more than he could ever have imagined wanting.

The hot wet heat of her was a drug and he lapped at her, long, slow and wicked. He teased the small bundle of nerves with the tip of his tongue and tortured her with powerful, deep thrusts of his entire tongue at her entrance. Her pleasure cascaded against his mouth and ears as she was thrust quickly to the brink of orgasm and he held her there for as long as possible, torturing her with his tongue and fingers, filling her, stretching her, teasing her, delighting her.

Her thighs quivered either side of his head, and every shift and sway of her body only served to increase his own arousal. He knew that he would have to take himself in hand later, but that was then, Erin was now, and she was all that mattered.

She tasted like woman, like lust, like all he'd ever need, he realised as his breath hitched in his throat and she cried that little breathy moan that let him know she was so very close to the edge. He knew from her body's response that no one had touched her here, no one had kissed her here and, Neanderthal that he was, that gave him more pleasure than was justifiable.

Yes, yes, yes.

With her words on the air above him, his tongue pressing and taunting her clit, Enzo pushed her into an abyss of stars that pulsed in time with her pleasure, and knew that he'd never be the same again.

Erin slowly opened her eyes, aware that she was in bed, and closed them again when she remembered how she'd asked him to stay last night. He'd been about to leave, when she'd reached for his hand. She just hadn't wanted to be alone after what they'd shared.

She turned onto her opposite side and reached for the imprint of where Enzo had spent the night, a little surprised to find it still warm. He must have only just left.

But he'd still left.

And in a way she was thankful. Because he couldn't be there for what she needed to do. Because even while she realised that there was no future for her and Enzo, that there simply *couldn't* be, she could still not continue to use him in any way.

Because he wasn't the irresponsible, careless playboy she'd thought him to be. She could see how he'd been shaped by his parents, could see the hurt and the depth of the emotion he tried to mask from a world whose eye had been trained on him almost since birth.

Snippets from their time together ran through her mind.

Rin doesn't seem to suit you.

Take what you need from me. Take your pleasure.

What I see when I look at you...a powerful, determined, fierce and beautiful woman.

All these things that he had said to her, given to her. This was not a man who *didn't* care. This was not a man like her father at all.

And no matter what happened from here on out, she knew that she could never be just another person that would betray him. That would take a single thing from him without his knowledge or consent.

And before she could change her mind, she sat down at her laptop on the desk in front of a small window looking out at the marina in Cannes, and started her email to Gio Gallo.

I've told Gio I'm out, Sam.

Are you sure?

Yes.

Enzo squinted angrily at the horizon from behind dark sunglasses. Here at the marina, he'd not been able to do as he'd wished, and drop into the frigid depths of the sea to shock some sense back into himself. So he'd spent far longer than was probably healthy in a very cold shower.

The problem was that things felt so genuine with Erin, that he was beginning to fall for the lies they had both woven around this relationship. And the fact that he wasn't actively running for the hills was becoming a serious problem. As perfectly illustrated by the fact that he'd spent half the night watching her sleep, not because she'd asked him to stay, but because he hadn't been able to drag himself away.

Erin arrived on the upper deck at that moment, looking fresh in wide-legged white linen trousers and a light blue linen shirt, her hair in a messy bun on top of her head and sunglasses dangling from her fingers.

Of course she looked the most innocent, the most natural that she had done since he'd first met her. Just when he was trying to remember her conniving manipulations. *Of course* he struggled with his body's instinctive, near *primal*, response to this woman. That was her plan, wasn't it?

'Good morning,' she said shyly, biting her lip, the artifice of her hesitation impeccable.

'*Buongiorno*,' he replied, rising from his seat to greet her. 'Cannes suits you,' he said with a forced smile.

'*Merci*,' she replied with a wry smile.

He went to kiss her cheek, but she moved ever so slightly, and when her lips found his, he held himself in check, when the palm of her hand rested on his chest, he prayed his heart would stay still. He wondered if he was imagining the shift between this morning and before and told himself off for being fanciful.

'You don't think so?' he asked, as she slipped behind the table onto the banquet seating.

'I like Cannes, but… Italy was special.'

He blinked, hiding his surprise at her answer.

'We have a party tonight,' he said, changing the subject.

'Another one?'

He mock-winced. 'Marcus has a lot of parties, but this one is important to him.'

'You've known him long?' she asked.

'Since university.'

'That's why your English is so good? Because you went to university in England?'

'Yes. My father was too notorious in America, and England was closer to Europe, so…' He shrugged off the end of the sentence. 'Marcus comes across as a bit of a buffoon, I know, but there is something bluntly honest about him which is important to me.'

He watched her closely, for any signs of a reaction to his description, but Erin just smiled and nodded.

'Then I will look forward to getting to know him more,' Erin said instead. 'As long as *I* can pick the dress this time,' she said pointedly.

He smiled when he was supposed to smile, and laughed when he was supposed to laugh, but all the while he couldn't stop himself from wondering where this was going. Could he really still see himself leaving her at the top of the aisle? To expose her to the glare of the world's press and their fierce judgement? Before he'd met Erin, he'd lived his life unsure and uncaring of his next steps, going wherever he fancied, wherever the next party was. But for the first time in his life, he didn't know where he was going and he didn't like it one single bit.

* * *

Erin walked into the large three-story club in the heart of Cannes's beachfront, feeling very self-conscious.

Enzo hadn't been as effusive as he had in the past, but Erin knew that he liked the way she looked in the flowing white dress she'd chosen for the evening. The pallor of her skin had warmed in the last few weeks beneath the Mediterranean sun and the white made her appear bronzed, so that *this time* when people turned to stare at them, she knew it wasn't because she looked hideous, or was an embarrassment. It was because she looked like she fit on his arm. And finally, she was beginning to feel that way too, which was a painful irony.

She'd received a one-word email response from Gio Gallo as she'd got dressed earlier that evening.

Understood.

And despite the fact that she knew she had lost Charterhouse for good, she knew she was doing the right thing.

For Enzo and for herself.

As for the future? Oh, she didn't think she could pretend to carry on as if nothing had happened, she certainly couldn't *marry* him. But she also wasn't quite ready to let him go just yet. So she'd hoped to claim just one night. One night as herself, as Erin, before she had to return home from Neverland. She wasn't sure she'd be able to tell him about Gio and what had brought her into his life, but she could certainly tell him that it wasn't his fault she was breaking their engagement.

'Darling,' Marcus said, to her when she and Enzo found him, 'you look *ravishing.*'

'Thank you,' she said, accepting his compliment with a genuine smile.

'Hello, I'm Cynthia,' she unnecessarily re-introduced herself.

'I know, we met before. On the Isola del Giglio?'

'Oh, did we?' Cynthia asked, oblivious to any awkwardness, or awareness of her own rudeness.

No matter what happened, Erin would never be friends with this woman, she decided.

'I'm so pleased you both could make it,' Marcus said. 'It just wouldn't have been the same without you. Champagne!' he shouted at the top of his lungs, making Erin flinch then laugh when a waiter in a black-and-white suit immediately appeared with a bottle on a tray with four glasses.

It might not have been how Erin was used to spending her evenings, but she wanted to try for Enzo's sake, for her own sake. She wanted this night to be perfect and these were his friends and they weren't all bad. The music was loud, and the crowd boisterous, but for the first time she didn't fear making a fool of herself or being the centre of attention for the wrong reasons. She wanted to borrow a little of Enzo's fun and try it on for size.

The club itself was spectacular. The Art Deco interior design suited the elegance not only of the location but of the attendees, and Erin found herself not only begin to relax but to actually start to enjoy herself. If Enzo seemed a little flat, she found herself dialling up her energy to compensate, not quite aware that she was doing so.

She made small talk with Marcus, it was impossible to do so with Cynthia, and she got talking to Alana, a lovely woman from Morocco who owned and ran an ethical clothing company which made her instantly think of Conxion.

Which in turn made her wonder what it was she would do now. Without Charterhouse. The company would now,

surely, be broken into a thousand different pieces, as Gio had promised. And she'd never have a chance to fix her father's mistake. For her mother. For herself too. It hurt, but not as much as it would have to hurt Enzo in the process.

She looked across at him, found him watching her. She smiled, but he didn't return it. Not immediately. She was about to go to him, but he waved her off with a 'don't mind me' look.

Something had shifted between them since the news of his father's engagement had broken. It was hardly surprising that he was finding it hard, she couldn't imagine what it must be bringing up for him. So, she sent him a reassuring smile and slipped away to the bathroom, hoping she wouldn't encounter any nasty gossips this time.

Enzo watched her go, weaving through a crowd dressed in more money than sense, and still she shone like the brightest ruby. Dark, complex, and powerful.

'Listen, I've got this investment thing,' Marcus said, the volume of his shout a little too much, making Enzo flinch.

Only a handful of people knew about his company, let alone a portfolio significant enough to keep him *off* the world's rich list. Sometimes it took more money than less to keep your anonymity. So, he wasn't entirely comfortable with Marcus bringing it up now. But he could see that his friend was drunk.

'I don't talk business when I'm drinking, Marcus, you know that.'

'I know, it's just that this is time sensitive.'

'Then it's *too* sensitive and I'm not interested,' he dismissed him.

Marcus side-eyed him as if gauging his mood.

'Listen, I'm sorry about your dad,' Marcus said more

quietly. He knew how bad things had been for Enzo over the years, and while they rarely delved beyond the surface, Marcus had seen enough.

He nodded, the only acknowledgement of Marcus's sympathy he could muster.

'Have you heard from your mum?' Marcus pressed.

Enzo gritted his teeth, this time shaking his head.

He hadn't. And that had—he was reluctant to admit—worried him. Usually she would have called him in hysterics by now and the sheer fact that she hadn't... And he didn't like worrying about her, because she had never really worried about *him*. And what he most especially disliked was sounding like a stroppy insecure child!

Last time he'd heard from her, she'd been sequestered in a chalet in Switzerland with a therapist and a spiritualist. 'I'm going to make it work this time, Zo, I promise. It's going to work.'

Maybe she was making it work. Maybe she had drowned herself in alcohol and pills. Who knew? All he could say was that he was distinctly and acutely uncomfortable with all these *feelings*. He didn't know what to do with them. Other than try and push them all back down.

'So, how's it going with the girl?' Marcus shouted into his ear above the music, his use of language making Enzo tense.

Erin wasn't a *girl*. She was...she was...

Coming up against a wall, he realised that truly, he didn't know what Erin Carter was. Master con artist, or not?

'Have you found out what she's after yet?' Marcus shouted again.

'No.'

'I can't believe she's managed to keep that quiet this entire time. She hasn't slipped up? Not once since Capri?'

Enzo didn't reply, hoping that his friend would just drop it.

'And I still don't understand why she signed the prenup. Is there a fidelity clause in there somewhere? Is she expecting you to cheat on her?'

'Marcus, I don't know,' he replied finally, giving up the fight with his frustration. 'Whatever it is she's after, she's not going to get it. And when she reaches the top of the aisle and comes face-to-face with the fact that I have absolutely no damn intention of marrying her, and instead, will leave her facing the music in front of as many guests and as many of the world's press as I can possibly muster in the next seven days, she will be humiliated and left with nothing. And then she'll realise that it was a mistake messing with me. *Everyone* will realise that it's a mistake to mess with me.'

And with that, he finished the last drop of his whiskey and stalked off, completely failing to see Erin where she stood in the shadow of the doorway, staring after him in shock.

CHAPTER TEN

ERIN'S SHAKING HANDS covered her mouth.

Whatever she's after, she's not going to get it.

I have absolutely no damn intention of marrying her.

She'll be humiliated and left with nothing.

Oh god.

He knew. No. He'd *known*. He'd known that she wanted to marry him from the beginning. That it had all been part of a horrible scheme. Her legs began to shake and she pressed back against the wall that had shielded her from Enzo's view. She took in a deep gulp of breath, not feeling like it was enough. Tears filled her eyes. Her mind swam with them, hurt, fear, horror, nausea.

What he must have thought…what he must have felt.

Guilt pinched and bit into her stomach, her heart twisting far more painfully than that.

He clearly didn't know about Gio's involvement. Or that she'd emailed to tell him that she wasn't going to go through with it. That she'd cancelled the deal the moment that things had become real for her. The moment she'd realised that he wasn't who she'd thought he was.

But it had never been real for him.

And when she reaches the top of the aisle…

That part felt especially painful because he *knew* what that kind of humiliation would do to her.

A sob rose in her chest and she tried to stifle it.

The ringing started in her ears and wouldn't stop.

It had all been lies. He'd been playing her this whole time. The helicopter? Had he really forgotten that she'd said she didn't like heights? And the shopping trip? Had that been a test? Test after test, setting her up just to fail. The dress that he'd suggested she wear to the party. The way he'd comforted her after.

Oh god…the intimacy she'd shared with him.

Their interactions rushed through her mind like the trailer of some awful movie.

And just like that, what had been special and precious, and incredible to her became sordid, and horrible. How far would he have let her go? Would he have slept with her if she hadn't found a way not to? Oh god, she could hate him for doing that.

Hurt and anger twisted her train of thought into turns that it would not have made before. And deep from within, far older than her time with Enzo, came another visceral pain. If he could do that and it be a lie, then he could never have cared about her at all.

And she'd cared enough to sacrifice the one thing—the *one thing*—that she'd been working to get back for *years*. She'd let everything go. Because of him, because of what she'd felt for him.

She was just like her mother. Lost and left with absolutely nothing because of a man.

The horror of it left her stunned, a ringing in her ears drowning out the music and the people in the club.

'There you are,' Cynthia announced as if the last thing she'd wanted to do was actually find Erin. 'He's looking for you. Worried you'd wandered off,' the other woman said,

already looking around the club to find someone else more important to talk to.

'Okay,' Erin said, nodding and wiping her cheeks, thankful that Cynthia was so uninterested as to notice her distressed state.

What should she do? Her passport and things were still on the yacht, so even if she wanted to leave, she still had to go back there. She could call Sam. She knew that her friend would help with whatever she needed—a private jet if she needed it, probably. But Erin was the one who had got into this mess. And she needed to get herself out of it.

She needed her things first, and then needed to leave. And what, just disappear into the night? As if none of this had ever happened? So she could become just some funny story that he could tell his friends and laugh about?

Yes, she had done a terrible thing, deliberately setting out to marry him for her own needs. But he hadn't needed to play along. He could have walked away.

But he hadn't. He'd wanted to use her too. He'd wanted to humiliate her and turn her into some cautionary tale. Anger shot through her, filling her, pushing at her skin, desperate to get out, to burn and scorch in the way she felt burned and scorched.

She didn't want him to get away with it, she didn't want him to walk away unscathed.

She didn't want him to walk away as if she didn't matter and he didn't care, she thought as her heart broke.

She smoothed her hair away from her face and stood up away from the wall, turning the corner, and came face-to-face with him, her smile freezing in place.

She took him in, the question in his gaze, that raised brow of his, the hard lines of his cheek and jaw, the mid-

night black of his hair, the rich depths of his gaze—a gaze she now knew hid secrets and lies as easily as breathing.

'There you are, *cara*, I've been looking for you.'

Enzo frowned as he saw something flash in Erin's gaze, but it was gone so quickly he couldn't be sure what it was. He was already out of sorts following his conversation with Marcus, and honestly for the first time in his life, he was ready to be nearly the first person to leave the party, not the last.

'I've been here the whole time,' she said with an elegant shrug, her smile a little forced.

'Is everything okay?'

'Oh, Enzo. Everything is just marvellous,' she said, slipping her hand through the crook of his arm, and leading him back towards the dance floor. 'We're here with your friends, in a gorgeous part of the world, in a fabulous club, having a *wonderful* time, no?'

Well, no. He wasn't having a wonderful time. He was something horrifyingly close to miserable, but as he had refused to let himself be miserable since about the age of ten, when his parents had made him pose for cameras on the steps of the courthouse of their second marriage, he smiled and let her lead him back to the dance floor.

Erin seemed to have found a wave of energy he'd not witnessed before now, and even Cynthia had begun to soften towards the happy, effervescent Erin Carter that had them all enthralled.

And he didn't like that either. An only child, one might have accused him of not learning to share his toys, but Erin wasn't a toy and he wasn't a child. She just didn't seem to be...*herself.* The Erin that he had come to know in the last few weeks. Even though the irony was that whatever Erin

was embodying right at that moment was precisely the kind
of woman that had attracted him before, he didn't like it,
didn't quite like what he was seeing. It made him feel unsettled.

That feeling lasted long into the early hours of the morning as the club wound down, many of the revellers flushed
in the face from alcohol or happiness as they all slipped
away to their respective beds for the night.

Erin took off her shoes and walked barefoot, her arm still
hooked into his as they made their way back to the marina.

'Did you have fun tonight, *amore mio*?' he asked, genuinely curious. It would seem that she had, but...*but*... He
had this nagging feeling that he couldn't shake that something wasn't quite right.

She turned to him and tugged his arm closer to her side.
'Yes, soooo much fun.'

'Are you drunk, *cara*?'

She laughed. 'No, why? I haven't had a drink in hours.'

He nodded, eyes narrowing on her before she laughed
again and tugged on his arm. Maybe he was projecting.
Maybe he was letting his mood impact his thoughts.

They reached the marina, the wood jetty bobbing slightly
beneath their feet as they boarded the yacht. Strangely it was
Erin who led the way to the upper deck, clearly not ready
to go to bed. He forced his eyes away from the seductive
sway of her walk as she went over to the wet bar.

'Would you like something to drink?'

'No, *grazie*.'

Erin shrugged, the careless gesture so foreign on her
body, he clenched his jaw. Something was wrong.

She poured herself a glass of wine and held it in loose
fingers as she turned a considering gaze on him, her head
cocked to one side, the smile off somehow.

'I think I'm ready,' she said, taking a mouthful of her drink.

'Ready?'

'Yes. Ready to have sex with you.'

The cough of shock lodged in his throat, before it escaped in a punch of breath from his lungs.

'*What*?'

She put the drink on the bar and closed the distance between them, looping her arms around his neck and pressing against his chest and torso. Brain short-circuited by the sudden and shocking feel of her, his hands automatically went to her hips, anchoring her to him or away from him, he wasn't quite sure.

'Let's have sex.'

Madonna mia, why did she keep saying that? And saying it *like* that?

This was as far from the Erin of earlier that afternoon as she could have possibly got.

'Erin—'

She pressed a kiss to his lips, teasing his mouth open with the seduction of her tongue. His body reacted on instinct rather than desire, making a mockery of what Erin wanted. The kiss waged a war between desire and disinclination, Erin only breaking the kiss when he refused to let it spin out of control.

The moue of dissatisfaction on her lips was almost cruel.

'What's wrong? Didn't I do it right?'

Something fisted his gut and the warning he'd ignored until that very moment screamed so loud in his ears, he flinched.

'What is this, Erin? What's going on?'

He looked at her, staring intently into her glittering eyes.

Was it alcohol that made them shine so bright? No, he realised with a shock. It was *tears*.

'*Dio*, Erin, what the hell is going on?'

'Surely I'm only giving you what you want, Enzo,' she
said as if she were offering him pocket money.

'I don't...'

'What? Don't you want me?' she asked, her voice quivering.

'Of course I want you. But not like this,' he stressed.

'Really? How *would* you want me, then? *Broken*?'

'Broken?' he asked, revolted by the thought. 'What the—'

'*Humiliated*?' she asked. 'Left with *nothing*?'

His words echoed on her lips sent a shiver of sheer horror down his spine.

'At the top of the aisle. In front of the media and your
friends.'

She'd overheard him. His conversation with Marcus. He
shook his head and let out the breath that had been locked
in his lungs for what felt like an eternity.

Erin watched as he pulled his tie loose from his neck in three
quick yanks and huffed out a bitter laugh. She wanted to
be surprised that he hadn't taken her up on her 'offer'. The
thought of it turned her stomach. But she'd known. In the
back of her mind and the quiet of her heart, she'd known
that he wouldn't.

And in that moment, all the anger and all the fight went
out of her. The fury that had fuelled her to get her to this
point burned out with a desperate last indignant flame before sinking back into thick smoke and charcoal in surrender.

'You heard the conversation with Marcus,' he stated.

'Yes,' Erin confirmed, ready to surrender everything to him.

'How fitting. It was after all how I found out about your intended deceit. And Sam? He is your lover, perhaps?'

'No,' Erin said, bruised by the bitterness in his tone and unable to bring herself to correct him.

He nodded to himself as if her answer hadn't really mattered to him. Standing there, the moon picking out the white in his shirt like a beacon, he looked impossibly even more handsome than ever, which was just cruel.

'What was this,' he asked, gesturing to what had just happened between them. 'Some kind of test?'

'Maybe,' she admitted, unsure herself now. 'Perhaps it was a bit like a helicopter ride, or a shopping trip. Or an awful dress,' she said, forcing the words out of her mouth.

He plunged his fists into the pockets of his dark trousers and turned away from her as if he couldn't bear to look at her.

'What was it? That you were going to get out of marrying me?' he asked, his gaze firmly on the night sea. The past tense he'd used made her flinch, distracting her from the thread of hurt she imagined in his tone.

Shame overwhelmed her. He'd wanted her broken, and that was how she felt.

'I could never quite work it out,' he confessed as if half impressed. 'You signed the prenup, so it wasn't money.'

'No. I… I was promised that if I married you then Charterhouse would be mine.'

'Charterhouse?'

'A publishing company.'

He frowned, finally turning back to her. 'The project you told me about? You did all this for a *business*?'

She hurt from the harshness of his tone, but knew she deserved it. 'It belonged to my family, before my father sold it.'

'What the hell does that have to do with me?' he demanded angrily.

She swallowed. 'I... Gio Gallo,' she whispered.

That seemed to stop Enzo in his tracks. He blinked as he processed the information, his face a reflection of his confusion.

'Gio Gallo? My grandfather?'

'Yes,' Erin said, nodding once. 'He owns it, and offered to sell it back to me if...'

She didn't need to finish her sentence. The rest was painfully clear by now.

'That man is nothing to me,' Enzo exclaimed. 'He wasn't when I was a child and isn't now. Why would he have any interest in who or when I married?'

'I don't know. He wouldn't tell me.'

'So, let me get this straight. You agreed to marry a complete stranger, in exchange for a company?'

She nodded. 'There were conditions,' she said, trying to explain. 'I wasn't allowed to tell you, otherwise I would have. And the business was...it was in my family for generations before it was sold. I made a promise to my mother that I would get it back. I wanted so desperately to make it happen.'

'That was supremely naïve,' he bit out, utterly unmoved by her motives.

She clenched her jaw, taking the critique as utterly deserved.

'I'm so sorry. I'm so, very sorry. I thought you were like him,' she said, needing Enzo to understand in part. 'At the beginning. I thought you were like my father. Careless and

lazy and flippant and selfish. I thought you were all the things that you had been painted in the press.'

'Does that make it okay to you?' he demanded.

'No. There is nothing I can say or do to make it okay,' she admitted truthfully. 'There is nothing about any of this that is okay,' she said, wiping the tear from her cheek, hating that he'd seen how affected she was by this. Hating that she *was* affected, when he didn't seem to care at all.

'Crocodile tears, *cara*? Really?'

'They're not,' she said quietly.

'Oh,' he scoffed loudly, his hands coming to a prayer position in front of his chest. 'You expect me to believe that this was real? That you fell in love with me along the way?'

His words were cruel and punishing and so much more painful because they were the truth. 'Yes,' she said, determinedly. Because this was it. She knew that. There was no coming back from this. He'd never see her again and it was her only chance to tell the truth. No more lies. Never again.

Enzo struggled and fought with the desire to believe her. But he didn't know which Erin she was. The innocent, the con artist, the seductress, the fury... He had seen so many different sides to her and that he had fallen for them all was acid in a wound so deep it knocked the breath from his lungs.

Her apology should have been meaningless. The declaration of love meaningless. But it wasn't. And that was warning enough.

'Annulment. Was that how you planned to get out of the marriage? I'm presuming you would have left me as soon as you got what you wanted?'

She held his gaze, refusing to hide a single one of her emotions from him now. They were as clear as the bright-

est stars in a clear night sky. And he wished to god that he
didn't see a single one of them.

She nodded.

Yes. That had been clever.

He had just one question left. He shouldn't ask it. That
he did it anyway was just proof of how low she had brought
him.

'Was anything you told me the truth?'

'Yes.'

Madonna mia, he wanted to believe her more than he
wanted his next breath.

'And for you?' Erin's quiet question exploded into the
night.

'What do you mean?' he asked, playing ignorant despite
knowing exactly what she had meant.

'Was any of it true for you? Somewhere in all the lies and
games, was any of it real? Because, in some ways, I was
more *me* with you than I have ever been, and I...' she said
haltingly, 'I wondered whether...maybe...'

'No,' he lied. 'None of it was true, and nothing was real.'

It couldn't have been.

It couldn't have been because that would mean he was
just the same as that small child he'd once been, standing
by himself, waiting to be enough, waiting to be loved for
who he was and not what he could do or give.

And he couldn't be that same sad child. He wouldn't.

He stared out at the darkness, the clouds covering the
stars and horizon in such a way that made him feel empty
and hollow. He didn't know how long he stayed like that,
but when he turned back Erin was no longer there on the
upper deck.

In some distant part of his mind, he was conscious of her
leaving the yacht and the marina, safe in the knowledge that

his staff were good and well paid enough to make sure that wherever she was going, she'd be safe and okay.

He didn't want to know where she went, he told himself. He didn't care. His overheard conversation had brought an abrupt end to a plan that no longer needed to be fulfilled. Whoever Erin Carter was, she'd learned her lesson.

As had he. When things looked too good to be true, they generally were.

And thrusting all thoughts of her from his mind, he turned his attention to the man who had been behind the whole thing. Gio Gallo. His mother's estranged father.

Now that was a target who could bear the weight of Enzo's anger. What on earth was the old man up to? He had, until now, shown absolutely no interest in either his daughter or his grandson. His *kin*. As far as Enzo was concerned, the man didn't deserve the time of day.

But clearly Gio Gallo had resorted to extreme methods to get his attention. For what reason? Enzo was *still* none the wiser. And neither did he care.

The old man's plans had been thwarted and that was enough. Enzo was done being manipulated by the people around him, he decided, digging his heels further into the solitary island he had put himself on long ago. The only thing that would make him feel better would be to return to his eminently enjoyable lifestyle as if none of this sordid mess had ever happened.

Erin wheeled her suitcase into the empty airport. It had taken her very little time to pack her bags, and write a note for Frederick, asking him to return all the clothing that she'd purchased that day in Positano using Enzo's card.

The member of staff that had found her a cab hadn't wanted to leave her on her own, but she needed to disen-

tangle herself from Enzo and anyone with him. It was three o'clock in the morning and after she had used her phone to buy herself a ticket on the first flight out from Cannes to Heathrow, she found the ladies' bathroom, checked that it was empty, locked herself in a stall and collapsed against the door, letting the tears fall. Fist pressed into her mouth, just in case anyone did enter the bathroom, she let the silent sobs wrack her body, from the inside out.

All the anger that she'd felt in the club, first hearing the ruthlessness of his plan had fled under the immense weight of her own guilt.

She had lost Charterhouse, but it didn't even compare to losing *him*.

She had seen him, standing there all alone on the upper deck of his yacht, and her heart had torn in two. She didn't believe him, when he said that it had all been lies. She knew that she'd hurt him terribly. And she deserved to see that, to know his pain on top of her own.

Oh god, how had she got this all so wrong?

It had started off wanting to help her mother. Wanting security. But she'd done that at someone else's expense. And she *knew* better than that. She did, she told herself as another tear rolled down her cheek. She had become just like her father, she realised with horror. Wanting something so desperately that it didn't matter who she hurt in the process. Only it did matter.

Her heart broke, not for herself, but for him. For the little boy that had been so appallingly used, by his parents, as if he were a chess piece in the game of their relationship. And she had done the same. Until she had seen differently. But it had been too late. He had been brutally hurt by her. And she knew that there was no coming back from that. And she'd live with the guilt of having done that to an admirable

man, a kind man, a funny man, a man who had brought her alive under his attention.

A man she loved.

Her chest ached and her tears ran and she ignored the phone buzzing in her purse until she couldn't. She checked the screen, hoping that it might be Enzo and hating herself for being disappointed to read the name.

Still, she hit the button to accept the call.

'Oh, Sam. I've really messed things up.'

CHAPTER ELEVEN

Enzo Rossetti stalked through the foyer of Gallo Group headquarters in Rome, utterly unaware that he was retracing Erin's earlier footsteps, four weeks to the day. The soothing tones of rose gold and cream had no impact on the furious Italian whatsoever.

Nothing had dulled the edge of his frustration. Ever since Erin had left, despite his words, Gio Gallo's name had been an earworm in his mind and despite all his intentions to ignore the man's foolish interference in his life, Enzo couldn't let it alone.

A member of Gallo Group staff pointed him towards an elevator with doors open and waiting. He'd always known about Gio Gallo. When he'd been younger, he'd looked for any piece of information he could find about the ruthless, determined man who had cut Enzo and his mother from his life.

Harsh words to describe his grandfather, but no less true. Gio had severed all financial, emotional, and legal connections between him and his daughter because he had disliked her choice of husband. Whether the man had been right about Luca Rossetti or not, that Gio Gallo had chosen to abdicate his responsibilities as a father, as a grandfather, was *unnatural*.

And feeling an unusual spurt of pride for his mother,

Enzo was pleased that she had defied Gio's overly zeal-ous rule. She wasn't the only one—there was apparently a cousin who had also been disinherited five years ago for exactly the same crime.

Marriage.

So why on earth had Gio sought to engineer *his*?

Was he, in his dotage, finally regretting his actions? Enzo scoffed. He doubted it.

But whatever his reasoning, why had he chosen Erin?

The latter, of course, was irrelevant and he told himself as he rose to the uppermost floor of the impressive building that he didn't care. He stepped out into a small but luxuri-ous waiting room where an assistant sat behind a large or-nate desk, attacking a keyboard with alarmingly red nails.

'Please take a seat,' she said without deigning to look up or even pause whatever war she was waging.

He barked out a laugh.

'*No, grazie*,' Enzo replied, walking straight over to the large doors bearing his grandfather's name, opening them and continuing on into the room.

The old man who was sitting behind the desk was much smaller than Enzo had imagined. The research he'd done had given Enzo the impression of height and width. But Enzo's fury began to ebb at the sight of slight shoulders and papery skin. Despite that, there was nothing aged about his gaze. The warning there was bright, clear, and fiercely intelligent.

'This is a rather impetuous start to our relationship,' Gio Gallo observed.

'We don't have a relationship,' Enzo hit back.

Gio shrugged as if his objection was irrelevant.

'Coffee?'

'Black.'

Gio stared back at him as if that were unnecessary in-

formation, as if no one worthy of his time would take it any other way.

Enzo didn't want or need any more coffee, but it might be better to have something to occupy his hands so that he couldn't throttle the old man.

And just like that, all his plans, his carefully constructed verbal attacks burned to ash in his mind and he was left with only one question. The question that had driven him here, despite his absolute conviction that he would have nothing to do with any of them ever again.

'Why did you do it?'

'I thought you would make a good match. She is perfect for you,' Gio replied without shame or prevarication; no denial or pretence as to not knowing what they were talking about. Enzo could respect at least that much. But the answer?

Enzo scoffed. *Perfect?*

'Why did you do it?' he asked again. Because despite his words, Gio had *not* answered the question.

Gio glared mutinously at him and Enzo glared back, finally dropping the mask of the careless playboy who would have thrown his hands up into the air and given up, made a joke, laughed it off.

'Ahhh. *There* you are,' Gio said.

Enzo refused to be unnerved by his words, or insight into his personality, instead clinging to the silence that Gio *would* fill eventually. They always did.

'Did she get to meet you? The real you?' Gio asked.

Enzo clenched his teeth together.

'Mmm. I thought she might. She's really quite an amazing young woman.'

Something about the proprietary way he spoke of Erin grated on him painfully.

'*You* marry her then.'

Gio smiled at that. A near laugh. Apparently, that was as far as the man got to humour.

The assistant brought in two espressos and left just as quickly and quietly.

'That's not part of the plan.'

'What plan? No games. No mysterious manipulations. Why do all this?'

'Because you are family.'

'Certainly not legally,' Enzo pointed out.

'My issues with your mother should never have involved you and for that I am regretful. I...made a mistake. And you paid for it. You appear, by your itinerant ways, to still be paying for it.'

Not sorry. Not at fault. He would have gone mad growing up with this man in his life, Enzo was sure. But still...there was an acknowledgement there that threatened to soften him, to ease his anger.

'She reached out to me,' Gio said, his piercing gaze pinned on Enzo.

'Erin?'

Gio arched an eyebrow.

'Your mother,' he clarified.

Enzo blinked.

'We talked.'

'Good for you,' Enzo said, knocking back the espresso and preparing to leave. This wasn't going as he'd wanted and he knew when to cut his losses.

'You are a strange combination of both of your parents,' Gio observed.

'You don't get to say that.'

'You are stubborn like your mother, and a coward like your father.'

'How dare you!'

The accusation roared from deep within Enzo to a place he'd rarely visited.

'I don't really have the luxury of time, or small talk, so I will do us both the favour of getting to the point,' Gio said cryptically. 'Unlike your mother, who clung desperately to whatever it was she wanted, you seem intent on throwing it all away. I'm guessing that's your father's influence.'

Shock whipped through Enzo like lightning. He wanted to argue, but he couldn't. He wanted to shout, but nothing came out. For a moment, they just stared at each other, as all the walls and barriers Enzo had used to protect himself began to crumble.

'No small talk, huh?'

'No, boy. No small talk. You cannot continue to live your life surfing the edges of everything you want.'

'I'm more than you think, old man.'

'Oh, yes, I know. I know about the secret investment company, the admittedly impressive wealth. You get that from *me,* by the way.'

'*Madonna mia,*' Enzo exclaimed in frustration.

'It's not a life. What you had. What you thought you enjoyed,' Enzo said. 'You ran away from anything permanent in your life and I wanted you to experience someone you couldn't shuck off so easily.'

'She would have left the moment she got what she wanted,' Enzo pointed out bitterly.

'I believed she would change her mind.'

Enzo shook his head, speechless at the man's presumption, hurting and furious that she hadn't changed her mind. That she hadn't stayed.

'I believed that she was someone who wouldn't abandon you or leave you,' Gio insisted.

'You had to pay her!' Enzo yelled, his anger loud and furious in the stillness of the room as he ripped open the wound that hid in his heart of hearts. Because he'd *wanted* Erin to be that woman. He'd *wanted* Erin to love him and not leave him, or abandon him. He'd wanted her to love him for himself, without conditions, strings, or bribes. Because damn it, he'd fallen for her.

'You should know that she dropped her claim on the publishing company,' Gio announced, probably aware of the impact it would have.

'What?' Enzo asked, shock tensing every muscle in his body.

'She told me to keep it. She chose you.'

'When?'

'Does it matter?'

Very much.

Not waiting for an answer, Gio pressed on. 'I received an email two weeks ago. Would you like to see it?'

Yes.

'No.'

Three weeks ago? That was before the party. That was before...

Gio checked his watch.

'I have a meeting.'

Enzo was being dismissed and entirely unsatisfied by his encounter, wanted to argue.

'I—'

'We are done here. For now. I would...' And for the first time since meeting his grandfather, Enzo sensed the smallest glimmer of vulnerability. 'I would like to continue to meet. Occasionally. When you are in Italy.'

Enzo glared at his grandfather, his world seesawing

around him, and unsure whether to lash out or cry out. He swallowed.

'I don't know.'

'Well, let me know when you do. You may leave.'

Enzo stood there for a full minute, but not once did his grandfather look up or acknowledge him. On the way out of Gio's office, he thought he saw an IV stand, with bags, half hidden behind the door that gave him pause.

'Get out,' Gallo commanded, having noticed his hesitancy.

And oddly enough, Enzo bowed to his grandfather's authority. Because for the first time since Erin had left, the little voice that had told him he had made a mistake had become a shout.

Erin looked out at the grey, windswept beach, so different from the near tropical colours of the Amalfi coast, and shrugged into her coat and scarf. An unseasonal cold snap had descended, fitting Erin's mood better, but she couldn't tell whether she felt better or worse to be so far removed from what she'd shared with Enzo.

She'd spent a week or so miserably haunting the small flat in London she'd rented after finishing university, but she'd needed to come *home*. Being in Italy and France had made her realise how much she'd missed it. Not London, but Falmouth. How much she'd missed her mother.

Arla Carter had left her alone for nearly two days before sitting her down at the beaten-up dining table with a cup of tea, nearly as strong as coffee, and told her to 'spill'.

Shame had kept Erin silent and guilt had kept her from being able to move on at all. It had been two and a half weeks since she'd left the marina in Cannes and she couldn't think of anything else.

I did something unforgiveable, Mum.

Arla had told her that nothing was unforgiveable. Unless it involved children or animals, and that had made Erin laugh just a little.

So, slowly, over a cooling cup of tea, Erin told her about the meeting with Gio, the deal he'd offered in exchange for Charterhouse, and then travelling to Capri. She told her mother about meeting Enzo, and what she'd thought of him. She told her about touring the coastline, about the romantic proposal. About the dress she'd worn that had drawn such horrible attention, and even though it had been by design she now realised, Erin told her of how he'd made her feel when she'd told him of the bullying she'd experienced as a teen.

She told Arla about Enzo taking her to Florence, about seeing the frescos and Giotto's bell-tower, just like her mother had always wanted. Erin told her about the muddying of her feelings and how she'd finally told Gio she wouldn't do it, and then, eventually, how she'd uncovered that Enzo had known all along.

'I... I'm so ashamed,' she'd confessed tearily, her lips wobbling as she tried to pull it all back in, the sadness that kept pouring out of her. 'Enzo didn't deserve what I did to him.'

Her mother had sighed and rubbed circles on her back, soothing the ache that held her entire body tight in a vice.

'You need to forgive yourself, my love.'

Erin had shaken her head.

'You do. You made a mistake.'

'It was more than a mistake, Mum.'

'Okay, you made the wrong choice.'

'I was just like Dad,' Erin had confessed, finally unearthing the deep heart of her hurt. 'I'm just like Dad. I just thought... I thought that...'

'That when we got Charterhouse back, it would all be okay?' her mother had finished for her.

Erin had nodded and cried even harder.

'Oh my love, I'm so sorry. I know how much you had to do for me in those first few years after we moved down here. I know how much we clung to that dream of recovering everything that we'd had before. I was… I shouldn't have let you do that.'

'No, Mum, I was fine—'

'No. It wasn't fine. You were a child. You shouldn't have had to do what you did. And you shouldn't have had to shoulder that burden or that silly dream. And for that, I'm sorry,' she said, taking a shuddery breath. 'But you need to know that you're nothing like your father,' Arla had said gently. 'Your father was a selfish man, it's true. He put his schemes above your needs and mine. But he never felt guilt or discomfort or regret. He never learned from his mistakes and never used them to shape him into becoming a better person. You? You are doing those things. And it's hard. It's painful to confront our mistakes. It's *hard* to forgive yourself and move on through that discomfort. But if anyone can, you can.'

Her mother's words had offered her a small light in the darkness. She'd been stuck, thinking the worst of herself, but if she learned from it, used it to guide her in the future, harnessed it to be better… No, it wouldn't bring back Enzo. But she couldn't do it for Enzo, she had to do it for herself.

'But, Erin, I don't need Charterhouse for security. I don't want Charterhouse for me. If you do, that's an entirely different matter. But that company has cost us as much hurt and upset as your father has. Perhaps it's time to let the past go and move into the future, fresh and new. Perhaps,' her mother had said, 'it's time to figure out what *you* want to do.'

As Erin looked out at an angry grey tide she realised that now that she didn't have Charterhouse hanging over her head, ideas were pouring in. There were so many people in Sam's network with exciting projects and businesses that she could contribute in small ways until she found the thing that she wanted to do. But the one thing she did know, truly know, was that she wanted to help other women find their path, to give women the support they needed as they found what it was they wanted to do with their businesses. To support them while they made mistakes and picked themselves back up again.

But underneath those ideas, the slow sparking of energy and peace she had found with her mother's forgiveness and her own, was the ache for Enzo. She wanted to speak to him, to laugh with him, to tease him and to know what he was thinking.

She missed his charm. She missed the lightness of being she had felt around him. She missed the balance she had found between Erin and Rin in his company. And even though he had told her that what they'd had wasn't real, that nothing they'd shared was true…she knew that what *she'd* felt was real and she wouldn't let anyone take that away from her.

In the distance a dog ran back and forth between its owner and the tide, chasing birds and stones and whatever else took its fancy. She sighed at the simple easy joy before shrugging deeper into her jacket, knowing that it was time to head back, so as not to worry her mother.

As she turned, her gaze landed on a solitary figure on the headland, the forceful winds pushing the long line of his coat from his body. Hair tousled by those same winds, and the harsh jawline made her think of a man who couldn't possibly be there, in Falmouth on such grey stormy day.

Wishful thinking never got anyone anywhere, she decided, cutting back up towards the path that would take her home. But as she drew closer and closer, the feel of the man's gaze heavier and heavier...she couldn't shake the feeling that it was...

Enzo.

For a moment, he thought she was a mirage. That after three weeks of thinking of little else, he had conjured her from his imagination. Sinking deeper into a thick coat, the red hair whipped around her like flames on a breeze that felt almost punishing after the Mediterranean climes. For days Gio Gallo's words had haunted him as vehemently as his thoughts of Erin Carter.

So much so he'd even spoken to his mother who was, perhaps most surprisingly of all, still in rehab. They'd talked. A little, not too much. But enough for him to verify Gio's statements.

But none of that retained a foothold in his mind as Erin Carter made her way towards him. She looked pale, the dark smudges beneath her eyes letting him know that it was highly likely that she was still punishing herself.

Guilt lashed him, the salt on the air irritating the emotional wounds he had opened in the last few weeks. Erin didn't deserve that. He was just as responsible, if not more so, for what had happened.

As she drew closer, her steps faltered, as if she'd only just realised that it was him.

Enzo.

He wasn't quite sure if she'd said it out loud, or if he'd imagined his name in her voice, but it soothed the restlessness he'd felt for weeks. She came close enough for him

to catch the scent of her perfume on the air before it was whisked away by the breeze.

Christo, he had missed her. The sound of her voice, the way her eyes glittered when she smiled, the guilelessness that he'd mistaken for an act. Or at least that he'd told himself he'd mistaken for an act.

In truth, he'd never have fallen for her if he'd genuinely believed her to be lying to him. And he had *fallen* for her. So deep and so far.

He scanned her face, soaking the sight of it into him like he might never get another chance. Which was true. Because he'd hurt her. He'd caused her pain. He'd sent her away, after using her as a pawn in a game *he* was playing. He'd done exactly what he'd accused her of doing and he was genuinely fearful that he might not deserve her forgiveness.

'Are you really here?' Erin asked, as if not quite believing her eyes.

'Yes,' he said, the words forced out through a throat thickened with emotion.

Her hand raised as if to touch him, but fell by her side as she looked down, her cheeks flushing for all the wrong reasons.

'I—'

'I had a few things I wanted to say, if that's okay,' he said. He knew he'd cut her off, but he was pretty sure it was another apology that he didn't really deserve. He'd looked up her father, looked up Charterhouse. He wondered if in the same position he would have been driven to do whatever it took to claim back what she should have rightfully inherited.

Erin nodded.

'Would you mind walking while we talk?' he asked, and when she shook her head, he stepped out onto the beach, her beside him, and *oddio*, he missed her hand slipping

into the crook of his arm. He took a deep breath, praying to get through what he needed to say before dropping to his knees and begging her to take him back into her life any way she'd have him.

'First I want to say that I'm so deeply sorry for the things that I said that last night on the yacht.'

'Enzo—'

'*Cara*, please. Let me finish?'

She nodded, eyeing him warily.

'I should never have held you responsible for a mess of my own making. I'm not saying that setting out to marry me for an ulterior motive was a good thing, but you were right. I didn't have to play along. And I'm sorry for the way you must have felt at me placing the blame at your feet.

'In my defence, I was shocked. I was already confused by things, by my feelings for you. And I just felt so awful. That you'd heard those things. To imagine you hearing what I'd planned to do, realising how that must have sounded to your ears. I felt unspeakably guilty. And in my guilt, I lashed out,' he confessed. 'I didn't want to admit that I'd got it wrong. I didn't want to admit that I could have stopped it at any time, because I didn't want to stop it. Because I didn't... I didn't want to let you go,' he said, clenching his jaw against the overwhelming emotions. 'With you, I'd had more fun, felt more alive, more interested, more *myself* than I had in years. And the thought of not having that anymore...' He trailed off with a shake of his head.

'You brought something new into my life. Fun, ease. *Care,'* he admitted, knowing that he had been careless for far too long now. 'I'd thought that maybe if I didn't care, then I wouldn't get hurt again,' he tried to explain. 'But I didn't realise what I was cutting myself off from.'

Erin looked out at the horizon, as if she wasn't sure she was ready to hear the answer to the questions on her lips.

'And what was that?' she asked.

'Love.'

She froze.

'*You*,' he added, her gaze returning to his in a heartbeat. And he smiled, a little sadly. 'I guess I fell into my own trap. Because I fell in love with you, Erin Carter. You are beautiful, yes, smart, funny, *sexy*, but you are also kind, and affectionate, and considerate. And while you have driven me to complete distraction, I have come to realise that there is nothing else for me. No one else. I love you,' he said, without gimmicks or untruths or fancy distractions. 'I have fallen utterly, irrevocably and helplessly in love with you,' he confessed, searching the stark blue eyes before him for signs of hope, for any hint that might put him out of his misery.

Erin's heart ached from his words. They were so much more than she could ever have imagined. No, there were no roses, no drones, no music, but there were no lies and no false praise. He meant every word.

'You forgive me?' she asked in wonder.

'Absolutely. Even if you don't think you could forgive *me*,' he said, his hands stuffed into the long pockets of his coat, holding it against him as the wind played with its tails.

'Enzo, no, there is nothing to forgive,' she said, finally giving into temptation and reaching up to cup his jaw. He leant into her palm, the heat from her body meeting the cool of his skin. He turned into her hand, and pressed a kiss into the centre, and it meant more than any of the kisses they had shared before. Because this was the first kiss from Enzo to Erin. And she didn't want it to be the last.

'Oh, I fell hard for you,' she said, tears pressing at the

edges of her eyes, and for the first time in what felt like a lifetime, they were happy tears.

'*Cara*, please don't tell me it's too late,' he begged, his hand gently closing around her wrist as if ready to keep her there with him, her hand against his cheek.

'No, Enzo. It would never have been too late. I would have waited for you, forever,' Erin vowed, truth zinging through her veins and written in gold on her heart.

'You gave up Charterhouse,' Enzo stated. It wasn't a question, and the only man that he could know that from was Gio Gallo.

She nodded, and looked out to sea, not because she didn't want him to see her thoughts and feelings, but because she wanted the calm of the horizon. Because while it was stormy, here on the beach, out there it was a single silver line.

'Yes. After you told me about your parents, I didn't, I *couldn't*, be another person in your life who did that to you,' she explained.

His eyes flared, gold flecks in deep dark depths. He pressed another kiss to the palm of her hand.

'Why didn't you tell me? When we argued?'

'Because it shouldn't have mattered. I was still in the wrong.'

He shook his head, understanding and regrets heavy in his gaze.

'Would you have told me? About it, about Gio?' he asked.

'Yes,' she admitted. 'Eventually. I think I wanted you for just a little bit longer. I think I wanted the *me* I was around you for a little bit longer too.'

'I understand that,' he confessed gently.

'Do you really think that we can put all this behind us?' she asked, hope a desperate twisting thing alive in her chest.

'I don't want to put it behind us. I want it to be a funny story that we tell our grandchildren, *cara*. About how I met a beautiful woman who had forgotten how to laugh.'

'And how I met a handsome prince who had forgotten how to love,' she added.

'Until you.'

'Until you.'

'I love you, Enzo Rossetti,' she said, letting that love fill her up from the inside until it shone from her eyes and her heart like light, radiating golden heat.

'Say it again, *cara*,' Enzo instructed, the smile on his lips almost heartbreakingly beautiful.

So, she threw her head back and shouted, 'I love you, Enzo Rossetti!' and then ruined it by descending into giggles and laughter, so pure and true that they would both remember it for the rest of their lives.

EPILOGUE

ERIN COULDN'T BELIEVE this day was here.

She looked at herself in the full-length mirror, the beautiful flowing ivory lace dress that clung to her torso and fell from her waist in cascading layers. Her hair, tumbling down around her shoulders in waves.

Her mother stood behind her, tears in her eyes. 'You look so beautiful,' she whispered, as she pressed a tissue to her face to stem the flow. 'But you're ruining my make-up,' she accused with only love in her voice.

They both laughed with smiles that wobbled with happiness and delight.

Her mother took her in her arms. 'I'm so pleased for you, Erin. But more than that, I'm just so proud of the woman you have become. It's incredible to see you go from strength to strength. I love you, Erin, but more than that I *like* you,' she said, her gaze full of truth and joy, Erin knowing it was the highest praise her mother could give.

Arla Carter's words touched her deeply.

It hadn't been easy. As predicted, the press *had* been full of headlines and pictures, and articles full of equal amounts of harsh critiques and praise. And just as one wave of the news cycle crested, another began to pick up speed. First, following their announcement that there wouldn't be a dou-

ble wedding, and then a second when Enzo's father's engagement broke apart beneath rumours of infidelity and money troubles. But together they had weathered the worst of it and delighted in the best of it.

Shortly after Enzo had visited her in Falmouth, they had travelled to Switzerland to meet with Amelia Gallo. It wasn't easy, there had been years of hurt and neglect. But Erin knew that it meant the world to Enzo to see his mother getting the help she needed and deserved.

And soon after, Gio Gallo had reached out privately to Erin, with a reworked offer regarding Charterhouse. And as hard as it was to let go of a childhood dream, Erin knew that turning it down was the right thing to do. She couldn't continue to follow her father's dreams, and nor could she hold herself to a promise she'd made to her mother before she'd known better. Erin had turned Gio's offer down, but instead made a counter-offer of her own; a visit between Erin, Enzo and Gio the next time they were in Italy.

He hadn't been able to make it today, and Erin suspected privately that it was because he wasn't well enough to travel. But Enzo's cousins Antonio and Maria had, and even though he would probably never acknowledge it out loud, the burgeoning friendship between the cousins meant a lot to Enzo.

So it would be a small group of people that celebrated her marriage to the Playboy of Amalfi, Erin thought wryly, and she wouldn't have it any other way. Marcus was there, Alana, whom Erin had met at that fateful party in Cannes, Samara had managed to come over for it—Enzo's look of shock when he realised Sam was in fact a woman was priceless. She'd brought with her several black-suited men and women that made her think of security guards.

And Erin had realised that the funny thing about her friendship with Sam was that it had never needed the trap-

pings of details, of things that Sam kept secret…because what they felt and what they did know about each other was enough. And Erin was just thankful that she could be part of this day, having been part of the chaotic plan that had brought her to Enzo in the first place.

She and her mother had taken a car to the church, and from there the day moved in bursts of incredible speed and moments of incredible stillness. Erin's mother walked her up the aisle of the very small, very ancient chapel in Capri where they'd chosen to exchange their vows.

The service, delivered in Italian and English, was short, but deeply sentimental, and Erin wouldn't have changed a single thing about it. They had each written their own vows and nothing could have prepared Erin for the overwhelming sense of love that rippled through her at his words.

You are my compass, my north, my south, my east and west, you are my guide and my companion. You are my home and I am yours. When you are lost, and whenever you are in need of rest, I am yours. When you are happy, joyful, and silly, I am yours. I will protect you, love you, honour you and cherish you with every breath I take. Because I am yours and I love you.

And when she'd given hers, she'd thought she'd seen the shimmer of tears in his eyes and knew how much her words meant to him.

I promise to stand beside you, no matter what adventures we weather—thrilling, or tough—because I am yours. I promise to stand beside you when things are good as much as when they are hard, when we are happy or sad, when we are hungry or full, when we are angry or laughing. I will stand beside you because I am yours and I love you.

They had kissed to applause and laughter, the perfect way to cement their vows and their union, and while she knew

it wouldn't always be plain sailing, that didn't matter, because they would face whatever came their way. Together.

Long after the last staff member had left the yacht anchored off the Amalfi Coast, Enzo Rossetti came to where his wife stood at the rails, looking out at the glittering coastline. He slipped his arms around her and gently rested her back against his chest, wondering how he'd got so lucky.

He held her in his arms, knowing they had all the time in the world and he realised that for the first time he didn't want to rush off somewhere new, he wasn't looking for some crazy distraction. He had everything he needed, right here, for the rest of his life.

He could barely credit all the things that had happened between them, to bring them here.

'What are you thinking about?' she asked, pressing cool fingers to his furrowed brow, trying to soothe thoughts she couldn't read.

'About secrets and lies,' he said with a heavy sigh.

'There will never be such things between us again,' she promised.

'Oh, *cara*,' he said, with mock gravity. 'There is just one more secret that you must keep. One that you can't tell anyone,' he said to her, pressing a kiss against his favourite part of her.

'What's that?' Erin whispered, her voice husky with desire.

'That the Playboy of Amalfi waited until his wedding night.'

'I did once tell you that I had traditional values,' she said, sighing as his palms found her breasts and his mouth found the delicate skin at the curve of her neck.

The whisper of a moan was stolen by the wind, as he

turned her in his arms, to feel the blazing heat of her gaze on him. The blush on her cheeks was pretty, not the painful, blotchy, mark of humiliation, but this one almost beautiful to see. He would have her wearing nothing else but that blush if she would allow him.

'No one would believe me if I told them,' she said, a smile on her beautiful lips. 'They'd think it a lie.'

'Because no one can resist the charms of the Playboy of Amalfi?' he teased with another kiss.

'Oh, I can resist your charms, Enzo Rossetti,' Erin said confidently and playfully. 'But I could not resist your heart,' she said, her words touching his soul.

'I didn't have a heart until you came along,' he confessed.

'Yes, you did. You were just looking for it in the wrong place.'

'Because even before I'd met you, it was yours,' he said and kissed her with all the love he felt for her.

That night, beneath the canopy of stars, he loved her and pleasured her until they were both utterly spent, and he was thankful that they'd waited. Thankful that this was the first of all the nights of the rest of his life to love her, worship her soul, spirit and body. It was the joy of his life that he could make such a vow to such an incredible woman. The woman who had come looking for a wedding ring, and found a happy-ever-after.

* * * * *

TYCOON'S TERMS OF ENGAGEMENT

CLARE CONNELLY

MILLS & BOON

PROLOGUE

CHARLOTTE'S FINGERS TREMBLED on the mouse of her computer, as she tried to process what she was seeing.

A deposit of fifty thousand pounds, on the morning of her twenty-first birthday. No message beside the deposit and the name identical to all the others: Papandreo.

Her blood turned to ice.

Her skin lifted in tiny little goosebumps.

Her eyes squeezed shut—but it didn't matter.

The numbers and, more importantly, the name, still swam inside her mind. She felt a tightening in her throat. A nausea that made her want to reach for the rubbish bin. Except she wouldn't give in to that feeling. She wouldn't give in to *any* feelings to do with her so-called father. After all, wasn't being a father more than just making a sperm donation decades earlier? And providing a huge amount of money in exchange for silence?

Because Charlotte Shaw was a very well-funded, dirty little secret. An illegitimate child who had known, for as long as she could know or understand anything, that her very existence was not only a mistake, but a cause of regret.

Worse, she'd ruined her mother's life.

Not her, per se, but by being conceived to a man who was married and very much in love with his wife—too in love to leave her, but not so much as to stay faithful.

Not only had there been a generous trust fund set up for

Charlotte, but each year, on the morning of her birthday, an amount was deposited into her bank account as a 'gift'. A guilt gift? More likely, as a reminder to Charlotte of the importance of staying silent.

Because the money her filthy rich 'father' had funnelled not only supported Charlotte, but more to the point, her mother, Mariah. Mariah, who'd been left heartbroken by the circumstances of Charlotte's birth—by having fallen in love with a man who wanted her to have an abortion. By falling pregnant to a man who would never, ever leave his wife.

Charlotte clicked out of the internet banking browser and stood up, sucking a gust of air into her lungs and trying to steady her nerves.

So what if he'd given her a veritable fortune? To him, it was negligible. Small change.

It didn't mean anything. She was still nothing to him and always would be. And that was just utterly and completely fine by her.

CHAPTER ONE

CHARLOTTE STARED BLANKLY at the lawyer. His words were somewhat amorphous, refusing to take any recognisable shape. Every now and again, though, she'd catch a hint of something that made her jaw drop.

Death of your father's wife.

Officially acknowledging you.

Your birthright—the possible inheritance of the Papandreo business.

If you were to marry—and please note, marriage is a prerequisite for taking ownership.

She nodded along, even though it made very little sense. Her mind had gone into a shutdown from the moment she'd arrived in the fancy law firm's boardroom and been greeted by three obsequious lawyers in custom-made suits, all bending over backwards to ingratiate themselves with her.

'Do you have any questions, Miss Shaw?'

Charlotte blinked across at the oldest of the men, with his steel-rimmed glasses and side-swept greying hair, and reminded herself forcibly that *she* was a lawyer, too. Okay, she wasn't a lawyer in the same way these dudes were. She worked in the charities sector and was more at home with staff in jeans and leather jackets, who brought in ramen noodles for lunch—because the salaries in their line of work were hardly anything to write home about.

But she'd done the hard yards in her degree, and she wasn't an idiot.

'So, let me get this straight.' She reached for the fine bone china coffee cup and took a sip, relishing the familiar hit of caffeine. 'You're saying that my biological father's wife has died.'

She left a gap, waiting for acknowledgement.

The lawyer to the left of the older man nodded once.

Charlotte compressed her lips. She always made the distinction of calling Aristotle Papandreo 'biological father', even though there was no other father in the picture—her mother had never re-married, or so far as Charlotte knew, even gotten close to dating. How could she, as a woman, who'd essentially become a shadow of herself, thanks to living through such a betrayal and heartbreak?

'And as a result of this, he now feels that the time is right to acknowledge my existence?' She faltered a little on the word 'acknowledge'. In truth, it caught in her throat like a blade. Such a simple word. Three syllables that hid a lifetime of hurt, because every day, every milestone, every birthday, every triumph without her father's acknowledgement had been a kick in the teeth. Over time, she'd hardened her heart and told herself she didn't even *want* to meet him, but that didn't stop the wound from seeping.

'Indeed.' The central lawyer—Charlotte wished she could remember any of their names—smiled, as if this was the sort of bountiful news she'd woken up desperate to hear.

Charlotte's eyes narrowed in a silent rejection of that premise.

'And he would like to meet me.'

'In due course, yes.'

'In due course' sounded like a cop-out to Charlotte. It sounded like a promise to be broken. A weak, watery sound-

ing out of the daughter he'd spent twenty four years refusing to know.

'I see.'

'The reason we're involved—' the blond man flanking
old guy's other side leaned forward, bright blue eyes latching on to Charlotte's, '—is that there are some other legali-
ties to be aware of.'

'You said something about the company,' she repeated,
sipping her coffee again, needing another touchstone to one
of the most important and familiar things in her life.

'The Papandreo Group is very old,' he said. 'The first
business was a bank, based in Athens, in the seventeenth
century. The majority of the family's wealth is controlled
by an ancient—some might say arcane—provision, which
is surprisingly still in effect.'

Charlotte moved her hands beneath the table and clasped
them in her lap.

'The right of ownership and control of the Papandreo
Group will pass to whichever descendant marries first, after
their eighteenth birthday.'

Charlotte nodded a little jerkily, though it made hardly any
sense. 'Are you saying that if I were married, I would legally
be able to take possession of the company?'

'Yes.' The blond smiled, nodding. 'That's exactly it.'

Charlotte's throat went dry. Her eyes filled with stars.
'But I'm not married.'

'No, and the company is being very successfully run by
your half-brother, Zeus Papandreo,' the older lawyer said,
as if this were all by-the-by, when in fact, he couldn't have
hand-picked a phrase more perfectly designed to inflame
Charlotte's strong sense of injustice than that which had just
been uttered. 'And you have your own career. Rather than
focusing on the stipulations of the company's bylaws, you
should consider the financial settlement Aristotle is propos-

ing to make in your favour, as well as his desire to publicly welcome you into the family.'

Charlotte could feel the screech rising in her throat. It was only with the strongest force of will she managed to contain it, to bite it back. She was in overload mode—too much information was being layered over way too many feelings, way too much anger and resentment, bitterness and hurt. She scraped her chair back and moved to stand behind it, digging her fingers into the soft leather. She was aware of their eyes, all on her, with a mix of expressions—from sympathy to surprise to interest.

'Thank you for your time, gentlemen. There's a lot there I need to consider.'

'Of course.' The blond rallied first, reaching into his breast pocket and removing a thick, white card, which he slid across the table. 'This is my number, if you have any questions, at any time. It's a lot to take in.'

'Yes.' Charlotte nodded as she picked up the card and pushed it into the back pocket of her skin-tight leather pants—a jackpot find from the local thrift shop. The store was just a short walk from her best friend Jane's apartment—which Lottie had moved into about a year before. 'I will.'

'Good, good,' the older man stood, rubbing his hands together, as if to congratulate himself on a job well done. 'Is there anything I should tell Mr Papandreo?'

'Tell him?'

'He asked us to report back to him. Would you like us to say—,'

Charlotte pulled a face, as if she were being stabbed. It hurt just as much.

Apparently, because her 'father' had now decided to acknowledge her, he expected her to gleefully fall in line and what? Be *grateful* to him? She shuddered with revulsion.

'There is *nothing*, and I mean *nothing* I want to say to that

man—and he should be very glad to hear it. Because, believe me, if I were ever to give him a piece of my mind, I doubt he'd recover from the shock.' She straightened, pleased to see their reactions, their surprise, and glad to have landed that hit. 'Though you are welcome to pass that message along, of course, in the interest of discharging your duties.' She turned and walked, with a confidence she wasn't quite feeling, towards the door of their boardroom. 'Thank you again for your time.'

She left without speaking another word, but they were all zooming and zipping around her head. The myriad of things she would have *loved* to throw at her father, without the intermediary of lawyers to take the sting out of it.

How she hated that man, and his smarmy, arrogant, overachieving son. How she *loathed them* and always had.

For the hurts Aristotle Papandreo had thrown at Charlotte all her life weren't just about how he'd refused to acknowledge her and shown no interest in knowing even a thing about her. No, it was worse than that. Because he had a son. A golden-boy child, who had grown up in his father's shadow, and his grandfather's shadow, who'd been raised in the mould of a Papandreo and swaggered with the confidence of a man who could do no wrong.

Aristotle had two children. One of them he put front and centre in his life, while the other he had constrained to an existence of secrecy and shame.

She stopped walking, Bank tube station in sight with its bright white light called to her reassuringly. But she ignored it, stepping backwards quickly and pressing her spine against the grimy stone wall of a sandwich shop, overflowing with lunchtime customers. It was a warm day and the stone was heated, but Charlotte hardly noticed.

She hated them.

Not just Aristotle, but Zeus as well. She'd hated them for many years.

And sometimes, she'd fantasised about how she could ever get even with them for how they'd hurt her and her mother. Sometimes she fantasised about how she might finally take her revenge.

Going to the press wasn't an option—Charlotte had made it a point of pride to *never* spend a drop of the money her 'father' gave her, besides the school fees, in which matter she'd had no say. But the one compensating point in all of this was that her mother, a shell of a woman in most ways, was able to live a life of unparalleled luxury. Charlotte would never do anything to risk taking that away from her.

She had no doubt that a man heartless enough to ignore his own child would not hesitate to make good on his threats and demand repayment of the entire confidentiality agreement settlement.

So publicising her link to the Papandreo family had never been an option.

In fact, she had never really been able to think of a single way she might reach out and wound them.

Until now.

The lawyers had given her the keys to the kingdom—they just had no idea how motivated she'd be to use them.

'The right of ownership and control of the Papandreo Group will pass to whichever descendant marries first after their eighteenth birthday.'

Her heart began to speed. Her mind whirled.

It was as preposterous as it was offensive. The very idea that being married somehow imbued a person with a merit they otherwise didn't possess made her insides twist. It was, as the lawyer had said, positively arcane. Then again, the Papandreo Group *was* very old, and bound by some arcane rules.

Far be it from Charlotte to question that now… No. She wouldn't question it. She'd see it for what it was in that moment, a gift. Because she knew what that company meant to her 'father' and 'brother', and she knew how good it would therefore feel to swipe it out from under them.

And she knew just how she was going to do it.

CHAPTER TWO

DANTE SAN MARINO literally felt the colour drain from his face. At the mere mention of the word 'marriage', he practically broke out into a cold sweat, so utterly traumatised was he by his first foray into that whole way of life.

Which had been the one and only failure Dante had ever had to live through.

He hadn't enjoyed the experience and had no interest in repeating it.

Particularly not with a woman he'd developed a very satisfying, no-strings relationship with over the past six months. At least, he *thought* it had been 'no strings', that they'd been completely on the same page regarding that. Now here she was, sitting opposite him, calmly asking him to marry her. Like they were choosing what to share for dessert.

'I thought I explained all this to you.' His voice rang with his trademark authority, a deep voice of easy command. He reached for his mineral water, keeping his eyes on the woman who, up until three minutes ago, he'd presumed he'd be taking back to his bed that night for yet another very satisfying session. 'Nothing about what we're doing is serious.'

Charlotte Shaw's wide-set green eyes met his without a hint of emotion. 'I'm aware of that.'

'And yet, you're proposing to me?'

The corner of her lips—painted a bright red and distractingly full, even now—lifted as if with mocking amusement.

'Not in the sense of a traditional marriage.'

He arched a brow. 'Is there any other kind of marriage?'

'Well, yes, actually. I'm glad you asked.' She reached for her own drink—an Aperol spritz that she'd had waiting on the table even before he'd arrived. As if she'd needed the Dutch courage, though Charlotte was unstintingly confident and independent—two of the qualities he admired most about her. 'There are marriages like this, for example.'

He suppressed a shudder at her casual reference to their 'marriage'. 'We're not getting married.'

'Hear me out,' she implored. 'You owe me that much, don't you think?'

Her question was like a lightning bolt, spiking through him. 'I don't owe you anything. What we've been doing has been mutually agreed upon and satisfying, but neither one of us gave more than we took.'

'True,' she conceded, with a dip of her head. Honesty was another trait he liked in Charlotte.

'You said you never wanted to get married.'

'I don't,' she reassured him.

'Then this makes no sense.'

Her smile now was not just a corner of her lips, but rather her whole, beautiful mouth, revealing her gleaming white teeth and that deep dimple in her cheeks—one of the first things he'd noticed about her, the night they'd met at a charity gala. Followed swiftly by her confidence and poise, by the direct way she had of staring at a person.

'You're the second person to say that to me this week.'

He arched a brow in silent enquiry and Charlotte waved a slender-wristed hand through the air. 'Oh, Jane thinks I'm quite mad, too.'

He furrowed his brow. He'd met Charlotte's best friend Jane on the same night he'd met Charlotte, though if pressed to describe her, he wouldn't have been able to say more than

that she had blond hair and had, he thought, been wearing a long, black dress. But he knew from conversations with Charlotte that the two women lived together, worked together and were basically inseparable. So the fact Jane *also* thought Charlotte had come up with some hair-brained, half-baked scheme boded well for Dante.

'Okay, so how about we just forget it and go back to what we do best.'

'Which is?'

Beneath the table, he pressed one foot out, stroking her calf, and saw the way her eyes widened in surprise.

'This.'

She bit down on her lower lip, massaging it with her teeth. His gut twisted for a whole other reason now, with a rush of blood heading south.

'Dante, listen to me.' Her voice was husky though and, when she reached for her drink, those beautiful hands weren't quite steady. 'I know this is just sex. That's one of the reasons I decided to talk to you first.'

His lips flicked with a quick, thunderstorm of dislike. *First* implied there were others to come if he said 'no'.

'I like having sex with you,' she said, as though they were discussing the weather. 'But what I like even more is that you and I are on the same page about a whole host of things.'

Dante's frown broadened. Because in many ways, they were complete opposites. Charlotte was a free-spirited bohemian who bought second-hand clothes and sponged off her best friend. He wasn't one to give expensive gifts but on the few occasions he'd suggested flying her with him to his island in the Med, she'd refused so much as the gift of a seat on his jet. Dante admired her pride, but not her hatred for capitalism and financial success.

'We're chalk and cheese, Shaw, and you know it.'

She laughed then, a sound that didn't help the whole blood-

flow situation. His cock strained against the zip of his pants and suddenly he wanted to dispense not only with this conversation but with dinner too, so they could get straight back to his apartment.

'Okay, yes, we're chalk and cheese. But that's what makes this plan so great.'

'Go on,' he said, his tone like iron despite a deep feeling of reluctance to continue this conversation.

'We don't really like each other,' she said, with a lift of one shoulder.

'I like you just fine.'

'You like sleeping with me,' she retorted, whip fast. 'This relationship is about sex. It has been since day one. I think you're arrogant, shallow, bossy, capitalistic and sometimes kind of rude.'

He laughed then, because the description was so bluntly, honestly and deservedly given.

'I also think you're as cold as ice.' She shuddered a little. 'A total closed book on anything beyond the superficial. And that's okay, because in bed, there's nothing cold about a damned thing between us. And that's what I'm here for.'

'Except, for the whole marriage thing?' he drawled, glad for her abrupt rendering of his character.

'Right,' she nodded. 'The thing is, I need to get married and quickly. It can't be a pretend engagement, or I'd just hire someone, with a watertight NDA. No, this has to be an actual, legal wedding. Except, I can't marry someone I like and I can't marry someone who might like me—I don't want the emotional complications right now. I need this to be easy.'

He nodded along like this all made perfect sense when, of course, the opposite was true. He tried to focus on the facts she'd hinted at but not revealed. Something like acid seemed to burn the back of his throat. He leaned forward, eyes pinning her, as years of fights and failings built inside of him

then burst like a storm cloud as his worst fear appeared before his eyes. 'Charlotte…are you pregnant?' The question came out calmly, although his pulse had ratchetted up about a thousand per cent.

Her own eyes widened with the same sense of shock he was feeling. 'What?'

'I mean, it's the twenty-first century, but it's the only reason I can think of for this sudden, desperate need to marry.'

'What the actual…?' She swallowed the curse word at the last minute, but her cheeks were flushed with pink. 'I'll have you know I was raised by a single mother. I would *never* get married just because I happened to be pregnant with some guy's kid.'

He arched a brow at her passionate, if slightly provocative, defence. 'Some guy being me?'

'Or anyone's,' she swore.

'And what if the guy—in this hypothetical scenario, *me*—wanted to marry, for the sake of the baby?'

Her jaw dropped, her eyes flashing with something he could have sworn was anguish before there was fire back in every line of her being. 'Then that guy—you—would have to take a serious course correction.'

'And what about the baby?'

She squared her shoulders, visibly calming herself down. 'What *about* the baby?' she demanded with hauteur.

'Call me old fashioned, but if a couple can make it work and raise a baby together, isn't that better?'

'Better than what?' Her eyes narrowed.

'The alternative.'

'Which is?'

'Single parenthood.'

'See, this is exactly what I'm talking about,' she said, looking at him like he'd sprouted two heads. 'This is why I could never *like* you.'

He laughed then, but with a sound of disbelief, as he shook his head. A waiter appeared and Dante ordered for both of them, without consulting the menu, adding a bottle of champagne for good measure. They were probably not going to be celebrating, but he was still hopeful they'd be putting this bizarre conversation behind them and moving to the bedroom portion of the evening before too long.

'You say things like that as though it's normal and it's not. Getting married is…totally personal and subjective and *no one* should get married for the sake of a baby, who can be raised just fine, as I am living proof thank you very much, without some ridiculous ceremony having been conducted between two consenting adults who would rather eat glass than get married.'

He sat back in his chair, loving the way the fire of her temper made Charlotte's eyes flash, and her lips move faster than normal. The way her soft, auburn hair bounced around her ivory face like flames flicked in a fire grate. And most of all, loving the way the swell of her cleavage lifted and fell with each rush of breath she drew in.

'We can agree to disagree, given that it's not relevant.'

Her lips gaped. 'Fine.' She glanced away from him, once more visibly trying to calm down.

The waiter returned with the champagne, went to uncork it but Dante shook his head dismissively and reached for the bottle. 'I'll do it.' He wanted to be left alone with Charlotte and sooner rather than later.

The waiter handed the recognisably expensive bottle across, so Dante could curl his hands around the ice-cold neck and unfurl the metal. Alone once more, he was conscious of the way Charlotte's eyes lingered on his hands as they worked, of the way she seemingly couldn't look elsewhere.

'Then if you're not pregnant, why the sudden urge to get married?'

She rolled her eyes in a gesture he found ridiculously juvenile but also somehow appealing. He ground his teeth, momentarily put off by that.

When this whole thing started off, it was easy as pie. They'd met through a charity function, hit it off and fallen into bed, despite the fact he'd been completely sexless since his divorce—hadn't even felt a hint of attraction for another woman, in fact. Charlotte had been different though. Beautiful, but impish and irreverent. He'd found her fascinating and, for no specific reason, he'd wanted her, like a lightning bolt bursting through him.

A great night ensued, with absolutely no promises. The only promise Dante felt he could ever give another woman was that he didn't do promises. But a week later, they'd bumped into one other at yet another event. This time it was the birthday party of a mutual friend—though Dante used the term loosely as Howard Kernshaw was more of an associate than friend. The same sparks that had ignited at their first meeting burst to life once more. They hadn't even made it back to his place—a broom closet at the venue had been pushed into service.

The next time, it had been the back of his limo, after leaving another charity event. But after that, a month had stretched without a chance meeting and despite no shortage of options in the women-who'd-happily-jump-his-bones department, he'd found himself totally unmoved. He just wanted another night with Charlotte. And then another. Craving in a way that he'd taught himself not to crave, not to want. Not ever, ever to need again.

And so, before he'd weakened, he'd come up with some black and white rules to protect himself if they were going to get involved. It had to be on his terms, but she had to know about them beforehand. This wasn't a relationship. It was sex. And so long as they both wanted that, both enjoyed it

and had fun together, he had no problems with the uncomplicated nature of their relationship.

Knowing how black and white this was meant they could also do *this* sometimes, too. Go for dinner, share pleasantries, swap superficial stories about their lives, but it was always surface level, as one might entertain a prospective colleague or client.

This—what she was doing now—was getting messy. Personal.

He tapped his fingers against his knee, willing his hard-on to calm the hell down, because it didn't matter that she was wearing that silky camisole top he adored the feel of, what she was doing now was moving the goal posts into what Dante considered an absolute danger zone—one he never, ever intended to enter again. God knew the first time had almost killed him. He still carried the wounds of that marriage, though he would never admit as much to another soul.

'I'm going to tell you something that no one other than Jane and my mother know about me.'

Her tongue darted out and licked her lower lip in a gesture that spoke, plainly, of nervousness. And he'd never, ever seen Charlotte nervous before. Not when addressing a swanky crowd of thousands of would-be benefactors. Not when he'd first approached her. Not *ever.*

'But before I do, I need you to promise me something.'

'Why?'

She rolled her eyes again. His fingers itched with a desire to reach for her and pull her into his lap, to kiss her until her eyes were rolling back in her head for a whole other reason.

'Because this is very, very confidential and needs to be handled sensitively.' She glanced around furtively, as though a dozen reporters might be about to jump out with boom mics in their faces.

'Okay, you have my word.'

'You won't tell anyone what I'm about to say?'

'*Cristo*, Charlotte, did you assassinate JFK or something?'

'Yeah, one of my little-known skills is an ability to time travel.' She bit into her lower lip, clearly so unsettled now that he took pity on her.

He reached out and topped up her empty champagne flute. 'I'm listening.'

She nodded, looked around once more, then started to speak. 'This is about my father,' she whispered, so softly he almost didn't hear.

'Your father?' He relaxed a little. He'd never heard her mention her father. He'd always presumed she didn't have one. Which was absurd, because everyone had both a mother and father in some form or another, but he'd presumed hers had died. Or that she had no idea who he was. Actually, he hadn't really put much time into thinking about it at all, or he might have asked. Except, that would have been breaking one of his rules. |So no, actually, he would never have asked.

She nodded once.

'What about him?'

'The thing is, I've never met him.' Her throat shifted as she swallowed.

'Why not?'

'His choice,' she said. 'And then, I suppose, mine. Not that he changed his mind, but even if he had, I would have taken great delight in screaming "hell, no" down the phone line.' Her smile lacked humour. 'But he didn't change his mind. He didn't ask. At least, not until recently.'

Dante's frown deepened. That was interesting. What might have occurred in a man's life that he would decide, out of the blue, to reach out to his twenty-four-year-old daughter? Then again, Charlotte was starting to make a name for herself on the charity circuit. He knew—not from her—that some big corporates had been headhunting her for a while,

offering eye watering salaries to have her come join them. Maybe the dropkick dad thought he could get some money from his daughter?

The conversation was veering dangerously close to the ground they always assiduously avoided. Personal details were anathema to them. He wanted to remind her of that, even when he'd agreed to have this conversation.

'I hate him, Dante.'

Dante tilted his head to the side, considering that. His own parents had died in a helicopter crash—along with his grandfather—when he was eight years old. He had loved them, as all children love their parents. He wished he'd had a chance to know them better, but there hadn't been the chance for that. His grandmother had raised him from that point on.

'I know that sounds harsh, but this guy...'

Charlotte was intelligent and fiercely determined when it came to the charities she championed, but there was a kindness to her that she worked hard to hide. For her to say she hated someone, he knew it was a big deal.

'He ruined my mother's life,' she finished carefully. 'And made it abundantly clear that he wished I'd never been born.'

Dante could only imagine living with that reality. It went some of the way to explaining why Charlotte had developed a tougher than nails exterior. She was a fighter. Evidently, she'd been fighting from birth.

'But now he wants to meet you,' Dante prompted.

'His circumstances have changed. His wife passed away recently. She was the reason I was a big, dirty secret.'

She dipped her head a little, her cheeks flushed.

'He had an affair with your mother?'

'A very brief affair.'

'I see.'

Charlotte shook her head. 'My mother loved him. She thought it was mutual, but he lied to her.'

He nodded, even though she wasn't looking at him. Her shoulders were hunched, and she seemed so small and fragile. Somehow, he felt the stirring to life of an ancient, protective instinct.

'Anyway—' as she glanced up at him, her green eyes had renewed focus and determination, '—he has this company and I can take control of it, but only if I'm married. So, I want to get married.'

Dante frowned, not following. 'But why?'

'Because it's my birth right,' she said carefully. 'He denied me my place in his life. He ignored me. He ignored my mother. He made us conceal my connection to him. But now, there's a way I can do something to fix that. No, not to fix it,' she amended. 'But to become impossible to ignore.'

Dante still wasn't following. What kind of company would Charlotte be interested in? Would she really care about taking up the mantle of a business just to have a place in her father's life?

'It's a valuable company,' she said, reaching for her champagne and taking a sip. 'I haven't had long to work it all out, but I'd plan to break it up, selling off parts of it and using the money for the charities I support. It could be life changing to so many people.'

Now, it was beginning to make sense.

'And it all starts with getting married.'

Dante's gut dropped to the floor. The protective instinct was still there, but she was asking the impossible of him. 'I'm never getting married again, Charlotte.'

There. He'd said it. It should have given him some relief, but all Dante felt was hollowed out, just like he had in the immediate aftermath of his divorce. For the first time in his life, Dante had had to face defeat and he hated it.

'This wouldn't be a real marriage, though,' she insisted, imploring him to listen with those wide eyes and generously

curved red lips. 'I mean, it would be *the best* parts of a marriage. Sex and privacy.'

Despite the pervasive ache in his belly, a smile tugged at his lips, even as he was shaking his head. 'It's not going to happen, Shaw.'

She closed her eyes and expelled a breath. 'What about your *Nonna*?'

He recognised her question for what it was: expert negotiating. Brutal and effective.

'You told me about her,' Charlotte reminded him and inwardly, Dante cursed. Because he *had* told her about Allegra San Marino. But it had been a brief conversation, months earlier. A rare lapse when it was Dante who'd briefly broken their rules. He was surprised she'd even remembered.

'You told me she's desperate for you to get married. That she's getting old and frail. That you wish you could give that to her.'

His eyes narrowed as the conversation replayed through his mind. 'And you told me I was barking up the wrong tree if I expected you to marry me. You told me you never planned to marry either.'

Charlotte nodded. 'Things change.'

'Not this. Not for me.'

'Dante, I don't know what happened between you and your wife—,'

Visions of his ex, Jamie, flooded his brain. Jamie when he'd first met her, so beautiful and innocent, Jamie on their wedding day, Jamie pregnant, Jamie losing the baby, Jamie pregnant again, another loss, another pregnancy, another loss. The endless round of doctors' appointments, of tests or hormone injections, of bed rest, of grief and a sense of failure and, finally, his refusal to try ever again because he couldn't—wouldn't—go through it or put her through it.

'What happened isn't relevant,' he said, curtly. Harshly.

He couldn't help it. His failed marriage struck a nerve. It always would.

'Okay, that's fine. I can respect that. But I'm going to go out on a limb and say you've got some baggage around it. I get it. Which is why I'm making it abundantly clear to you that I don't want either of us to think of this as a marriage. It would just be…a mutually beneficial arrangement.'

'No.'

She pouted, lost in thought. He felt a groan building in the pit of his gut. He didn't want to have this conversation with Charlotte. He wanted to take her home, to his bed, and kiss her senseless then make love to her all night long. That's what they were. That's what made sense.

But if she kept insisting on this damned marriage, he knew it would be the end.

The whole premise of this was uncomplicated—and she was going ahead and complicating it in a way he really resented.

'Let me ask you this. How can you be sure your father is being honest?'

She furrowed her brow.

'You clearly don't like the guy. And he obviously hasn't had your best interests at heart all this time. So why do you think the whole "get married and I'll give you the business thing" is for real?'

'It wasn't my father who told me about the clause; it was his lawyers.'

Dante shrugged. 'So?'

'They're not going to risk their licences by lying to me.'

'I cannot think of any company that would have marriage as a prerequisite to ownership.'

'It's a very old company.'

He shook his head, dismissing that. Something about this

wasn't adding up, and Dante didn't like things that didn't make sense.

'Look, Dante, I need to know you won't say anything.'

His nostrils flared with indignation. Did she take him for a gossip? 'I've already given you my word.'

She lifted one hand placatingly.

'My father—that is to say, my biological father—is,' she glanced around, making sure no one was close. 'Aristotle Papandreo.'

He shook his head in a natural reaction to that. Aristotle Papandreo was Charlotte's father?

'I see you've heard of him.'

Who hadn't?

'I've met his son,' Dante said, slowly, connecting the dots then nodding once. 'In fact, I've met your father, too.'

Charlotte looked *hurt*. Wounded. Like an animal being hunted. She covered it quickly, but not before he saw the look of betrayal in her eyes.

She shrugged though, like it didn't matter.

'Are you telling me you can take control of the Papandreo Group just by getting married?'

She bit into her lower lip. 'Getting married *before* Zeus Papandreo does.'

Aristotle's brows shot upwards. 'Well, that shouldn't be a problem. The man's hardly known for his interest in commitment.'

'But he's obsessed with that company. He'll do whatever it takes to keep hold of it.'

Dante grunted. It was a lot to take in—the kind of curve ball he could have had no way of predicting.

Before Jamie, he might have tried to help Charlotte. In fact, he knew he would have. Before Jamie, he'd been a completely different person. But now, Dante knew better than to even start trying to fix things.

'I'm sorry, Charlotte,' he said, and he really meant it. 'There is one thing I know for absolute certain. I'm never getting married again.'

He stood up, ignoring the dull, twisting of regret deep in his core, because this was—and had to be—the end for them. It had just been sex—easily replaceable, in theory—yet he didn't relish the idea of never seeing her again. Which was all the more reason to get the hell out of there.

He reached down and tilted her chin, meeting her eyes. 'Good luck, *cara*. I hope you find what you're looking for.'

And then, he walked out, because it was the right—and only—thing he could do.

CHAPTER THREE

CHARLOTTE WOULD HAVE preferred to take a few nights to lick her wounds after Dante's rejection. She thought she'd inured herself from that kind of pain—and she hadn't realised that his saying 'no' to her proposal would genuinely hurt, given the super casual nature of what they'd been doing. But somehow, she'd gotten used to the idea of him being around. Not in a 'real' sense, but just as someone she could hook up with whenever she wanted.

It would have been nice to just stay home—well, technically at Jane's house, because Charlotte had just sort of ended up living there when her lease had ended—and absorb all of the body blows she'd been dealt lately, but she knew she was already living on borrowed time.

She'd just presumed Dante would just fit in with her plans. After all, he had almost as much reason to go for a fake marriage as she did.

His grandmother was the only family member he had left, and she was getting very old and frail. According to Dante, she'd made no effort to hide how much she wanted him to get married again and start having adorable little Italian babies. Dante had looked concerned when he'd admitted as much to Charlotte and Dante San Marino was *not* a man to look anything remotely like concerned, generally.

He was ridiculously confident, almost toxically alpha, arrogant to the point of infuriating, whip smart in a way that

sometimes hurt her brain, and richer than sin, to boot. A combination of old family money and new business nous, meant he was constantly in the finance papers for this deal or that.

Charlotte had offered him an easy way to give his grandmother what she wanted, without any of the complications he clearly wanted to avoid.

And he'd still said 'no'. Which left her up the proverbial creek without a paddle and no time to spare if this was going to work. She needed a husband and she needed one now.

So, instead of staying home and watching box sets with a huge tub of ice cream, Charlotte had slipped into a Stella McCartney dress she'd found on eBay the summer prior, pushed her feet with their newly-painted toenails into a strappy pair of sandals, grabbed a glittery clutch and zhushed her hair, before stepping onto the street and hailing a cab.

The event at the swanky art gallery wasn't one she routinely went to, though she was invited every year. However, it was a fundraiser for a children's hospital, so technically it was a good work opportunity—any charity function had, by definition, a guest list full to bursting with people willing to donate to good causes.

Tonight, though, her focus wouldn't be on schmoozing London's elite. No, she had to work fast, if she was going to find a man who might be willing to marry her—without expecting any kind of romance or relationship in the mix.

Fortunately, finding a shallow would-be husband amongst this crowd wouldn't be too hard. The Roman Numeral set tended have a few rank and file members who would be sure to fit the bill.

Her dress was silky and fell to a couple of inches above the knees, showing the creamy translucence of her skin. She walked confidently in her heels—a virtue of being short and having to go to a lot of these sorts of things, she could probably have run a marathon in a pair of three-inch spikes.

'Name?' Through the foyer of the hotel, and at the entrance to the ballroom, a woman in a stunning one shoulder lime green dress greeted Charlotte expectantly.

'Charlotte Shaw.'

The woman ran a manicured nail down the list then nodded. 'Miss Shaw, welcome,' she waved inside the room. It was a swirling hive of activity and voices. Conversation, laughter and gossip, no doubt. If you'd been to one of these things, you'd been to them all.

She drew in a deep breath, steeling herself, as she always did, to be Charlotte Shaw. Not Lottie, who was more comfortable lounging around in her pyjamas and watching reruns of Friends, eating Thai takeout. But Charlotte Shaw, who'd gone to a prestigious girls' school, an even more elite university, graduated with impressive academic marks and received invitations to join some of the top tier firms in the country. Charlotte Shaw who had made a name for herself in the charities sector. That version of herself was expected to be polished, professional and sophisticated. She pasted a smile to her face and breezed in, as though she had not a care in the world, when in fact, she cared very, very much about how quickly she could wrench the Papandreo company out of the hands of the man who'd been such a monumental jerk to her and her mother.

Dante almost hadn't come to the damn event, but given the enormous amount his hedge fund had donated to the charity, it had seemed in poor taste to not at least put in a brief appearance. He generally left this sort of thing to his assistant, so he wasn't really even sure why he'd felt compelled to put on a suit and come and mill with some of London's filthiest rich elite. Not for pleasure, certainly.

And not for company, either.

He knew he'd want to meet someone else, at some point.

Another woman he could sleep with, anyway. But the problem was, Charlotte had been such a perfect fit. Not just because of the way things were between them in the bedroom, but because she so perfectly matched his total non-desire for a serious relationship. As soon as he'd explained where he was at, in terms of women, she had echoed his thoughts. Spelling out her need for independence. Saying they shouldn't get deep with each other, and that it was fine to just call a spade a spade and admit that they were essentially using each other for sex.

Excellent.

And not something, in his experience, that many women would go for.

So, as his eyes scanned the room, and he continued to listen to a high-level conversation about bitcoin, he did a double take to see Charlotte locked in conversation with a guy who basically looked as though he would lick the soles of her shoes if she asked it of him. And marry her?

Dante stood a little straighter, eyes narrowing.

Charlotte's hand reached out, touched the guy's forearm. He was vaguely familiar. Something in steel? Shipping? Dante had met him at an event, some time ago.

Charlotte laughed, her red hair moving like a wave around her face, so his gut rolled, because he knew how it would feel—soft—and smell—sweet. She was clearly wasting no time in finding someone who *would* fall in with her marriage plans.

The realisation hit him like a tonne of bricks. She had approached Dante, first, and he'd refused her. So here she was, the very next night, looking for an alternative. Something she'd no doubt have no trouble doing.

Only, he didn't want her to marry someone else. He didn't want her to get married at all. Which was pretty damn hypo-

critical, given that he'd sworn off the whole idea of marriage himself. But so had she.

Charlotte didn't want this. She was doing it for revenge, and for altruism, and she'd asked him for a *favour*. Because she could trust him to go through the motions of the engagement and the wedding. She trusted that she could rely on him and, in exchange, it wouldn't get messy.

She'd even dangled the only carrot that would ever, every induce him to even halfway consider marriage: his *Nonna*.

Allegra had put her own life on hold—her grief too—to raise Dante. She'd been a living saint all his life and the one thing she wanted, the one thing that would allow her to live out the rest of her days in peace, would be knowing that he'd opened himself up to love. That he was still capable of wanting things like a family.

That wasn't true, but Allegra didn't need to know that.

Here, Charlotte was offering him a way to protect his grandmother from the legacy of his failed marriage, to give her some hope, at least, that he might live the kind of life she'd always dreamed of. Because Allegra San Marino had put family above all else and she always said it was her greatest achievement.

The man Charlotte was talking to said something else and this time, when she laughed, she leaned forward, stood onto the tips of her toes and whispered something right back in his ear. Something the guy really, really liked, by the looks of it. His grandmother slipped from his mind as he saw red. She was flirting with the man and he was eating it up. It wasn't hard for Dante to connect the dots—and have them join all the way up to these two falling into bed together.

Dante was moving even before he realised it, even before he made any kind of decision to move. He stepped right away from the bitcoin conversation and strode through the suits and tuxedos, the brightly coloured dresses and clouds

of perfume and hairspray, until he was within touching distance of Charlotte. He wasn't thinking. This was instinct, pure and simple. It might have been just sex with them, but that didn't change a thing. Charlotte was his and there was no way he'd let her hook up with anyone else.

'We need to talk.'

Charlotte's pulse went from limp and lackadaisical to tsunami speed and power in the space of an instant. She'd know his voice anywhere.

Grant Mayberry, who she'd been sizing up—and on the brink of discounting—as a potential convenient husband, threw a quizzical look over her shoulder. She could see in his features the same response she'd seen time and time again at this kind of event, when people came face-to-face with the great Dante San Marino.

Fear, trepidation and a little hope—because Dante held some serious purse strings and, for the right investment opportunities, wasn't afraid to use them. How many times had she excused herself from a boring, impromptu elevator pitch aimed at Dante, about something or other that needed funding?

'Dante,' Grant stuck out a hand. He had small fingers, but she'd already registered that, when she'd scanned for a wedding ring. 'Nice to see you again.'

Dante dipped his head once in silent acknowledgement before transferring his gaze to Charlotte. 'Now.' His voice rang with command but also something new. Anger?

He looked unbearably good in a bespoke, jet-black suit jacket, snowy white shirt and crisp black bow tie. His dark hair was brushed back from his brow and he smelled like his cologne—a citrussy fragrance that never failed to curl her toes.

'Actually, no,' she batted her lashes at him, ignoring the way her whole body seemed to spark to life at the sight of him.

'Think again,' he said, a warning in his voice that sent a *frisson* of desire up her spine.

At the same time, Grant said, 'That's fine, Charlotte. We can have that drink later.'

A muscle jerked in Dante's jaw and his eyes didn't leave her face. The intensity of his look was making the hair on the back of her neck stand on end.

'I'm thirsty now,' she said, turning back to Grant, flashing a megawatt smile. 'And Dante and I really have nothing to say to each other.'

But Grant evidently knew what side his bread was buttered on—or at least, which side he hoped it *might* be, because he was already backing away, smiling obsequiously at Dante.

'Oh, for goodness' sake,' she muttered under her breath before whirling around. 'I suppose I should be glad,' she hissed. 'I don't think I could handle being married—even just on paper married—to such a coward.'

Dante's smirk was infuriating.

'You think this is funny?'

The smile dropped. He glared at her again. 'Believe me, funny is the last thing I find this situation.'

She glared right back. 'Well, then, it's just as well that it's none of your business. You turned me down, that's fine. I accept it. But don't get in the way of my husband browsing now, please.'

'Husband browsing?' he repeated with incredulity. 'Are you even hearing yourself?'

She rolled her eyes, then wished she hadn't when she felt the way his whole body tensed in response.

'You cannot simply choose a random man and get married.'

'Oh yeah? Why not?' She crossed her arms over her chest, her temper spiking so that now her pulse was thundering for a whole other reason.

'Because it will make you miserable.'

He stared at her as though he was choosing his next words with care. Or maybe like he was fighting something, inwardly. Either way, she didn't have time for it.

Charlotte sighed. 'It's out of my hands. I need to do this—and fast.' She turned, to walk away, because standing there and staring at him was like trying to hold your ground on quicksand—impossible. She wanted to reach out and touch him, to wrap her arms around the waist she knew to be toned and taut, to hold him close to her body and just breathe him in, before lifting up and teasing his lips with hers, brushing them lightly…but she didn't. Instead, she began to walk towards the bar, hating the way her frustration had morphed into something else. Something unforgivably like regret, because she hadn't wanted to walk away from him at all.

But a hand on her wrist stopped Charlotte mid-step and a light tug had her turning back to face him.

His face was the very definition of 'thunderclouds' but she didn't get why. Unless he was actually *jealous*? Jealousy, though, had no place in their relationship. They both knew that.

Then again, if she'd seen some gorgeous woman draped over him, eagerly hanging on his every word, she might have felt a stirring of that emotion despite what they'd promised each other. That was a normal biological impulse, she reasoned, as ancient as time itself.

'I am not going to let you marry someone you barely know.'

'You're not going to *let* me?' she repeated, voice squeaking.

He made no attempt at apology.

'Dante, you don't get to "let" me do anything.'

'Want a bet?'

She stared at him, not comprehending.

'If you are determined to go through with this—,'

'Which I am—,'

His nostrils flared. 'Then we'll do it your way.'

Silence crashed around them. She stared up at him, her heart racing as she tried to understand what he was saying.

'You've changed your mind? I thought you didn't want to get married.'

'Believe me, I don't.'

She ignored the flicker of pain, familiar rejection crushing her insides, and straightened her spine. 'Then fine, leave me alone.' She pulled on her wrist but he didn't let go. Instead, he pulled her closer, so she bumped right into his chest.

'But I see no reason why us getting married has to fundamentally change the parameters of our relationship.'

Her heart stammered.

'We have spent six months sleeping together and successfully avoided any emotional entanglement.'

'Agreed.'

'Then our marriage will be the same.'

Her heart slammed into her ribs. Every cell in her body began to tremble and shake. *Married.* It was something she'd sworn she'd never, ever do. Never love a guy. Never marry. But Dante was just talking about a continuation of what they already had. It was easy. Everything she wanted.

'You're saying yes?'

'Provisionally, yes.'

'Provisionally?' she arched a brow, then made a show of looking around. 'I need a firm answer. Because one way or another, I'm walking out of here with a husband tonight.'

His jaw visibly shifted as he ground his teeth. 'You are walking out of here with me, tonight, Shaw.'

She arched a brow. 'You seem to think you have a right to boss me around.'

His nostrils flared. 'You're asking me for a favour, I'm telling you how it will work.'

'How, exactly?'

He looked around then, as if only just becoming aware of the attention they were drawing. 'Not here. Let's go back to my place where we can talk in privacy.'

'Talk?' she prompted, with a small half-smile.

His eyes bore into hers. 'Oh, don't get me wrong, Charlotte, that will just be for starters. I don't even want to think about how you might have spent the night if I hadn't happened to be here.'

She drew in a deep breath. 'You think I would have gone home with him?' she asked, incensed by the assumption.

'It sure as hell looked like that was his plan for the night.'

'Yeah, well, it wasn't mine,' she huffed out. How could he even think such a thing?

'Then you'll have no problem with me making it very clear to him, and anyone else who might have been on your radar?'

'Making what clear?'

'That you're mine, Charlotte. At least, when it comes to this, anyway.'

And before she could ask him was 'this' meant, he dropped his head and claimed her mouth in a kiss that was as harshly angry as it was passionately, addictively hot…

CHAPTER FOUR

CHARLOTTE COULDN'T THINK of a single time when they'd driven in silence. Usually, they at least went through the motions of making small talk, of going over one another's days, their current projects, some acquaintance or other they had in common. Never anything too deeply personal, just surface level information that acquaintances might swap at a dinner party.

They usually ran like a well-oiled machine, until the moment they stepped inside his South Kensington home and ripped each other's clothes off.

But this trip was deathly quiet. As if they were each holding their breath. Or maybe, in the case of Dante, trying to take back the agreement they'd just forged with the kind of kiss that would be all anyone talked about for days, because it had been so intimate and so...steamy.

Yesterday, he'd been as completely and utterly opposed to marriage as any human being possibly could be. And now? Now, he'd practically insisted on it.

She glanced across at him, her mouth going as dry as the desert as the reality of their situation slammed into her for the first time. Until then, it had been almost hypothetical. She'd been so focused on the idea of finally being able to avenge her mother, to tilt the scale of justice back in her favour, that she hadn't really thought about what it would be like to be married.

His legs were wide set, his thighs thick and masculine. Beneath the expensive fabric of his suit trousers, they were roughened by dark hair and deeply tanned. His chest was taut and muscular, which she knew was courtesy of the martial arts training he'd done for years. He had a gym in his place equipped with all the necessary accoutrements. She'd gotten him to show her some self-defence moves one morning, but the exercise had quickly devolved into them making love on the gym floor.

Her cheeks flushed at the memory, and at that exact moment, he turned to look at her, his eyes like onyx, darkly glittering and mysterious. His face, all chiselled and angular, with that square jaw and stubbled chin, looked every bit as tautened by tension as it had back at the charity event.

'You might want to rethink the way you're looking at me, Charlotte.'

Her lips parted. 'How am I looking at you?'

'Like you want me to finish that kiss?' He glanced at her. 'Believe me, that's on the agenda. But first, we need to talk about this.'

She bit into her lip. 'What's to talk about? We're getting married.'

'Yes,' he agreed, no mention of it being 'provisional' now. 'But getting married, having sex, living together. That's a lot of potential for blurred lines, which I know we are both keen to avoid—,'

'Living together?' she interrupted quickly. 'That hadn't even occurred to me.'

'Hence the conversation we're about to have.'

'Right,' she nodded, glancing at his face. 'I mean, yeah. We could live together. Your place is big enough for us to be able to keep to ourselves.'

He nodded once. 'My thoughts exactly.'

And she hated that. She hated acquiescing so easily to

him, letting him call all the shots. Even when he was doing her a favour, she still resented his easy authority.

'You were right, yesterday. I have my reasons for wanting this to work.' He glanced out the window, then back at her, his lips a grim line. 'It is imperative that my grandmother believes I have fallen in love and decided to throw myself into the whole concept of a happily ever after.'

She ignored the way something in the region of her heart clutched in response to his obvious concern for his *Nonna*.

'This has to seem real,' he said, the words almost dragged from him against his will.

'I agree.'

'So when we go tell her, we'll act like a couple.'

She bit into her lower lip. 'When *we* go tell her?'

'She'll never buy it otherwise.'

'Right.'

'It's not a big deal,' he muttered. 'A few days in Italy, maybe a week, so she can see this is legitimate. And then we're done.'

'Yeah,' she said, nodding slowly.

'In terms of the wedding,' he lifted his shoulders. 'I am more than happy to leave the details to you. If you want the whole big circus, that's fine. Or if you'd prefer to simply get married and leave it at that, I'm fine with that, as well.'

She frowned. 'I presume your grandmother would want to be there.'

'I suppose so, yes, but at the end of the day, as long as she thinks I'm in love again, she won't mind the details either.'

'A small wedding, as soon as we can legally arrange it, with our closest friends and family. Yes?'

'Fine.'

'Okay.' She expelled a soft breath. 'Anything else?'

He flicked at his black bow tie until it opened, then undid

the top button of his shirt, revealing a hint of his tanned chest and hair.

Her heart rate accelerated. The predictable physical response to this man was none the less powerful for being expected.

'I'll have a prenuptial agreement drawn up.'

She wrinkled her nose. 'That hadn't even occurred to me. What kind of lawyer does that make me?'

'A trusting one,' he said.

'I'm not interested in your money.'

'It's to protect you as much as it is me.'

She was about to point out that she had very few assets, but of course, that wasn't true. Not only was there the trust fund her father had set up for her, but there was also the matter of the Papandreo Group, which was worth trillions.

And once they were married, it would be hers.

All hers.

Satisfaction seared her, so hard and fast it stung.

'In terms of our personal relationship,' he was continuing. 'So long as we maintain the status quo, I can't see any problems developing.'

'And the status quo is…'

'We keep it simple,' he pointed out. 'You and I don't talk about anything serious or personal. Sex is sex, everything else is irrelevant.'

A small smile lifted the corner of her mouth, but inside, there was a familiar coldness spreading through her organs. 'We're good at that.'

He nodded once, his eyes dropping to her lips, lingering there, making her heart slam against her ribs.

'We must almost be home,' she said, a little breathlessly.

His glance flicked over her shoulder, to the window, then back to Charlotte's face. 'This is my street.'

Relief exploded. With the details of their deal ironed out, she was desperate to finish what he'd started at the charity event.

It wouldn't have surprised Dante if Charlotte turned out to be a witch. When they touched, it almost felt as though a spell had been cast over him. The brush of her fingers over his body was incendiary, but her lips were even more so. He felt as though his veins had been pumped full of molten lava. And it had been like this between them from the very first night.

It had been a release. And a relief.

After Jamie, he hadn't slept with anyone else. He hadn't wanted to. Although he had always thought of himself as a red-blooded guy with pretty consistent needs, in the end, he'd started to dread sex with his wife. Not because the sex had been bad. It was sex, after all. But because of the heaviness of expectation that came with it—the hope that she'd conceive and that this time, the baby would be okay.

Spontaneity and sensuality had gone by the wayside, in favour of monthly cycle tracking and recommended positions for conception. Each month that passed without success had made him feel like a failure. But worse was when the test showed a positive result, only to ride a rollercoaster of emotions for weeks, then go through the grief—and guilt—of knowing they were losing the baby.

They'd split and he'd been celibate. Not by conscious choice, rather by natural attrition. He wasn't interested in something he'd come to associate with heavy personal pain.

He worked. He went to work functions. He worked some more.

And then there was Charlotte and, for the first time in a long time, he'd felt a stirring of something unexpected and almost unfamiliar.

Desire.

Simple, white-hot, uncomplicated lust.

Passion.

Need.

It was like being brought back from the dead. She touched him and he felt himself burning up. She kissed him and his whole world tilted sideways.

What they had was exactly what he needed.

He just hoped this marriage of theirs wouldn't mess anything up.

The last thing he wanted was to screw up another woman's life.

But Charlotte wasn't looking for anything more from him. She'd made that clear, right from the start, and she'd made it clear when she'd rolled out this whole proposal. She was asking him for a favour. Their marriage was a means to an end. Their sexual chemistry was the cherry on top.

He pulled at her dress, suddenly impatient to see her, to feel her naked body against his. The fabric was soft and she shivered as he lifted it over her head then threw it to the living room floor. Her hands mimicked his, pushing at the buttons of his shirt until it parted down the middle, running her hands over his chest, teasing his hair roughened nipples as they moved to his shoulders then dropped the shirt to the floor.

He swallowed a curse as he shoved a hand into the waistband of her underpants and cupped her neat rear, pushing her against his body and holding her there, hard up against his arousal, his voice gruff as she began to move, rocking her hips, like she couldn't wait for him to be inside her.

That made two of them.

'I want you,' she said, undoing his belt, then his zip, pushing his boxer shorts down with his pants. He stepped out of them then lifted her quickly, wrapping her legs around his

waist as he took the few short strides to the leather armchair and sitting down on it, Charlotte straddling his lap.

He loved it when she rode him. *Loved it.* She was so right, with her long, red hair draped over her shoulders, her pert, neat breasts at his face height, so he could lean forward and flick them with his tongue, tease them with his teeth. His hands cupped her bottom, pulling her towards his arousal.

She swore as she tilted back her head, her cheeks flushed pink, and he grinned, moving his head to the sensitive flesh at the side of her breast and sucking there, flicking her with his tongue, pulling away only when he'd left a dark purple mark of possession. A kinky, desperate need to make sure she understood that she was his. Just for this night, and just for sex, nothing more.

'Dante,' she groaned. Now she eased up, just far enough to remove her underpants and then bring herself back over his length. Her eyes holding his as she bit into her lower lip and pushed down on his length. Her tight, wet muscles slicked around him, squeezing him, making heat build at the base of his cock, spread through his whole body. 'Please,' she cried out, as she finally settled hard in his lap, taking him in completely and staying perfectly still while she adjusted to the size of him.

They'd had a conversation about condoms in their first week together. They were both safe, and she was religious about taking the pill. *I don't ever plan to have kids.*

He loved doing this with her, without a condom. He loved feeling every part of her.

He was addicted to this.

Sex without the need for a baby. Sex, just because you wanted it. Sex, because they were two passionate people, driven by biological urges and for no other reason.

She cried out and he gripped her hips, holding her right there, burying himself deep inside her, before running his

hands over her body, all of her, feeling, touching, finding his cravings for her unabated even then, when he was on the brink of satiation.

He dragged his mouth over her breasts, her collarbone, to her shoulder, where he nipped with his teeth and then found her mouth, or perhaps she found his, hungry, desperate, aching for her. She arched her back and shouted his name into the room, her hair cascading like a fiery wave. He could only stare at the sight she made, at the beautiful, passionate, spirited woman she was.

He groaned then, because her explosion, her muscles squeezing so hard, was the tipping point for him and there was nothing he could do to stop it. He held her tight as he came, the shockwaves rocking through both of them, pulling them apart even when they were as physically close as two people could ever be.

Charlotte's smile was slow to spread, but it seemed to come from deep inside of her. Since the meeting with her father's lawyers, she'd had a big ball of nerves in her belly, a stress and frustration that she just hadn't been able to ease.

But Dante had known how.

Dante with his beautiful body that always seemed so perfectly in sync with hers.

She blinked down at him to find him staring hungrily at her—unapologetically—his eyes full of admiration, so her cheeks glowed with warmth.

'Thank you,' she said, lifting one shoulder in a half shrug. 'I needed that.'

He laughed. 'That's mutual.'

She pressed a hand to his chest, feeling the thundering of his heart. 'I'm actually starting to think being your pretend wife could be kind of fun.'

His smile slipped a little, as if he'd forgotten all about their

fake marriage. She wanted to ask why he hated marriage so much, what had happened with him and his ex-wife, but that would break one of their first cardinal rules—no serious stuff. So she pulled away from him instead, placing a quick kiss on his lips as she stood, her body tingling all over.

'I'll be right back,' she murmured, grabbing her clothes and swishing her hips exaggeratedly as she left the room.

In the bathroom, she stared at herself in the mirror, a fingertip tracing the pink patches his stubbly beard had left, and the dark purple bruising he'd pressed just to the side of her breast. Something fierce and strong arced inside of her, a pleasure that was like magma. So hot and animalistic, so ancient and prehistoric, it seemed to resonate from deep, deep within her.

Before Dante, Charlotte had seen a few guys. Never serious. Never more than a casual date, here and there. Sex, sometimes. She'd always pushed herself to stay in control, to know that no matter how much she enjoyed someone's company, she could walk away any time. That she had that power.

Her finger pressed into the bruise mark and she frowned a little.

She wasn't stupid.

Dante was dangerous.

Not himself, per se, but the connection they shared. While it was true that they didn't have a lot in common, it was also true that the power of the sexual chemistry was deeply addictive. The kind of addiction that made it hard to imagine turning your back.

One day, it would lessen though. It would fade. It had to.

Until then, she just had to take great care to neatly compartmentalise how they were physically with the whole marriage concept. He was right about blurred lines and how problematic that could be. But Charlotte had had a lifetime

of practice at keeping people at arm's length. Dante might have been dangerous, but she was up for a challenge.

No matter what, once she had the Papandreo company, she would walk away from him, come what may—and then, Charlotte would have everything she'd really wanted in life. Her independence, and the destruction of her horrible, hateful father and brother.

Dante San Marino was a heck of a lot of fun, in the meantime. But beyond that, he was nothing to her. Nothing.

CHAPTER FIVE

IT WAS NOT a call he relished making, which explained why he'd put it off for as long as he could.

In the two days since agreeing to marry Charlotte, Dante had had the prenuptial agreements drawn up and given notice of their intention to marry at the registry office, whereby setting the clock ticking on the twenty-nine-day waiting period until they were legally eligible to marry.

He hadn't told his grandmother yet, but he'd arranged to visit her for a week and told her he wouldn't be alone. The less she knew in advance, the better—he wouldn't put it past her to turn up on his doorstep demanding answers if he informed her, ahead of time, that he was bringing a woman.

He'd done just about everything he needed to do and the wedding was now hurtling towards him like an asteroid from which there was no escape.

Not that he'd want to escape, anyway. He'd given Charlotte his word and he would never renege on that.

Which meant there was just one thing left to do, and it could no longer be put off. Not if there was a chance someone at the registry office might tip off the press about Dante San Marino's impending marriage. As one of the richest men in the world, there was a not inconsequential amount of speculation surrounding his private life—something he'd guarded even more fiercely once he and Jamie had split.

Jamie.

His gut rolled with the complex emotions he felt whenever he thought of her, reaching for his phone and pressing her name before he could back out of this. The thought of Jamie hearing about his wedding from anyone but him sat inside him like a lead balloon. He'd already hurt her enough for ten lifetimes.

She answered on the fourth ring.

'Hey, stranger.'

As always, her voice pulled at something in his chest. He cleared his throat. 'Jamie, hi.'

'You sound cross. Is everything okay?'

Jamie knew him better than anyone on earth. The fact she could correctly deduce his mood after hearing just a couple of syllables showed that to be true.

'Do you have a minute?'

'For you, I have five minutes, at least. What's up?'

He stood, prowling towards the window, bracing an elbow on the glass and staring down at London, the Thames writhing through it like a big, pewter snake.

'There's no easy way to tell you this. I'm getting married.'

Her sharp intake of breath might as well have been a whip against his flesh. He winced, wishing he could take back the words. Wishing, no matter what he'd just told himself a minute ago, that he could renege on this whole stupid deal.

Nothing on earth was worth hurting Jamie for.

'Oh. Erm, congratulations.'

She sounded like she was about to cry.

'Listen, Jamie,' he began, aware that his accent had thickened, as it always did when he was battling the depth of his emotions. His failures where his ex-wife was concerned.

'It's okay.' She cleared her throat. 'We're divorced. I didn't expect you'd be single forever.'

Silence fell, a staticky, heavy silence that, to Dante's ears,

was prickly with accusations, no matter how kindly she was letting him off the hook.

'I did,' he said, simply. 'You know that.'

'Yes.' Another clear of her throat. 'So, who is she?'

He thought of Charlotte and something fizzed in his gut for a whole other reason. Where everything with Jamie was heavy and charged with dreadful guilt and grief, Charlotte was the exact opposite. When he thought of her, he felt levity and lightness, happiness and simplicity.

'No one you know,' he said, though perhaps that wasn't true. After all, they all moved in similar circles. 'Charlotte Shaw.'

'Never heard of her,' she said.

Dante suspected that would change. Not just with their marriage, but when the truth of her parenthood came out and she took possession of the Papandreo Group.

'What's she like?'

'She's—,' he searched for the right words, and drew a blank. What could one say to their ex-wife about their future wife? 'You'd like her,' he finished, after a beat.

'I'll take your word for it,' Jamie said, a little wistfully. The implication was clear: we'll never meet.

More silence. He smothered a sigh. They'd divorced and that was for the best, but the guilt over how he'd failed Jamie followed him still. He wished he could have given her what she wanted. She had deserved better. He shifted his weight to the other foot, pressed his palm to the glass, feeling the cold smoothness and picturing Jamie.

'Do you love her?' It was barely a whisper, the softest words, a question into the darkness.

He closed his eyes on a wave of feeling. Panic, regret, remorse, guilt.

'Never mind. I shouldn't have asked—,'

'No,' he said, because he'd failed Jamie so often, so many

times, and at least he could give her this. He had told Charlotte that this would be their secret, that it was imperative that nobody else knew the truth, but Jamie, he realised now, had to stand outside of that bubble. 'We're not in love, Jamie.'

Her sigh was a gust down the phone line. 'Then why?'

'There are practical reasons for our marriage.'

'She's not pregnant, is she?'

He heard the awful, awful fear in those words and wanted to rip out his heart. 'No.'

'Okay. I mean, I shouldn't—I'm sorry—I'm asking things I have no right to ask. I'm just—blindsided.'

'I should have texted you first, prepared you better.'

'We're divorced. I honestly never expected you to stay single, Dante. It's fine.'

'This isn't like what we were, Jamie.' That was the God's honest truth. Jamie and he had been little more than teenagers when they'd met and their relationship had been one of growing up together. They'd been friends, first and foremost. They'd never had the kind of explosive sex that he and Charlotte shared. He knew Jamie needed to hear that truth, but he felt something unexpected in saying those words—he felt the sting of having betrayed Charlotte, who deserved better than to be minimised to save another woman's feelings.

He ground his teeth, hating the complexity of this. It was exactly the kind of situation he'd sworn he'd never again be in.

'It's fine,' she said, again. 'I'm happy for you.'

She sounded the exact opposite of happy.

'I just wanted you to hear it from me.'

'I appreciate it. And I always like to hear from you,' her voice took on a wistful edge. 'I have to go now,' she said, the words quivering a little, as though she were fighting tears. 'We'll talk later, okay?'

She disconnected the call before he could respond.

He closed his eyes, trying to picture Jamie, to imagine her face, but it was Charlotte's eyes that lanced him, clear, inquisitive, endlessly fascinating. He groaned, dropping his forehead against the glass and staring down at the city, kicking himself mentally, for the hundredth time, for agreeing to this.

'This is very comprehensive,' Lottie said, flicking a glance across the kitchen counter, to where Dante was placing a selection of antipasto on a serving platter. It was hardly gourmet cooking, but she was still impressed by the way he was assembling antipasti, as though he did such things on a daily basis.

'The platter?' he asked, following her gaze.

She laughed. 'The prenuptial agreement, but the platter too.'

His grin made her stomach twist. 'Better to be safe than sorry.'

She turned the page and jolted upright.

Section 7—children.

She pressed a finger to it then looked at him again. 'Children?' Her voice was a little high pitched.

'We're having sex and getting married. It seemed like a wise precaution.'

'But we're not having children. I'm on contraceptives.'

'Sure, but it's better to be—,'

'Yes, yes, safe than sorry, I heard you before.' Her eyes widened and out of nowhere, something clutched in her belly, at the thought of carrying a baby—their baby—to term. She shook her head, panic quickly overtaking it. 'I don't want children.'

'We've discussed this,' he reminded her, putting down a slab of feta cheese and coming to the other side of the counter, bracing his hands on the top. 'Neither of us wants kids. It's all good. But sometimes, accidents happen and the point

of a prenuptial agreement is to safeguard against any possible contingency. Okay?'

She returned her attention to the document, moving her finger as she read the stipulations. There was nothing particularly unexpected, she realised, her nerves calming a little. Provisions as to custody in the event of a divorce, the fact neither parent could remove the child from the country without written permission of the other, the allocation of a set amount by Dante in a trust, a provision for consultation when it came to matters such as healthcare and education. She nodded as she continued reading, her throat dry but breathing returning to normal.

'Okay, that's all fine,' she said with a lift of her shoulders, turning the page and landing on the far less controversial question of assets.

By the time she'd finished reading, Dante had moved the platter between them and poured two glasses of red wine. She eyed her glass, the deep, burgundy liquid beautiful to look at.

'So?'

'So, it's fine. Thank you for organising it. Do you want me to sign it now?'

'No rush. Take it to a lawyer, get a second opinion.'

'I'm quite capable of understanding a document.'

'I wasn't implying otherwise,' he said. 'You are always so quick to see the worst in me.'

'No, I'm not. But I am a lawyer, you might remember, and there's nothing in here that concerns me.'

'You are not a family lawyer,' he continued, in that slightly patronising tone he had, that always made her glad their relationship was purely physical. 'There might be items your lawyers want included that mine haven't thought of. There's no downside in taking some extra advice.'

She compressed her lips, trying to suppress the frustration she felt at his superior tone. 'Sure,' she said, because it was

easier than arguing. And also because, on some level, his advice was sound. Getting legal advice never hurt. In fact, it was one of the first things she counselled anyone to do, because lawyers often saw things in a way that could prevent difficulties in the future. She forced a smile, even when she hated to concede the point to him.

'How's the wedding planning going?'

She arched a brow. 'Wedding planning?'

'Dress. Flowers. That kind of thing.' It sounded a little ludicrous to hear a man like Dante, who was all pure alpha, talk about the pretty wedding requirements.

'So, because I'm the bride I have to organise the flowers?'

He stared at her with a look of total non-comprehension. 'Do you want me to do it?'

She pressed her lips together now to stop a laugh from escaping. She had to admit, to herself at least, that the idea was kind of ridiculous.

'I do not know my roses from my lilies, but if you have some aversion to it, I can get my assistant to handle it.'

She opened her mouth to object, but then it occurred to her that the idea of having an assistant organise all the details was one sure fire way to keep their wedding just as it should be: meaningless. Something they had to go through for the sake of legally marrying, and little else.

'I'll hire a wedding planner,' she said, tapping a finger on the prenuptial agreement. 'I don't know why it hadn't occurred to me before now.'

He lifted the glass of wine towards her and when their eyes met, something charged the air between them. Static electricity lifted the hairs on the back of her neck. She looked away again quickly.

'To our wedding, then,' he said. She couldn't help but detect the grimness in his voice. To wonder, again, at what had happened in his first marriage to make him so deathly

against the whole institution. Questions, questions, questions that she would never ask.

But that didn't mean she couldn't read his feelings and sympathise with him.

'I can't thank you enough for this,' she said, softly.

'It is not just for you, Charlotte. This wedding benefits me too, remember.'

She nodded, clinking her glass to his then replacing it on the benchtop.

'In fact,' he said, taking a sip of his drink before echoing her gesture. 'My grandmother is expecting us next week.'

Charlotte's eyes flared wide. 'When you say expecting us—,'

'To stay with her,' he said.

'Oh.'

Her pulse went all thready and something like anxiety stormed through her, because keeping Dante at arm's length was fine when they were alone, but in the presence of his *Nonna*, she'd have to do a much better job of acting enamoured with the man. And she'd have to know more than the superficial stuff about him.

'Dante, when you say 'next week', you don't mean we're staying with her for a whole week, do you?'

'She wants to get to know you.'

Charlotte's eyes swept closed. 'That's what I was afraid of.'

'You knew this was part of the deal.'

'Yes, it's just—,' her voice tapered off as she tried to explain. 'Don't you think there's a risk, in spending so much time with her?'

'What risk?'

'Well, that she'll see through us, for one thing.'

His eyes glittered with determination when they met hers. 'It's up to you and me to make sure that doesn't happen.'

'I mean, I'm obviously going to try, but—,' She bit into her

lower lip, eyes meeting his, as some sort of presentiment of disaster drifted across her. 'You and I know that *not* getting to know each other properly is sort of how this all works,' she gestured from herself to him, with the sinking sensation that she was standing on the edge of a big, gaping void. 'If we're going to pull this off, I think we sort of have to...go over more than just the basics.'

He shrugged.

'You don't think there's a problem with that?' she pushed.

'You seem to be presupposing that the more we get to know each other, the more we'll like each other. What if the opposite is true?'

She burst out laughing at the unexpectedly grim—but re-assuring—take on their situation.

'You've already said you don't like me,' he pointed out. 'You know me well enough, after six months of sleeping together, to realise that there is precisely zero risk of us developing feelings for one another. We are simply not wired that way.'

'Nonetheless, I think we should be cautious about this.'

He arched a brow, clearly sceptical. 'How so?'

'Well,' she pondered that. 'Like if I come up with some questions for you to answer. Things I'll need to know, that aren't too personal. That way, it's less of a conversation and more of an...'

'Interview,' he interrupted, expression giving nothing away.

'Yes,' she agreed.

'That's fine. If that's your preference, Charlotte, we can do it your way.'

She nodded, as if in agreement, but inside, her nerves were starting to zip and jangle, because this was more complicated already, than she'd wanted. 'Are you sure I have to go meet her? You can't just take a photo of me? Tell her I'm busy working?'

'She knows I would never marry someone she hadn't met.'

It was *so* damned sweet, so thoughtful and respectful, that Charlotte's eyes stung with the unexpected ache of unshed tears. 'You're really close to her, huh?'

'She put her life on hold to raise me,' he pointed out. 'I respect and love her, yes.'

Charlotte took a sip of her drink; it was full-bodied and spicy. 'How old were you when—,' she left the question unfinished, the implication nonetheless clear. So much for avoiding personal conversations.

'Eight.' And before she could ask him how his parents died, he supplied, 'in a helicopter crash.'

She grimaced. 'That's awful.'

'Yes. It was a mechanical failing. It went down quickly, landed hard. My parents, my grandfather and the pilot all died on impact.'

'Oh, Dante,' she shook her head a little, reaching across and covering his much larger hand with her own. He stared down at them, as if he'd never seen hands before, then pulled his away. But his eyes lingered on her own hand for several beats.

'An engagement ring,' he said, with a single nod of his head. 'I'll organise that tomorrow. Do you have any preference for style?'

And just like that, she was doused in ice-cold water, reminded of the strictly pragmatic nature of their relationship. Not only that, but she was also reassured by the way he'd acted like a safety rail, when she'd had a momentary lapse in judgement and briefly forgotten the way things stood with them.

'Something simple,' she insisted. And then, for clarity, 'Not flashy.'

'Not flashy?'

'You know, not some massive diamond that's going to weigh me down all day.'

He frowned. 'Why not?'

It was so like him to just presume bigger was better that she couldn't help rolling her eyes. 'Because I don't like that kind of thing.'

'Nice kinds of things?'

'A simple gold band will be fine.'

He stared at her like she'd lost her mind. 'No one will believe that's what I would choose for you.'

'Then why are you even asking me?'

'Because it should be something you want.'

'Then I've told you what I want.'

'Something boring.'

'No, something simple.' She lifted her shoulder. 'Apart from anything, I think it's in poor taste to wear some huge rock when I'm working in the not-for-profit sector.'

'You make no sense.'

She laughed. 'I make perfect sense; you just don't understand me.'

'No, you are a contradiction,' he insisted. 'You went to expensive schools, a prestigious university. You raise hundreds of millions of dollars each year, from people like me, yet you are so disdainful of wealth. Why?'

'Because it's so unevenly distributed,' she said, shaking her head at how he couldn't comprehend that. 'Don't you think there's something kind of gross about how much money you have? When there are people out there sleeping in cars?'

'Yes,' he surprised her by agreeing instantly. 'Which is why I donate to your charities and many others.'

'Well, you do at least have a social conscience,' she said, ignoring the way her heart did a funny little triple beat. 'I still don't want a huge chunk of diamond on my finger.'

He groaned but she knew she'd gotten through to him. 'Okay. It doesn't matter, anyway. It's just for show.'

'Right. Like a costume.' It was fake. Something she'd wear, then return at such time that their marriage was no longer useful to either of them and they went their separate ways. 'Just make-believe,' she added, wondering why she felt the need for that extra reassurance.

CHAPTER SIX

IN THE END, the decision was simple. Despite Charlotte's stipulations, Dante looked at all the rings the exclusive jeweller had to show him. He amused himself by imagining how she'd react if he went against her wishes and chose the most ginormous, perfectly-formed diamond solitaire they had, just to annoy her. It was tempting. Very tempting. Tempting to give her the kind of ring most women would surely love?

But he had no interest in deliberately thwarting her—he seemed to aggravate her enough just by being himself. So he asked to see the plain bands, and having looked over those, and still not been satisfied, he was on the brink of going to a different jeweller, when a new tray of rings were presented.

And it hit him, right in the middle of the solar plexus. The only ring he could possibly choose for her. Granted, it was fussier than she said she wanted, but the second he saw it, he just knew it was perfect for Charlotte.

And for some reason he couldn't put his finger on immediately, that really mattered to him.

He supposed it was because rings were significant, even when the marriage itself was fake. His mother's wedding ring was still in his possession. It had been recovered after the crash and his grandmother had kept it safe, all those years, until he met Jamie and was ready to propose.

She'd worn the ring then and had always imagined that their daughter might wear it, too.

Now, that ring was in a safe—cursed, in Dante's opinion. But he knew it was not an insignificant thing to give a woman an engagement ring, even when the marriage was just for show.

'That one,' he said, pointing to the large emerald solitaire, surrounded by a circlet of white diamonds and set in a petite platinum band. 'It's perfect.' It was elegant, petite and sparkling, just like Charlotte, and the colour of the gem was just exactly the same as her eyes. 'It's made for her.'

'Very good, sir. Would you care to see the matching necklace?'

He laughed then and nodded. Apparently, he wasn't above irritating his soon-to-be-wife, just for the sake of it.

Charlotte had gone to a lot of trouble to make sure everything about tonight screamed whatever the opposite of romance was. She'd chosen her most casual pair of jeans with a slouchy grey t-shirt that did nothing for her figure, scrubbed off all her makeup and scraped her hair back into a tight ponytail. All the lights in Jane's place were switched to their max setting, not so much bathing the apartment in a golden glow as floodlighting it in bright white. She'd made no effort to tidy up, and she'd ordered Indian food from the restaurant down the street, that always used too much garlic in everything, because nothing screamed unromantic like garlic breath.

Because this was the night before they flew to Italy, and his grandmother, and it was their last chance to get to know each other better. Not only that, but Jane was also away in Athens, meaning they'd be home alone. There was no way she was going to let the essential *tête-à-tête* be mistaken for anything other than what it was—a study session.

What was that expression about perfectly laid plans?

Because for all Charlotte's efforts to look like she hadn't made any effort, the second she wrenched open the door, it didn't matter. None of it mattered.

Dante stood there, all way-too-handsome-billionaire in his tailored suit pants and crisp white shirt, tall, slimly muscled, dark and handsome, mysterious and brooding. Her heart popped, her pulse stormed and she wished, more than anything, that she'd at least glossed her lips.

Why, though? He took one look at her and dragged her against his body as though they hadn't seen each other for a year, not a day, and kissed her so hard and fast that if she *had* been wearing lip gloss, it would all have been smudged off immediately, anyway.

His hands lifted to the back of her hair, pushing at the elastic until it fell away, and then his fingers tangled in the long, red ends, tilting her head back so he could kiss her so much better, so much harder. Her body felt as though it had been hit with a burst of lightning. She tingled from head to toe. He smelled so good, so masculine and earthy. His shirt was a thick cotton, and it was warmed by his body. She pushed at it, lifting it out of his pants, so her fingers could connect to his bare chest.

'*Cristo, cara*,' he muttered, as she undid his zip and grasped him in the palm of her hands.

She pulled away from him, looking upwards. 'Do you want me to stop?'

He looked down at her with something dark in his eyes, something that might have been resentment or fear, but her blood was pounding so hard and fast that all she could think—and feel—was the tumultuous rush of her own needs, overtaking everything else. Or maybe it was yet another way to prove to herself that, first and foremost, this was really just about sex. There was nothing else here, nothing more serious or complicated.

Smiling slowly, she dropped to her knees, the harsh curse that slipped from his lips only making her body throb with need because there was such a heady power in how quickly she could do this to him. She moved her head forwards, his

hands in her hair stilling, his whole body frozen, as she took him inside and teased him with her tongue, her lips, until he was crying her name.

Only then did his hands move, slipping from her hair to her arms, lifting her quickly, bringing his mouth back to hers as he lifted her and wrapped her legs around his waist in one movement, stepping forward so her back was braced against the wall. Then, he drove into her, his voice rough and deep, her own cry one of absolute surrender and perfection. Her whole body was on fire, tingling, aching, needing. Her skin felt almost too sensitive to bear. When he took one of her nipples in his mouth and pressed his teeth against it, she sobbed because the pleasure was so utterly exquisite it was almost too much to handle.

His name was a mantra in her mind but she kept it there. Just his name. Just for her. She bit down onto her lower lip, rather than cry it out as she wanted to. And then, she was tumbling off the edge of an abyss. The pleasure an enormous tsunami swallowing them both up and roaring through the apartment with its own pounding, desperate ferocity.

They stood there, breathing fast and loud. Bodies sheened in a hint of perspiration. Eyes wide, lips bruised, the fast-paced urgency of their love making new even for them.

But it was just sex, she reminded herself, as she forced a smile to spread across her face and lifted a hand to his cheek. Casual, meaningless, easy-to-walk-away-from sex.

'Thanks,' she said. 'I think I needed that.'

His eyes flickered with something but then he was easing her down to the ground, face neutral. 'Did something happen?'

She glanced up at him, confused.

'A bad day?'

'Oh.' His concern did something trippy to her insides. She shook her head. 'I just—,' What? Meant that she needed reassurance that this was just physical? 'It doesn't matter.'

His lips quirked into a quick frown but then he turned away from her, looking deeper into the apartment. He'd never been here before. It was Jane's place, though Jane always insisted that Charlotte should treat it as her own. But that wasn't why she hadn't brought him here before. It was her private space. Hers and Jane's. Their sanctuary from the world. Charlotte had never actually brought anyone here. So why had she agreed for him to come over tonight?

When he'd suggested it, she hadn't even thought to question the location. It had been a simple, 'I can come to you. What time suits?' kind of question and she'd simply focused on the matter of timing, texting him that as well as the address.

But now that he was here, all big and beautiful and expensive looking, Charlotte felt as though the bubble of her sanctuary had been ever so slightly burst.

'This is where you live?' he asked, as he moved into the living room and looked around. He'd tucked his shirt back into his pants and refastened the zip—he looked precisely as untouchable as he always did.

She tried to see the apartment through his eyes, but didn't like the hint of vulnerability that brushed over her. He glanced over at Charlotte and her stomach dipped. Not wearing make-up or nice clothes had been a stupid, stupid decision, because both had always served as more than fashion choices. For Charlotte, they were armour. A way to keep her real self hidden. To present what she wanted to the outside world. And now, she'd let Dante see so much of her. Too much.

She swallowed past a heavy lump in her throat, glancing around the room again.

'It's my best friend's place,' she said, haltingly.

'Jane,' he supplied.

She shouldn't have been surprised he remembered her name. Dante was nothing if not a details man.

'Yes.'

'Have you lived here long?'

'I mean, I used to stay here all the time, before I actually gave up my lease and moved in.'

'Why did you give up your lease?'

Charlotte pulled her hair over one shoulder, heat sparking in her veins once more at the way his eyes fell to her fingers and lingered there. Such an innocuous gesture, yet he stared at her as if she'd just performed some kind of burlesque routine.

Then again, she'd greeted him at the door and fallen to her knees, so she kind of had, Charlotte thought, with a faint blush spreading over her skin.

'I—,' she swallowed again. 'I don't think your grandmother will ask that,' she said, pleased she'd been able to bring their conversation back to the whole purpose of this visit. 'I ordered in. Are you hungry?'

His eyes rested on her face a little longer, as though he were probing beyond her words, into her brain, trying to see her inner most thoughts, but Charlotte smiled brightly and turned away, walking into the small kitchenette and removing two bowls.

'I hope Indian is okay. The place around the corner does great curries. Jane and I are obsessed.'

She was babbling.

'Is this her?' He came into the kitchen, holding a framed photograph of Jane and Charlotte. They were laughing hard at something the waiter—who was taking the photo—had just said.

Just the sight of Jane was reassuring. 'Yeah, that's her.'

'I vaguely remember her from the night we met.'

Charlotte pulled a face.

'What?'

'You "vaguely" remember her?'

He glanced at her. 'What's wrong with that?'

'It's just—Jane's probably the most beautiful woman who's ever lived. I doubt you only "vaguely" remember her.'

He stared at her as though she'd started to speak another language. 'Is she?' He looked down at the photo again, frowning a little. 'I suppose she's beautiful, yes.'

'You suppose she's beautiful?' Now it was Charlotte's turn to stare at him in bemusement. 'You've got to be kidding me?'

'I was a little distracted by the woman beside her,' he said with a shrug that made her stomach go all squirmy and weird.

She didn't reply. She didn't want to keep talking along these lines. She had never been jealous of Jane's beauty—partly because Jane couldn't help it, she'd just been born that way, but mostly because Charlotte knew the headache Jane's looks had caused her. Jane couldn't go anywhere without men falling at her feet and she hated that kind of attention.

A pang of remorse sparked in Charlotte. At this very moment Jane was in Athens, trading on her stunning looks, to lure Zeus Papandreo into a situation that would delay his own ability to find a bride. It had been the added security Charlotte had needed, to buy herself some time to pull this off.

It was a security she still needed, she thought. While Dante had agreed to go along with this plan, anything could happen between now and the wedding date. She wasn't going to take any risks by letting Zeus have a head start. No. She needed Jane to stay in Athens and keep him occupied, so that he couldn't get married before Charlotte.

It was all so preposterous, but she refused to let the company slide. She could only imagine the look on her mother's face when she went home and told her what she'd done. Finally, payback, after all those years of hurt and rejection. Of the intense heartbreak that had defined Mariah Shaw's life.

She'd hated asking Jane to do this for her, but there was no one else in the world who knew the truth of Charlotte's

parentage and no one else would be such a reliable bait to arrogant, womanising Zeus.

Jane had assured Charlotte she could handle him and Charlotte was sure Jane was right. At least, she really, really hoped she was.

'How did you two meet?'

'In school,' Charlotte said, scooping some rice into their bowls before adding the curry. 'Do you eat everything?'

He nodded.

'No allergies?'

'Planning to dispose of me once we're married?' He asked with a hint of amusement.

She grinned. 'Ah, yes. An excellent plan. Why didn't I think of that?'

He laughed. 'Sorry to tell you, the prenuptial agreement means even if I were to die during our short marriage, my assets would be held in trust.'

'Who for?' she asked, genuinely curious.

'What do you mean?'

'You're an only child. Who's the beneficiary of the trust?'

His features shifted a little, his expression briefly haunted, pained. She ached to reach out and smooth away the lines on his brow. To hold his face in the palms of her hands and kiss him, gently, reassuringly. She kept dishing up the curries instead.

'Because we can help you structure it so that charities receive it,' she said, glancing at him, offering an impish smile to help him through whatever was causing him pain.

'My ex-wife inherits everything,' he said, after a beat.

Charlotte's fingers slipped and the spoon dropped to the counter, leaving a lurid orange blob of butter chicken sauce against the white melamine. She turned quickly, grabbing a sponge to clean it—she knew how it could stain if left un-

checked. But mainly, she needed a moment without Dante's intelligently assessing eyes boring through her.

Because he'd surprised her.

And on some level, he'd made her feel…something she didn't want to feel. Something Charlotte knew better than to analyse.

'Has she re-married?' She was pleased her voice came out pretty close to normal.

'No.'

'Does she have children?'

He closed his eyes briefly, shook his head. No verbal response.

Interesting.

But being interested in him was *bad*. Unsafe. Not what they were doing.

'Did your grandmother like her?'

At that, his lips tugged into a half-smile. 'Yes.'

There it was again! That pang of something unpleasantly sharp, like a blade, right in her side.

She lifted the bowls and nodded towards the living room, where there was a small table in the bay window.

'Would you mind grabbing some water?'

He followed behind holding two glasses and, once at the table, he sat without touching his fork. 'Jamie—that's my ex-wife—and my grandmother were very close. She took the divorce hard.'

Charlotte arranged her features into an expression of sympathy. It wasn't hard to feel it, but at the same time she wished she didn't.

'Why did you break up?'

There. She'd asked and it was something she probably needed to know. Only, that wasn't *why* she'd asked. She'd let curiosity get the better of her and she was annoyed at her own weakness.

'It's complicated.'

'We've got all night,' she reminded him.

'It's personal.' His eyes lifted to hers. The blade was back, only this time she perfectly understood why she felt it. He was delineating boundaries—just as they'd agreed they would—but this time it felt like rejection. As though he were dismissing her.

'Okay.' She tried to infuse a casual breeziness into the two syllables. 'Is there anything about that situation I should be aware of?'

He took a sip of water, his expression neutral, but there was a tick in the lower part of his jaw. 'My grandmother doesn't know the details of what happened, so she's unlikely to ask you. If it comes up, we should just stick to the line that you've helped me get over it.'

Her heart twisted sharply, unexpectedly, unwantedly. Because that one little lie revealed so, so much about Dante. Namely, that he wasn't over his ex-wife. That he thought he might need help to get over her. Charlotte tried not to think about it, not to unpack it, but the simple, throwaway sentence had lodged right in her sternum. He must have cared for his ex-wife a lot. She didn't know what had happened between them but, suddenly, Charlotte was aware of one thing for absolute certain. She'd never compare to Jamie. Not in Dante's eyes. Just like her mother had never been enough for her father and she, Charlotte, had never been enough for either of her parents to properly love her.

Dante was someone else who would always look at her and wish she was someone else.

She blinked down at her curry, but Charlotte was no longer hungry. Nonetheless, she speared a piece of broccoli and swooshed it around in the sauce. 'What else do I need to know?'

* * *

If this were a genuine relationship, and if he was planning on spending any more nights sleeping at Charlotte's, he would have already ordered a new mattress for her barely-double bed. How she got any sleep on that lumpy thing was beyond him.

Dante sure as hell hadn't been able to sleep. And not just because the size of the bed meant that every tiny movement either one of them made brought them back into contact and his body didn't seem to realise that they'd already slept together—twice—that night.

No, his body was firing with a whole heap of needs, apparently. And Charlotte was *right there*, in a soft, tiny camisole and boxer shorts. Her pale skin so smooth and silky. How he'd ached to just reach for her and start kissing those pillowy lips until she kissed him back and wrapped her arms around him… God, he wanted her.

So, he'd given up on sleep, given up on the bed, and taken the few steps into the living room to make himself a strong coffee—something he'd learned early on in this whole thing that he and Charlotte both shared a love of. He took the mug back into the living room, eyes landing first on the table at which they'd shared dinner and, after talking of Jamie, a whole heap of black and white biographical information.

What did you want to do when you were a kid? What did you study at university? What's your favourite restaurant?

He now knew that Charlotte liked Indian food but preferred pizza, that she loved to travel and had a huge bucket list of destinations, that she had turned down each of the headhunting calls she'd received in order to remain in the charity sector, that she loved designer clothes but only shopped at thrift shops and that she believed she had developed some kind of foot mutation that allowed her to live almost permanently in high heels and not feel their pinch.

Their conversation after Jamie had been like an extension of any of their others. Surface level and polite. Both instinctively avoiding anything that might dig too close to feelings. Anything that might inspire more questions than they wanted to answer.

He hadn't asked her about her mother, because he'd just known it was a no-go area for her. And besides knowing the other woman's name, and that she and Charlotte saw each other pretty regularly, he didn't need to know more.

Not for this to work.

He dragged a hand over his stubbled jaw, briefly contemplating exactly what 'this' was.

It had never occurred to him to get married just to appease his grandmother and assuage her concerns. But in recent months, with her health taking such an obvious decline and her worries for him clearly at the uppermost of her thoughts, no matter how often he sought to reassure her, Dante didn't, for even a moment, doubt that this was a good course of action.

He would never have concocted it, nor would he have suggested it, but Charlotte's needs so perfectly dovetailed with his own—and her insistence on all the barriers that he wanted kept in place meant they could rest assured that this was all perfectly business-like.

Except for when they touched, he thought with a hint of self-mockery. '

He took a sip of coffee, grimacing as the bitterness hit the back of his palette.

The problem was that Dante San Marino, amongst other things, ran a huge hedge fund. He analysed risk for a living and he was damned good at it. Which wasn't to say he didn't take risks. Some of his biggest wins had been off the back of deciding to stare uncertainty in the face. But he'd

always been prepared to gamble with money—because he had a lot of it.

But with his personal life it was different.

He'd gambled once, personally, and lost everything. More than he'd even known he'd had to give. He'd lived with a myriad of soul-destroying emotions for way more years than he should have, because he'd wanted to give Jamie absolutely everything in life.

Their marriage had almost destroyed him. Maybe it had. But work had brought him back. Work had been his touchstone, always. The arena in which he felt completely in control. Where he could click his fingers and make whatever he wanted happen.

Charlotte was too much of an unknown. He had to make sure he kept his walls in place, to keep her at arm's length, because there was no way he'd ever risk going through anything like he'd felt with Jamie.

It was just as well Charlotte felt exactly the same as he did.

Nonetheless, aware that she was sleeping in a room down the hall—though God knew how in that monstrosity of a bed—he grabbed a pen from beside the fruit bowl and scrawled a quick note on the back of an envelope:

I'll send a car to bring you to the airport tomorrow. D.

Just as he was about to leave, he remembered the ring. He hesitated a moment before pulling it from his pocket and placing it beside the envelope. He'd originally planned to give it to her over dinner, but why? What would the point of that have been? There was no need for romantic gestures with them. It was better to keep it unceremonious and simple, just like this whole relationship.

He pulled the door shut quietly behind him, not bothering to wonder why he was so keen to avoid waking her up.

CHAPTER SEVEN

THE SUNLIGHT CAUGHT the ring and made it glow like a dragon's eye, as Charlotte placed her hand on the railing of the plane steps and began to ascend them. True to his—written—word, Dante had sent a limousine to collect her that morning, just a few hours after she'd woken up and instinctively reached for him, needing his touch, wanting him, craving him. A short search of the apartment had revealed the note and the ring box.

And though the ring was utterly, incredibly beautiful, and not ostentatious rather than just perfect, she'd had a strange heaviness in the pit of her stomach ever since seeing it.

Because it was *too* perfect. Because it was just the kind of ring she might have wanted to choose if this had been real and she didn't want Dante to just get that about her. She didn't want him to be able to have that sort of insight. It unnerved her and made her question their ability to keep one another at arm's length, no matter how often they promised each other they would.

Except, it was obviously just a fluke. He'd probably walked into the jeweller, asked for something not-too-diamond-y and chosen the first thing he'd been presented with after that.

She paused, a few steps from the top of the plane stairs, throwing a glance over her shoulder back to the airport runway, looking at the car that had driven her here. The ring itself wasn't the sole reason she felt so weird and uncertain this morning.

It was everything about last night.

Things he'd revealed without meaning to. Things she'd wanted to admit to him, that she'd never told anyone other than Jane. It was the way they'd fallen asleep together—a first. But at some point in the night, Charlotte had woken up and realised he was still there and despite her every effort, something nice and warming had slid into place inside of her. Something she didn't ever want to feel because of a man but couldn't help in that moment.

For a little while, last night, she'd felt as though she were part of something special. As though she were part of something and someone. All her life she'd vowed to never want that. To never put herself in a position like her mother had, of relying on a man. Of relying on anyone, other than Jane. With Jane, she'd allowed herself to trust, to love, to rely.

But Jane was different.

Something had happened when they were young that had connected them, like siblings, but stronger. They both felt that bond and would always feel it.

Again, a hint of guilt shifted through her when she thought of her best friend and she crossed her fingers, hoping that she was more than a match for Zeus Papandreo's brand of arrogant charm.

Yes, she trusted Jane with her life. But there was only Jane.

The truth was, Charlotte's mother had been completely destroyed by her love affair gone wrong. She'd been cast out by her own family and her mental health had suffered throughout her life. Charlotte had, from a young age, been aware of the ravages her mother endured, but had been unable to help and had known, all the while, that she was to blame. That her existence had caused that pain. That ache. That brokenness.

Mariah, for her part, had tried to do her best for Charlotte, but Charlotte knew something that no child should ever have to grapple with—that her mother didn't love her. She couldn't

bring herself to. Because Charlotte was half Aristotle, she was a constant, living reminder of what Mariah would never have. Charlotte had been sent to boarding school, presumably to stop reminding Mariah of that romance. And from that point on, Charlotte had begun to train herself in living her most independent life and relying on nobody.

'Good, you're here.' Dante's voice popped through the bubble of her memories. She turned back towards the door of the private jet, stomach twisting at the sight of him. In another suit, despite the warmth of the day. Though as she watched, he removed the jacket and draped it over one shoulder. 'Are you coming?'

She ignored the double entendre. Or barely registered it. He'd caught her in a moment of heart vulnerability, when the past and all her wounds, were right at the surface of her mind, so she had to fight hard to wrap a protective cloak about herself and assume a look of nonchalance that befitted this scenario.

'Yep,' she said, after a beat, forcing a smile to her face and taking the rest of the steps, until she was on the little platform just outside the door.

'Good. The flight is ready for take-off.'

'Okay.'

Charlotte went to step inside but Dante didn't move, so the moment she did, they were close enough to touch and all the air in her lungs seemed to urgently need to escape. Her fingertips tingled with a desire to feel him. To brush over his hair or his shoulder. To dig into his neat hips.

'You need a new bed.'

It was the last thing she'd expected him to say. Her eyes widened as she glanced up at his face, frowning. 'I do?'

'Hell, yes. That thing barely passes as a bed.'

She laughed then, a natural and spontaneous sound. 'What's wrong with my bed?'

'Apart from the fact it's tiny and feels like it could break at any second, the mattress is lumpy.'

She laughed. 'Are you serious?'

'Deadly.'

'I would have thought you could handle a few bumps, Dante.'

His jaw clenched. 'I can sleep on a wooden floor if I have to. But not every night. You shouldn't be sleeping on that bed.'

'It's fine. It came with the place.'

He made a sound of disgust. 'Charlotte, you cannot be serious.'

'It's *fine*,' she repeated. 'Far better than lots of women have.'

'So you're going out in sympathy with Britain's unhoused population?'

She pulled a face.

'Because I can't see how you having a bad back and sleepless nights does anything to help anyone…'

'You'd be surprised what you can get used to. I don't even feel the springs any more.'

He shook his head. 'You can afford a new bed, can't you?'

'It's not about that.'

'This doesn't make sense.'

'Of course it doesn't make sense *to you*,' she said, shaking her head. 'Dante, tell me this,' she posited. 'How many cars do you own?'

He shrugged. 'I don't know.'

'But more than one,' she said, with confidence.

'Cars are collectible.'

'Cars are a terrible investment. They lose value the second you take them out of the showroom.'

'I don't collect them to make me money. I collect them because they're collectible.'

'And I'm not casting aspersions on your lifestyle choices,

even when I fundamentally disagree with them. I'm just saying—we're different people. And that's okay.'

'Good quality sleep is important for your health,' he continued, in a tone that reminded her a little of a headmaster.
'I don't know how you get anything done in the day after
spending the night on that piece of junk.'

She laughed again. 'You're ridiculous. It's totally fine.'

'It is not—,'

She pressed a finger to his lips. 'You're forgetting that
I probably weigh half what you do,' she said. 'The bed really doesn't bother me like it does you. But if it makes you
feel any better, you don't ever have to be in my bed again.'
As soon as she said it, she felt a strange, twisting ache, like
she'd just closed the door on something that she'd actually
really enjoyed. Having him in her space. Having him in her
bed. Warning sirens blared, but she ignored them. She was
in total control of this.

'Deal. My place it is from now on.' He looked down the
plane and nodded slightly. 'Take your seat, Shaw. It's show
time.'

In Dante's opinion, Charlotte Shaw always looked good
enough to eat. Scratch that. Pretty much any man on earth
would share that same view. But today, of all days, she looked
particularly, mouth-wateringly delectable, in skin-tight white
pants and a silky blouse that was just the perfect fit on her
slender frame, tucked in at the waist, but billowing a little
above, so he caught a hint—but not quite enough—of the
outline of her breasts. Her feet were encased in her usual sort
of shoe—heels—and her hair was long and loose around her
face, all fiery and wild, in a way that made him ache to drive
his hands through it.

Unbidden images of her from the night before raced
through his head. Just inside the door of her flat, for Christ's

sake he hadn't even been able to get three steps in the door, down on her knees. Taking him deep in her mouth, those perfect lips wrapping around him. He'd thought he'd died and gone to heaven.

Had she honestly been planning to marry someone else? Any guy who'd agree to her proposal? The thought turned the blood in his veins to ice. It was interesting to contemplate how much he hated that idea, even when he knew that their relationship was shallow, limited to sex, by mutual agreement.

'Hello, earth to Dante,' she clicked her fingers in his face, her expression now one of schoolmarm impatience. 'Are you even listening to me?'

'I wasn't,' he said, without a hint of apology.

Her brows lifted.

'Don't be hurt. I was thinking about you instead,' he said, voice gruff and deep, laced with the desire that was flooding his body.

Her cheeks glowed pink and her tongue darted out to moisten her lower lip, before she dragged it between her even white teeth. 'Down, boy,' she muttered, but her pupils were huge and he knew—because they'd been doing this for long enough—that she was finding it as hard as he was to ignore the sexual chemistry that fogged the air between them. 'This is study time,' she reprimanded in a mock cross tone.

'You're right. What have I missed?'

She pursed her lips in exasperation. 'Dante, we've been talking for ten minutes. Have you really not been paying attention?'

Had it been that long?

He pulled a face, shrugged and grinned. 'Start at the beginning,' he suggested, enjoying the way she rolled her eyes.

'I just gave you a very succinct biography of your life, which I've committed completely to memory I'll have you

know. But what I don't have much of an idea of is your grandmother.'

'My grandmother?'

Charlotte nodded. 'We didn't actually cover her last night.'

'Didn't we?' Dante felt the hint of misgivings. They'd done an exceptional job the night before of going over the basics. Actually, more than the basics. They'd gone over the essentials, the bread and butter facts a bonafide couple would know about each other. Just enough to get them out of trouble if his grandmother were to launch into some kind of interrogation. Which was not completely out of the question, given how much stock she put into Dante's 'happiness'. Never mind that her idea of happiness—a big, Italian family—didn't match up with his—no personal risks and being as successful as anyone could hope to be professionally.

'Nope. I mean, the fact that she raised you, that you respect and love her, but nothing else.'

'What do you want to know?' There was scepticism in his tone though, because he didn't want to keep having these kinds of conversations with her. He'd presumed they were done.

'What are her hobbies?'

He leaned back in his chair, giving that thought.

'Like, does she knit? Play bridge?'

He laughed then, shaking his head. 'You have the wrong idea about her.'

'So, what's the right idea?'

'For one thing, she's not someone who's giving in easily to the idea of aging. She might be an octogenarian but you wouldn't know it to look at her.'

Charlotte was silent, pointedly waiting for him to continue.

'She loves fashion,' he said, thoughtfully, remembering the whirlwind trips they'd take to Rome each year, so she could re-stock her wardrobe with the latest couture. 'It's her

one indulgence. She's always dressed immaculately. She always has been.'

Come to think of it, the same could be said for Charlotte. Except for last night, when he'd turned up at her place and she'd looked so beautifully mussed up, all casual and relaxed, that something had exploded inside of him. Her hair was the only concession to her inner-wildness, a mane of red that couldn't ever be fully tamed. God, how he loved to wrap his fist around it, to feel those curls spring against his palm.

'Okay. But what's she like?'

'Like?'

'Yeah.'

'What do you mean?'

Another roll of those deep green eyes. 'Is she funny? Intelligent? Was she cross with you as a child? Does she cook?' She asked shrugging. 'How would you describe her?'

He furrowed his brow, considering that. 'She was never cross with me,' he said. 'Which isn't to say I didn't deserve it.' A half-smile crossed his lips. 'I was always getting into some kind of mess.'

'You?' She sounded incredulous.

'Surely that cannot come as a surprise to you.'

'Well, yes, actually.'

'Why?'

'Because you're just not someone I can imagine ever breaking the rules.'

He laughed then. 'You're kidding?'

'No. You're hyper disciplined. It's part of what I like about you.'

'You mean one of the few things you like about me?' He teased because she'd said, that night she'd proposed to him, that she didn't actually like him at all.

'Right,' she nodded. 'Can I ask you something else?'

'You're done with my grandmother?'

'No, it has to do with her.'

He should have expected that. The sight of one of his air stewards entering the main body of the jet was a welcome relief.

'Can the interrogation wait until after refreshments?'

'By refreshments, please tell me you mean coffee.'

'I've got a theory, by the way,' he said, as the steward approached and placed a tray on the table between them. He saw Charlotte's eyes light up because there was indeed a pot of thick, dark coffee and two small cups.

'Oh, thank heavens,' she muttered. 'My machine wouldn't work this morning.'

He frowned. 'It was working fine for me.'

Her eyes lifted to his and something sparked in their depths. Something uncertain, or accusatory. 'What time did you leave, anyway?'

'I didn't look at the time,' he lied. 'Right around when I could feel my ribs bruising up thanks to your nightmare of a mattress.'

She rolled her eyes. 'You're such a snob.'

He laughed again. 'Which brings me back to my theory.'

'Oh god. Do I want to hear this?'

He grinned. 'You drink too much coffee.'

She visibly blanched.

'But I think it's because of your bed.'

She groaned. 'Not this again.'

'I'm serious. How can you possibly get a good night's sleep in that thing?'

'I will not have my love of coffee maligned. Nor my bed for that matter. And I have to tell you, you're the first man to complain about it.'

For the briefest of moments, every single part of him froze. Every. Single. Part. Even the parts that were in charge of keeping his blood pumping and his lungs inflating. It was

like someone unseen had waved a big magic wand and turned him completely to stone. Only for a moment. But her words were like magic—black magic—because out of nowhere, he was forced to contemplate the men who'd come before him. And he wasn't an idiot. There had been men. How many, he had no idea—that was just precisely the kind of information they didn't discuss.

And what did it matter? She hadn't been a virgin when they met. Beyond that, who cares?

Still, just the idea of the men who'd been with Charlotte, who'd gotten to drive her wild, who'd made her groan with pleasure, made him feel…angry. Angry like he'd felt the night he'd agreed to marry her.

Except, he realised now, it wasn't just anger. It was more complicated than that. It was a swirling vortex of darkness. Of jealousy—yes, he was jealous—and dislike. It was hatred and envy. It was ego and competitiveness. A need to know that he was the best, he was different. It was a soul-deep wish to be able to somehow go back in time and change everything around. But how the hell could he? Besides, he'd been married to Jamie and some of those years had even been happy ones, before their inability to conceive had soured every aspect of their lives. It was an errant, totally undeserved, unwarranted and unwanted reaction. A purely emotional response that he quickly talked himself out of. This was just casual. Fun. Nothing serious. Charlotte could sleep with whomever she wanted and so could he, when this was over.

'Coffee?' She prompted, having poured her own cup and now hovering the spout of the pot over his.

He nodded once. 'Please.'

'I sleep fine,' she said. 'It doesn't matter how much coffee I drink. When I'm tired, I sleep.'

He grunted, still not sure he was capable of more than a single syllable response.

'So, your *Nonna*. What should I call her?'

'Allegra,' he said, glad he didn't sound like the swirling darkness that was still inside of him, even as he tried to control it.

'What did Jamie call her?'

He sat up straighter, instantly uncomfortable. If imagining Charlotte with another man was unpleasant, hearing her refer to his ex-wife was even more so. '*Nonna*. But they'd known each other a long time.'

Her features did something funny. Something slightly resembling the whirlpool inside of him, before she smiled serenely and reached for her coffee cup.

'How did you meet?'

'My *Nonna*? I imagine shortly after my birth,' he said, deliberately misunderstanding.

'You and Jamie.'

He hesitated. 'My grandmother isn't going to ask you that.'

'I'm asking.'

His stomach tightened in an unmistakable warning sign. *Do not answer.* They weren't going to do this. Questions for the sake of thoroughness were one thing, but he had no intention of opening this particular door. But then again, it was a simple enough question. It was probably somewhere on the internet, in one of the pieces that had been written up when they'd gotten married.

'At an art gallery opening.'

Charlotte nodded thoughtfully. 'She's an artist?'

He shook his head.

'A patron of the arts?'

'She was a waitress.' He told himself to stop talking, but somehow found himself saying, 'Some guy kept hitting on her. He'd had too much to drink, wouldn't take no for an answer. Jamie ended up pressing her tray—filled with dainty little egg and caviar cups—at his chest. She got fired. I intervened.'

Charlotte's eyes widened but otherwise her features were unreadable. A perfectly controlled mask of casual interest, as befitted their perfectly casual interest in one another.

'And you fell in love?'

Again, he hesitated. 'Yes.'

He saw the way her brow beetled, the question in her eyes, and he felt an answering question inside his chest. He had loved Jamie. He'd cared for her, immensely, and he'd known she needed him—ever since that first night. What was that, if not love?

'I was young,' he heard himself say, remembering that night. 'And she was so different to anyone I'd ever known. Right away, I felt as though I needed to protect her. To keep her safe.' The word 'safe' sat in his throat like a boulder, because it was something he'd thought about for a long time. Why hadn't he been able to keep his parents safe? His grandfather? Why hadn't he somehow protected them from the accident? Why couldn't he go back in time and fix everything? He blanked the unsettling thoughts, frowning as he kept speaking. 'There was such a vulnerability to her. A raw realness that I'd never seen. I mean, all the girls I went to school with were so polished and confident, so sure of themselves and their place in the world. Sometimes, I felt like Jamie was walking around without a clue where she was going.' He feigned a shrug, but everything felt stiff and heavy. 'She was alone in the world. Orphaned, like me, but no *Nonna* to take her in. We had a lot in common on that front.'

'That explains why she and your grandmother were so close,' Charlotte said gently.

He clammed up. He had to.

Because if he didn't, he'd start talking about why having a family mattered so damned much to Jamie. Why she couldn't just let the idea go. Why it had almost driven her mad, the desperate need to conceive and to hold their baby

in her arms. Why she'd needed, more than anything, to feel that she belonged to a family, not just a partnership.

He felt his jaw tick as he turned away and looked out of the window. The seatbelt sign had been switched off right before the steward had appeared with morning tea and Dante took advantage of that now, unfastening his belt and standing abruptly.

'Excuse me, I'm going to check in with the flight deck.'

Charlotte didn't turn to watch him go, even though she was very, very tempted. And confused.

And…something else. Something she knew better than to think about, because it was part of the emotional toolkit she kept buried way, way down in the back of her brain. It was a part of her she wasn't even sure she had access to. She'd cut off the blood supply so long ago, for her own sake.

Because she wasn't going to turn into her mother.

Ever.

Nonetheless, Dante's words had seemed to be spilling out of him, almost against his will, and she was as mesmerised by the picture he painted as he seemed to be by the memory of Jamie and the feelings she'd evoked in him.

Something else had been perfectly clear to Charlotte, too.

The fact that when he'd described the women he'd gone to school with, the women he'd implied were a dime a dozen because he knew so many of them, Charlotte knew he saw her as one of them. Just like he'd enumerated. She was outwardly confident, composed, put together. Never in need of saving by anyone, ever.

Even now, when he'd stepped in to do her a favour, it was on her terms. Her rules. And her choice. She'd *chosen* him first, but if he'd stuck to his guns on the whole turning her down thing, she'd have found someone else and married them instead. In other words, she was happy to rely on someone

for help, so long as that someone knew that they were temporary and dispensable.

But the idea of Dante as a fixer, a saviour, took hold in her mind, and other parts of his personality started to make more and more sense. Suddenly, she could see him as someone who would want to swoop in and make someone's life better, who wouldn't be able to sit with injustice and unfairness. Was that the reason he'd had a change of heart regarding this marriage? She could have sworn he'd been jealous, but maybe that was ultimately irrelevant? Because not only was he fixing something for Charlotte, but also for his grandmother.

It all made complete sense. It was suddenly so logical and obvious as to why he had agreed to this.

But understanding him like this, seeing this side of him, represented a danger she feared it was too late to back away from. For the last six months, she'd been absolutely convinced that they were, as she'd said to him, chalk and cheese. She'd told herself, again and again, that their values and aspirations were completely different. That he was superficial and shallow, driven only by a capitalistic desire to earn more and more money.

But what if she'd been wrong about him? What if beneath that arrogant, self-assured exterior was a man who had a heart and who wanted to do the right thing by the people he cared about?

And why did understanding that about him leave her with an ache in the pit of her stomach, long after he'd left the cabin?

CHAPTER EIGHT

'SHOOT. CAN YOU give me a minute?' she asked, after reaching into her handbag and pulling out her cell phone. There were missed calls from Jane, and a text asking Charlotte to call her.

From the now open door to the airplane, Dante looked back at Charlotte, who was standing midway down the aisle.

His eyes roamed her face, a frown tweaking his lips. 'Of course. Is there a problem?'

She glanced back down at her phone and the text from Jane asking for Charlotte to call her. 'I hope not,' she said, then lifted a finger in the air. 'I won't be long.'

'I'll wait in the car. Take your time.'

She sunk back into one of the sumptuous leather seats, the plane engines having finally whirred to a stop and fallen silent.

Jane answered quickly. 'Finally!' she said down the line. 'I've been waiting for you to ring.'

'Sorry, I was on a flight.'

'To where?'

Charlotte bit into her lip and some warning light in her mind told her not to go into it now. Jane wouldn't approve of what Charlotte was doing. Oh, she knew Charlotte intended to get married, obviously, but not to Dante.

Not that Jane didn't like Dante. But the fact that he and Charlotte had been sleeping together and how messy it all

had the potential to be would make Jane want to swoop in and warn her away from some guy who'd been happy to have a sex-only relationship and was suddenly going to become her husband. And Jane wouldn't have been wrong.

'That…doesn't matter,' Lottie said, wishing her voice had sounded a little less frantic. But the enormity of what she was trying to do suddenly hit her like a tonne of bricks. Not just marrying Dante and somehow keeping everything between them as easy and unemotional as they both wanted—needed—it to be, but also the corporate coup she was attempting to mount.

'Is everything okay?'

'Fine. What's up?'

'I—,' Jane's voice faltered and concern for Jane immediately eclipsed everything else Charlotte might have felt.

'Is it Zeus?' She demanded swiftly. 'Are you okay?'

'I'm…yes. Of course. Why?'

Lottie sighed gratefully. 'I've just—I've been worrying that maybe I sent you on a quest to the lion's den. I couldn't live with myself if he hurt you too Jane.' God knew it was the truth, from the depths of her heart. What Jane had been through had traumatised her. Charlotte didn't want to add to that.

'He's not going to hurt me,' Jane said, with valour and determination in her words.

'God, I hope not. I wouldn't trust him as far as I could throw him.'

'He's not like we thought, Lottie.'

Jane's voice wobbled a little, her tone was soft and sweet. Something twisted inside Charlotte. Something dark and angry. Something laced with indignation. 'Oh?' She managed to say, but the word was bitten out with a hint of her feelings of betrayal.

'He's actually quite…nice.'

Charlotte jerked to a standing position, striding part way down the plane aisle, before stopping and thrusting a hand onto her hip.

'At least, he's not the complete piece of work we'd always presumed,' Jane continued meekly.

It was too much. Too much for Charlotte to hear. And from Jane of all people. Jane who was the one person that was always in Charlotte's corner. The one person she thought of as *her* person, who was supposed to fall in completely with Charlotte's thoughts, on almost everything. Certainly on the family members who'd screwed her over so totally all her life.

'I beg your pardon,' her voice shook with outrage. 'No one who goes through women like that is "nice".'

'I'm not saying he's perfect.'

'You hardly know him,' Charlotte pointed out logically, trying to reassure herself, as well as make Jane see sense. 'You've only been in Athens a few nights.'

'I know,' Jane replied crisply. 'I guess I just have a sense for—,'

Charlotte continued to walk towards the door, standing at the top of it and looking down on the scenery. The private air strip was in the middle of Tuscany and the hills rolled away from them on either side. 'Listen,' she said quickly. 'Nice or not, he's my sworn enemy and you're my best friend.' She tried to lighten her tone, to suppress the fact she was feeling let down by the one person she'd always been able to trust. 'I want that company,' she reminded Jane. 'And his father Aristotle has given me the perfect way to get it. To rip it out from *both* of them. It's not about Zeus. It's about my mother. What they took from her and took from me. It's about payback. It's about what I deserve.'

Damn straight, she added for good measure.

But a moment later, she had cause to regret her outburst, because Jane sniffed and whispered, 'I know.'

'Oh, God. Jane. You're crying. What's happened? Please, tell me. I can't bear for you to get hurt.'

'I just—,' Jane's voice wobbled some more. Down on the tarmac, Dante was standing beside the car, his shirt sleeves pushed up to his elbows, revealing his tanned skin. Her mouth went dry, despite her concern for her best friend.

'I want you to have everything you want, Lottie, you know that. But…'

Charlotte squeezed her eyes shut, because this was so completely, perfectly understandable, coming from Jane. Jane who had cried when they were fifteen and a butterfly had gotten trapped beneath a window right as someone had slammed it down—just the tip of its wing, enough to give the hope of salvation. But when Charlotte had thrust the window back up, the butterfly had been too crippled to fly. It had half-flapped but fallen to the ground. Jane had reacted immediately, bursting into tears at the sheer cruelty and unnecessariness of it. She was too, too kind.

'You don't want to hurt him,' Charlotte said, softly, knowingly. 'You're too kind,' she said, shaking her head, as Dante turned to her and put a hand on his hip. A gesture of impatience if ever she'd seen it. She had to focus Jane on the task at hand and then get off this plane. 'Look, he'll get over it. He'll get over you.'

'But not losing the business,' Jane whispered.

Charlotte brushed that aside. 'He'll still be worth a stinking fortune. He can rebuild, do something else. He can use the same damned name, for all I care.' She bit into her lower lip, trying something else, though feeling guilty for pushing Jane into something she clearly had issues with. 'Let me put it this way. What do you think he'll do if he gets married before me?'

There was silence.

Charlotte tightened her grip on her phone. 'Do you think he'll give one iota of thought about me?'

More silence.

'Of course he won't.' She imagined that future with a shudder. 'He'll take his triumph, his ownership of all things Papandreo, and that will be the end of it.'

'I'll stay for a week,' Jane conceived after a beat, sighing heavily. 'One week, to give you a head start. After that, I'm leaving Athens, and Zeus, and I don't ever want to hear his name again, okay?'

'A week?' Charlotte groaned, thinking of the time they were about to spend with Dante's grandmother. What if Allegra San Marino hated Charlotte? What if she didn't live up to the precious Jamie? What if Allegra disapproved of the marriage, Dante decided there was no longer any point to this for him and Charlotte was right back to square one?

But what if the opposite was true? What if Charlotte put on the performance of a lifetime this week, and Allegra San Marino *loved* her. To the point where there was no way on God's green earth that Dante could even consider walking away from her. Then, she'd be confident that no matter what, this wedding would go ahead, just as soon as legally possible.

'A week,' Charlotte repeated, fortified by the confidence that she *could* do this. She got people to part with millions of dollars for her charities, every day of the week. She was great at convincing people of things, great at winning them over. 'Okay, okay. I can work with that.' And she could. She had to.

Charlotte had grown up around money. Not just because of the tens of millions of pounds her biological father had squared away to bribe Charlotte's mother into silence. Charlotte's mother had bought a big old house in the Cotswolds and decorated it in a style that would have made Martha Stewart swoon. If she couldn't have her heart's desire, she

could at least live in the kind of house that people would drool over.

Not only that, but Charlotte had also gone to school with a host of girls from monied backgrounds. Girls whose parents were royalty, nobility, celebrities, or in the case of Jane, world-famous human rights lawyers. People who had a fortune at their fingertips and weren't afraid to show it.

Deep down, Charlotte had always, always despised that kind of ostentatious wealth. She'd hated it. She'd hated the inequities, the essential imbalances in the world, the sense that so many people were living without and so many just had way too much.

She'd turned her nose up at all of them, had bonded with Jane over their love of high street clothes. Although Charlotte had developed a preference after school for couture, though only if she could find it in a charity shop and thereby feel she was somehow playing out a sort of Robin Hood-esque fantasy.

And she particularly loved getting the overly wealthy to part with their money, to help those most in need.

So while she was perfectly *au fait* with the world of wealth, she hadn't been expecting a place like this when Dante had said he was bringing her home. It wasn't so much ostentatious as biblically perfect. It was as if the Garden of Eden had been brought back to life, right here in the foothills of Tuscany. The whole property was surrounded by thick, lush pine trees, making it impossible to see beyond them. But as the car entered through the wrought iron security gates, gravel crunching beneath the tyres, the property opened up to reveal gentle undulations, so darkly green they were almost impossible to believe. There were more pine trees inside, too, but here they were dotted over the lawns, creating long, dark shadows that would be utterly perfect to sit beneath on a too-hot summer's day. She could practically feel

how the grass would be cool, the air degrees more bearable there. She turned to face Dante, face showing surprise. 'This is where you grew up?'

His eyes raked her face. 'You're surprised.'

And wasn't that the truth? She felt an unexpected hangover from the flight. The sense that Dante wasn't at all as she'd thought. And now Charlotte was here with him, at his family estate, being forced to grapple with that on the fly.

'You just—,' her voice faltered, and she grimaced. 'I suppose I am.'

'Why?'

She turned back to her window and looked out once more, as the car cruised past a pond with a small timber jetty. Birds flew low over the pond, dipping down from time to time, as if looking for small fish.

Out of nowhere, she imagined Dante as a young boy, sitting on the jetty, feet dangling in the water.

'It's just so,' she sought for the right word. 'Natural.'

He made a sound, a gruff syllable of agreement. 'And?'

'You're—,' she turned back to look at him and something shifted into place, like all the lenses of a kaleidoscope being brought into focus. She was wrong to be surprised. Dante San Marino was nothing if not elemental and wild. True, he concealed that side of himself in his bespoke Sa-ville Row suits and urbane, arrogant manner, but she'd seen otherwise. She'd seen the side of him that was untamed and raw. Formed by the elements and totally wild, in so many ways. Best not think of that now, though.

'Never mind,' she said, focusing her attention through the middle of the car now, between the two front seats and the front windscreen. As the car swept around a corner of the drive, an amazing citrus grove came into sight. Not filled with small offerings, either, but rather, enormous, bushy cit-

rus trees, heavy with blossoms, ready to start growing fruit. She could just imagine how sweet it would smell.

Beyond the grove was the house and at the sight of it, Charlotte lost her breath completely.

It was the quintessential Tuscan villa, with the sand-coloured lime washed walls and terracotta tiled roof. But it was also enormous and gracious, with a hot-pink bougainvillea scrambling up one side and large pots standing sentry at the double width front door, each with an established fig tree.

'Dante,' she whispered, eyes wide, lips parted, unconscious of the way he was staring at her. 'It's so utterly perfect.'

He made another gruff sound. 'That's one way to win your way into my grandmother's affections.'

She blinked, trying to focus, to remember what she was doing here. Remembering that she needed to bring her A-game and that that started now.

Fortunately, it would not be at all difficult to show an admiration for this place. It was truly like heaven on earth.

'It's incredible,' she repeated, turning to face him. Out of nowhere she felt a wash of unexpected feelings, a rawness, and tears threatened.

She swallowed the ridiculously vulnerable emotion away. 'Are you ready?' She infused the words with a confidence she wasn't sure she felt.

His eyes roamed her features, and she had the unsettling sense that he'd perceived her momentary wrong-footing. But he smiled then, reached down and put his hand over hers. 'You're going to be a brilliant fake fiancé. Try not to worry, *cara*.'

Cara. Not Shaw. Somehow, just that single term of endearment threatened to undo a part of her she desperately needed to hold onto. Which was absurd, because he'd called her this

before and it hadn't made her heart beat like a trapped bird against her ribcage.

What on earth was happening to her?

As she stepped out of the car and was immediately enveloped by the heady fragrance of citrus blossoms, sunshine, nectar and pollen—so overpowering her nose tingled with the suggestion of a sneeze—she knew the answer.

Magic.

This place was sheer and absolute magic.

Allegra San Marino was both exactly like Charlotte had imagined, but also the complete opposite all at once. As Dante had described, his grandmother was incredibly elegant, in a pair of cream, wide-legged trousers and a pale-yellow singlet, that showed her toned arms and tanned skin. But she was also naturally very beautiful, with dark grey hair that she had coiled into a bun at the base of her neck and skin that looked to have been very well cared for all her life. She had eyes like Dante's, so dark they were almost black but glittery and perceptive, watching Charlotte from the moment she stepped from the car.

Allegra moved out of the shadows of the front entrance, onto the small, tiled portico.

Her nails were neat but manicured, and her smile was broad and welcoming, even when there was a hint of something in her eyes that spoke of doubt. Worry.

Which made precisely zero sense. If there was anyone on earth who was more than capable of handling themselves, it was Dante.

Even if he was hotter than Hades and richer than sin, and therefore probably batting off fortune hunters with a stick, this was *Dante*. A man who didn't suffer fools gladly and who would never be taken advantage of by anyone.

Whether because he too perceived a slight hint of concern

in his grandmother's features, or just because he'd primed himself to give an award-winning performance from the minute they arrived, Dante was at her side even before Charlotte realised he'd gotten out of the car He had one arm around her waist as he pulled her to his side and leaned down to whisper, 'This will not work if you look like you're about to get a root canal, Shaw.'

He was right, of course. There was a lot riding on the next week. She had to nail this. She glanced up at him and tried to imbue her features with an emotion she'd never personally felt—nor wanted to feel—love and smiled wide.

Apparently it worked. Or at least Dante registered the change, because his eyes widened for a moment, his lips compressed and the fingers at her side dug in a little, almost as if he couldn't help but tether himself to something real and physical, before walking forwards, his arm around her waist bringing her with him, whether her legs would oblige or not.

'Darling,' Allegra spoke in accented English, presumably out of deference to Charlotte. And Charlotte was glad. While she spoke passable Italian, it had been a while since she'd used it, and she suspected it was pretty rusty. 'Welcome, welcome,' she cooed.

Dante dropped his arm from around Charlotte's waist for a moment, so he could wrap his petite grandmother in an embrace and kiss her cheeks. 'It is good to see you, my Dante,' she said, face lighting up as if a thousand globes were behind her eyes. 'But you look too thin. You are not eating enough,' she tsked, then turned to Charlotte. 'He is never well looked after, except for here.'

Charlotte suppressed—just—a laugh, as she nodded and assumed an expression of serious contemplation. 'He is at risk of fading away,' she murmured, thinking the exact opposite. While there wasn't an ounce of unnecessary fat on Dante, that was because his body had been sculpted into a

form of muscle and strength. He was definitely not a waif. Allegra just had whatever the grandmotherly equivalent of rose-tinted glasses was.

Dante arched a brow and even though he didn't speak, Charlotte could practically *hear* his thoughts. *You've never complained about my body before.*

True that.

'And you have brought someone home with you,' Allegra continued, walking, with a slight limp, until she was close enough to look properly at Charlotte.

'Yes, *Nonna*. I wanted you to meet Charlotte, so that we could tell you our news, in person.'

Allegra went quite still, not quite touching Charlotte, though it had been her intention, Charlotte deduced, a moment ago. 'Your news?' She turned back to Dante, her back ramrod straight.

Dante was similarly still, assessing. This, after all, was the moment of truth for him. To see how well his grandmother would take the engagement and if it would alleviate the worries that he'd confided in Charlotte the older woman had been experiencing.

'We're getting married.'

Allegra paled a little, looking from Dante to Charlotte and back again. 'I'm sorry. Did you say—are you actually engaged?'

Her eyes dropped to Charlotte's hands, which were shaking a little. The ring was right there though, sparkly and beautiful, and, she realised, just the kind of ring Dante's grandmother would expect him to give the woman he loved. A gold band would never have sufficed. Not if this was to seem genuine.

So he'd chosen something big and stunning, whilst still keeping to her request that it not be a diamond that could be seen from outer space.

'To this woman?' Allegra repeated, glancing at Charlotte. Charlotte felt sympathy for Allegra because this news had clearly come totally out of the blue.

A muscle ticked in Dante's jaw as he stepped forward. Charlotte had thought he might be going to comfort his grandmother, to offer her support, but instead, it was Charlotte he crossed to, wrapping an arm back around her waist and pulling her to his side. She partly resented it—because it was just the kind of thing a man might do if he thought a woman needed his protection, for him to act like a shield, and that was definitely not Charlotte's shtick. She didn't need anyone and never would.

At the same time, his show of loyalty—even when she knew it was make-believe—was as warming as it was unnecessary.

'I know this must seem like a surprise,' Charlotte murmured, wondering if it was making things better or worse for her to speak, but knowing that she had too much riding on the success of this introduction to risk a negative impression. 'Dante insisted we tell you in person.'

'I wanted you to meet my fiancé,' he said, eyes crinkling at the corners as he looked down at Charlotte, doing an impersonation of a totally besotted fiancé that was every bit as spot on as her own had been a few moments earlier.

'I presumed you must be bringing a lady friend,' Allegra said, apparently bringing her surprise back in control. 'I just didn't know how serious it would be. My darling,' she approached Charlotte now, eyes blinking rapidly. 'Forgive me for my reaction. My grandson has always—how do you say it? Played his cards at his chest?'

Charlotte smiled kindly, relieved that the first hurdle was actually more of a minor speed bump.

'We've only just become engaged,' she promised. Then, with sincerity, 'You're the first person we've told.'

Allegra's eyes lit up. 'This calls for a celebration,' she clapped her hands together. 'Rosaria! Rosaria!' Her voice was loud and she turned quickly, striding back inside the doors of the house. 'Prosecco on the terrace,' she called, before whirling around to face them. 'How wonderful. Now, come on, I must hear absolutely everything,' she said, finally reaching for Charlotte and drawing her into an embrace. 'Welcome, my darling girl. Welcome to our family.'

Charlotte smiled, even when it felt, strangely, like a small part of her was withering and dying in response to such unexpected and wholesome kindness. And love. The kind of love she'd always shunned because it was easier to shun love than it was to seek it and know the pain of rejection.

CHAPTER NINE

IT BECAME ABUNDANTLY clear to Dante, within about ten minutes of arriving on the terrace and sitting down to enjoy a platter of food and bottle of ice-cold prosecco that his grandmother had managed to make appear so swiftly, that no matter how prepared they'd thought they were, it was definitely not going to be enough.

Not if they were going to get through this week unscathed.

Not if they were going to be able to convince his grandmother that they were truly in love. The kind of love where you knew not only the surface level, biographical details of a person's life, but also the dust and grime that resided in the nooks and crannies of their personalities.

Allegra was too skilled an investigator to outright ask for such details. No, she bided her time and dug around the edges. Watching with those eyes that reminded him, just briefly, of a crow's looking for a morning feast.

She might have left eighty in the rear-vision mirror several years ago, but Allegra could still run rings around just about anyone, intellectually. Something Charlotte was evidently recognising. She'd had one sip of prosecco then swapped to water, apparently deciding she needed to keep her wits about her.

Dante reached for a piece of bread and dipped it in oil— oil that he knew would have been produced from his grandfather's prized trees, on the southern edge of the property.

The trees were planted when Alberto had been a boy, by Alberto and his father, and they ran in straight lines from the base of the hill and halfway up it. It was the perfect vantage point, Alberto had once told Dante proudly, for the sun to catch the trees and make them grow lush with fruit. The oil was the most robust and spicy Dante had ever tried. Every year, Allegra would send several large, glass bottles to his home. It barely lasted six weeks.

'And how come I am the first to tell, eh? Not your own parents, *cara*?'

Charlotte glanced at him and he felt her reluctance, as surely as his grandmother would. Inwardly, he winced. Charlotte would need to get better at covering her reactions if she wanted to be able to keep her secrets.

'We'll go to Charlotte's mother next,' Dante smoothed over the slight bump.

'How come not first?' Allegra persisted.

'Are you complaining, *Nonna*? I would have thought you'd be thrilled to get the news before anyone else.'

'I am. But also curious.' She glanced back at Charlotte. 'You'll have to forgive me, Charlotte. At my age, I've learned to ask the questions I have when I have them. You never know if you'll get another chance.'

Charlotte's lips twisted with something like amusement. 'That's a trait I'm afraid we have in common. Dante will tell you that directness is something I have to constantly work to curb.'

He knew she was just forging a connection with Allegra but something about her statement made his insides harden with a need to reject that. Because it was completely inaccurate. Fortunately, he could see a way to kill two birds with one stone. 'You know there is not a single thing I would change about you, *mi'amore*,' Dante corrected, reaching out and putting a hand on Charlotte's knee. Then kicking him-

self because somehow, even here with his grandmother just a few feet away, his body went into overdrive at Charlotte's proximity, at the feel of her warm leg through the fabric of her pants, so he was suddenly forced to think of any number of unpalatable events just to get his body to *stop* stirring with unmistakable hunger.

He felt like some kind of out-of-control hormonal teenager, all over again, except even more out of control than the first time had ever been for Dante.

He ground his jaw, which made it a little harder to hold the carefree smile in place.

'The truth is,' Charlotte's voice faltered a little. 'My mother won't be that thrilled and we wanted to just take a little while longer to enjoy the news—to share it with a happy audience—before we broach the subject with her.'

A question readily sprung to Dante's lips but he stopped himself from asking it, just in time. Because naturally, as the doting fiancé, this was something he should already know.

'Why on earth would your mother not be happy?' Allegra asked, a hint of indignation in her voice. 'Is there a problem with my grandson, I wonder?'

'As if there could ever be a problem with Dante,' Charlotte volleyed back a similarly coy, affectionate response and Dante's gut rolled with something like admiration. She was a skilled actress, that was for sure. 'My mother just doesn't really approve of marriage. I was raised to see it as the exact opposite of what I should aspire to in life,' she added. Something in her voice told Dante that, though she was acting the part of his fiancé, this admission was the absolute truth.

And like any other truth she'd revealed to him during their acquaintance, it only served to spark a thousand more questions he wanted answers to.

'Interesting,' Allegra said. Dante recognised that tone. It was her prelude to more questions. More interrogation.

He knew he should say something to protect Charlotte, to move the questioning on, but out of a purely selfish desire to know more he didn't. He sat back in his seat, as though he were the most relaxed man on earth and moved his arm from Charlotte's knee to drape along the back of her chair instead, his fingers absentmindedly drawing circles against the silk of her blouse.

'And why should she hate marriage so much?' Allegra pounced, sipping her champagne and leaving a dusty pink lipstick mark at the top of the glass. 'Particularly when you have found someone who evidently makes you as happy as my Dante does.'

'My mother never had the good fortune to meet someone like Dante,' she admitted, with a small shrug of her shoulders that would have dislodged his touch if he had any interest in allowing it to do so. 'Perhaps if she had, she'd feel differently.'

'Your father?'

Here, Dante felt a prickle of compunction. It was a step too far. Despite his interest in the subject matter and what Charlotte was revealing about herself, he knew this was not a conversation she wanted to have.

'*Nonna*,' his voice held a warning, but Charlotte was answering anyway, as if he hadn't spoken.

'They weren't married and I wasn't planned. I've never met him.'

The words formed cool, logical statements. There was nothing in them that spoke of heartbreak. But he felt it. There was something in the way her whole body had gone stiff and sharp, the way she looked like she was holding herself together with sheer willpower alone.

'That might explain it,' Allegra said with a nod, then her face softened into a smile that was both content and devas-

tated. 'I was fortunate enough to meet the love of my life, though I had to wait a good while.'

'Oh?' Charlotte asked, He felt her exhale, as if sensing that the danger had passed.

'I was thirty by the time Alberto and I met. But I knew. I just knew.' Her smile was wistful. 'Like with you and Dante.'

Dante glanced at Charlotte and he was sucked back in time to that charity gala, when he'd seen her across the room and just *known*. Not that she was the love of his life—never again. But that she would be important, in some way. That he wanted her with the force of a thousand suns.

He was grateful Charlotte didn't look at him, because he wasn't sure what his features would reveal.

'Alberto was very like him, you know,' Allegra continued. 'Sometimes, I look at Dante, and I see so much of my husband, his grandfather—,'

Dante's heart turned over. His grandmother had never said that to him before.

'It's more than how they look, though. They are both so fiercely determined, so driven, so moralistic and strong, courageous too. Has he told you about the night he got lost in the woods?'

'*Nonna*,' his voice held a warning, but Allegra continued, unabashed.

'He was only nine. He had just moved here and after…the accident,' her voice faltered, 'well, it was a difficult time. He left the house, without me knowing, after dinner.'

'There was a cat,' he said, remembering the night. 'I followed it.'

'You disappeared,' she said. 'And I didn't realise, until the next morning. It was the middle of winter and he was out there in just his pyjamas. Can you imagine?'

'You must have been terrified.'

'I was terrified, he was not.'

'It was an adventure,' he said, with a lift of his shoulders. 'I am sure you shaved ten years off my life.'

'You seem to be doing just fine on that score,' Dante said.

Charlotte did glance at him then and though she smiled, he saw the slight hint of mockery in her eyes. The teasing impishness that was the perfect antidote to the strange barrage of feelings his grandmother was washing over them.

'He speaks very highly of you, Allegra.'

'Well, I'm not surprised. I do feed him very, very well and he was always a greedy child.'

Charlotte laughed and Dante felt warmth light every single part of him. He glanced away, towards the rolling hills, seeking comfort in their familiarity. Hoping that, with that one glance, he could see and feel just like he always did when he came home. Only, he'd never been home with Charlotte before.

'Now, darling, Dante knows the schedule I keep, but for your benefit, we have an *aperitivo* here each day around seven. Dinner is served at eight. Once upon a time, I would have insisted on a walk around the estate, following dinner, but I'm not quite up to that, these days. You, naturally, should enjoy the property, though. Dante knows the best paths. I do not eat a big breakfast, but there is always coffee and fruit, and Rosaria will make you anything you'd like. For lunch, we—,'

'*Nonna*,' Dante interrupted with an affectionate smile that was just about the *last* affectionate anything Charlotte could take from Dante. She'd gone from knowing they needed to give a stellar performance to feeling like she was drowning in a sea of confusion. Because he was *so good* at playing this part and she was *so good* at bouncing right back off of him, that it all felt so incredibly natural and dangerously, terrifyingly real.

She needed some space and she needed it immediately.

'You'll work it out,' Allegra confided.

'I had thought you would enjoy staying in the east wing, but a newly-engaged couple likes, more than anything, some space, so I have asked Rosaria to set up the pool house for you. It should be done, by now.'

'*Nonna*,' Dante's voice was lined with warmth. 'Please stop making Rosaria run around like this. Charlotte and I can take care of ourselves.'

'Oh, nonsense. You know she loves to fuss.'

'I know she loves you and would do anything you asked of her.'

Allegra's smile was one of genuine pleasure. 'Yes, dear. But lucky for her, I feel quite the same. Now, off you go, I'm going to take a little nap before the evening.'

Dante reached down and pressed a kiss to his grandmother's cheeks.

'I'm glad you came home, my darling. It never feels quite right without you.' Then, turning to Charlotte, 'And I am very pleased to meet you, Charlotte. You are quite lovely and I can see for myself how happy you make him. It has been a long time since he's been happier. I've wondered, sometimes, if he'd ever—,'

Charlotte felt Dante bristle beside her.

'But no matter. He is happy now and you must hurry up and get married, so I can once again feel a baby San Marino in my arms.' She clapped her hands together, totally unaware of the way Dante seemed to have almost stopped breathing. But Charlotte was. She felt it. She saw it. She just *knew* the throwaway line was wreaking havoc with his senses. 'I'm not getting any younger, you know,' she waggled a finger in their faces, laughed, and turned, leaving them alone on the terrace—Dante with a face that was ashen beneath his tan and eyes that swept shut just as soon as he could be sure his grandmother would not notice.

'Dante?' she moved to stand in front of him. 'Are you okay?'

He almost seemed to sway. She wondered, briefly, if he might be about to faint and quickly did the calculations on how someone of her size and stature might save a falling Dante from cracking his head against the ground.

But a moment later, he opened his eyes and seemed to stare right through Charlotte, almost like she didn't exist. 'I'm fine.' His smile was tight and dismissive, ice-cold and laced with rejection. It was in such stark contrast to the way he'd been looking at her whilst Allegra put them through their paces. Like the sun being rolled over by thick, grey storm clouds. She couldn't help but shiver.

'You don't look—,'

'I said, I'm fine. I just need a breather from all that fakery. I'll get Rosaria to show you to the pool house. Excuse me.'

'The pool house' was a heck of a misnomer, if ever there'd been one, Charlotte thought, as the housekeeper—a woman in perhaps her late fifties—showed Charlotte through the grounds. It was a short walk from the main house, over a red brick path that was lined on either side by lushly overgrown lavender bushes, fragrant with their bristly purple flowers reaching towards the sky. She reached for one as she passed, lifting it to her lips and trying to take some kind of comfort from the familiar scent. Her mother had a line of bushes, not dissimilar to this, surrounding her potager.

In truth, she needed to stay completely focused on the moment to keep Dante's harsh words from her mind. And the effect they'd had on her—acting like a lead weight so she was sucked ruthlessly quickly out of the lovely, warm, accepting bubble Allegra had so easily created for them on the sunlit terrace.

'It is not locked,' Rosaria said, her accent far thicker than

Allegra's. 'There is no need. The estate is secure.' Her smile beamed. 'You can press this button,' she gestured to a small white panel near the door. 'Any time. It connects to the house-keeping team.'

'Oh, good. So, it won't just bother you?'

'Not at all. There are a few of us, but Allegra prefers me above all else,' Rosaria said, her cheeks flushing with pleasure.

'How long have you worked here?' She asked.

'Oh, a very long time, now,' she said, rocking back on her heels a little, as if considering that. 'About a summer before—,' she glanced towards the house and lowered her voice. 'The accident.'

Charlotte's eyes narrowed. 'So you knew Dante back then.'

Rosaria nodded.

'So very sad,' she murmured, not meaning to pry, even when she totally did want to pry.

'A great tragedy. Allegra has never really been the same. Only with Dante does she light up, again. And for a while, with—,'

'Jamie,' Charlotte supplied, to save the other woman's obvious reluctance to mention Dante's ex-wife. 'It's okay,' she reassured her. 'I know how much she meant to Allegra. And Dante, come to think of it,' she said, glad that the words emerged without any hint of jealousy—as was appropriate, given that this was a fake relationship, admittedly with a serving of sex on the side.

'Yes, but now they have you,' Rosaria smiled brightly. 'Such wonderful news.' She glanced over Charlotte's shoulder. 'Should you need anything, just press the button.'

And with that, the housekeeper was gone.

Dante wasn't proud of himself for running away, but that was, nonetheless, exactly what he did. Despite the heat of the day, he set off from the villa in a long-legged stride that

carried him through the rose garden, past the koi pond and the potager, over a large field that sometimes housed goats and, finally, to the olive grove, with the lines and lines of thick-trunked trees and their silver leaved foliage.

There was something so familiar about this part of the estate, from the trees themselves to the way they smelt, to the sound of the leaves, rustling in the last afternoon breeze. He strode between their trunks, memories of his childhood particularly thick here, dousing him with a sense of history he wanted to fight.

He hadn't hesitated to bring Charlotte here. Obviously, it was the only way to convince his grandmother he was happy, that she could finally stop worrying about him. To give her the gift of complacency at the end of her life. But then, he hadn't really properly prepared for the reality of Charlotte being at his family home. Of seeing her dazzle his grandmother with her charm and quick wit. Of seeing her wrap the older woman around her finger, so to speak. He hadn't been prepared for how completely at home she'd seem here, how much she'd almost seem to belong.

In a way Jamie never really had.

Jamie had always been so nervous, like a meek little mouse, scared to break anything, scared to say the wrong thing, even when Allegra had blunted all her more forthright instincts and been gentle and soft.

No, Jamie was very different to Charlotte. But she'd still belonged, Dante reassured himself, with a slick of unpleasant disloyalty making him remember the past properly. Jamie had been his wife, his other half. And as such, she'd become a part of the family.

Why hadn't that been enough for her? Why couldn't she just accept that they weren't able to have children and move on?

He shook his head in frustration, dragging a hand through

his hair, thinking back to their marriage. Trying to pinpoint the exact moment he'd recognised what was happening. How fruitless it was to keep trying because she was starting to hate him. To resent him with the kind of bitterness that could never be erased. Whatever love there'd once been between them had died and they had both been simply going through the motions. Whether out of sheer stubbornness or loyalty, he couldn't say.

In some ways, it felt like a lifetime ago.

But when his grandmother had mentioned children, on the terrace this afternoon, he'd had a trauma response, plain and simple. Every part of him had seized up. He'd panicked. And he'd taken that out on Charlotte, Punishing her when she'd done nothing but play the part of his fake fiancé with absolute aplomb. Even when that had involved sharing more about herself than she might have liked.

She'd done her best for him and he'd thanked her by being rude and obnoxious.

She deserved, at the very least, to know why.

CHAPTER TEN

THE POOL HOUSE looked to have been built more recently than the main villa, which had the markers of being genuinely old. Whereas this might have been added some time in the last few decades, she guessed, going by the finishings. However, it had been constructed in a style that was faithful to the period of the main house, with walls that matched and the same terracotta tiles. The gardens surrounding the pool house were established, filled with lush trees and hedges, giving it even more of the eden-esque feeling that shrouded the whole estate. But at the front, near the door, was the pool. Not like a normal suburban pool, this had more the feel of a lake, except she could see it was man-made. The shape was irregular, designed to look like it had been formed by the earth, and it was large enough to easily swim proper laps. She moved towards the water, absentmindedly crouching down to feel the water with her fingertips.

The sun was dropping lower in the sky. Charlotte glanced towards the main house—part of which was just visible from where she was—and contemplated the *aperitivo* hour Allegra had nominated. What exactly would she say if Dante still hadn't reappeared?

The whole point of this trip was to convince his grandmother that they were in love so she'd stop worrying about him. Well, Charlotte thought they'd done a pretty good job of that so far, but Dante had totally flipped out. She replayed

the afternoon in her mind, trying to pinpoint the precise moment it had all become too much for him, and drew a blank. The best she could guess was that it had been Allegra's parting remark about having children.

So what?

It was just an old lady's wishful thinking—and there was nothing surprising in the sentiment. Dante himself had told Charlotte how much family meant to Allegra. Naturally, she'd like to see her grandson creating more of that very same thing—family.

It didn't matter that he didn't share those aspirations. He'd told Charlotte he never wanted children. Fine. But why let his grandmother's comment get so far under his skin?

Unless it hadn't specifically been that comment. Allegra had also waxed lyrical about how happy Dante seemed, how she wasn't sure she'd seen him happier. For a man who was clearly still hung up on his ex, maybe that had been too much?

I just need a breather from all that fakery.

Fakery.

Charlotte's frown deepened as she made her way back into the house and into the bedroom, where someone had unpacked her suitcase already. She removed a chic emerald-green dress from the wardrobe and held it against herself.

Armour.

Protection.

It was a stunning, simple dress in which she always felt her best. And she needed that tonight, because Dante's comment had *hurt* her.

It had cut her to the core. In a moment of warmth, when she'd expected at least gratitude and relief, and at most triumph, he'd belittled their accomplishments. No. He'd belittled *them*. She pulled her hair over one shoulder as she contemplated that.

There was no 'them' and yet there was. Even though they weren't a couple, in the traditional sense, they'd been sleeping together, casually, for months. That, in and of itself, required mutual respect. In that moment, he'd disrespected her. After all, their 'fakery' for Allegra wasn't Charlotte's idea, it was Dante's. Dante who wanted to assuage his grandmother's concerns and set her mind at ease for the final chapter of her life. Dante who *wanted* the fakery. Who'd insisted it needed to be done well.

Charlotte swallowed past an odd lump that had formed in her throat.

In the bathroom, she undressed and took a quick shower, running the loofah over her body until it was sudsy and soft, trying to push his comment to the back of her mind. Trying to partition it off, as she had so many other hurts in her life.

But none like this.

None of the men she'd casually dated before Dante had *ever* hurt her. Charlotte had never put herself in the position where they might. It had been the very definition of casual. Fun and easy, but the moment it had stopped being either of those things, she'd ended it and gotten on with her life. Charlotte was not someone who required the company of a man—she would always have preferred to be single than feel that she needed to have someone else in her life. In any event, she had Jane and her work, and the people she helped through that work. That had always been enough for Charlotte. It had had to be. There was no way she'd ever allow herself to be weak like her mother. To be hurt and discarded as her mother had been.

No, when it came to men, Charlotte called the shots. She took what she wanted for just as long as it suited her and then she walked away.

She supposed she should also thank her birth father for that. After all, if he hadn't treated her mother so badly, and

his wife come to think of it, perhaps Charlotte wouldn't have developed such a tough outer shell. If he hadn't spent a lifetime ignoring her, financially compelling her to stay hidden, to conceal her true identity from the entire world, maybe she would have believed in the possibility of love and happily ever after. Charlotte was glad that wasn't the case though. It was so much easier this way. So much better.

The problem was she couldn't walk away from Dante. Even though this didn't feel casual, easy or fun now. Even though this was the exact moment she might ordinarily choose to paste a smile on her face and say something like, 'Great knowing you, see you later!' She couldn't do that and keep the company.

Charlotte groaned, dropping her head forward and pressing it against the cool tiles, blindly reaching out and turning off the water.

This had been a *stupid* idea. A very, very stupid idea. Asking Dante to be her fake husband had seemed like the right choice, at the time. But they had too much other stuff going on, even when it was just physical, to make it easy to keep things light.

She should have found someone new, offered them money in exchange for marriage, and had them sign a watertight non-disclosure agreement. Not that it would have mattered, anyway. The lawyers hadn't stipulated that the marriage had to be a love match. Just a marriage, in the legal sense of the word. She could have married any guy off the street to meet the terms.

Another groan, as she pushed the shower screen open and reached for a large, fluffy white towel, wrapping it around herself and patting her skin dry.

She glanced at her reflection in the mirror, amazed when the face that stared back at her looked so completely like herself. There was no hint of her remorse and inner turmoil

on the familiar arrangement of her features. Outwardly, she just looked like Charlotte Shaw.

Fakery indeed.

She pushed open the door that joined the ensuite bathroom and the bedroom and startled because Dante was sitting on the edge of the bed, legs spread wide, elbows pressed into his thighs.

She made a sound of genuine surprise and he looked up, but slowly. Or maybe it was that everything was moving in slow motion, all of a sudden?

A gentle breeze brushed over her skin, courtesy of one of the open windows.

He looked at her with those dark eyes that saw too much, but Charlotte wasn't really sure he was seeing anything.

'Good,' she said, brightly, with more of that perfect fakery. 'We need to get to your grandmother's.'

'Yes,' he said, nodding once. 'But first, we should talk.'

Her stomach dropped to her feet.

Talk.

Fear gripped her heart; ice flooded her veins. This was all getting too complicated. Too hard. Too…real. She didn't want him to bare his soul to her, even when a part of her did want precisely that. And she sure as heck didn't want him to say he was sick of the 'fakery' and that they should end this. Either way, talking was *bad*. It was everything she avoided. And him, too, she wanted to remind him.

She swallowed quickly. 'That's not necessary,' she assured him, looking around for the dress she'd discarded earlier. Dante had moved it, from the bed to the back of a nearby chair. 'There's nothing to talk about.'

He frowned, but she turned away at that moment, dropping her towel and reaching for some underwear from the drawers.

She felt his eyes on her but more than that, she felt the pull of his doubts. She felt the part of him that wanted to explain

why he'd snapped like that, and she felt the part of him that just wanted to accept her easy rationale.

Her dress was next. She slipped it over her body, then turned to face him. He was sitting right where he'd been a moment earlier, but his head had angled to follow her. Only when he looked at her, Charlotte had the feeling he was hardly seeing her at all.

'Dante, do you still want to go through with this?' She asked the question with a tummy ache of doubt and worry. If he said no, she'd have to fly straight back to London, to start husband hunting. She could find someone else. She would have to.

So why did the very idea leave her ice cold? Was it because Allegra had been so warm and welcoming, and Charlotte hated the idea of the older woman learning that it had all been a deception? Or did it have more to do with Dante and the idea of never seeing him again?

He dragged a hand through his hair and stood, walking towards her then. She was reminded, powerfully and overwhelmingly, of their size difference.

He pressed his palm to her cheek, cupping it, angling her face to his, so their eyes met, and the breath in her lungs seemed suddenly too hot. 'I gave you my word,' he said, simply.

Which should have reassured her, but it really didn't. She was starting to realise that Dante was someone who wanted to fix everything and that included his grandmother's happiness. She knew it to be true. She'd used it as a bargaining chip. To motivate him to agree to this. But what if he was prioritising his grandmother's happiness above his own? What if this whole arrangement was actually a huge mistake for him? She was using him to get what she wanted and she'd known just which lever to pull to get him to agree. How could she not regret that now?

'Yes, but I can give it back,' she said, hating that her voice wobbled slightly to her ears. 'We don't have to do this. I can find someone else to play my fake husband.'

His eyes closed, as if he was physically rejecting that idea, but Charlotte knew that not to be the case.

'I'm serious, Dante. This wasn't supposed to be a big deal. I just chose you because you were there. We were sleeping together. It made sense.'

He made a noise then, one she couldn't interpret.

'It's just pretend,' she said, wishing she believed herself one hundred per cent. 'Fakery, like you said.'

His eyes opened then, lancing her with their intensity. 'You are very, very good at it.'

Why did that sound like an insult? She shrugged one slender shoulder. 'So are you.'

His smile was ice cold, totally lacking in the warmth she'd seen that afternoon, and her heart hurt. Hurt in a way she was terrified of. Hurt in a way she ran a mile from. In fact, that's exactly what she wanted to do. To pack her bag and get out of there. Tell Allegra it had all been a big mistake and just go home. Forget she was a Papandreo. Forget the fact her father had ignored her for her entire life.

But how could she?

The most important thing in her world was the acquisition of her father's company. Righting a wrong that had been perpetuated against her, time and time again, and also against her mother. Wasn't revenge worth almost any cost?

And if Dante were to become collateral damage? A voice in the back of her mind demanded.

Only, he wouldn't. She'd make sure of it. After all, they'd been sleeping together for six months and had no difficulty in keeping things simple and easy—in making sure their feelings didn't enter the equation. They'd just keep doing the same thing now.

'Dante, we don't need to talk. We don't need to dig deeper, to share secrets. Remember? That's our rule and it's a good one. If this is going to work, and we're both going to emerge unscathed, we need to keep things compartmentalised.'

'And those compartments are?'

'Well, I would like to think we can keep doing this,' she said, lowering a hand and brushing it over his pants, dragging—somehow—a flirtatious smile up from the pits of her belly. No mean feat when she felt as though her insides were being shredded. 'But as for the marriage, it's really just a professional relationship. We struck a deal. We know what the requirements are. Neither of us want the lines to get blurred, right? We've said that before and we both still think it?'

'Are you asking me, or telling me?'

She hesitated. Great question. Of course. 'Telling you,' she insisted, even though the insistence was more a case of bravado than anything else.

'Okay.' He took a step backwards, his expression totally unreadable. The second he put physical space between them, her whole body trembled with a deep and profound sense of loss. Of need. Of grief.

She spun away, terrified all of a sudden by whatever was happening. Because despite what she'd just said, Charlotte was not sure she could even *find* the lines they'd initially drawn, let alone keep to them. Which was all the more reason to *pretend*, she reminded herself. She had to pretend until it became second nature and everything felt normal again.

'Why don't you freshen up while I finish getting ready?' she suggested, her voice almost totally normal seeming. 'You grandmother will be expecting us.'

He left the room without another word.

If there was one thing Dante hated in this world above all others, it was a sense of having lost control. He had always

been able to bend things—including people—to his will. Through hard work, determination, charm, intelligence and the fact he'd always had money at his disposal, he'd been able to make pretty much any situation work to his advantage. Of course, having lost his parents and grandfather the way he did had shown him that control was not always possible—or he would have somehow found a way to bring them back to life. He had no delusions of God-like grandeur, but for the most part, he exercised discipline over all aspects of his life.

His marriage had been a notable exception.

No matter what they'd tried, which doctors they'd consulted, they had never been able to conceive. It hadn't mattered what reassurances he'd given Jamie, their lack of fertility had destroyed her and ultimately their marriage.

Though not on the same scale, a similar sense of spinning wildly off course was hurtling through him now and had been all evening.

He'd gone to the pool house with every intention of telling Charlotte about his marriage, the divorce and their reasons for it. But she'd stone-walled him straight off the bat, making him wonder if his instincts to confide in her—to enable them to play their roles more easily—was wide of the mark.

She'd seemed brittle, though. She said one thing, but he *felt* something else coming from her, he just couldn't quite put his finger on it.

And whatever it was, whether ambivalence or regret, or something else entirely, there was no sign of it now. From the moment Allegra had welcomed them back to the main house, Charlotte had sparkled. There was no other word for it. She'd smiled and laughed, amused and charmed. He found it impossible to look away from her. She simply shone.

Allegra saw it, too, he was certain of it.

His grandmother was someone else who shone, and always had, and it was like two bright, buzzing fireflies had

found each other. They spoke of art and music, discovered a shared love of opera, swapped anecdotes about the performances they'd been to. Charlotte spoke about her work and the passion she felt for helping people—aware that she came from a privileged background and that she felt a duty to enrich the lives of people who were not so fortunate.

To look at her that night, he wouldn't have possibly been able to guess that there was even a hint of doubt in her about what they were doing. Nor that she'd seemed somehow uncertain, earlier, in the pool house.

She was a total contradiction.

He was out of control.

And he hated it.

He hated it during the dinner—the more she sparkled, the more he glowered—and he hated it even after they'd left, when Charlotte's performance slipped and she became herself again, and he sensed the same reservation in her he'd felt earlier, in the pool house.

They walked side by side, down the path to the cottage, in a silence that was not, in Dante's opinion, companionable. In fact, each step they took only added to his sense of being out of control—and pissed off.

'You know,' she said, as they approached the pool house and the lights cast a soft golden glow on them. 'I really don't get you.'

He glanced at her, jaw clenched. In that moment, he didn't get himself, either. 'No?'

'You're the one who brought me here.'

'Your point?'

'You could have come on your own and told her about me.'

'She would have thought that strange.'

'Okay, fine. But you still could have left me in London. We didn't have to do this together.'

'In order to convince her...'

'There's no way that lovely woman, who thinks the sun shines out of you, would ever doubt your word, Dante,' Charlotte hissed. 'You could have come on your own.'

'I'm still at a loss as to the point you're making.'

'You brought me here and I'm doing my absolute best to be the perfect imaginary fiancé, but you're not pulling your weight.' She jabbed a finger into his chest, then. 'I don't know what's going on with you, but you were like a stone all night tonight. I had to basically spin plates on my fingers to keep your grandmother from noticing.'

He grimaced at her fair charge.

'So? What's the problem?'

He'd never really seen Charlotte angry before, but she was a passionate woman, and this side of her was just the flip-side of that passion.

'You did a good enough job of convincing her for the both of us.'

'Not this again,' she groaned. 'You really are unbeliev-able, do you know that?'

'How so?'

'You keep accusing me of being good at what you've asked me to do, like it's some kind of failing. This is our deal, isn't it?'

'Yes,' he agreed, his gut tightening. He hated everything about this, suddenly. Being here, under these circumstances. Fighting with Charlotte. Being her fake fiancé. Knowing that they'd gone too far to undo any of it.

'Well then, why aren't you doing your bit?'

He clamped his lips together, searching for a way to explain.

'God, Dante,' she threw her hands in the air, frustration obvious. 'You need to get yourself together or this is never going to work.' She turned, to walk away, but he reached down and grabbed her wrist, spinning her back to him.

Fire sparked in the depths of her eyes. 'What?'

Frustration burst through him, like a lightning bolt. Fierce and bright, burning him all over.

'What?' she demanded, so he felt her frustration, too.

'Damn it, Charlotte,' he said, the words far from cold.

'Why? Damn what?'

'You act like this is easy. You act like—,'

'Like what?' she shouted, then lowered her voice. 'I act like we agreed I would act. How you're supposed to be acting.'

That was true. So why was he finding it so hard to play the part? Why couldn't he just roll up his sleeves and treat her like a beloved fiancé? Why was it that the more time they spent together, the more he found acting that part impossible?

'You wanted to make your grandmother happy and I'm trying. Isn't that what you want?'

What he wanted? He had no idea any more. It all seemed so stupid. But then he thought of Allegra and how hard she'd found his marriage breakdown, how she'd pined for his happiness ever since. He thought of how she'd been after her stroke, six months earlier—right before he'd met Charlotte, in fact. He thought of how hard she'd fought to recover. All the physical therapy sessions, the cognitive work, so the only lingering sign of her stroke now was the slight limp she carried.

'You've turned to stone again,' she snapped and pulled her hand free.

'I'm not stone,' he muttered.

'You're acting like it.'

He moved closer to her, putting his hands on her hips, staring down at her with all of the frustration that had taken up residence in his body. 'I am more than happy to demonstrate how wrong you are,' he said. Suddenly, all he could think about was the physical side of this and how everything made sense when they were together. How if they made love,

he wouldn't have to think about the confusion inside of him. Because when they were in bed, he was back in control, driving her wild, mastering her completely.

'Oh yeah?' she asked, still angry, but also, breathlessly. The same tug that dominated Dante was clearly throbbing through her, too.

His response was to stare down at her, his eyes probing hers, until her lips parted and her cheeks were flushed.

'Fine,' she muttered. 'Show me.'

He didn't need to be asked twice. He leaned down and lifted her around the waist, throwing her over his shoulder, ignoring her sound of surprise. Suddenly, he was all neolithic cave man, and she was his conquest. Nothing mattered but this.

Afterwards, he'd face the music, whatever it might be, but for now, he just wanted to be with her and make the rest of the world, his questions, doubts, uncertainty, be utterly, completely silenced.

CHAPTER ELEVEN

CHARLOTTE WAS OUT of breath and out of fucks to give. She really was.

She'd been fuming mad after their dinner with Allegra, but it hadn't even been Dante's fault. Sure, he'd sat through the meal like an inert lump, for much of the time speaking only when spoken to and hardly evincing a loved-up fiancé vibe. But it was how much Charlotte *noticed*—how much she *cared*—that had really gotten under her skin.

She had genuinely enjoyed getting to know his grandmother—a woman with whom she had a great number of overlapping interests, in fact. But all night, half of her brain had been focused on Dante. Wondering about him, worrying about him, stressing that this whole fake engagement had been too much to ask of the man.

A man who clearly had a saviour complex, who'd seen a woman in distress, in need of 'rescuing', even though that was the very last thing she'd ever knowingly convey. Even though it was the last thing she wanted to feel or need. Had she guilted him into this? She'd known just which buttons to press—his worry for his grandmother—and she'd used that to her advantage. His first instinct had been to run a mile. Had it been the correct one?

But then, what about this?

Beside her, Dante lay on his back, staring at the ceiling, his cheeks flushed, his chest moving with each breath he

took and expelled. *This* was something neither had wanted to step away from, just yet. They hadn't been ready.

Another thing that terrified her.

Dante turned at that moment and caught her looking at him. He didn't smile. His face remained as it had before. Stony. Cold.

In contrast to the white hot way he'd just made love to her. Hard, fast, desperate, passionate, as though she was the beginning and end of his universe. As though he craved her with an almost life-sustaining passion.

Only, no, she was wrong. He wasn't completely cold. She knew that now. She'd probably known it for a long time, but seeing him with his grandmother, and here in Tuscany, it was impossible to pretend any longer. He might have acted like an emotional automaton but, beneath the surface, he did have a heart. And she suspected he knew how to use it. He would never use it with her, but it was there, beating and warm.

So he wasn't cold, so much as confused or distracted. Like something was weighing on his mind. As it was on hers. But the problem was, Charlotte didn't want to talk about it, because her gut instinct was that talking about it would make everything so much worse.

And yet…that damned part of her, that was constantly at war with common sense, was banging into her brain, pushing against what she knew she should say and do and what she *wanted* to ask.

She bit into her lip, as if to physically stop herself from asking him anything.

But Dante was moving, shifting onto his elbow, so he was facing her and looking at her with an expression that was half grim, half accepting.

'I need to tell you about my wife.'

Something tightened in the very centre of Charlotte's

chest, as if a vice had been applied to her organs. She shook her head, but no other denial came out.

'Partly, because you deserve to know. Partly because it will make this easier. And partly, because I just…want to tell you.'

Her lips parted at that last sentence. It seemed to Charlotte that Dante had been waging the exact same war she had—a battle between good intentions and wants.

She pressed a finger to his lips. 'I don't need to know.'

'Why are you fighting this?' he pushed. 'Do you think that knowing this about me will fundamentally change what we are?' His eyes scanned hers.

How did he know that? How could he understand the tightrope she was carefully walking, even when she'd exercised such diligence in concealing anything that might give her away?

'I'm not afraid,' she lied.

'Listen to me, Charlotte. I want to tell you for that exact reason—so you can understand why I am the way that I am. Why I will never really get married again—not in the real sense of the word. Why this,' he gestured from his chest to hers. 'Is all we can ever be.'

'You say that like I'm asking for more.'

'I say it like a man who can read the situation, *cara*.'

Her spine prickled with goosebumps.

'We're good together,' he said, simply. 'In another world, if we were different people, with different pasts, we could make something truly good come out of this. But we've both lived lives that have made us want to run from love.'

She drew in a deep breath. 'Dante, stop. You're grossly misunderstanding what I want.'

His lips twisted. 'I know you do not love me, don't worry. But we both see the danger here. It is the only reason I can

think of that we are both so desperate to keep reinforcing our rules. Why we keep insisting it's just about sex.'

'It is—,'

'Yes,' he interrupted. 'And I am about to explain why, for my part at least.'

She glanced down at the crisp white sheet between them, dropping her hand from his lips and giving up on arguing with him. In other words, letting the curious part of herself win the battle, finally. But that didn't matter. Charlotte would win the war. She would protect herself with every last fibre of her being.

And in doing so, she'd protect Dante, because they both wanted the exact same thing—security. A guarantee that this relationship would leave them unscathed.

'For the first year or two of my marriage, Jamie and I were very happy together. We were young and in love, and we had everything we could possibly want in life. We travelled, we connected, we spent as much time together as we possibly could—which was, actually, not that much because I worked a lot then. As I do now,' he conceded.

Charlotte's stomach felt mushy. She didn't want to hear this, even though she was hanging on his every word, with some kind of masochistic fascination.

'I've often wondered if that was part of it.'

'Part of what?' she prompted, when he didn't continue.

His eyes latched to hers, but in a manner that made her feel he wasn't really seeing her any more. He was back in the past, looking at Jamie, looking at himself, in that oddly distorting way memories had.

'Why she was so desperate for more?'

'More? Are you saying she cheated?'

He shook his head. 'Jamie would never do that.'

Something barbed her side. Hurt. Betrayal. Jealousy. Sharp

enough to seem like an electric shock. He defended her automatically. Spoke of his ex-wife with reverence.

Charlotte blinked away, hating her visceral response to that. Hating that he could evoke anything like that in her.

'Then what?' Her voice emerged a little gravelled.

'She wanted a baby,' he said, the words heavy and scathing.

'Oh.' Charlotte frowned. 'I see.' She didn't. While she'd known for a long time that she'd never get married, or have children, she also knew that many people out there felt the exact opposite. A lot of people grew up with that biological urge to procreate hard-wired into their brains.

'I doubt it,' Dante muttered, looking at her now with something in the depths of his eyes that made her head hurt. Or was that her heart? Because for a moment, he looked truly vulnerable. Sore. And she yearned to reach out and draw him into a hug. To tell him that it was okay. That no matter what he was feeling, it would all be fine eventually.

She stayed right where she was though, one hand forming a fist at her side, beneath the sheet, where he wouldn't see it. She dug her fingernails into her palms so hard she knew they'd form little crescent moon indents.

'She wanted a family,' he said. 'And I loved her enough to give her anything. I didn't have strong feelings, one way or another, back then. I was focused on my career and then on Jamie. It was enough for me.'

'But it wasn't for her.'

He shook his head. 'She'd always wanted a big home, filled with people, bursting at the seams of love. And I wanted to give that to her. I would have done anything, Charlotte. Anything.'

She nodded, slowly, because she was pretty confident that Dante didn't have children. It wasn't the sort of thing he'd

have failed to mention, after their various conversations surrounding the matter of permanence.

'We tried.'

Her heart panged at the oblique reference to his sex life with the other woman. She tried to blot it out and focus purely on the admission he was making, and on how hard it was for him to get this out. On the fact that she suspected this was not something he'd told many people, if anyone.

'We tried for a long time, taking comfort from all the websites that said you shouldn't be worried until after twelve months, that it didn't necessarily mean anything was wrong. And then, we began the testing and then the IVF.'

Sympathy swirled inside Charlotte. 'What happened?'

'Charlotte had a condition that made it difficult to conceive naturally. IVF was successful, on multiple occasions, but each time, she miscarried.'

'Oh, no,' Charlotte whispered, tears sparkling on her lashes, despite her intention to keep everything about Dante at arm's length. 'I'm so sorry, that's awful.'

'Yes, it was. Awful. Disheartening. Our marriage turned into an endless round of trying to conceive, failing, succeeding then losing the baby, just a constant pressure. Jamie was obsessed and the more she wanted, the more I felt a weight that I almost couldn't bear.' He drew in a deep breath. 'I felt like a failure,' he muttered. 'The one thing my wife wanted and I could not give it to her. All the money in all the world, all the best doctors, and we could not succeed.'

'What about surrogacy?' she whispered.

'We tried it. Our surrogate lost the baby.'

'Oh, Dante,' a tear slid down her cheek. 'I don't know what to say.'

His eyes lifted to hers and his lips tugged downwards. 'I'm not telling you because I require sympathy, nor because I think there is anything you can say that will alleviate this,

here, that I feel,' he pressed his fingers to the space between his rib cage and Charlotte's blood ran cold at the clear allusion to his love for his ex-wife. 'I have been torn apart by guilt for so long, I don't know any other way to feel.'

'Guilt?'

'I couldn't give her what she wanted, don't you understand that?'

'Yes. I do. And while that's very sad, Dante…it's just, not your fault.'

'I couldn't fix it.'

Vulnerability for him weakened her heart. 'Believe it or not, even you, the great Dante San Marino, cannot fix *everything* in the world.'

He looked away, his jaw locked in an expression of determination, if ever she'd seen one. Of dismissal, too. He wasn't willing to hear what she was saying, nor to take it on board.

'Dante, if the shoe were on the other foot, and it was you who had a medical reason for not being able to create a pregnancy, would you have wanted Jamie to feel bad about that?'

A muscle jerked in his jaw.

Charlotte shook her head. 'I don't mean to say *anyone* should feel bad. Not you, not Jamie. Sad, yes. Disappointed, but not bad. This was nobody's fault.'

'My reason for telling you is because I need you to understand that when we broke up, it was the end for me. Not just of my marriage, but of any possibility of ever moving forward. Of ever opening myself up to caring about another person, to the possibility of hurting them, to the possibility of not being able to fix whatever they might need me to fix.'

Charlotte's heart twisted with sympathy.

'My work is my life.'

Charlotte nodded softly. She felt the beginning of a strange sensation, like a splintering in the region of her heart, but there was also warmth and a need to comfort Dante, even

when her own world was strangely unfamiliar. 'My reasons are very different to yours,' she said, slowly, thoughtfully. 'But you were right before. I'm as determined as you are to never get seriously involved with anyone.'

He looked at her as if he didn't quite believe her and yet he wanted to.

'My mother was completely destroyed by what my biological father did to her. She loved him so much—honestly, she still does. All her life, she pined for him.'

'But she had you,' he pointed out. 'That must have given her some consolation.'

She made a noise of rejection. 'You think?'

He was quiet, watchful.

Charlotte let out a small sigh. 'Honestly, Dante, my mother went between hating me and ignoring me. I was a constant reminder of what she'd had and lost.'

A harsh invective flew from his lips. 'Charlotte—,'

'It's fine,' she lied, trying to summon a casual smile. 'I stopped waiting for her to love me a long time ago. I stopped wishing my father would acknowledge me, want to know me. I stopped looking to anyone else to care about me, whatsoever. If it weren't for Jane, I would be completely alone,' she added. 'Which is fine, because that's kind of how I've always known it had to be. I was only a teenager when I came to understand something I'd probably instinctively known for even longer. The only way to avoid being hurt is to never, ever trust another person with your heart.'

He nodded, as if in total agreement, but there was a sympathy in his eyes, a look of pity that she hated.

'Really, you don't need to worry.' She forced a bright smile more successfully now. 'I'm an excellent actress, but everything that happens up there is purely for your grandmother's sake. We both need this ruse to work, Dante—and while I'm not asking for your heart, I am asking for your trust.

We both are.' Her smile began to feel brittle. 'So, we're all good, right?'

It took him a beat to answer, but when he did, he nodded. 'Yeah, we're all good, Shaw.' But God, how she wanted him to call her *cara* in that moment. And what kind of a liar did that make her?

After five days in Tuscany, at his grandmother's villa, with Charlotte in full-blown fiancé-for-hire mode, Dante was in desperate need of a break. He'd thought that telling her about Jamie, their fruitless quest for a baby, the toll that had taken on his marriage and his life, might have somehow fundamentally changed their dynamic, but it hadn't. He felt this oppressive need for her, all the time. And while he kept telling himself it was just physical, all this time together was making her crave other things, too. Like the stories she so artfully weaved. The way she laughed. The way she was so kindly solicitous with his grandmother. The way the afternoon sun bounced off her hair, making it look almost like lava. Or the way she *adored* Italian food, savouring absolutely every meal that was produced, eating it in a way that was so sensual and downright sexy they often barely made it into the pool house before he started ripping off her clothes, kissing her like it was the one thing he'd been designed for.

Sometimes, they didn't even make it to the pool house.

Sometimes, they didn't even make it out of the house.

Once, his grandmother had found them kissing, just outside the front door and promptly slammed it shut again, causing them both to laugh like teenagers.

Cristo, what was happening to him?

'I've been thinking,' Allegra San Marino cut into his thoughts, topping up their glasses of mineral water and gesturing to the evening antipasto platter spread out before them.

'Uh oh,' Charlotte teased. 'This sounds important.'

Allegra wiggled her brows. 'I have a proposal.'

'We're already engaged,' Dante pointed out.

'Yes, that's right. You're getting married, in London, in three weeks. Correct?'

'Yes,' Dante agreed.

'But what if you were to get married here?'

'Here?' Charlotte looked from Allegra to Dante and then to the gardens surrounding them.

'Oh, yes, of course. It is far nicer than some registry office in England.' Allegra shuddered, as though the very thought was truly awful.

'We can do another ceremony,' Dante offered. 'Later.'

'Darling, I might not have "later",' Allegra said, gent-ly though, as if she was worried he didn't understand the complication her health presented.

Charlotte's features softened.

'Unless there is a reason you feel the need to marry so quickly?' Allegra pushed.

He saw Charlotte's cheeks heat as she computed his grandmother's meaning. She was as subtle as a sledgehammer.

'No, Allegra,' Charlotte said, gently, though, reaching over and putting her hand on Allegra's. He looked at their hands and wondered at the strange, twisting feeling in his gut, the sense of being out of control, unsure of himself suddenly. He didn't like it. He also didn't like the things Charlotte had revealed to him earlier, the depths of emotional neglect she'd had to live with, the fact she'd been made to feel unwanted by everyone in her life. While Dante had lost his parents and grandfather at a young age, he'd never known anything but love from them before hand, and afterwards from his *Nonna*. He drew his gaze back to Charlotte's face, wishing she could have known that same feeling of affection. Wishing she'd had more security in her life. Wishing she had it, even now. 'The only reason is that we don't want to wait.'

His eyes bore into hers, as that statement shifted around inside of him.

He knew she was just saying something to placate Allegra. To ensure they could still go through with their swift marriage. To meet her requirements of inheriting the Papandreo empire. But that didn't mean her statement was entirely false.

Dante found, on some level, that thought absolutely terrified him. He *couldn't* wait. He didn't want to. No matter how he felt about marriage, about his marriage to Jamie in particular, this was all so different. Charlotte was different, their relationship was different and the marriage they'd planned out was something else entirely.

Simple.

Straightforward.

The same rules that had kept them both happy and safe for the last six months were still in place. Even more so now. The more they each got to know the other, the more those rules made sense. The more they both understood why they had to be followed.

'Ah, young love,' Allegra agreed, though her disappointment was impossible to miss.

He had been pleasantly surprised by how much his grandmother had taken Charlotte into her heart. By how much she clearly admired and respected the other woman.

She'd loved Jamie, too, but it had been a different kind of love. To Jamie, Allegra had served almost as a second mother. Someone who Jamie could turn to when she needed holding up. This interaction with Charlotte was more mature and level. Almost as though they were friends and equals. In fact, there was a confidence about Charlotte that, now that Dante thought about it, had been one of the things he'd noticed first. He'd watched her from afar, seen the way she was with other people, and he'd felt a shockwave of electricity, pounding towards him.

'You know,' Allegra said, slowly, thoughtfully. 'I'm tired today.'

Dante was immediately watchful. 'Are you okay?'

'Fine, fine,' she waved a hand through the air. 'As wonderful as it is having you here, I don't entertain often these days. I'm a little worn out.'

Dante felt a rush of regret. 'Of course. I should have known.'

'Nonsense. I wouldn't change a thing. The only reason I bring it up is that I thought I might have a quiet night.'

Dante frowned. Something about this seemed almost pre-arranged.

'I hope you don't mind, but while you've been here, Rosaria has been arranging dinner at the pool house for you.'

Charlotte rolled her eyes with easy affection. 'Has she?'

'I get the impression we're being managed, don't you, *cara*?' he asked Charlotte, eyes glancing to hers and then bouncing away again immediately afterwards, because the bolt of lightning that burst into him seemed almost to sear his skin.

'I think that might be the case,' she said with a good-humoured laugh.

'Oh, you two,' Allegra said, standing, wagging her finger towards them. 'You're being quite unkind to me!'

Dante shook his head.

'Walk me to my room, Dante. If you'll excuse us, Charlotte?'

'Of course,' Charlotte agreed good-naturedly, a smile still playing about her lips. A smile that, if he'd allowed his gaze to linger on it, might have robbed him completely of breath.

'Just wait a moment,' Allegra said, lifting her finger to hold Dante where he was before disappearing into her bedroom. A moment later, she returned, holding a black, velvet pouch.

'I would like you to give this to Charlotte for me.'

Dante took the pouch, frowning. 'What is it?'

'A gift.'

'I presumed as much. But of what?'

'It's a necklace, if you must know.'

'A necklace? May I?'

She nodded once, her lips pursed as Dante opened the pouch and tipped the contents into his palm. It was like being dragged back in time. He remembered this so vividly from his childhood. On a delicate platinum chain sat a diamond pendant, shaped like a teardrop. He remembered his mother wearing it, often. She'd loved it. And when Dante had, as a little boy, asked her if she wore it because she was sad and it looked like a tear, she'd considered that for a moment before replying that in fact, if you turned it upside down, the pendant looked like half of a love heart. She'd told him that she loved it because it was a reminder that she was one half of so many other people—that for everyone she loved, she was loved back.

He'd always remembered that, as one of the first times he'd been corrected—and happily so.

'This was my mother's.'

'No,' Allegra said, gently. 'It was my mother's. She wore it, I wore it, your mother borrowed it—and would no doubt own it, by now, had they not—,' she tapered off, blinking quickly. 'I would like Charlotte to have it.'

'*Nonna*, I know she won't accept it,' he said.

'Then you must make her.'

'I don't know if you've met Charlotte, but I haven't got a hope in hell of making her do anything she doesn't choose.'

'Then make her choose to wear it. For me, Dante.'

He stared at it, his heart pounding. He couldn't say why, but somehow, it just felt so meaningful.

'Why don't you give it to her?'

'It should come from you.'

'Why?'

'Because you have the other half of her heart,' Allegra pointed out.

His lips parted in surprise. 'My mother's story.'

'Yes,' Allegra's expression softened in memory. 'She told me about your question. You were such an observant, literal boy, darling. We giggled about it, at the time, but the more I've thought about it over the years, particularly after that day, the more truth I've seen in her words. This is one half of a heart and whomever wears it should always be reminded that someone else is in their heart just as much as the reverse could be said.'

He squeezed his palm over the necklace and tried to think straight. Tried not to let emotions colour his judgement—because he was torn between acting like himself and the man he was supposed to be—a desperately in love fiancé.

'It's a beautiful gesture,' he said, clearing his throat.

'The necklace has always meant so much to me. On my darkest days, when I am missing them most of all, I have worn it and your mother's story has brought me such comfort.'

'Then you should continue to have it, to wear it.'

'I don't need it now. Don't you see, Dante? Charlotte is my comfort and my hope. All things I didn't have, until so recently.' Her smile dazzled him, or perhaps it was the lie he had dragged his grandmother into that was blinding him with shame. 'Seeing the two of you together—I know now that you are loved just as much as you deserve. More than that, I know you love. I cannot tell you how relieved I am.'

'*Nonna*,' he began. But what could he say? Deny it? Tell his grandmother that he'd only ever loved one woman and that had been an unmitigated disaster?

Only, even if he'd wanted to say that the words wouldn't form in his mouth. He couldn't make his tongue cooperate.

'Thank you,' he said, simply, pushing the necklace into his pocket.

'You'll give it to her tonight,' Allegra insisted. 'Promise me.'

He ground his teeth. 'Of course, *Nonna*.' He leaned down and kissed her cheeks. 'Sleep tight.'

CHAPTER TWELVE

ALLEGRA SAN MARINO hadn't just pulled strings to have their dinner served at the pool house. She'd spooled a whole ball of yarn.

Rosaria was overseeing matters, but there was a team of other people, dressed in formal black tie. A table had been placed on the edge of the water with a long white tablecloth draped over it. Candles sat not only atop the table, but also on the tiles surrounding the pool, glowing golden against the dusk sky. And there were more candles still, somehow floating on the surface of the water, bobbing and flickering like little magical sparkles. A string quartet was over the other side of the water, playing the soft strains of a modern acoustic song, but without the lyrics, and the air was heavy with the intoxicating fragrance of garlic and cheese.

'Ah, you're here,' Rosaria clapped her hands. 'Sit, sit.' Her smile beamed.

Charlotte glanced up at Dante, her heart in her throat.

It had been…a week. At every turn, she'd done her best to both perform like a superstar, showing herself to be just the kind of fiancé his grandmother would think worthy, whilst also remembering, and reminding them both, that this was just make believe. Which was not particularly easy, given how romantic and stunning this part of the world was.

But this was the cherry on top of the impossible pie she'd been managing all week.

She thought she'd hidden her groan but a bemused glance from Dante showed her that in fact, she'd audibly revealed her disbelief.

So much for disappearing into the pool house and pretending to read a book.

'Have I mentioned that my grandmother is a force of nature?'

'It's something I've noticed for myself. But this…' she gestured to the table, grimacing a little.

'Would you prefer to be alone?' Rosaria, hovering nearby, had apparently noticed something was amiss.

Feeling rude and ungrateful, Charlotte was quick to shake her head. 'Of course not. I'm starving.'

'Ahh, good,' Rosaria beamed once more. 'Then please, do sit.'

This time, at her command, they walked towards the table. Dante moved to one of the chairs and pulled it out, gesturing for Charlotte to be seated. She hesitated, something about the moment seeming almost too big for them. Too special. Too…romantic.

'*Va bene*?' His voice was close, his accent deep. Goosebumps lifted over her body.

She realised, when she glanced over her shoulder and looked at him, *why* the moment was so overwhelming.

While they'd had dinner before, they'd never done something so overtly romantic. It was like walking into one of those carnival rooms of mirrors, where everything showed as distorted and confusing. She couldn't really see what they were any more. A combination of the week they'd shared, Allegra's obvious pleasure and acceptance, the looming wedding, the fact their physical connection was anything but slowing down… Charlotte felt as if the world was tilting in the wrong direction.

She sucked in an uneven breath, her eyes holding his.

He shrugged though, his features wearing a mask of amusement. 'Just…go with it,' he suggested. But the trivial nature of his comment was completely undermined by the way he leaned down and placed a kiss against the bare skin of her shoulder, making her stomach clench in instant, unmistakable desire.

'Dante,' she whispered, his name so much more than two syllables joined together. It was both a plea and a freak out. A desperate need for reassurance—that everything was going to be okay. In response, he brushed his hand lightly over her shoulder. She sucked her lower lip between her teeth, staring at him fully.

'It doesn't mean anything,' he said, with absolutely no idea how those words scored against her skin. After all, he was just reiterating something they'd both said, time and time again. It wasn't his fault that those words now felt like weapons.

'Of course not,' she agreed, pleased her voice emerged so steady and normal.

'You're beautiful, Charlotte,' he said, simply. Her heart skipped a beat and then another, until she felt as if everything was all wonky.

'No, this is beautiful,' she said, unevenly, trying, desperately, to hold onto something pragmatic in the face of all this splendour. 'I'm just me.'

His response was to tilt her chin, lifting her face towards his, then kissing her gently on the lips.

Her heart went into overdrive. She sat down quickly, mainly to escape the intensity of his gaze and the feelings he was so easily stirring inside of her. Or maybe it wasn't him, so much as the week they'd shared. Charlotte felt as if a match had been struck, regardless, and she wasn't sure she knew how to put out the flames.

As she sat, his fingers brushed her shoulders, like he wanted to reassure himself that she was there. A moment later, he was

taking the seat opposite and she tried to smile like everything was normal when inside she was awash with feelings.

'How long do you think your grandmother has been planning this?'

'From the moment we told her our news, probably,' he said, with a rueful shake of his head.

'Is she okay?'

'You mean her limp?'

'Actually, I meant her going to bed early.'

'Clearly a ruse,' he pointed out with an arched brow.

'Right,' she nodded. 'Of course.' She frowned. 'And the limp?'

He didn't answer right away. One of the suit-wearing waiters appeared with a very expensive looking bottle of champagne and began to pour the wine into their long stemmed glasses.

Once they were alone again, Dante leaned forward. 'She's come a long way since the stroke, but she can't quite get her left foot to work how it should.'

Charlotte blanched. She couldn't imagine Allegra having a stroke. The woman was so very vital, so alive, The idea of her brain misfiring, of her potentially losing her body's mobility and her mind's agility, just seemed so completely impossible.

'She was lucky,' he said, reaching across and putting his hand on Charlotte's, offering a comfort she strangely really did need.

Charlotte stared back at him and it was like a huge hole had opened up right beneath her. She was in free-fall, with nothing to grab hold of.

'Dante…' she said, softly, slowly. This was too much. It was all too much.

'To fake engagements,' he said, reaching for his champagne and lifting it towards hers. He was trying to reassure her, she recognised. To underscore the thing they'd agreed

to all along. But it did nothing of the sort, because Charlotte could *feel* the contradiction in that. This week she'd started to feel that no matter how hard they tried, it was almost impossible to fight the fact that their relationship had some elements to it that were very, very real. In fact…almost all of it was.

She needed to pull herself back from the brink, because she was on a surefire path to heart-break central, if she wasn't careful. And Charlotte was always very careful.

She could think of one way to douse these romance flames in ice cold water, though she didn't relish the prospect of what she was about to do.

'So, the other day,' she began, reaching for her champagne and taking a sip for good measure. 'When you were telling me about Jamie…'

She'd expected his whole demeanour to change, like it had in the past whenever mention had been made of his marriage, or divorce. The only change though was a slightly resigned expression that crossed his features.

'I thought you would have more questions, in time.'

She lifted her brows. 'And that's okay with you?'

'I decided to tell you about us, Charlotte,' he murmured, with no idea how his casual use of the word 'us' to describe his marriage to another woman cut through all her insulation and shielding. 'I presumed that wouldn't be the end of it.'

'Oh.'

'So,' he asked, casually now, like he was okay with all of this. 'What did you want to ask?'

She massaged her lower lip with her teeth. 'I guess, I'm wondering how she is now. Do you ever talk to her?'

He rubbed a hand over his jaw. 'I spoke to her about a week ago.'

Something sharpened inside of Charlotte. 'You did?'

'Sure.'

'Okay. It's just—you say that like it's normal, to be on those kinds of terms with your ex. A lot of people aren't.'

'Our marriage didn't end because we stopped caring for one another. We just couldn't be together.'

Charlotte moved one hand beneath the table, so she could fumble with her fingers in her lap, away from his perceptive gaze. 'I see.' And she did. Everything about Dante suddenly made so much sense. She'd known he was still hung up on his ex, in some ways, but she hadn't realised the extent of how much he loved her.

'I called to tell her about our engagement,' he said, gently. 'I didn't want to risk that she might hear of it from someone else.'

Charlotte's heart twisted. That was very fair and very chivalrous. And completely like Dante. 'Did she take the news okay?'

He hesitated a moment and then nodded. 'As well as could be expected.'

'Is she seeing anyone else?'

'Not at the moment.'

Charlotte thought about that. 'You told me that you intended to leave your fortune to her and any children she might have.'

He nodded, as if her question wasn't implied.

'She doesn't have children?'

'No.'

'So…'

'She will.'

'I thought you said she couldn't?'

'She'll adopt.'

'How do you know?'

'Because in the end, it's what she suggested with me.'

Charlotte shifted in her seat, a little surprised by that. 'And you said no?'

'I didn't think it would work.'

'Why not?'

'Because,' he said, still not shutting her down, even when his features had grown taut with tension and he was wrapping his fingers so tightly around the stem of his champagne flute she thought it might snap. 'I knew that even if she were able to adopt, the baby would only be a reminder of what I hadn't been able to give her. I have no doubt we both would have loved them, but I don't think it could have saved our marriage. Not after so much loss and resentment.'

'Did she resent you?'

'Yes.'

'She said that?'

He paused. 'She didn't have to.'

Charlotte closed her eyes against a wave of pity and something else. Something that moved like a groundswell through her, a surge of recognition and understanding that made her pulse erratic and her head spin.

Because there was not a thing Dante could say that would change how she felt. There was not a single part of her that would ever get over him.

She toyed with her fingers as piece by piece, she began to understand something that she'd probably known since the very first moment she met him. Or at least, since that very first kiss, that very first night when he'd held her and she'd glimpsed a light, in the distance, a shimmering promise of what could be, if only she were brave enough to reach for it.

She'd been as brave as she could allow herself to be—trying to reach for Dante, whilst also holding herself back. Telling herself that everything they shared could be boiled down to a casual physical relationship when it was, with hindsight, so much more.

'You've never told me about your past, you know,' he said, conversationally, like the whole world wasn't explod-

ing down around her ears. She barely even heard him over the cacophony of noise.

'What?'

'Lovers, boyfriends, a trail of broken hearts left in your wake?'

She blinked rapidly. There were no such men, because she'd always been incredibly careful. And that caution had extended to keeping her relationships utterly temporary.

Not once had she been tempted to prolong a fling.

Not once had she woken up buzzing with a need to find her phone and text someone. To see them again.

Not until Dante.

She glanced towards the pool, staring at the flickering candles, her throat throbbing with the sensation that her heart had taken up residence there.

'You've never asked.'

'We agreed we wouldn't talk about any of that.'

'That's true.'

'Yet, here we are,' Dante murmured, then, with an exaggerated grimace. 'You know my darkest secrets.'

'My darkest secret is that my most significant relationship is with Jane,' she said, a half-smile on her lips when she thought of her best friend.

Dante's lips flickered in the hint of a frown. 'Your best friend?'

'Right. But really, we're more like sisters—like family. There's nothing I wouldn't do for her and she'd say the same about me.' Charlotte glanced down, her stomach twisting with guilt at what Jane was currently doing for her. The feeling that she'd thrown her bestie to the wolves—or rather a very specific wolf—wouldn't go away.

'There's no guy that broke your heart, that made you this way?'

'What way?'

'Determined not to settle down. Self-protective.'

'You say that like it's a bad thing.'

'It's not,' he murmured, but his frown deepened. 'Except, I feel like you have so much more to give, *cara*. If only you'd let yourself.'

'I'm okay with how things stand.'

He reached over and took her hand, lacing their fingers. Butterflies burst into her veins, their wings flapping and making her body shiver from the inside out.

'You think that because your father didn't love you, no one ever will?'

Her lips parted on a harsh exhalation. It sounded indignant, but in truth she was shocked. That he'd understand her so well. That he'd verbalise her fears so concisely. That hearing him say it would unstitch something deep down inside of her.

She looked away, towards the pool and, in the distance, the string quartet. They were playing beautifully—but neither Charlotte nor Dante were listening properly at all.

'I think it's not worth the risk,' she said, unevenly, because Charlotte didn't know what she felt any more and what she'd be prepared to risk, if there was any chance of being with Dante—of really being with him. Of being free to love him and being loved back by him.

But it was all so impossible, wasn't it? She didn't know how to love—not without fear, not without mistrust—and he wasn't prepared to try, after what had happened with Jamie. That was why they had all their rules and boundaries. For more than six months, they'd kept each other at arm's length, telling themselves they were safe from consequences because they refused to let this thing get out of hand. But what if it wasn't so easy to control? What if their relationship had developed a mind—and heart—all of its own?

'One day, you might meet someone who changes your mind.'

Her heart slammed into her chest. Someone else? Did he have any idea how impossible that was to contemplate? Just the idea of opening herself up to another man was like pouring acid over her skin.

'Do you think *you'll* ever let yourself fall in love again?'

His eyes lifted to hers, speared them, held her gaze for so long, her breath seemed to be stagnating inside of her. She waited as if everything she was hinged on his answer to this one, all important question, and she didn't really understand why. Only, she knew that whatever he said next was meaningful and important.

'No,' he answered, eventually, shaking his head a little and removing his hand. Ice flooded her whole body. 'I will never let that happen.' He glanced away from her, towards the band, so she had a full view of the way his jaw was clenched and her stomach dropped to her toes.

He would fight love, even if he thought he felt it, because he was determined to avoid what he'd gone through with Jamie. He would fight love, even if it was sitting right across the table from him, looking at him with unmistakable longing.

There was no way he would ever want to hear the revelation she'd just had.

There was no way she could tell him.

He wouldn't allow himself to return her feelings, but he'd feel obliged to her, for the rest of his life, just because of who he was, just because of how he seemed to think it was his job to save people.

Well, Charlotte would never become a problem he had to save.

She was brave, she was strong, she was independent and, no matter what, she wasn't going to burden Dante any more than he'd already been.

* * *

Long after the dinner plates had been cleared away, they sat on the edge of the pool, feet resting on the first step, knees touching, beneath the starlit sky.

For Charlotte, there was such a finality to this evening, though it was their second to last night in Italy and not their last. It just felt like a new beginning, even when it was a goodbye of sorts.

She'd come here believing herself completely immune to love and now she knew she wasn't. Dante, and this magical, beautiful villa, had opened up that side of her and she supposed she should be grateful.

But in many ways, she also recognised she had a life ahead of her just like her mother had lived. Alone, lonely, pining for the one man she'd ever loved, knowing she couldn't have him.

Dante wasn't married, and she wasn't even sure if he was still in love with his ex-wife, but it was clear that his marriage to Jamie was going to prevent him from ever being able to move forward. So, in all the same ways Aristotle Papandreo had been unable to return Charlotte's mother's feelings, Dante was unable to return hers.

'I have something for you,' Dante said, his voice deep, cutting through her thoughts.

She glanced across at him and her heart, newly awakened, lurched with the fulness of her love. 'You do?'

'It's from my grandmother. She wanted you to have it.'

She kept her features neutral, but she heard the distinction he insisted on making. It wasn't from him. There was no significance to whatever this was, at least, not so far as they were concerned.

'Here.' His voice, though, was heavy with emotions. He pulled a black velvet pouch from his pocket, held it in his hands a moment and then passed it across to Charlotte. She felt it between her fingertips, the friction of velvet on fine

metal. Curiously, she opened the drawstring and carefully fished out the contents.

A stunning, enormous teardrop diamond was held on a very fine white gold chain. She stared at it for a long time, trying to understand why Allegra would give her such a beautiful piece of jewellery. For even though Charlotte generally despised ostentatious pieces, and this was certainly emblematic of wealth, there was something delicate and beautiful about it. Something that overcome any distaste she might otherwise have felt.

'It's beautiful.'

'Yes.'

'I mean, it's way too much,' she said, trying to infuse her tone with teasing lightness when her heart was weighing her down so completely. 'But I love it, anyway.'

She stared at it, aware that a heavy silence enveloped them, making Charlotte acutely aware of the lapping of the water around her calves.

'It's a family piece,' he said, the words devoid of emotion, but in a way she knew was carefully cultivated. 'It was my great grandmother's, then my grandmother's. My mother loved it and wore it often.'

Charlotte drew in a quick breath, closing her fingers over the necklace for a few brief seconds before slipping it back into the bag, drawing the string tight and holding it towards Dante. 'I can't accept it.'

His dark eyes flashed to hers. 'You have to.'

She shook her head. 'It's too valuable. Too sentimentally important,' she corrected. 'It's very kind of her, but that's not what we are.'

His lips pulled to the side. 'She thinks we are.'

Charlotte's eyes closed. 'Of course she does, but she's wrong.' Oh, how it hurt to say that!

'I want you to have it.'

Charlotte blinked and stared at him, her heart rabbiting hard. Did he have any idea what effect that sentence had on her? If he cared for her, if any of this was real, she would take the necklace and wear it every day close to her heart. But it just wasn't right.

'I'll wear it tomorrow,' she said, softly. 'So she can see me in it. But after that, you can have it.'

'You won't even think about keeping it?'

'Dante, you just told me it's an important piece to your family.'

'We have other important pieces.'

'This is—too much.'

'Think of it as a thank you,' he said. 'A bonus, for a job very well done.'

She was caught so completely off guard by the transactional nature of his statement that she lost any ability to mask her feelings, to hide how shocked—and hurt—she was by the very idea of that. For a moment, she was sure it was written all over her features, before she managed to flash him a bright smile, as though her heart wasn't splintering into a billion tiny fragments.

He closed his hand over hers, pushing the velvet pouch towards her chest.

'She loves you,' he said, quietly, voice deep. Was she imagining the way those words seemed to come right out of the middle of him, like they were a part of him. Was it just wishful thinking that imbued them with something else? Maybe a little of his own feelings too?

Yes. Of course it was wishful thinking. She loved him and she was desperate for him to love her back. Desperate, just like her mother had been, all Charlotte's life.

The kind of desperation that had the ability to turn to bitterness, if you weren't very careful.

'She's a very special woman.' Her voice sounded rigid to her own ears. 'I'm sorry I won't get to see her again.'

Something crossed Dante's features. 'I wouldn't be so sure.'

Charlotte's heart twisted. 'No?'

'We're getting married, Charlotte. We haven't talked about a divorce—there will be other events, in the future, with my grandmother. I'm sure of it.'

'Oh.' She blinked quickly. She wasn't sure she could muster the emotional fortitude to keep pretending. Not now that she knew how much of her act had been real. 'Yeah, I guess you're right.'

'So, keep the necklace. Wear it whenever she's around. It will make her happy.'

She bit into her lower lip, staring at the black velvet pouch.

'It will make me happy.'

And really, what wouldn't she do to make him happy? She glanced across at him and he smiled. Every part of her began to tremble with just how much she felt for this man. He leaned forward a little and she matched his gesture until their lips met and they were kissing beneath the ancient, star-lit sky, surrounded by the fragrance of citrus blossoms and night flowering jasmine. She kissed him, finally realising that he was the love of her life and he'd never, ever know it.

They'd promised each other this was a meaningless marriage of convenience, a transactional, mutually beneficial arrangement, devoid of any truth or emotion, and damn it if she wasn't going to keep acting her heart out and pretend that was still the case—even when it hurt more than she could ever put into words.

CHAPTER THIRTEEN

CHARLOTTE HAD ALWAYS loved London. It was a part of her, stitched into her soul, and had been from the first time she and Jane had come to town together, exploring it as teenagers, jumping on the tube and travelling around wherever the Piccadilly or Jubilee or Northern lines decided to take them.

But the moment Dante's jet touched down in the city, and they slipped into his limousine bound for South Ken-sington, a darkness had settled around Charlotte. A sense of reality. A feeling that everything they'd shared in Italy had been some kind of dream that wouldn't translate to this life, to this place.

There, she'd felt so close to him, regardless of what they'd said from the start. There, neither had had work commitments, or other obligations. They'd been together from morning until night. They'd slept in the same bed. They'd shared every meal, every pot of coffee, every laugh, every swim, every little bit of it. And even without understanding what she was feeling, until that night by the pool, she'd intrinsically known that it was a very special time. That he made her feel special, even if he didn't love her.

But back in London, with work to consume them both and the inevitable taking over of the Papandreo company, it was easy to believe things would change between them. Or rather, go back to what they'd been before. Sex but otherwise, a polite distance.

The thought left her cold, when she suspected it should have been reassuring.

They travelled in silence, but Charlotte was too wrapped up in her thoughts and worries to notice or care. But as the car pulled into his street, Dante made a sound of surprise. She glanced at him, and then followed the direction of his gaze, to where a woman was standing outside his house.

A tall, brunette, dressed in a skinny jeans, hi-top sneakers and a pretty camisole top.

Something in Charlotte began to sink. 'Someone you know?'

He glanced at her, frowning a little. 'You could say that.'

Her heart sank further as a premonition took hold.

'Jamie,' he said, and when the car pulled up, he turned to face Charlotte. 'I'm not sure why she's here. Wait here while I go and see.'

Charlotte's chest seemed to tighten. 'You want me to wait in the car while you talk to your ex-wife?' She shook her head. 'I don't know who should be more annoyed about that—her or me.'

He grimaced. 'What would you prefer?'

Irritation flicked at her souls. 'We're getting married, Dante. You can't hide me forever.'

He looked at her with a sense of confusion. 'I'm not hiding you. I'm trying to protect you.'

Her nostrils flared; she seriously doubted that.

'From your ex-wife?'

'I have no idea why she's here. What mood she's in.' Something about his statement had her pausing her own indignant thoughts and homing in on him and his mindset. She knew enough to understand that his marriage had been an emotional minefield at the end. And evidently still had the potential to be.

'It's fine,' she said, glancing away. 'I'll go and get some

groceries,' she said. 'Go, talk to her.' She forced a smile. 'This is none of my business.'

He nodded, accepting that. Her heart splintered. She watched him get out of the car and walk towards his ex-wife. She watched them hug. She saw him smile and she felt like an outsider, looking at two people who belonged together. She felt—broken. As the car pulled away from the kerb, a single tear slid down her cheek.

Dante didn't glance in her direction once.

All Dante could think of was getting rid of Jamie. Which surprised the hell out of him. This was his one-time wife. Someone he'd once loved. Someone he'd probably thought he still loved, up until maybe a few months ago, when he'd realised he rarely thought of her, didn't miss her and had started to truly accept the necessity of their divorce.

It wasn't that he was against the idea of seeing her again. And he sure as heck didn't want to hurt her. But he'd been looking forward to getting Charlotte back to his place and pulling her into his arms and kissing her just like they'd kissed in Italy—often and thoroughly. He wasn't ready for the little holiday bubble they'd created to burst just yet. Even when he knew it inevitably would, because this, here, was their real world and their real lives. Reality would intrude, but he'd hoped it would be the kind of reality that shifted a little to accommodate the way things had changed between them.

The fact that theirs wouldn't be a real marriage no longer mattered. It would be real to them, real in its own way. No love, but respect, friendship, sex, shared interests and a deep understanding of one another and why those barriers mattered so much. And neither of them wanted children. There was more than enough here to warrant them marrying, yes, but also staying married. After all, why mess with a good— no, great—thing?

'Hey, you,' Jamie broke into his thoughts, smiling up at him. But it was a sad smile, the kind of smile he'd seen plenty of before.

'Jamie, have you been waiting long?'

She shook her head. 'Allegra told me your flight schedule.'

He closed his eyes. She'd spoken to his grandmother?

'I see.'

'Can I come in?'

He glanced towards the door, surprised by how vehemently he wanted to demur. This was where Charlotte lived now. It was the physical representation of their bubble. But this was *Jamie*. A woman he'd shared more love and loss with than he could put into words.

'Of course,' he said, putting a hand in the small of her back as he guided her up the stairs. He thought of Charlotte though, as he unlocked the door. Wondering what she would buy at the stores. Wondering if she was as carefree about Jamie's being here as she seemed and hoping she was. Because he knew one thing for certain. He never wanted to hurt her. She'd known too much hurt and rejection in her life. He would not be a person who added to that.

'So,' he said, once they were inside. 'How are you?'

'I'm—okay,' she said, lifting her shoulders.

'Okay, good.' He frowned, not wanting to ask her what she was doing at his house.

'Allegra says she's nice,' Jamie murmured, not quite meeting his eyes.

'Jamie, you didn't tell my grandmother anything about my relationship with Charlotte, did you?'

'You mean the fact that it's fake?' The words had a hint of something in them, something he'd never heard from Jamie. Anger? Accusation?

'It's not fake.'

'Right, but you're not in love.'

He'd never love anyone again. That was a mantra he'd held close to his chest for so long, it had weaved its way into his being, so it didn't occur to him to dispute that.

'It's just a practical marriage, right? Something to do with your business, I'm guessing. Everything always comes down to that for you.' There was bitterness in her voice.

'In fact, it's Charlotte's business,' he said, distractedly, because his mind was starting to rattle and screech. There was an odd, panicked background hum going through his mind, making it impossible to think straight.

'Charlotte's business? You're doing this to help her?'

He forced himself to focus. Or try to. 'It's mutually beneficial.'

She frowned. 'Okay then. Well, that's not why I'm here, anyway.'

'No?'

'I wanted to tell you *my* news.'

'You have news?'

'I'm adopting.'

He stared at her, surprised. 'You are?'

'Yes. I was hoping I would meet someone else, someone to do this with but…something about the fact you're moving on, marrying someone else, made me realise that I've been living my life in a kind of stasis, just waiting for everything to change. It's not going to. I can't have kids, Dante. I can't. My body just won't cooperate.'

He grimaced, old griefs and guilts swirling through him.

'It's taken me a long time, but I accept it. And the truth is, I'm excited again. Somewhere out there is a baby, or a toddler, a little person who *needs* me, and we're about to become a family. At least, we will once I've jumped through all the legal hoops,' she added with a small laugh.

'I'm happy for you, Jamie,' he said, lifting a hand and putting it on her shoulder. Once upon a time, she'd been his

other half. At least, he'd thought she had, but then again, his experience had been limited. In fact, the more he thought about it, the more he realised that wasn't the case. She wasn't his other half. She had been someone in his life, someone he cared for and wanted to make happy, but they'd never stood toe to toe, arm in arm, meeting life's challenges together. They'd never been partners, in the true sense of the word.

He drew in a shallow breath, as something in his noisy, cacophonous brain shouted at him, demanding to be examined. Something about other halves and people who completed you in every way, something he refused to think about or focus on. Now or ever. Because if a relationship breakdown with someone who wasn't your other half had the power to wound you as theirs had him, how bad would it be with your true soulmate?

'I know the timing is lousy,' she said. 'I mean, you've just gone and spent a week with Allegra. It's just…' She tapered off, shrugging her shoulders. 'This is you and me, Dante. As it turns out, I wasn't really looking to meet someone else.' She sucked in a deep breath. 'I can't imagine raising a child without you. Whenever I think about it, think about my family, you're there with me. A part of it. A part of me. I know what you said back then, when I brought this up…'

He stared at her, wondering if he was imagining this. Wondering if somehow, he'd conjured up a version of Jamie that didn't actually exist.

'What are you saying?'

'I'm saying that I want us to try again.' She expelled a long, slow breath. 'I know how unbearable it was, in the end. I know how much of a toll it took on both of us. But I'm different now. I've finally accepted this situation. And with that, I think we could just go back, be like we were before.'

This was the last thing he'd expected to happen today and the last thing, he realised, that he wanted.

'Jamie,' he sighed softly. But she was moving, lifting her hands to his chest, touching him right there where his heart was thumping.

'Just think about it,' she urged. 'You don't need to settle for marrying someone you don't love. I don't care what the business benefits are—you deserve to be happy. I want to make you happy.' She lifted up onto her tiptoes and kissed him then, like they'd kissed a thousand times before. Like they'd kissed in their marriage, every single damned day.

But with each shift of her mouth, cell by cell his body shut down, turning to ice. Just a few seconds later, he stepped back and shook his head. 'I don't need to think about it, Jamie. I'm pleased for you—so pleased that you're finally going to get your dream of being a mother—but I'm engaged to someone else.'

'And that's the only reason you won't consider this?'

'No,' he said, gently. 'You and I were great, for a while. We really were. But I think we both know that over time, we fell out of love.'

Her smile was ghostly. 'No, we didn't,' she whispered. 'You just wish that were the case.' She moved to the front door. Dante didn't see any point in disputing the facts of their relationship even when he knew, in every fibre of his being, that Jamie was wrong. He didn't love her now and he was starting to wonder if he ever really had loved her—in the way a man should love the person he intends to spend the rest of his life with. 'Think about it, Dante. I'm offering you the world.'

Except his world had changed shape a lot since meeting Charlotte and he didn't have to think very hard to realise why...

Charlotte took a long time at the grocery store. She tried checking in with Jane, grabbed a coffee, ambled up and down

each aisle, before finally paying and making her way back to Dante's. She deliberately prevaricated, because she wanted to give Jamie and Dante time to talk.

Because she wasn't planning to look like some jealous girlfriend, even when jealousy was practically eating her alive.

The driver was waiting for her in the parking lot. As she approached he stepped out to help her load the bags into the trunk. When they pulled up outside Dante's Charlotte hesitated for a moment before hopping out and grabbing the shopping. The driver offered to help once more, but she demurred. It was only four bags. She could manage.

She approached the house with her head bent, so didn't see the movement at first. It was only when she lifted her gaze to the door, frowning and wondering what happened next, that she saw that Jamie was standing out the front. Waiting.

She tried to smile, but everything suddenly felt onerous. Way too hard. She approached the other woman with a sinking feeling in the pit of her gut.

'Hi. You must be Jamie,' she said, a little unevenly.

'Yeah, that's me. And you're Charlotte.'

'Uh huh.'

'Allegra speaks very highly of you,' the other woman said, glancing over her shoulder a little guiltily, towards the house.

Allegra, Charlotte noted. Not Dante.

'She's very sweet.'

'Yes, she is. They both are,' Jamie continued. 'I know Dante has this big, tough exterior, but beneath it, he's such a softie.'

Anger flooded Charlotte. If she was a cartoon character, steam would have started spurting from her ears. To be told anything about Dante rankled. When it really shouldn't! Naturally Jamie knew him better than Charlotte. But a hot possessive streak was overtaking every rational part of Charlotte's brain.

'Anyway,' Charlotte said, lifting the bags a little higher. 'I'd better get this in the fridge.'

'Wait,' Jamie's voice was urgent now. 'I just need a moment.'

Charlotte's throat ached suddenly. Her shoulders felt weighted down.

'Dante is a great guy,' she said. 'I don't know exactly what's going on between the two of you, and why he feels like he has to help you with this whole fake engagement or whatever, but before you make him go through with it, I thought you should know something.'

Charlotte could hardly breathe.

The insults just kept coming.

The fact that Dante had told Jamie about their arrangement—or, at least, that they weren't a real couple. The fact that Jamie was implying Dante didn't actually want to go through with it. That it was all because he felt a sense of obligation. The very bottom fell out of Charlotte's world.

'I'm still in love with him,' Jamie said. 'He's not the kind of guy you easily get over. And the thing is, I think he still loves me.'

Charlotte blinked at the other woman, wondering if she had any idea how much this was hurting her to hear.

'That's between you and Dante,' she said. 'If it's true, though, I would never stand in his way.'

Jamie puffed out a breath of relief. 'Oh, good. That's exactly what I was hoping you'd say. Will you tell him that? Tell him he's off the hook, Charlotte?'

Charlotte stared at the other woman, not trusting herself to speak. She just nodded, as a thousand childhood fears and hurts slammed right back into her.

Feeling unwanted.

Surplus to requirements.

Loving someone and wanting, wishing, hoping they would love you back, when they just didn't have it in them.

Thrust upon someone who wished she'd never been born.

There was second-hand trauma, too, when she thought of her mother and how she'd loved a man her whole adult life who'd already been in love with someone else.

It had destroyed her mother and Charlotte knew it would destroy her, too.

'Thank you so much,' Jamie cooed. 'Allegra's right. You're quite lovely.' And with that, the harbinger of Charlotte's doom spun on her sneakered heel and sashayed elegantly down the street.

'Cristo, you took your sweet time,' Dante muttered, a moment after hearing the front door shut and dragging a hand through his hair as he came into the foyer to find Charlotte standing there, holding paper bags, staring into space.

She looked…pale.

'Are you ill?'

Her eyes slid to his, staring at him, her lips parted, her cheeks almost paper white.

'Charlotte, for the love of God, sit down, please, before you pass out.'

'I'm okay,' she husked, her brow furrowing. 'I have to put these in the fridge.'

But she made no attempt to move. She just stared at him, as if she'd never seen him before.

Concern became a tide, surging through him. Whatever was happening he needed to know immediately. He needed to fix it. Even accepting that he couldn't fix everything for everyone, he knew he would try for Charlotte. He knew she deserved that.

'Charlotte?'

'I met Jamie,' she blurted out, her brows knitting together.

He swore under his breath, crossing to her, needing… something. He didn't know what. So he took the bags, at the very least, to relieve her of their weight, and placed them onto the tiled floor.

'When did you meet Jamie?' he asked, focusing on that, first.

'Just now. Outside.' She shivered. 'She waited for me.'

He felt something odd—a panic he hadn't known before. An anger, too, that his ex-wife had somehow slipped right inside the bubble he and Charlotte had made in Tuscany. He'd known reality would intrude, but he hadn't expected *that* kind of reality. He didn't want it.

Charlotte's lip tugged between her teeth. 'You told her about us.'

He bit back a groan, swiftly followed by a curse. 'Yes.' He couldn't, after all, deny it.

'You told her this is a fake relationship,' Charlotte nodded. If he could have gone back in time and sewn his lips shut to stop that revelation escaping, he would have.

'I told her that, yes.'

Charlotte nodded, but her shoulders were slumped and she looked confused. Or wounded. Which was so much worse.

He moved quickly then, putting his hands on her hips, needing to hold her, hoping that would help her understand. 'When I called to tell her we were engaged, she was upset. I told her that our marriage was of a practical nature. I told her we weren't in love.'

It was what they'd agreed to, what they'd said to each other over and over again, so why did Charlotte now look as though he'd physically wounded her?

'I didn't know you'd told her. Or anyone. I wasn't prepared…'

'It's just Jamie,' he promised. 'She won't tell anyone. I trust her.'

Charlotte's eyes opened and lanced him with the directness of her stare. 'It's not about that.' She drew in a deep breath. 'I can't do this.'

The words were simple enough, but he didn't follow her thought process. 'Talk about Jamie?'

She shook her head. 'Marry you.' This time, she whispered, the words almost drowned out by the rushing of blood through his ears. 'I'd never forgive myself, Dante.' Her lips twisted in a bitter half-smile. 'You're off the hook.'

'Off the hook?' he repeated, wondering where the hell she'd have gotten the idea he *wanted* to be off the hook.

'Yes. You can go back to Jamie. You should be with her. Be with who you love. You should be happy.'

He swore then. 'Is that what she told you?'

Charlotte turned away from him, pulling out of his grip, moving back towards the front door. His heart accelerated. His head ached. *Don't leave me.*

'It's not true, *cara.* I don't want to be with her.'

Charlotte shook her head, but didn't turn back to face him. He swore inwardly. When she reached the door, he moved quickly, pressing his hand over hers, on the doorknob, refusing to let it turn, imprisoning her body with his own.

'Charlotte,' he dropped his mouth to the sweep of her neck and pressed his lips there, feeling the familiar taste of her, the fluttering of her pulse. 'I want to marry you.'

God, he hadn't even realised how true that was until he was on the brink of losing her.

She turned then, her body trapped by his, every inch of her connected to him.

'Why?'

He stared at her, the simple question likely requiring a simple answer, but he found he couldn't easily locate one. 'Because it's what we agreed,' he said, knowing it wasn't right. Knowing it didn't sum up how he felt and what he wanted.

'Yes, it's what we agreed,' she spat, but with something like anger. 'We agreed we would get married. That it would be practical and simple. That neither of us would want more than the easy relationship we'd developed.'

'Right,' he said, ignoring the maelstrom of uncertainty in the pit of his gut. 'Exactly.'

'No, not exactly,' she retorted with an angry sound.

But why was she so angry? Because of Jamie? 'Look, I'm sorry she came here. I'm sorry she spoke to you. But—,'

'It's not about her,' Charlotte said, eyes huge in her face, as she stared at him with an emotion he didn't understand. Like she was silently imploring him to understand something utterly foreign.

'Then what is it?'

'It's about us.'

'Us?'

Her eyes filled with tears.

'It turns out, I was wrong.'

'About me?'

'About everything,' she groaned. 'I can't marry someone who doesn't love me. Someone who probably loves someone else.'

'I don't love her,' he said quickly. 'I honestly don't know if I ever did.'

He didn't push himself to question why he was suddenly so certain of that.

Charlotte's eyes closed and her features momentarily crumpled, in a way that damn near broke his soul in half. 'My father never wanted me. My mother never wanted me. I can't marry someone who deep down doesn't really want me either. Not enough.'

He opened his mouth to dispute that, to tell her he did indeed want her in his life, in some capacity, so long as they

could control their expectations, so long as it was easy and simple.

But how could he say that? Nothing about them was simple, and it probably hadn't been for a long time. They'd been fooling themselves that they could play with fire and not get burned.

'I should *never* have suggested this to you.' The words landed against him like blades.

She pressed a hand to his chest and sucked in a deep breath. For a moment he wondered if she was going to change her mind. But she pushed at him. Not hard, but hard enough for him to get the message. Back off.

Now that he wasn't holding her she was able to open the door and slip through it without giving him even a second to reply.

He just stared at the door, her words thundering through him, over and over and over.

Jamie's reappearance in his life was nothing short of bizarre. As was her insistence that they were in love, when the truth was, whatever love they'd felt for one another had died slowly—over the course of years—leaving only the warm affection of two people who had once shared a sort of teenage love.

A childish love.

A love that hadn't been strong enough to withstand the trials of real life.

A love that had never been meant to go the distance, whether they'd had children or not. But regardless of whether or not he loved Jamie, the pain of their marriage was real. All of it. Knowing that she was suffering and he could do nothing to alleviate it, watching her become a shell of her former self. Wanting the best for her but not being able to deliver that.

The pain was something he'd been running from ever since.

The way it had made him vulnerable. How he'd hated that. He'd promised himself he'd never be in that position again. Yet here he was, staring at a closed door, feeling as though his entire body had been split in half. Feeling as though every single cell in his body was on fire.

Feeling as though his entire reason for being had just walked out the door.

Which was exactly why he didn't chase after her. Exactly why he let her last statement hang in the air, defining and ending their relationship all at once.

I should never have suggested this to you.

The first time her mother had forgotten her birthday Charlotte had been devastated. She'd cried all day, weeping into her hands, whilst still hoping that maybe, just maybe, a phone call would come through to the school. A present, like the other boarders got on their birthdays.

Something.

Anything.

Proof of love.

But nothing had arrived. And the bricks of acceptance had begun to form inside of her. So too the ability to take hurt and rejection and calcify it into something strong and permanent, adding to the wall of strength that she knew she'd need in life.

This pain, though, was something else. Despite her best efforts, despite everything she knew about life and love and all the warnings she'd given herself, she'd fallen hard in love for Dante San Marino. And he didn't love her back.

He liked her.

He respected her.

He loved sleeping with her.

But where she had failed in the pledge she'd made herself, he'd held fast to his, keeping his relationship with Charlotte in the exact same box it had been in all along.

When she'd got home from his place, she was utterly exhausted and it was only as she flopped into her lumpy bed that she realised she'd left her bags at his place. With her toiletries, her toothbrush and the beautiful teardrop diamond necklace Allegra had insisted she have.

Tears leaked out of the corners of her eyes, as she accepted yet another failing. Another person who'd found a chink in the wall she'd thought was impermeable and worked her way into it.

Because Charlotte had come to love Allegra, too, and their beautiful home in Tuscany. Damn it, at some point, she'd started to love them all. To love the life she thought she and Dante might share.

Pain seared her, familiar but foreign, because she loved Dante more than and differently to anyone she'd ever known.

And she could never, ever be with him.

All night, Dante thought about Charlotte. All night, he tossed and turned, and fumed, and swore, and then tossed and turned some more, because nothing made sense and everything was wrong.

Everything.

Sometime around dawn, he gave up on even attempting to sleep and made a strong dark coffee, carrying it onto the terrace, staring out at the street with a heaviness in his chest he couldn't shake.

He drank it and thought about Charlotte. He also thought about Jamie and the mistakes he'd made in his first marriage. He thought about how he'd tried to be the husband she needed, instead of thinking about if he was the husband she deserved. Because he hadn't loved Jamie enough—not

to withstand what life had in store for them—and she had deserved so much more.

Just like Charlotte did.

But whenever he considered that and contemplated Charlotte being with someone else, someone who could love her without hesitation and reserve, his brain practically exploded. His heart, too.

How could anyone else love her more than he did? How could anyone else give her more than him, when Dante was willing, he realised, to give her his entire life and soul if she'd accept it.

He cursed into the early morning air, draining the last of his coffee as he turned and stalked back into his house, pausing only to pull on some clothes, before storming out onto the street and towards—he hoped—his future.

Charlotte had slept hard in the end. She supposed because she'd worn herself out crying and feeling and bitterly regretting everything. Wishing she hadn't said anything to Dante. Wishing she'd stuck with their marriage plan. Wishing she'd just gone through with it and kept her feelings hidden, because at least then she would have been with him.

And surely that would have made her happy, on some level?

Except it wouldn't have. Because she'd done enough of that in her life—loving someone and walking on eggshells because you knew their feelings for you were conditional.

She couldn't do it again.

Not with Dante.

Not with a man she loved as she loved him.

How stupid she'd been to let it get so far.

Then again, what choice had she had? She realised now that she'd probably fallen in love with him that night they met. What else explained the uncharacteristic way she'd gone

home with him? And then hooking up with him again and again and again. Throwing caution to the wind and craving someone as if her life depended on it.

She'd told herself it was just physical because she'd needed to believe that. She'd told herself she couldn't stand him, because that had felt safe and sensible. But both of those things had been lies.

She had to put this behind her. She had to start fresh. She had to prove to herself she was strong. That this wouldn't break her—even when it felt as if it was pulling her apart completely.

As the sun rose, she pushed out of bed, showered and dressed with care.

Her bags were at Dante's and while she could have sent someone for them, she wanted to prove to both of them that she was okay. Or maybe she just wanted to give that to Dante, because she knew how he'd be beating himself up, worrying about her, worrying that he'd hurt her like he'd hurt Jamie and even though it was true, that her heart was breaking, that wasn't his fault.

He just didn't love her.

It was as simple as that.

Ignoring the aching in the centre of her chest, she left the apartment and looked left, then right and lifted her hand to hail a cab.

He ran.

He ran faster than he'd ever run before, his legs burning, his eyes filling with stars, because the cab driver had dropped him at the wrong end of the street and he'd been too distracted to notice at first. And now that he knew what he wanted to say to Charlotte, he had to say it then. And there. It was a long, straight street, and he picked up speed quickly, so he saw her emerge from her front door, hail a cab and

slip into it. Saw the cab slide away from the kerb and drive away from him.

He swore, his lungs burning from the exertion of running like this, but there was no way he was going to let her go. No way in hell. Not now, when he finally understood himself.

Finally, there was an intersection, and blessedly, a slow-moving learner driver was paused hesitantly at it. Dante put on an extra burst of speed, reaching the cab and thumping the driver's window with his open palm.

The guy pressed a button, so the glass dropped. 'Y'alright, sir?'

'I need a moment with your passenger.'

The driver flicked a glance to Charlotte in the rear-vision mirror.

Dante turned his attention to her and through the still closed glass of her window said, 'It's important.'

She'd been crying, he realised. Her pinched face was still pale but it was tear streaked now and her lips were a bright pink, like she'd been biting them incessantly.

'Charlotte,' he said, the word like a desperate, anguished plea.

The car behind them honked, jolting her into action. She said something inaudible to the driver, then pushed out of the car, so the driver was free to move forward into the intersection.

The driver of the car behind gave them a rude gesture as he passed.

Dante didn't care.

'When I told Jamie about us, I was still clinging to what we'd agreed our marriage would be. I didn't even feel bad telling her, because it was something you and I said frequently to one another. While I had no intention of broadcasting it to all and sundry, I truly didn't see any harm in one person knowing the truth.'

Charlotte's jaw clamped. 'I don't need to know.'

'And then, as soon as I said it, I regretted it,' he insisted. 'I felt like I'd betrayed you.'

'You did betray me,' she whispered, eyes blinking furiously now. 'Our relationship is *our* business.'

'But don't you see, Charlotte? I've spent more than six months furiously denying, even to myself, that we even *have* a relationship.'

She closed her eyes. 'I know.'

'I think you and I are both guilty of that. How many times did we proclaim that this is "just sex" when it hasn't been that since our first night. And maybe it wasn't even then?'

Charlotte wasn't saying anything back, but she wasn't storming off either.

He grabbed her arms and held her. God, how he loved her. How he needed her to understand that.

'When you suggested this marriage, I ran a mile, because I was so terrified of admitting to myself how much I wanted to say "yes". And then, I saw you with someone else and realised what I was in danger of losing. I knew I had to put my fears aside and go through with it. But even then, I was pretending it was just about your company and my grandmother. I pretended our marriage would be a means to an end. A pleasurable one, but certainly not a marriage with the power to destroy me. Not a marriage that could make me wither away, like my first marriage did.'

She made a sound—a groan or a soft, aching plea.

'All along, you've been so different. Different to anyone I've ever known. I can't get enough of you. I can't walk away from you. Hell, I haven't been able to stop thinking of you since the first moment I met you. Charlotte Shaw, without me realising it, without me intending it, you have become the most important person in my world. You have become my absolute everything. There is no one else I want to marry

more than I do you and not for any reason other than the fact I am completely, unquestionably, unfathomably in love with you. All of you. Every part.'

Her lips parted in surprised, and her eyes looked at him as if to say, 'do you mean this?'

It was something. Not enough, but a start.

He grabbed her hands, lifting them towards his lips.

'In Italy, all that pretence fell away. We could no longer spin the lie that we were just sex. There was nowhere to hide. No way to disguise what we were feeling. At least, that's my interpretation of it.'

She bit into her lip and suddenly, Dante felt as if he might have sprinted so far out on a limb that couldn't actually support him. It was entirely possible that she didn't feel the same way about him. That he'd been wrong about everything. But that didn't matter. He still needed her to know how he felt. Because Charlotte deserved to know that she was loved. That to someone, she was the most important, vital, necessary person in the entire universe and always would be.

No matter what happened, he needed her to be free of the misconception that she was unlovable. If he didn't give her that, at least, he would always, always regret it.

'You are the sum total of everything. Everything I want in life. You are my love, my beating heart, my burning breath, my waking thought, my dreams, my need, my all.'

She closed her eyes as she let out a small sob and somehow, without her saying or doing anything to signal that she was agreeing with him, he just *knew*. In that way one knows how their other half is feeling. He dropped to his knees, right there on the sidewalk, clutching her hands.

'Charlotte, what I would like, more than anything, is for you to marry me. Not for your father's business, not for my grandmother's sake, but because you feel exactly as I do. As though there is no life you want to lead that doesn't have me

in it. Because you want to be my wife, as much as I want to be your husband. Because we're made for each other, my darling, and always will be.'

Her tears splashed against the back of his hand and he laughed softly, because she was nodding and laughing then, through the tears, and saying something that he was pretty sure was, 'Yes, Dante, yes. Of course I'll marry you. Of course I love you.'

He stood up and wrapped his arms around her waist, lifting her into the sky and kissing her then. Kissing her hard and fast and with all the love that was throbbing through his body. And then, he lifted her, cradled her against his chest and began to walk back to their home. Kissing her. Holding her. Knowing that he would never, ever let her go now. They were utterly, perfectly. Finally just as they were supposed to be and Dante wouldn't have changed a single damned thing about it.

CHAPTER FOURTEEN

FOR AS LONG as she'd known Jane, Charlotte had always understood that one's happiness directly affected the other, and when she went back to the flat, several days after Dante's declaration of love, because she needed fresh clothes, it was to find Jane huddled up on the sofa, surrounded by an absolute sea of used tissues, ashen and, well frankly, a mess.

Jane.

Her Jane.

Jane whom she'd presumed had stuck to their arrangement and come home and simply gotten on with her life. Jane whom she'd been wanting to tell her exciting news to, just as soon as she was ready to step out of her love bubble and incorporate someone else into it.

Jane who'd gone to Greece to do Charlotte a huge favour and was now absolutely, completely destroyed.

The first thing Charlotte did was message Dante:

Change of plans. I have to stay here a couple of days.

Dante had responded, I'll come over.
She'd replied, And risk this lumpy bed?

Anything for you.

Charlotte had taken one look at Jane and known there was absolutely no way she couldn't make Jane her complete and utter focus. She and Dante had their whole lives to live and Charlotte would never be able to forgive herself if she didn't find a way to fix whatever had gone wrong for Jane.

Only Jane wouldn't talk.

She was almost catatonic.

From time to time, Charlotte was able to get some toast into her, or a cup of tea, or a glass of wine, but only if she sat there beside Jane and kept reminding her to lift whatever it was to her lips and eat or drink.

Finally, a few days after Charlotte had come home and found Jane like this, her best friend had come out of the shower, wrapped in a towel, sobbing and started to talk.

She told Charlotte everything, body wracked with the force of her grief, as she explained how quickly she'd realised that Zeus was so different to what they'd imagined. How gentle and kind he'd been to her. How much he'd brought her back to life. How much he'd fooled her into thinking he was her safe place and always would be. How she'd fallen in love with him. And finally, how cruel he'd been to her on their last morning together.

Oh, Jane hadn't called him cruel. She'd berated herself over and over, for how much she'd deserved it and how she only hoped he would be able to find happiness, but for Charlotte it was like a red rag to a bull.

She could hardly see straight she was so incensed.

Not only that, but she was also missing Dante like a limb.

Two things became abundantly clear to Charlotte, after Jane's confession. One: she had to see her fiancé again. Two: she had to make that pig of a man Zeus pay for what he'd done to Jane.

A quick phone conversation with Dante and the plan was made—they'd leave for Athens the next morning.

* * *

'Are you sure you don't want me to come with you?' he offered, at the base of the Papandreo offices, with their shiny marble tiles and tall ceilings.

She squeezed his hand. 'I appreciate the offer, but this really is something I have to do on my own.'

A frown smudged across his lips. 'But you don't.'

'I do,' she replied. 'I love you, in every way, but this is my problem, my mistake, and I'm going to fix it on my own.' She kissed him quickly. 'But wait here, because I'm pretty sure I'll need a drink afterwards. Or something even more distracting,' she said, kissing him again, her gut rolling because she knew she would never, ever get enough of him.

'Okay,' he said. 'Whatever you need, I'm here.' And he always would be.

She took the lifts to the executive floor and approached a bank of elegant receptionists. One glanced up and made eye contact, offering a tightly dismissive smile.

'I'm here to see Zeus Papandreo,' she murmured.

'I'm sorry, Mr Papandreo is busy.'

'Busy?' she repeated, shaking her head. 'I don't think so.'

'If you'd like to leave your name and some details regarding your concerns, I can...'

'Do you value your job?'

The woman compressed her lips.

'I ask, because I have a feeling Mr Papandreo will have no hesitation in firing you if he finds out you didn't let me see him.'

'I—I'm sorry,' the woman said.

'This is an urgent family matter,' Charlotte said, crossing her arms over her chest. 'Now, which office is his?'

Only, that was obvious, by the way the receptionist glanced towards it.

'Excellent.' She began to stride towards it, but the recep-

tionist was standing. 'Wait, wait!' She called. 'At least let me notify him that you're here.'

Jane slowed her walk—it was the only concession she'd give.

She heard the receptionist's rushed explanation to Zeus, and then a quick call of, 'You can go in, but he only has a few minutes!'

Charlotte didn't even think about the fact she was coming face-to-face with her brother. She couldn't.

She didn't think about the fact that the man she was about to meet shared half of her DNA. That she'd wondered about him for years.

All she cared about was the hurt her best friend had suffered and how much they were both to blame.

She pushed the door inwards, her anger at fever pitch.

From the moment he turned to face her, it was obvious that Zeus hadn't expected Charlotte. 'You,' he exclaimed, staring at her with a tense line across his shoulders.

'You! Well, if I didn't hate you before, I sure as hell have a reason to now.'

His laugh was dark. 'Are you kidding me?'

'Nothing about this is remotely amusing.'

'You're telling me!' She saw the moment he registered her engagement ring and what it meant. She'd won the race. Though she wasn't technically married, she was engaged and short of obtaining a special exception—almost impossible to have granted—Zeus would have to wait out the same month-long period that she and Dante were. Meaning that if he hadn't already filled out the legal paperwork for a wedding, there was no way he'd beat her down the aisle.

She'd won. The company was, legally, bound to be hers.

'You're engaged?' he demanded.

'And you're utterly vile,' she threw at him, worry for Jane making her unable to think straight.

He looked indignant. 'You sent your best friend to Athens to seduce me so you could steal my company and I'm vile?'

Shame made her blood curdle. She'd done that. She'd really done it. She couldn't even recognise the woman she'd been that day, after the appointment with the lawyers. She'd been so devastated, so angry, so furious. She hadn't thought anything through, least of all the potential for collateral damage. When heaven knew there'd been enough of that already.

But his accusation put her on the defensive, so she said, 'Yeah, well, you sent her home utterly messed up, so what are you going to do about it?'

He visibly recoiled, his features showing shock, pain, hurt, worry. Yes, worry. Only then, he stood straighter, tightening his features into a mask of non-concern, as he said, dismissively, 'I'm sure she'll recover.'

Charlotte was *furious*. 'Are you? Well, that shows how well you know her, because I've never seen Jane like this. Not even after Steven,' she threw at him, referring to the man who'd date raped Jane years earlier and ruined her ability to trust any man afterwards. But then, she closed her eyes, because Charlotte had known how vulnerable Jane was and she'd still asked her to do this. 'And it's my fault,' she continued. 'I'm the one who begged her to do this. I'm the one who pushed past her objections. Who pleaded with her because I knew that she would never say no to me. I used her,' Charlotte now was guilt-stricken. She crossed her arms but it didn't keep the chill at bay. 'And now, I have to fix it.'

His features were like storm clouds. 'Some things can't be fixed.'

She was appalled. How could anyone not love Jane? How could he not appreciate what a gift she was?

'You're not even going to try?'

'Why would I?' he demanded.

'So, you don't love her?' she threw down the gauntlet.

'I can't see what business that is of yours.'

There was something in that, that caused Charlotte to hope, because it wasn't an outright denial. 'I'm making it my business.'

'That's not your prerogative.'

God, but he was a smarmy, arrogant piece of work.

'This makes it so,' she said, taking great pleasure in showing him her engagement ring, then narrowing her eyes. 'You care about this company.'

He glared at her.

'You want to keep it?' she pushed.

He thrust a hand onto his hip.

She sucked in a breath, surprised by how easy she found it, in the end, to give up on her plans. Anything for Jane, though. 'Well,' she said, carefully, intentionally. 'I will walk away, sign whatever I need to in order to give up my stake in it, if you promise to at least go and *talk* to her.'

His features, momentarily, showed surprise, but then he was all arrogant, unreadable man-mountain again. 'I thought you wanted the company badly enough to do anything?' he challenged.

'I want my best friend to be happy more,' she said, with a withering and derisive scowl. 'I would give up anything for her, as she would for me. Did you even know that's what she was planning to do?'

He didn't respond, so Charlotte pushed on.

'She was coming home to tell me that she loved you. That she thought I'd love you, too. That she wanted us to be friends. She knew it might mean losing you, but she was going to put you and me first, because that's the kind of person she is. And if you truly don't see that,' she glared at him one last time before stalking towards the door and wrenching it open. 'Then you don't deserve her.'

* * *

'Wait.' Zeus caught her at the elevator bay, and his voice was as imperious as it was commanding. But Charlotte was suddenly exhausted. And worried about Jane. And wracked with guilt. Nothing—no revenge, nothing—was worth this. What had she done?

She turned to stare at Zeus, utterly forlorn and completely furious, all at once, but the look on his face stopped her from letting the curse of invectives go.

His face was…she couldn't describe it. If she had to choose a word, she'd say he was just as forlorn as she was. Just as concerned.

'You say she's messed up.' His voice was raw and his eyes were half-closed, as if he couldn't bring himself to even look at her.

'Yes. She's ruined. By you.'

A muscle jerked in his jaw and then, his shoulders dropped, as he glanced downwards at the floor.

'I didn't want that.' He dragged a hand through his hair. 'Or maybe I did. I was so angry with her. So hurt. I was—,' he swore then. 'Oh, God, Charlotte. I was an absolute fool.'

'Yes,' Charlotte agreed. 'I suspect you were.' But because she knew a thing or two about love, and mistakes, she stepped forward and did something she thought she'd never, ever do. She put a hand on her half-brother's shoulder and squeezed it. 'But you can fix it, if you want to.'

He shook his head. 'You don't know what I said. How I behaved.'

'I know enough,' she contradicted, but gently. 'And I know that the reason Jane is so devastated is because she loves you, too.'

His eyes widened.

'Go and fix it,' she said, and when the elevator doors

pinged open, she gestured for him to precede her. He didn't need to be told twice.

'You think she loves me? Even after what I said?'

'I know Jane is the most forgiving and loyal person that's ever lived.' Charlotte took a step forwards as the doors pinged shut. 'But the same cannot be said for me, Zeus. If you ever hurt her again, if you ever so much as make her eyes *think* about watering up, you will pay for it. Understood?'

His eyes widened and then he laughed, shaking his head.

'What?' She asked. 'You think I'm kidding?'

The doors pinged open and her eyes landed on Dante, who'd been waiting downstairs, a silent, comforting presence if she needed it. Her heart exploded.

'No. I think I'm glad she has you. I'm looking forward to getting to know you, Charlotte.'

'Fix everything with Jane and we can go from there.'

And she meant it. It was a time for fresh beginnings and Charlotte realised that that applied to her and Zeus, as well.

In the end, it was Jane's idea. *If we have a joint wedding, then neither of you technically got married first,* she pointed out.

And so it was that six months later, at Allegra's villa, that Charlotte stood shoulder to shoulder with her very best friend in the entire world, a woman who was more like a sister to her than a friend, as they each said their vows to the men they loved, and were loved by, more than words could express.

The ceremony was witnessed by friends and family, though they tried to keep it intimate and small, to focus on the people they wanted to spend time with, most in the world.

Aristotle Papandreo was there, as the father of both a bride and a groom, and so was Charlotte's mother. It was something Charlotte had spent a long time worrying about. But in the end, it was Dante who'd reassured her, reminding her that they were their own people, and had to handle their own

feelings and behaviours. She couldn't control them. She just had to trust that for the first time in her life, they would both put her first and allow the wedding to be about her, not them.

And thanks to a carefully delivered warning from both Dante and Zeus, that was exactly what happened.

Which wasn't to say Mariah and Aristotle didn't interact. In fact, towards the end of the reception, Dante happened to walk past as they were locked in conversation and couldn't help hearing Aristotle say, 'I loved my wife and I could never have left her. But if you think, for one second, that I didn't love you, too. That I haven't thought about you…'

Dante shook his head, wondering at the possibilities that might open up, wondering at the future, and what it might hold. Love, apparently, had a way of finding its way through even the most closed-off of hearts. And wasn't he delighted about that?

Almost a year after their wedding, on a balmy summer's night, Dante returned home and Charlotte, who'd been watching the clock, waiting for his arrival, pounced immediately.

'Thank goodness you're here.' But the news she'd been waiting to deliver died on her lips, at the bemused expression on his face and the way he was holding his phone.

'What is it?' She asked, instead.

He passed the phone to her. 'Take a look for yourself.'

She read the text message—from Jamie—without even a hint of jealousy. There was no reason to envy the other woman. Her relationship with Dante was in the past and he left Charlotte without any hint of doubt as to how he felt for her.

Dante, I wanted you to be the first to know. I'm engaged. Broderick proposed last night, and Nathan and I are both thrilled. Lots of love, always xx

Charlotte's smile was like the sun, shining out of her. Jamie had adopted a little boy—Nathan—who was now four years old and in nursery school.

'Broderick is his teacher,' Dante explained.

'Yes, I knew they'd been dating. It's wonderful news.'

'It is,' Dante agreed, latching his hands behind Charlotte's back and pulling her close, kissing her until stars filled her eyes.

'And it's perfect timing.'

'It is?'

'Oh, yes.'

'Why, exactly?'

'Because I have some news of my own and I know you'll be able to enjoy it all the more, given how happy Jamie is.'

His brow furrowed.

'Dante, guess what?' she said, when he remained silent.

He waited, so she laughed, then took his hand and guided it to her still flat stomach.

His eyes widened. His jaw dropped. He stared at her like he didn't know which way was up. 'Are you saying…are you…?'

'Yep. We're having a baby.' And she pushed up onto the tips of her toes and kissed him. Kissed him like the moon was flooding her veins and the world was spinning just for them. 'We're having a baby,' she repeated, and she felt his whole body shift with what could have been a laugh, or a sob, or a sigh.

'We're having a baby,' he said, this time, and then he laughed. Tilting his head back and filling the room with the sound of sheer, unadulterated pleasure.

A feeling Charlotte echoed deep inside her heart.

Allegra was at the hospital for the birth. So too were a heavily pregnant Jane and Zeus. Aristotle and Mariah arrived within

a couple of hours of the baby's delivery. Charlotte couldn't help looking around the spacious, yet crowded, room and thinking how blessed she was. How full of love and laughter, support and encouragement her life now was.

These were her people. Her team. They would always be there for her. For Dante. And now, for their daughter Carina, named after Dante's mother.

They stayed for hours, doting on the little baby, until Charlotte could hardly keep her eyes open any longer and Jane suggested they give her a rest.

She was asleep within minutes, even before Dante had returned from walking them out.

The next morning, she woke and looked at their baby with such a swelling of love in her chest she thought it actually might form a bubble and carry her away. But then, Dante was there, and she was grounded again, in the best possible way. Anchored to her life, her love and to the dreams of happiness that had somehow become a reality.

'I have something for you,' he said, kissing her forehead gently.

'You've already given me everything I ever wanted—and then some.'

'Nonetheless, I bought this for you some time ago.' He reached into his pocket and pulled out a rectangular velvet box.

She took it frowning and cracked open the lid.

And stared at the necklace inside. It was a perfect match to her engagement ring, but it was also somehow so much *more*. The emeralds were each surrounded by diamonds, and there were more diamonds along the chain, making it bling in a way she suspected would be visible from the moon.

'Dante…' she looked from it to him, frowning.

'Do you have any idea how many rings I looked at that day?'

She shook her head, bemused. 'What do you mean?'

'You told me it couldn't be a diamond rock, but I knew I wanted it to be special. Unique. Chosen just for you. This, my darling, reminded me so much of your eyes and your strength. I knew you had to have it,' he said, tapping her engagement ring.

She closed her eyes on a groundswell of emotion. 'I thought you must have just grabbed the first thing you saw.'

He shook his head. 'Even then, I knew it meant something. That it was important. Though this,' he nodded towards the necklace, 'I bought to irritate you.'

'To irritate me?' she repeated.

'I thought you would hate it, and I quite liked the idea of that. And then, when I saw how much you loved your ring, I lost my taste for the joke.' He cleared his throat. 'And now, I wonder if you might love the necklace, as you loved the ring. I wonder if you would keep it and think of this day—the start of our daughter's life, the start of our time as a family…'

'Dante, I love it. I truly do. I love it because you bought it for me. I love it because you gave it to me. I love it because it's stunning,' she said on a small laugh. 'Thank you for this. And everything.'

He leaned down, brushing his lips over hers. 'All the thanks are mine,' he retorted. 'You have fundamentally changed me, Charlotte. I cannot imagine what my life would be like, had we not met.'

She shuddered a little. 'Let's not think about that.'

'No, let's never think about it. We did meet. We did marry.'

'And we made all our dreams come true.' She added, just as their baby woke and made a soft little sound that brought a tear to Charlotte's eyes.

'That is, indeed, the truth.'

* * * * *

MILLS & BOON®

Coming next month

ENEMY IN HIS BOARDROOM
Emmy Grayson

'Leave and I'll sue you and your firm for breach of contract.'

Her fury washes over me, hot and potent. It hits my skin, slips beneath. The air sharpens, not just with anger, but with the one thing I swore I would never let myself feel for this woman again.

Desire.

We stare each other down, wills clashing, breaths mingling. Her lips are parted, her breathing growing more ragged with each passing second.

I should let her walk out. Put as much distance between us as possible and never contact her again. No woman has ever tested my control, let alone made me want to throw the rules I live by out the window. She's dangerous.

But letting her walk away would be failing. And AuraGeothermal needs her expertise.

'Make your choice, Miss North.'

Despite the blush of embarrassment in her cheeks, she tilts her chin up. Damn it if I don't respect her for standing her ground.

'You've already made it for me, Mr. Valdasson.'

Continue reading

ENEMY IN HIS BOARDROOM
Emmy Grayson

Available next month
millsandboon.co.uk

Copyright ©2025 by Emmy Grayson

COMING SOON!

We really hope you enjoyed reading this book.
If you're looking for more romance
be sure to head to the shops when
new books are available on

Thursday 20th November

To see which titles are coming soon, please visit
millsandboon.co.uk/nextmonth

MILLS & BOON

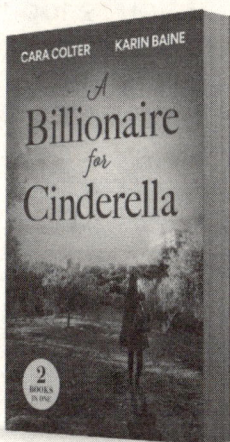

A STYLISH NEW LOOK FOR
MILLS & BOON TRUE LOVE!

Introducing

Love Always

Kandy Shepherd
Scarlet Wilson

Christmas
in
London

2
BOOKS
IN ONE

CARA COLTER   KARIN BAINE

A
Billionaire
for
Cinderella

2
BOOKS
IN ONE

Swoon-worthy romances, where love takes centre
stage. Same heartwarming stories, stylish new look!

Look out for our brand new look
OUT NOW
MILLS & BOON

FOUR BRAND NEW BOOKS FROM
MILLS & BOON MODERN

Indulge in desire, drama, and breathtaking romance – where passion knows no bounds!

2 BOOKS IN ONE

WANTED: A FIANCÉ
PIPPA ROSCOE   CLARE CONNELLY

2 BOOKS IN ONE

Business Meets Pleasure...
Louise Fuller   Millie Adams

2 BOOKS IN ONE

Christmas **Baby Bombshell**
Sharon Kendrick   Caitlin Crews

2 BOOKS IN ONE

Bound to a Bride
NATALIE ANDERSON   ANNIE WEST

OUT NOW

Eight Modern stories published every month, find them all at:

millsandboon.co.uk

afterglow BOOKS

Afterglow Books is a trend-led, trope-filled list of books with diverse, authentic and relatable characters, a wide array of voices and representations, plus real world trials and tribulations. Featuring all the tropes you could possibly want (think small-town settings, fake relationships, grumpy vs sunshine, enemies to lovers) and all with a generous dose of spice in every story.

♪ @millsandboonuk
@ @millsandboonuk
afterglowbooks.co.uk

#AfterglowBooks

For all the latest book news, exclusive content and giveaways scan the QR code below to sign up to the Afterglow newsletter:

SCAN ME

afterglow BOOKS

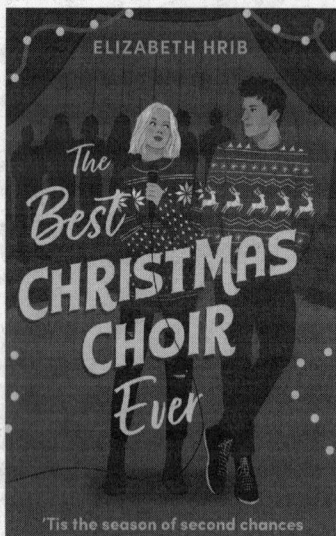

ELIZABETH HRIB

The Best CHRISTMAS CHOIR Ever

'Tis the season of second chances

❤ Second chance

💻 Workplace romance

🎁 Festive romance

OUT NOW

To discover more visit:
Afterglowbooks.co.uk

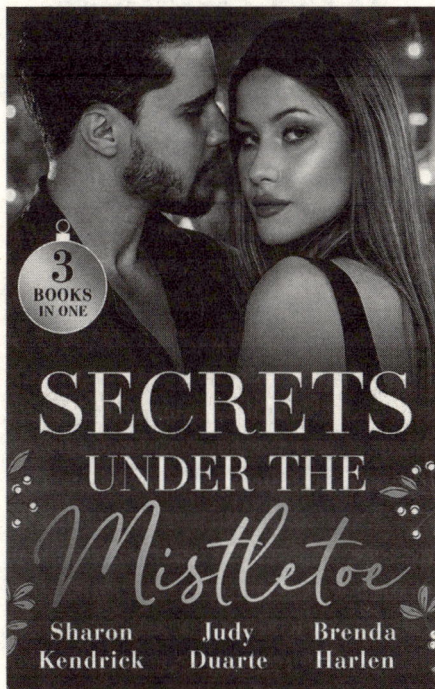

OUT NOW!

3 BOOKS IN ONE

SECRETS
UNDER THE
Mistletoe

Sharon Kendrick **Judy Duarte** **Brenda Harlen**

Available at
millsandboon.co.uk

MILLS & BOON

OUT NOW!

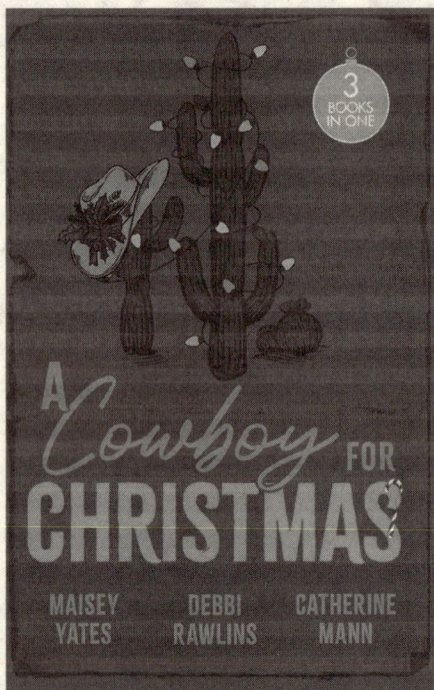

3 BOOKS IN ONE

A Cowboy FOR CHRISTMAS

MAISEY YATES   DEBBI RAWLINS   CATHERINE MANN

Available at
millsandboon.co.uk

MILLS & BOON

LET'S TALK

Romance

For exclusive extracts, competitions and special offers, find us online:

🅕 MillsandBoon

𝕏 @MillsandBoon

📷 @MillsandBoonUK

♪ @MillsandBoonUK

Get in touch on 01413 063 232

For all the latest titles coming soon, visit
millsandboon.co.uk/nextmonth